BEFORE THE
POISON

ALSO BY PETER ROBINSON

The First Cut

Gallows View

A Dedicated Man

A Necessary End

The Hanging Valley

Past Reason Hated

Wednesday's Child

Final Account

Innocent Graves

Blood at the Root

In a Dry Season

Cold Is the Grave

Aftermath

Close to Home

Playing with Fire

Strange Affair

Piece of My Heart

Friend of the Devil

All the Colors of Darkness

The Price of Love and Other Stories

Bad Boy

BEFORE THE
POISON

PETER ROBINSON

WM
WILLIAM MORROW
An Imprint of HarperCollins*Publishers*

BEFORE THE POISON. Copyright © 2012 by Eastvale Enterprises Inc. All rights reserved. Printed in the United States of America. No part of this book may be used or reproduced in any manner whatsoever without written permission except in the case of brief quotations embodied in critical articles and reviews. For information address HarperCollins Publishers, 10 East 53rd Street, New York, NY 10022.

HarperCollins books may be purchased for educational, business, or sales promotional use. For information please write: Special Markets Department, HarperCollins Publishers, 10 East 53rd Street, New York, NY 10022.

A hardcover edition of this book was published in 2012 by William Morrow, an imprint of HarperCollins Publishers.

FIRST WILLIAM MORROW PAPERBACK EDITION PUBLISHED 2013.

The Library of Congress has cataloged the hardcover edition as follows:

Robinson, Peter, 1950–
Before the poison / Peter Robinson. — 1st ed.
   p. cm.
ISBN 978-0-06-200479-6
I. Title.
PR6068.O1964B44 2011
823'.914—dc22

2011015538

ISBN 978-0-06-220468-4 (pbk.)

13 14 15 16 17   OV/RRD   10 9 8 7 6 5 4 3 2

To Sheila

BEFORE THE
POISON

1

Famous Trials: Grace Elizabeth Fox, April 1953, by Sir Charles Hamilton Morley

GRACE ELIZABETH FOX ROSE FROM HER BED AND DRESSED WITH THE AID OF her young attending officer Mary Swann at 6:30 AM on the morning of April 23, 1953. She ate a light breakfast of toast, marmalade, and tea, then she busied herself writing letters to her family and friends. After a small brandy to steady her nerves shortly before 8:00 AM, she spent the following hour alone with the chaplain.

At thirty seconds before 9:00 AM, Mr. Albert Pierrepont and his assistant entered Grace's cell, and with his usual polite deference and dispatch, Mr. Pierrepoint tied her hands behind her back with a soft calfskin strap and escorted her the short distance to the execution house directly above. It had been raining during the night, and the stone steps were dark and slick with rain. The small party entered the house, where the governor, the doctor, and two witnesses were already waiting, at 9:00 AM precisely. According to later accounts, Grace comported herself with great dignity throughout, and she never faltered in her steps or uttered a sound, except for a brief shudder and audible inhalation of breath when she first saw the rope.

Once at the gallows, she was placed in position over the chalked *T* on the trapdoor, and the assistant pinioned her ankles with a leather strap. Mr. Pierrepoint took from his pocket a white cotton hood, which he placed over Grace's head, then he carefully and gently adjusted the leather-sheathed noose around her neck. When all was to his satisfaction, he stepped back, removed the safety pin, and pushed the lever away from him in one sharp, swift motion. The trapdoor opened and Grace fell to her death. The whole business, from the cell to the eternal hereafter, took no longer than fifteen seconds.

After a brief examination by the prison doctor, Grace's body was left hanging for the regulation hour, after which time it was removed and washed, then an autopsy was performed. The findings were that she died instantaneously of a "fracture-dislocation of the spine at C.2 with a two-inch gap and transverse separation of the spinal cord at the same level." The pathologist also found "fractures of both wings of the hyoid and the right wing of the thyroid cartilage." Grace's larynx was also fractured.

The following day, after Grace's sister Felicity had formally identified the body, a coroner's inquest reported her death: "April 23, 1953, at H.M. Prison, Leeds: Grace Elizabeth Fox, Female, 40 years, Housewife of Kilnsgate House, Kilnsgarthdale, in the District of Richmond, Yorkshire (North Riding). Cause of Death: injuries to the central nervous system consequent upon judicial hanging." The governor entered in his daily log the simple words, "The sentence of death on Grace Elizabeth Fox was carried out by means of execution," and Grace's body was buried within the prison grounds.

OCTOBER 2010

I had promised myself that when I turned sixty I would go home. Laura thought it was a great idea, but when the day finally came, I was standing at her graveside in the New England rain, crying my eyes out. All the more reason to go, I thought.

"In two hundred yards, bear right."

I drove straight on.

"In four hundred yards, bear right."

I continued driving under the canopy of trees, leaves falling and swirling around me. The screen froze, then flickered and dissolved, re-forming into new shapes that didn't in the least resemble the landscape I was driving through.

"Please turn around and turn left in three hundred yards."

I didn't think this could be true. I was sure that my turning still lay about half a mile ahead to the left. It was easy to miss, I had been told, especially if you have never made it before. Sat navs obviously behave strangely in Yorkshire. I decided to leave it on and find out what it said next.

I slowed to a crawl, kept my eyes open, and there it was, a gap in the drystone wall on my left, which resembled a neglected farm track more than anything else, though I could see by the tire marks that someone else had been that way recently. There was no signpost, and an old wooden farm gate hung open at an angle, broken away from the rusty hinge at the top. The opening was just about wide enough for a small delivery van.

It had turned into a gorgeous day, I thought as I guided the Volvo through the narrow entrance. The hidden dale opened up to me beyond the overhanging trees like some magical land never seen by human eye before. The car bumped over a cattle grid and splashed through a puddle. It was hard to believe the deluge that had almost washed me off the road between Ripon and Masham, but that's Yorkshire weather for you. If you don't like it, my father used to say, wait ten minutes or drive ten miles.

"Please turn back now," the sat nav said. I switched it off and continued along the lane.

The grass was a lush green after the heavy summer rains, the pale blue sky dotted with fluffy white clouds, the trees resplendent in their muted autumn colors of gold, lemon, and russet. They might not be as dramatic as the fall leaves in Vermont, but they have a beauty all of their own, nonetheless. My window was open a few inches, and I could hear the birdsong and smell the wet grass.

I was driving west along the valley bottom, just to the right of Kilnsgarthdale Beck, which was running high, almost bursting its banks. The whole dale was probably no more than half a mile wide and two miles long, its bottom a flat swath of about two hundred yards, along which the beck and the lane ran side by side. Grassy slopes rose gently to a height of about fifty feet or so on either side, a silvery stream trickling down here and there to join the beck, and tree lines ran along the top of each side. A few cattle grazed on the slope to my right, which I guessed was attached to a farm out of sight, over the hill. Kilnsgarthdale is a small, secluded dale flanked by woods and drystone walls. You won't see it on any but the most detailed of maps.

I passed a ruined stone barn and the remnants of a drystone wall, which had once marked the boundary of a field on the opposite hillside, but there were no other signs of human habitation until I neared Kilnsgate House.

The house was set about twenty yards back from the lane, on my right, beyond a low drystone garden wall with a green wooden gate in need of painting. I paused and looked through the car window. It was hard to see much more than the chimneys, slate roof, and the tops of a couple of upper windows from the lane, because the rest was obscured by trees, and the sloping garden was quite overgrown. I had a curious sensation that the shy, half-hidden house was waiting for me, that it had been waiting for some time. I gave a little shudder, then I turned off the engine and sat for a moment, breathing in the sweet air and luxuriating in the silence. So this was it, I thought, my journey's end. Or its beginning.

I KNOW IT SOUNDS ODD, BUT I HAD SEEN KILNSGATE HOUSE ONLY IN PHOTO-graphs up to this point. During the entire purchase process, I had been involved in a massive work project back in Los Angeles, and I simply hadn't had the time to jump on a plane and fly over for a viewing. The whole business had been handled by the estate agent, Heather Barlow, and a solicitor, transacted via e-mails, couriers, phone calls, and wire transfers.

Kilnsgate House was by far the best of many I had viewed on the Internet, and the price was right. A bargain, in fact. It had been used as a rental property for some years, and there was no present occupant. The owner lived abroad and showed no interest in the place, which was held in trust for him, or her, by a solicitor in Northallerton. There would be no problems with onward chains and gazumping, and all those other odd practices the English go in for when buying and selling houses. I could move in, Mrs. Barlow had assured me, as soon as I wanted.

She had brought up the issue of isolation, and I saw now exactly what she meant. This had posed a problem, along with the size of the house, when it came to renting the place to tourists. I would be cut off from the world here, she had said. The nearest neighbors lived over a mile away on a farm, over the other side of the hill, beyond the tree line, and the nearest town, Richmond, was two miles away. I told her that was fine with me.

I got out of the car, walked through the creaky gate, then turned and stood by the wall to admire the view of the opposite daleside. About halfway up stood a stone ruin of some sort, framed by the trees, half buried in the hill. I thought it was perhaps a folly of some kind.

The only other thing that Mrs. Barlow had been particularly concerned about was my attitude toward the grand piano. It would be possible to move it out, she said in one of our many telephone conversations, but difficult. There would be no extra charge for it, of course, should I decide to keep it, though she would quite understand if I did want rid of it.

I couldn't believe my luck. I had been about to order an upright piano, or perhaps even a small digital model. Now I had a grand. All I would need, Mrs. Barlow went on, surprised and pleased by my acceptance and excitement, was a piano tuner.

Although I was unaware of it at this point, Kilnsgate House also had a history, which would soon come to interest me, perhaps even to obsess me, some might argue. A good estate agent, and Heather Barlow was good, clearly becomes adept in the art of omission.

———

I WAS TIRED AFTER MY LONG JOURNEY. I HAD SPENT THREE DAYS IN LONDON after my flight from Los Angeles, a confusing period of jet lag punctuated by lunches and dinners with old friends and business acquaintances. I had then bought a new Volvo V50 Estate—a good car for northern climes—at a showroom a friend had recommended in Camberwell, and driven down to Bournemouth to spend two days with my mother. She was eighty-seven and still going strong, proud of her son and anxious to show me off to all her neighbors, though none of them had heard of me except through her. She couldn't understand why I was returning to England after so long—it had only gone downhill even more over the years, she insisted—and especially to Yorkshire. She had hardly been able to wait to get out of there, and when my dad, bless his soul, retired in 1988, they had bought a bungalow on the edge of Bournemouth. Sadly, the old man only got to enjoy three years of retirement before succumbing to cancer at sixty-seven, but my mother was still hanging in there, still taking her constitutional on the promenade every morning and her medicinal bottle of Guinness every night.

If pressed, I realized that I wouldn't have been able to explain to my mother, or to anyone else, for that matter, why I was returning after so long. I would perhaps have muttered something about coming full circle, though what I was hoping for was more of a fresh start. Perhaps I thought that I could accomplish this time what I hadn't been able to accomplish in my first twenty-five years here, before I went off to America to seek my fortune. The truth was that I hoped, by coming back, that I would discover why I had felt such a deep and nagging need to come back, if that makes any sense.

Now, as I stood before the large house I had bought, suitcase and computer bag in hand, I started to feel the familiar fear that I had overstepped the mark, that gut-wrenching sensation that I was an impostor and would soon be found out. The reality of the house intimidated me. It was much larger than I had imagined, rather like some of the old English-style mansions in Beverly Hills. To enjoy such luxurious excess in Southern California had seemed perfectly normal, while back here, in jolly olde England, it seemed an act of encroachment on something that was not, by right of birth, mine. People like me did not live in houses like this.

I grew up in a rough part of Leeds, only fifty or sixty miles away geographically, but a million miles away in every other sense. When I was younger, affluence and privilege had always been more of an affront to me than the source of wonder it seemed to so many Americans, who thought the castles and history and royal family quaint. My family was more of a *Royle Family* than a "royal" one. I never forgot that my ancestors were the ones who had to tug their forelocks when the lord of a manor house such as Kilnsgate rode by, nose in the air, and splattered them with mud.

In my youth, I had been an angry young man, if not quite a card-carrying Communist, but now I didn't really give a damn. So many years in America had changed me, softened me—central heating, air-conditioning, a beautiful split-level penthouse apartment in Santa Monica, complete with a hardwood floor and a balcony overlooking the Pacific and a large dose of that "everyone-is-created-equal-and-any-one-can-be-president" bullshit.

But the change was only superficial. Some things run far deeper than material comforts. I must admit, as I stood and surveyed my magnificent new home, I could feel the old socialist, working-class values rise and harden into a big chip on my shoulder. Worse, I could feel again that deep-rooted, unnerving sensation that I *didn't deserve* it, that such houses were never intended for the likes of me, that I would wake up in the morning and it would all be gone, and I would be back where I belonged, living in a back-to-back terrace house on a decrepit council estate and working down the pit or, more likely these days, not working at all.

I had once tried, in my cups, to explain all this to Laura the night I won my one and only Academy Award—that I didn't deserve it, that at any moment the bubble would burst, everyone would realize what a phony I was, and I would be put back right where I belonged. But she didn't understand. To her American mind, of course, I deserved the Oscar. The Academy wouldn't have given it to me otherwise, would they? So why didn't I just accept the damn thing and enjoy the party like everyone else? Then she laughed and hugged me and called me her beautiful fool.

————————

Kɪʟɴsɢᴀᴛᴇ Hᴏᴜsᴇ ᴛᴏᴡᴇʀᴇᴅ ᴏᴠᴇʀ ᴍᴇ. Iᴛ ʜᴀᴅ ᴀ ᴛʏᴘɪᴄᴀʟ ᴇɴᴏᴜɢʜ Dᴀʟᴇs facade, from what I could see as I walked up the path between the trees and the overgrown lawn, a broad symmetrical oblong of limestone with a hint of darker millstone grit here and there, two windows on either side of the front door, the same upstairs, and a slate roof. There was an arched stone porch at the front, with wooden benches on each side, which reminded me of the entrance to an old village church. I guessed that it was a useful area for taking off muddy boots after a day's grouse shooting or riding with the hunt. There was even an elephant's-foot stand for walking sticks and umbrellas.

Above the lintel was a date stone carved, ᴊᴍ 1748, which I took to be the initials of the original owner. The keys were taped under the bench on my right, as Mrs. Barlow had promised they would be. She had also said she regretted that she couldn't be there to greet me, as she had an urgent appointment in Greta Bridge, but she promised to call by around six o'clock and see me settled in. That gave me plenty of time to get acclimatized and have a good look around, though I was beginning to regret that I hadn't stopped to pick up some supplies at the co-op I had passed on my way through Richmond. I didn't want to have to go out again tonight, not now that I was here, but I hadn't eaten since lunchtime, and my stomach was starting to rumble.

It took me a few moments to turn the large key in the dead bolt, but I managed, picked up my cases again, and walked into the hallway. It was more of a large antechamber or vestibule, by the looks of it, and it took up most of the central part of the front of the house. A small stained-glass square high above the door split the sunlight into blue, red, yellow, and purple beams that seemed to shift, kaleidoscope-like, as the trees outside swayed in the breeze and cast shadows with their branches and leaves.

I had seen photographs of the interior, of course, but nothing quite prepares you for the impact of the real thing. Size, for example. Like the exterior, it was so much larger than I had imagined that I felt intimidated at first. In my memory, English houses were small and cramped. But I was standing in a high-ceilinged room large enough for a party, with a broad wooden staircase directly in front of me leading to the upper landing, with railed galleries and doors leading to the bedrooms. I could imagine a host of people in Victorian dress leaning against the polished wooden railings and looking down on some theatrical performance, a Christmas pageant, perhaps, presented below, where I was standing, by unbearably cute children and costumed young ladies demonstrating their accomplishments.

A couple of well-used armchairs stood near the door by an antique sideboard, and a grandfather clock with a swinging brass pendulum ticked away to the left of the staircase. I checked the time against my wristwatch, and it was accurate. The walls were wainscoted to waist height, above which they were covered by flock wallpaper. A chandelier hung from the high ceiling like a fountain frozen in midair. All the wood surfaces shone with recent polishing, and the air smelled of lemon and lavender. Several gilt-framed paintings hung on the walls: Richmond Castle at sunset; two horses at pasture near Middleham; a man, woman, and child posing by the front of the house. None of them was especially valuable, I thought, but nor were they the kind of cheap prints people pick up at a flea market. The frames alone were probably worth a fair bit. Who could afford to leave all this behind? Why?

The gallery directly ahead of me, at the top of the stairs, was flush with the downstairs wall, which had one door on each side of the stairs, in perfect symmetry. There were also doors to my left and right. Taking the suitcase that contained my toiletries and what few clothes I had brought with me, I climbed the slightly uneven and creaky wooden stairs to seek out a suitable bedroom.

Two large bedrooms took up the front of the house, one on each side, mirror images across the gallery, and I chose the second one I peeked in. A bright, cheerful room, with cream, rose-patterned wallpaper, it had windows at the front and side, four in all, letting in plenty of sunshine. A selection of sheets and a thick duvet lay folded neatly on a wooden chest at the foot of the bed. The room also had a pine wardrobe, a dressing table, and a chair, with enough space left over to hold a tea dance. There were no pictures on the walls, but I would have fun searching around the local markets and antique shops for suitable prints. A second door led from the bedroom to the en suite toilet, washbasin, and glassed-in shower unit.

One of the front windows had a small padded seat, from which I could see over the garden trees to the opposite daleside, the beck, the folly, and the woods beyond. It seemed a pleasant little nook to curl up in and read. From the side windows, I had a view back along the dale where I had just driven. I could see that, even though it was only four o'clock, the afternoon shadows were already lengthening. Without even bothering to make the bed, I stretched out on the mattress and felt it adjust and mold to my shape. I rested my head on the pillow—the sort that was thicker at one end than the other, and reminded me of an executioner's block—and closed my eyes. Just for a moment, I could have sworn I heard the piano in the distance. Schubert's third Impromptu. It sounded beautiful, ethereal, and I soon drifted off to sleep.

The next thing I knew someone was knocking at the front door, and the room was in darkness. When I got up, found a light switch, and checked my watch, I saw that it was six o'clock.

"Mr. Lowndes, I assume?" said the woman standing at the door. "Mr. Christopher Lowndes?"

"Chris, please," I said, running my hand over my hair. "You must excuse me. I'm afraid I fell asleep and lost track of the time."

A little smile blossomed on her face. "Perfectly understandable." She stuck out her hand. "I'm Heather Barlow."

We shook hands, then I stood aside and asked her to come in. She was carrying a shopping bag, which she set down on the sideboard. I hung her coat in the small cloakroom beside the door, and we stood awkwardly in the large vestibule, the grandfather clock's heavy ticking echoing in the cavernous space.

"So what do you think now you're here?" Mrs. Barlow asked.

"I'm impressed. It's everything you told me it would be. I'd invite you into the den or the living room for a cup of tea," I said, "but I'm afraid I haven't explored downstairs yet. And I don't have any tea. I do have some duty-free whiskey, mind you."

"That's all right. I know my way around. I ought to. I've been here often enough over the past few weeks. Why don't we go into the kitchen?" She picked up the shopping bag and raised it in the air. "I took the liberty of nipping into Tesco's and picking up some basics, just in case you forgot, or didn't get the chance. Bread, butter, tea, coffee, biscuits, eggs, bacon, milk, cheese, cereal, toothpaste, soap, paracetamol. I took a rather scattershot approach. I'm afraid I have no idea what you eat, whether you're a vegetarian, vegan, whatever."

"You're a lifesaver, Mrs. Barlow," I told her. "Food completely slipped my mind. And I'll eat anything. Sushi. Warthog carpaccio. As long as it's not still moving around too much."

She laughed. "Call me Heather. Mrs. Barlow makes me sound like an old fuddy-duddy. And I don't think you'll find much sushi or warthog in Richmond." She led me through the door to the left and switched on the lights. The kitchen, along with its pantries and larders, ran along the western side of the house and it was the most modern room I had seen so far. It certainly appeared well appointed, with brushed-steel oven, dishwasher, fridge and freezer units built in, a granite-topped island, nice pine-fronted cupboards, and a matching breakfast nook by one of the windows. All I could see was darkness outside, though I knew I must be facing the end of the dale, where it dwindled into a tangle of woods beyond the drystone wall. The cooker was gas, I noticed, which I much preferred to electric because it gave me more control. There was also a beautiful old black-leaded fireplace—though I doubt, these days, that it was real lead—with hooks and nooks and crannies for kettles, soup pots, roasting dishes, and witches' cauldrons, for all I knew.

Heather started to unload her shopping bag on the island, putting those items that needed to be kept cool into the fridge. "Oh, and I know it's very impertinent of me, but I also brought you this," she said, pulling out a bottle of Veuve Clicquot. "I don't even know if you drink."

"In moderation," I said. "And I love champagne. I rarely drink a full bottle on my own, though. Shall I open it now?"

"No, please, I can't. I have to drive. Besides, it needs chilling. It would be criminal to drink warm champagne. But thanks, all the same." She put the Veuve in the fridge and glanced around at me. "I wasn't sure, you know, whether you'd be alone, or perhaps with someone. You never mentioned anything personal in our conversations or e-mails, such as children, a wife, or . . . you know, a partner. Only, it's such a large house."

"I'm not gay," I told her, "and I'm quite alone. My wife died almost a year ago. I also have two grown-up children."

"Oh, I *am* sorry to hear that. I mean, about your wife."

"Yes. She would have loved it here." I clapped my hands. "Tea, then?"

"Excellent. You sit down over there and let me take care of it."

I sat and watched while Heather filled the electric kettle and flicked the switch. She was a joy to behold, and a long way from being an old fuddy-duddy. An attractive woman in her early forties, I guessed, tall and slim, with curves in all the right places, and looking very elegant in a figure-hugging olive dress and midcalf brown leather boots. She was almost as tall as me, and I'm six foot two in my stockinged feet. She also had a nice smile, sexy dimples, sea green eyes with laugh lines crinkling their edges, high cheekbones, a smattering of freckles over her nose and forehead, and beautiful silky red hair that parted in the center and cascaded over her shoulders. Her movements were graceful and economical.

"How much do I owe you for the groceries?" I asked her.

"All part of the service," Heather said. "Consider them a welcome-home present." She dropped two teabags from a box of Yorkshire Gold into a blue-and-white Delft teapot and poured on the boiling water, then she turned to me. "England *is* your home, isn't it? Only you were never entirely clear."

Sometimes I wasn't too sure, myself, but I said, "Yes. As a matter of fact, I'm a local lad. Leeds, at any rate."

"Well, I never. My mother came from Bradford. Small world."

She pronounced it "Brad-ford." Everybody from Leeds pronounces it "*Brat*-ford." "Isn't it, just?"

"But you've been living in America for a long time, haven't you? Los Angeles?"

"Thirty-five years, for my sins."

"What did you do over there, if it's not a rude question?"

"Not at all. I wrote film scores. I still do. I just plan on doing more of my work over here from now on. After I've taken a bit of time off, that is." I didn't tell her what I hoped to do during my time off. Talking about a creative project can kill it before it gets off the ground.

"Film music? You mean like *Chicago* and *Grease*?"

"No. Not quite. They're musicals. I write the scores. The sound tracks."

She frowned. "The music that nobody listens to?"

I laughed. "That's probably a good way of putting it."

She put her hand to her mouth. "I *am* sorry. That was *so* rude of me. I mean, I . . ."

"Not at all. Don't bother to apologize. It's what everybody thinks. You'd miss it if it wasn't there, though."

"I'm sure I would. Might I have heard any of your music?"

"Not if it's the kind you don't listen to."

"I mean . . . you know . . ." She blushed. "Don't tease. Now you're embarrassing me."

"I'm sorry." I named a couple of the more famous recent films I'd scored, one a huge box-office hit.

"Good Lord!" she said. "Did you do *that*? Really?"

I nodded.

"You worked with *him*? What's he like?"

"I don't actually spend much time with the director, but Mr. Spielberg is a man who knows what he wants, and he knows how to get it."

"Well, I never," she said. "Pinch me. I'm talking to someone really famous, and I didn't even know it."

"Not me. That's one of the advantages of what I do. I don't get famous. People in Hollywood, in the business, know my name, and you see it in the credits. But nobody recognizes me in the street. It's sort of like being a writer. You know the old joke about the actress who was so dumb she slept with the writer?"

Heather smiled. The dimples appeared. "No," she said. "But I do now."

"I'm sorry. I didn't mean to be crude. I'm just . . . you know, sort of anonymous."

"But surely the money must be quite good? I don't mean to be even more rude and pry, but I do know that this house certainly wasn't cheap."

"The money's good," I agreed. "Enough so I don't really have to worry too much, though I do need to keep working for a few more years yet before I can even consider retirement."

"If I may say so, you haven't picked up much of an accent in your thirty years in America."

"I suppose not," I said. "I never really thought about it. Maybe I spent too much of my time in the local drinking beer and playing darts."

"They play darts in California? In a local pub?"

"Of course. The King's Head."

"Is it like a real English pub? All I've seen are those dreadful phony places they have in Spain and Greece."

"It's what the Americans think an English pub *should* be like. Lots of junk all over the place, padded banquettes, walls cluttered with old photos and posters, Winston Churchill, British bobbies, Union Jacks, the lot."

"Well, I never." Heather poured the tea and carried it over, sitting opposite me at the smooth pine table, careful to put down a couple of coasters before setting the cups and saucers on them. I won't say she was gazing at me with stars in her eyes, but I was definitely elevated in her view. "I got these, too," she said mischievously, offering me the packet of McVitie's chocolate digestives. "Bet you couldn't get these in California."

"Bet you could," I said. "They have a little 'shoppe' at the King's Head. You can buy HP Sauce, Marmite, Branston Pickle, and Bisto. Probably McVitie's chocolate digestives as well."

"Amazing. Anyway, I think you should find everything in working order," Heather went on, clearing her throat and getting back to business. "As I told you in one of my e-mails, the house is centrally heated. I set the thermostat to a comfortable level. It's in the hall, so you can adjust it yourself if you need to. Watch out, though, the heating bills can be high. Using the fireplaces should help. The door to the coal cellar is under the stairs, and that's where the firewood is kept. The telephone and Internet connections are in working order—at least, according to the man from BT—as are the satellite television and DVD player you ordered, across the hall. And that's about it. Oh, before I forget, there's a form and instructions for getting a television license. I don't know about America, but you have to have one here, or they fine you."

"I remember," I said. "My dad always used to complain about paying it. They used to send those little vans with the revolving aerials on top to catch people who hadn't paid."

"They still do. And they're a lot better at it these days. Anyway, I think you can do it online, if . . ."

I said I'd been doing most of my banking and bill paying online for years now, so that raised no problems. "I'm sure everything's fine," I said. "The owners certainly seem to have left a lot of stuff behind. I didn't expect quite so much."

"Yes. Well, I did warn you. I can arrange for anything you don't want to be taken away. But we all wanted a quick sale. You, too, as I remember."

"No problem. If there's anything I don't want to keep, I'll get in touch and maybe you can help me get rid of it?"

"I'll do what I can. Would you like the guided tour after tea, or should I leave you to explore on your own at leisure?"

As pleasant a tour guide as Heather Barlow I could hardly imagine, but I had a craving to be alone in my new home, to learn its surprises, stumble across its hidden nooks and crannies, discover its smells and creaks for myself, and to experience it for the first time in the way I expected to continue living here: alone. "I'll explore by myself, if you don't mind. Unless you think there's anything I ought to know."

Heather hesitated. "No . . . er . . . not that I can think of. Nothing. Any problems, you can always ring me at home or at the office. I'm sure you have the details already, but I'll leave you my card in case." She dug into her leather handbag.

"Is something wrong?" I asked.

"No. Why? What makes you ask that?"

"You just seemed a bit flustered by my question, that's all."

"Did I? I can't imagine why."

"Is the house haunted or something?" I asked, smiling. "I mean, it's so old I can imagine all sorts of things happening here over the years. Serving maids having the master's baby in secret, you know, all sorts of hush-hush upstairs-downstairs business. Ghostly governesses. Mysterious children. Something nasty in the woodshed. Maybe a gruesome murder or two?"

"Don't be silly. Whatever makes you think that?" Heather Barlow toyed with her hair, wrapping a long strand around her index finger. "You *do* have a vivid imagination. Mind you, I suppose that's exactly the sort of thing an American *would* say."

I smiled. "Touché."

She sipped some tea, then smiled back. Her pale pink lipstick left a mark on the cup. "Do you believe in ghosts?"

"I don't know," I said. "I haven't seen one yet."

"But you've only just arrived. You haven't spent a night here."

"I don't see why people should see ghosts only at night, do you? Anyway, I was just wondering, that's all. It's no big deal. I'm not scared or anything. It's just that in America you hear about these queer things happening in England. Mary Queen of Scots slept here, headless bodies, haunted houses and all that. It comes with the territory. People think it's quaint. Like the King's Head."

"Yes, well, I have always thought Americans are rather gullible as regards some of the more fanciful flights of British history," Heather Barlow said, with a dry laugh to take the edge off the criticism. "I shouldn't worry about ghosts if I were you. They don't come with *this* territory. At least, nobody has ever reported seeing a ghost in this house, night or day. All old houses have their peculiar histories, of course, their terrible memories and their darker moments, perhaps, but they don't necessarily manifest themselves as ghosts. And this may also be one of the few houses in the county where Mary Queen of Scots most certainly did *not* sleep. Now I really must go. My husband will be wondering where his dinner is." She finished her tea and stood up. Was there an angry edge to her words? Was she mentioning her husband for my sake? Did she think I was flirting with her?

I followed her toward the front door, took her coat from the cloakroom and helped her into it. She dug in her pocket for her car keys. When she found them, she turned to me with a new smile fixed in place and held out a square of cardboard. "You'll need this if you drive into town. It's a parking disk. Just set it for the time you arrive and display it on the dashboard. You've got two hours."

I took the disk. "Thank you," I said. "Thanks for coming by, and thanks for everything you brought. Especially the champagne."

"You're most welcome," she said, "though if you drink it all yourself, the next time you see me you may be more grateful for the coffee and paracetamol. Good night." And with that she dashed off, leaving me to stare at the closed door for a few moments, until the sound of her car starting shook me out of it. Then I shrugged and went back into the kitchen. I was impressed with Heather Barlow. She had gone out of her way to welcome me to Kilnsgate.

"Well, Laura my love," I said as I picked up my teacup and held it in the air in an imaginary toast. "Here we are. Home at last."

2

Famous Trials: Grace Elizabeth Fox, April 1953, by Sir Charles Hamilton Morley

I N HIS 1946 ESSAY "THE DECLINE OF THE ENGLISH MURDER," MR. GEORGE Orwell noted several common elements of the type of murder that provides the greatest amount of entertainment and satisfaction for the English public. In particular, he identified domestic life, sexual passion, paltry amounts of money, and the fear of scandal. While the murder of Ernest Fox does contain a number of these elements, it performs a subtle alchemy on them and presents us with something far more complex and substantial.

Nothing about the Fox affair was what it seemed. Ostensibly a reserved, educated, and considerate wife and mother, Grace Fox was, in fact, in the throes of a passionate adulterous liaison with a man—nay, a *boy*—young enough to be her own son. On the surface a devoted wife, she did, according to the evidence presented against her at her trial, poison her husband not only once, but *twice*. What kind of woman could do such a thing? Well may you ask.

We must, however, put ourselves in the jury's place and ask ourselves, on the basis of the witness testimony and evidence presented, whether indeed Grace Fox was the monster depicted by the prosecution, or was she, in fact, a decent woman driven to an extreme act of evil by a cold, cruel, and uncaring husband, and by the unexpected passion and hope unleashed in her by her young lover Mr. Samuel Porter? Our interest in a crime lies not so much in what is abnormal about it, but in those elements we may share with the criminal. Can any one among us, especially those members of the fairer sex, say that Grace Fox was so different from the rest, that she was set apart by anything other than her desperation, her impulses, and her poor judgment?

Most murders may well be sordid and commonplace affairs, but once in a while a murder grips the imagination of the public due to the characters of those involved and their heightened circumstances in life and within the communities they inhabit. This is just such a murder. While the details may well be vulgar, even gruesome, the ordinary human tragedy they reveal is what truly grips the audience.

It is not that Grace Fox used some hitherto unknown or exotic manner of dispatch; she did not, she used poison. It is not that she showed unusual cunning or intelligence in her planning; on the contrary, she was quite easily apprehended. It is not even that she demonstrated anything unique as regards motive. The age-old love triangle lay at the heart of it all.

But as Grace Fox sat in court day after day, silent and unmoving as the witnesses for the prosecution were paraded before her, never flinching as the cruelest and most intimate details of her thoughts and feelings were laid bare in the cold light of the courtroom, we felt that we were in the presence of a great enigma. For there she sat, beautiful in the simplest of clothes, her dark waves tied back from her pale, expressionless face. Was this, we wondered, the face of a cold-blooded killer?

OCTOBER 2010

My grief is a sharp blade. It pricks me when I least expect it, digs deep into me, stabs and twists, on and on like a cat worrying a bird. I might be shopping in a supermarket or eating a meal in a restaurant, and my eyes begin to burn with tears, my chest constricts. Once or twice, concerned shop assistants have worried that I was having a heart attack and offered to call an ambulance. Perhaps, in a way, I was.

That first night at Kilnsgate House, it was a dream of Laura that woke me. At least I think it was. Not a recurring dream; I don't have those. And it wasn't a nightmare, either, except that the emotions associated with its simple images shook me the way nightmares do.

Laura was laughing over a board game with her brother Clayton—Monopoly, I think—while I was in the next room with the door open, sorting through my things. I had to leave forever that day and would never see Laura again, though I had no idea why, or even whose idea it was, and I didn't know what to take with me and what to leave behind. Their unfeeling laughter penetrated me to the core. I was staring at an old black-and-white photograph of me and a school friend whose name I couldn't remember. In the photo, I was sitting proudly on my brand-new sled, and he was standing by me. We both wore mitts and woolly hats with pompoms. I remembered that my father had made that sled for me, remembered trudging around the scrap-metal yards with him searching for the runners. It had gone like the clappers until I ran it into a tree one day and was lucky to escape with a broken arm. The sled wasn't so lucky. Perhaps it was all a bit *Citizen Kane*, but there I was in the dream looking at this old photograph, crying my eyes out, my life in tatters for no reason I could understand, while my wife and her brother were laughing in the other room over who was buying Madison Avenue. I awoke with a sense of guilt and panic that soon turned into deep sadness and vague anxiety. The digital clock said it was 4:24.

Insomnia was hardly a novelty for me since Laura's death, especially with the added confusion of my new surroundings, the wind howling outside, the rain lashing against the windowpanes, the water dripping from a broken gutter onto a hollow, echoing surface. The house itself, like Caliban's island, was full of noises. Creaks in the old wood. An eerie whistling sound. A window rattling in its frame. A groan. A sigh. What sounded like anxious footsteps pacing up and down the corridor outside my bedroom. Lying there, unable to sleep, I began to feel quite scared, the way you do at 4:24 AM in an eerie old house, imagining all kinds of terrible creatures of darkness on the prowl. I could hear the sound track in my mind, a low-budget horror movie I had scored in my early days, all edgy strings, shrieking brass, and staccato percussion. I remembered Heather Barlow and our talk of ghosts.

My anxiety persisted, and in the end, when I thought I could hear the sound of a child crying, I knew that waiting for sleep was futile, so I slipped out of bed, got dressed, and headed for the stairs. I think I even searched under the bed first. There was nothing there, of course, nor was there anybody in the corridor, and only my own footsteps made the ancient floorboards creak. No crying child. No abandoned governess hanging from the rafters. Nothing. Too much M. R. James. Or was it Henry James?

It had been my intention, when I first got up, to go down to the kitchen to make myself a pot of tea, then perhaps sit and read for a while until I felt tired again, but I was so edgy by the time I got downstairs that I changed my mind. I knew I shouldn't, but instead of putting the kettle on for tea, I poured myself a stiff tumbler of duty-free Highland Park, something to take the edge off, to calm my nerves.

I had reconnoitered the downstairs of the house very quickly the previous evening after Heather's visit, so I knew that the television room was on the eastern side, the opposite side of the vestibule from the kitchen. Perhaps I was risking the wrath of the television license people, as I hadn't sorted that out yet—perhaps they had a van lurking down the lane right now—but I didn't care.

I flipped through the DVDs I had bought in London, mostly old British classics, some I had seen in my youth, or later, and a few others I hadn't seen at all but had always wanted to watch. The TV set was a good one—I had chosen a brand name I knew I could rely on—and its fifty-inch plasma screen fit comfortably on the far wall. The picture was excellent, the Blu-ray player and surround sound ideal. I settled with my whiskey into the reclining armchair, which was the perfect distance away to re-create being in a cinema, only I didn't have to put up with obnoxious people talking behind me, texting on their mobiles, crinkling cellophane bags, or with my feet crunching popcorn and sticking to the cola-flooded floor.

In the end, I decided on *Brief Encounter*. For many years it had been one of my favorite films, and as it began, I sipped my whiskey, snug in my armchair, a blue-and-white-striped blanket I'd found in one of the cupboards wrapped around me, legs propped up on the footrest. The wind raged outside, the bumps and creaks continued within, and I tried to push the sense of uneasiness from my mind as Trevor Howard and Celia Johnson played out their tragic and so-very-English little drama in the old Carnforth railway station against Rachmaninoff's lush romantic piano concerto.

I AWOKE IN THE ARMCHAIR WITH A STIFF NECK AT ABOUT NINE O'CLOCK IN THE morning, the heavy curtains blocking out any early sunlight there might be. When I shuffled to my feet and flung them open, I saw that last night's wind and rain had washed and scrubbed the landscape clean. It was all blue sky, green grass, and silver limestone again, all planes, curves, and angles, like an abstract landscape, autumn leaves drifting across. A David Hockney Yorkshire Dales, perhaps. Even better than I had imagined it would be.

The TV screen was still showing the menu for *Brief Encounter* with a snippet of Rachmaninoff playing over and over again. I couldn't recall getting to the end of the film. Half my whiskey was still in the glass on the arm of the chair. I walked into the vestibule, expecting to find a newspaper jammed in the letter box and letters all over the floor, but there was nothing, only the refracted light through the stained glass dancing on the walls and carpet.

I wandered into the kitchen and checked the cupboards, but I soon realized with a sinking feeling that there was no coffeemaker. Heather Barlow had brought me a vacuum pack of Douwe Egberts filter roast, and the previous owner may have left me a grandfather clock, a grand piano, and any number of other odds and ends, but no one had left me a coffeemaker, alas, not even a simple Melitta filter or Bodum cafetière.

Starting to panic a little—I can't function without my morning coffee—I tried desperately to think of a solution. There was a roll of paper towels, which looked strong enough to work as a filter, so I put the kettle on and doubled up a piece. When the kettle had boiled, I spooned what I thought was enough coffee onto the paper and tried to hold its edges over a cup with one spread hand, while I poured, slowly and carefully, with the other. It didn't work very well, and the soggy paper dropped to the bottom of the cup, though fortunately it didn't burst open. I left it there for a few minutes then used a spoon to try to fold it and lift it out and drop it in the rubbish. The result in the cup tasted a bit like metallic dishwater, but it was better than nothing.

As I sipped the dreadful liquid, I realized that I was hungry. Despite all the food Heather Barlow had brought me, I hadn't actually eaten anything but a chocolate digestive since the previous lunchtime. Luckily, I'm a fair cook—Laura and I often had to share cooking duties due to the vagaries of our respective jobs—so it was no great chore for me to whip up a plate of bacon, a cheese omelet, and toast. After that, I felt much better and decided I needed a cup of tea to take away the taste of the coffee. Morning sunlight streamed in through the east-facing window and bathed the kitchen in gold. I decided I liked it the way it was and wouldn't make any changes there. I wasn't too sure about the rest of the house. It was time to make my daylight inspection.

I carried my tea with me and walked through the door beside the stairs into the living and dining area at the back of the house. It was big enough to hold a society ball. The grand piano at its center was an old Steinway, its black-lacquered surface chipped in places, ivory keys worn over the years, and stained yellow, like English teeth. It looked as if a dog had been chewing on the legs. It didn't take me more than a few notes to realize that Heather Barlow had been right about finding a piano tuner.

At the eastern end of the room, to the right of the piano as I faced the back windows, the tan three-piece suite was arranged in a spacious semicircle around the glass-topped table in front of a huge stone fireplace. I found myself mentally claiming the chair on the right, angled so that it showed the view, with just enough flat space on the arm to rest a glass without its falling off.

At the western end stood another fireplace and a simple, sturdy dining table with eight chairs, though there was space enough for more; a large mirror hanging on the wall; and a swing door leading through to the kitchen on the left. Perhaps I would throw large dinner parties when I got to know a few people. I loved to cook for company. The walls were painted in light earth, terra-cotta, and desert shades, all a bit Santa Fe, but I saw no reason to change that. I had always liked Santa Fe. I guessed that the room had probably once been divided into two, perhaps even three, but I liked the openness, the sense of light and space. A hangover from life in Southern California, perhaps.

This was the back of the house, facing the dale's northern slope, and it had no side windows. There were, however, two large picture windows, one by the dining area and another by the three-piece suite. At the center, between them, French windows led from the room into the garden, where an ornate circular wrought-iron table with six matching chairs stood on a stone patio under the shade of a copper beech. A perfect spot for a barbecue, another item to add to my list.

I went outside. Though there was a definite autumn chill in the air, it was pleasant enough to sit for a while in my sweater, sip my tea, and watch the leaves fall. Other than the slight rustling or scratching sound they made as they fell, it was quite silent. There was a little garden shed, and on inspection I found the usual tools, weed killer, spiders, and plant pots. Perhaps I would take up gardening. There was no wall at the back. The garden simply sloped up from the patio through long grass to the tree line. I imagined sitting outside in spring and summer enjoying morning coffee, toast and marmalade, reading the papers, watching the flycatchers and warblers, robins, finches, and thrushes flit from tree to tree, listening to the blackbird's song. How my father would have loved it. How Laura would have loved it.

Then two large magpies flapped across the garden, and the moment was gone, the spell broken.

I WAS PLANNING TO WORK ON A NONFILM PROJECT, A PIANO SONATA I HAD BEEN thinking about since Laura's death. This was to be a major, long-term project that music people would listen to, I hoped, and even remember me by. Even though I had the grand piano, I would still need a study, somewhere I could park my laptop, send e-mails, check Web sites, and contemplate the fruits of my labors. One of the spare upstairs bed-rooms, I thought, would suit me perfectly.

The obvious choice was the other corner bedroom at the front of the house, but that, I decided, would make an excellent guest bed-room. It was the same size as the one I had chosen and also had en suite facilities. There was a double bed, bedside tables with lamps, and a large oak wardrobe, the heavy, old kind with a full-length mirror on the door. For some reason, it gave me a shiver up my spine. Perhaps I had once imagined monsters hiding in an old wardrobe and emerging when the lights went out? I gave it a wide berth. The cornices on the ceiling were elaborate bacchanalian swirls of grapes and laurels, as in my own bedroom.

I found myself drawn to one of the smaller back rooms—there were four of them in all, opening off the corridor that split the upstairs back half of the house into two, ending in a leaded-glass casement window looking out over the back garden.

The room I chose was a plain, small room right at the back, per-haps at one time a sitting room, study, or sewing room, with nothing much to recommend it on the surface, except that it had windows at the back and side. But there was something about the atmosphere, a feeling, a tingling sensation in my spine, something I couldn't put my finger on, that drew me to it and made the decision for me.

It bothered me because I don't usually get feelings like that. I sup-pose I consider myself to be a fairly rational being—for a musician, that is—an atheist with no particular belief in life beyond the grave, or in a spirit world. But nor had I ever been the sort of person who pooh-poohed anything beyond the merely solid, physical and concrete. I had met enough gurus and religious freaks in L.A., and I knew that the inexplicable happened, and that science and logic didn't have an explanation for everything. I had no idea where my inspiration for music came from, for example, but that didn't stop me from grabbing it and working on it. Whatever decided me, the small back room it was, and I was happy with my choice.

The walls were a pleasant, nondescript shade of pale blue, and a small oil painting of the folly across the dale, looking roman-tic and somewhat sinister in the moonlight, hung over the tiny fireplace. There was a worn armchair that had probably been there since the house was built, and beside it stood a small oval table inlaid with mother-of-pearl, on a level with the chair arms, where someone might rest a cup of tea, a book, or a nightcap alongside a candle or small shaded lamp.

Most important as far as I was concerned, there was a chair and a wobbly rolltop escritoire, made of walnut, which was just about big enough for my laptop. The inside contained a number of pigeonholes and a little drawer. All empty. I wondered if there was a secret compartment, as I had seen so often in movies, but I searched everywhere and found nothing. All I had to do to make it stable temporarily was wedge a folded sheet of paper under the guilty leg. Then, when I acquired some suitable tools, I could set about putting it right permanently. The top would be suitable for keeping a row of reference books handy.

There was also an old glass-fronted wooden bookcase filled with several shelves of coverless Everyman editions, poetry by Keats, Shelley, Byron, and Wordsworth, Lamb's essays; novels by Dickens, Thackeray, and Jane Austen; along with a number of cheap, ancient, musty-smelling hardcovers by writers nobody has ever heard of, the kind with no dust jackets, water damage, and bent edges that you can buy by the boxful at charity shops like Oxfam or Sue Ryder.

When I opened the glass door and smelled the old books, I was immediately transported to the huge bookshop I had discovered in Milwaukee many years ago, a warehouse of a place, floor after floor and room after room of dusty books piled everywhere, torn and stained covers, a smell of mold and damp sawdust. Laura and I had spent an hour there and had come out with two carrier bags full—everything from old sixties paperback editions of Updike, Roth, and Nabokov with lurid covers, to a tattered bicycle repair manual and a pocket Japanese dictionary. We had laughed all the way back to the restaurant, mostly because, if we really thought about it, that hour we had spent in the musty old bookshop was literally our first date. I had asked her to lunch with me the night before, and we had stumbled across the place on our way there.

See how easily distracted I am by memories of Laura? These are the blind alleys I suddenly find myself wandering down, the cul-de-sacs of lost love, where the grief waits with its sharp blade, jabs at me all of a sudden like a mugger in the night and makes my eyes burn. These are the deserted plazas of the heart, my very own boulevard of broken dreams. Get a grip, you sad old bastard, get a grip.

"Problem, Mr. Lowndes?"

I was standing outside the bank a couple of hours later, getting in the way of the people queuing for the cash dispensers, when I saw Heather Barlow.

I smiled. "Chris. I told you."

"Chris, then. But you seem a bit discombobulated."

"You could say that." I gestured toward the bank. "They won't let me open an account without a utility bill. I told them I've just moved in, and I haven't received one yet, and I need a bank account so I can pay my utility bills. They don't seem to get the irony of it. They don't care. They say it's the Bank of England's rules to protect them from terrorists and money launderers. Do I look like a terrorist or a money launderer?"

Heather looked me up and down. "Well, you could probably pass for a money launderer, but a terrorist, no, I don't think so."

"And when I told her I felt like I'd just been in a Monty Python sketch, she pulled a face and said, 'Who?' "

Heather laughed.

"I'm glad someone thinks it's funny," I said. "Look, I need a drink. In fact, I think I need two. And maybe some lunch. Care to join me?"

Heather glanced at her watch. "Why don't we go to the Black Lion? It's just down Finkle Street here. They do a decent pub lunch."

"Lead on."

We entered a narrow street beside the bank, pedestrians only, except for local delivery vans, and walked passed a row of shops, including a butcher's, a charity shop, and a post office. "What will you do about the banking?" Heather asked.

"I suppose I'll leave things as they are for the moment. I can put

everything on plastic and have it paid off by my U.S. bank until I get a
utility bill." I shook my head. "I even threatened to take my business to
another bank. Guess what the girl said?"

"What?"

" 'You'll have no luck there. They're worse than we are.' "

"You're not in Los Angeles anymore."

"You can say that again."

"It's just here."

We walked through the door and down the short flight of steps into
the pub. To the right was a flagged dining area, and one of the tables
near the window was free. The room wasn't quite a basement, but I still
got the sensation of looking up at the people passing by outside.

Heather took off her coat and shook her hair, then sat down. "How
about I get us each a glass of champagne," I said, "and we can have that
toast?"

Heather laughed. "You can try," she said. "More realistically, I'll
have a glass of white wine, please. Dry, if they ask."

When the polite young barmaid asked me what I wanted, I chick-
ened out of the champagne and asked for a pint of Black Sheep and a
glass of dry white wine. Yorkshire pubs have come a long way during
my lengthy absence, but perhaps not as far as chilled Veuve Clicquot
for lunch. The menu was chalked on a blackboard over the fireplace
at the back of the dining room. Heather decided on chicken casserole,
and I ordered the "monster" fish and chips. My cardiologist would
probably have had something to say about the fried food, but at least
it was fish, not the ubiquitous roast beef. Against Heather's protestations, I paid for both the drinks and meals at the bar.

"We might as well drink a toast to your new home, anyway, don't
you think?" said Heather, raising her glass. "Even if we don't have any
champagne." We clinked glasses.

We chatted easily for a while as we waited for our food, Heather
telling me more about the ins and outs of local life, where to get this,
why to avoid that, how to do this, where the fitness center and swimming pool were located. Our meals arrived, my battered piece of fish
hanging off the plate at both ends. Heather laughed at my expression.
"Get that in L.A.?"

"We did have a fish and chop, as a matter of fact, but they mostly served Pacific snapper *en papillotte* and seared mahimahi with a guacamole *roulade*."

I washed the fish down with Black Sheep and everything tasted good. When you're living away from England and people ask you what you miss the most, you usually say, quite spontaneously, the pubs and the fish and chips. It was interesting to learn that there was more than a grain of truth in that.

"How are you finding the house?" Heather asked. "Anything you want rid of?"

"I don't think so. Not yet. Apart from some old books, and I can take them to the Oxfam shop myself. No, it's fine. A lovely place. I'm sure I'll settle in well enough. I have one question for you, though."

"Yes?"

"Who was the owner? I didn't really pay much attention to the paperwork, to be honest. I let my lawyer deal with it. But when I looked it over I saw that the owner was listed as a partnership of solicitors."

"That's right. Simak and Fletcher."

"What does that mean?"

"Exactly what it says. Kilnsgate House has been held in trust by Simak and Fletcher for many years now. There was enough money in the estate to pay for the upkeep. They acted as the owner's agent in the sale."

"So that's why it's their name on the deeds and contracts?"

"Yes."

"And you don't know the family who owned the house before?"

"There's been no family there for years except occasional paying tenants. Not since long before my time."

"It seems a bit odd, though, doesn't it? The anonymity. Everything shrouded in secrecy and mystery."

"You're reading too much into it. It happens more often than you'd think." We ate in silence for a while, then Heather said, "So you're not too lonely up at Kilnsgate?"

"Well, I haven't had any company yet, but no. Too much to do to be lonely. Why don't you and your husband come over for dinner some evening? Bring the children, too, if you have any. The more the merrier. I'm not a bad cook, though I'm a bit out of practice, and I have to get used to the different ingredients over here."

"All right," she said. "That's an excellent idea. We can have seared mahimahi with guacamole *roulade*."

"Now you're making fun."

"Couldn't resist."

"I promise you something very English. How's that?"

"What makes you think I don't like mahimahi? Do you think we're all boring backwoods provincials up here?"

"I don't think you're boring at all. How about Saturday?"

"Let me check and give you a ring. No kids, by the way. You mentioned you had two?"

"Yes. Boy and a girl, Jane and Martin. Both in their early twenties. They both went off to university within a couple of years of each other—one to Stanford, the other to Johns Hopkins. Now they're settling down. Jane's pursuing a medical career in Baltimore, still single, and Martin's in computers, married, with one child already."

"That makes you a grandfather."

"Yes, but I'm a very young-looking one."

She smiled. "I can see that. So neither plans on coming to live with you over here?"

"God, I hope not," I said, then paused. "I didn't mean that to sound so bad, like I don't love them or anything, and I certainly hope they'll be visiting. But I'm looking for a bit of peace and quiet. There's something I . . . I've got work to do, and I just, you know, need to be on my own for a while, to sort myself out. It seems the last twenty years or so we didn't slow down enough to see the world going by, and Laura's death was such a blow. I don't really think I've come to terms with it yet."

"Of course not," said Heather. "I didn't mean to pry."

"It's all right." We ate in silence again for a few moments, then I said, "What you mentioned yesterday about houses having their secrets, their darker memories. What did you mean?"

"I'm not sure that I meant anything in particular. It was just an off-the-cuff remark."

"I don't think so. I mean, it didn't sound like that. It sounded a bit ominous, as if you know something I don't."

"Why do you ask? Did something happen? Has someone said something to you?"

"No, nothing like that. It's just a feeling." I drank some more beer. "You do know something about the house, don't you? Is it something to do with the owner wanting to remain anonymous?"

Heather laughed, but it sounded a little more nervous and less musical than her previous laughter. "I really don't know much about that at all," she said.

"But there is something?"

"Well, yes, I suppose you could say that. A little ancient notoriety, perhaps."

"Like what?"

"It was a long time ago. I don't really know any of the details."

"But it's not the kind of thing you rush to tell prospective buyers?"

She seemed to relax at that and leaned back in her chair and sighed. "It's nothing, really," she said. "Neither here nor there. But you're right, I suppose. It's not something you advertise. Discretion just becomes second nature in this business."

"What is it? Will you tell me now? I promise not to ask for my money back."

"Of course. You've bought the place now, after all, haven't you? Signed, sealed, and delivered. Kilnsgate House used to belong to a local doctor, a GP, I believe. This was in the war and during the early fifties, you understand. A long, long time ago. Before I was even born."

"I understand. What happened?"

"His wife poisoned him."

"And what happened to her?"

"She was hanged. Quite a cause célèbre at the time, but a bit of a flash in the pan, not much remembered these days. That's all I know. Honest." She grabbed her coat and bag from the other chair. "And now I really must be getting back to the office. Thank you for lunch. Hope to see you on Saturday. I'll ring tomorrow."

———————

I SAT IN THE LARGE DARK ROOM AT HALF PAST THREE IN THE MORNING PLAYING the third Schubert Impromptu, the one in G-flat major, on the out-of-tune grand piano, a tumbler of whiskey balanced precariously at one end of the keyboard. I had found the sheet music among a collection in the piano stool. Someone had made notes in the margins in a neat, tiny hand. Bad dreams and strange noises had woken me yet again—wind in the chimneys, the usual creaks and groans from the woodwork and the boughs of the trees outside. It would take me some time to get used to it. The apartment in Santa Monica had been quiet.

As usual, when I awoke in the middle of the night I missed Laura the most. The sense of loneliness is sometimes so intense that I can find no reason to get up in the morning, no reason to play or write music, no reason to do anything. I drink, perhaps a bit too much, but I don't think I'm an alcoholic. Don't get me wrong. I'm not suicidal. I don't want to end my life, even at my lowest ebb; I just want it to ramble along smoothly and indifferently without any effort or participation on my part. And perhaps Kilnsgate House is just a bit too perfect an environment to indulge in that lassitude. I have to keep reminding myself that I have come here to work as well as to heal. This is my chance to be remembered for composing something other than music nobody listens to.

Schubert's beautiful andante sounded so badly mangled that I had to stop playing. Luckily, I had found a piano tuner in the yellow pages, and he had agreed to come over the following day. It meant I would have to stay in, as he couldn't guarantee the exact time of his arrival, but it would be worth the inconvenience to have the Steinway in good working order.

I picked up my whiskey and went to stand by the French windows. I could see only the vague silhouette of the tree line against the night sky beyond my own reflection in the glass; there were few stars visible through holes in the clouds, but they shone brightly. Here, the darkness was almost as total and overwhelming as the silence.

As I stood, I thought about what Heather Barlow had told me that lunchtime and how it had subtly shifted my perspective on Kilnsgate House. I know it all happened a long time ago, and that many people have lived in the house since then. The place has no doubt seen numerous happy moments, and the halls have echoed to the sound of children's shouts and laughter, not screams and cries. But that vague something I had sensed in what was now my office, and in other nooks and crannies, the feeling I had that the house had been *waiting* for me, that it had secrets to tell me, somehow took on a new perspective now that I knew a tragedy had occurred here. Perhaps I was imagining it all with the benefit of hindsight. I wasn't used to living in old places full of other people's memories. Everywhere I had lived in L.A. was new.

Knowing didn't really alter my feelings. It didn't disgust me or frighten me. If there *were* ghosts, I thought, they were pretty harmless. I knew why Heather had kept it from me. She was a practiced sales-woman, and there's no point in even hinting at something unsavory about what you're selling. There are no doubt people who would balk at living in the house of a murderess and her victim, no matter how long ago the events took place. But not me.

I didn't think I was enjoying some sort of vicarious thrill in the world of the sensational and the macabre, but I *was* interested. I have a naturally curious nature, and it intrigued me that the house I was now living in, now *owned*, had once been home to a murderess. I knew nothing about these people and their lives—or deaths; Heather hadn't been very forthcoming about the details. But I wanted to find out more. Put it down to having too much time on my hands. Let's face it, even if I was going to work on a piano sonata, there was only so much time in a day I could spend on it. And with no one around to talk to, and not much else to do except read, watch TV, and work on DIY projects—a slap of paint here, a new door handle there—I would have plenty of time to research a forgotten piece of local history.

I took my drink with me into the TV room and flipped through my selection of DVDs. In the end I settled for *Billy Liar*. It was *my* story, after all, except at the end I would have gone to London with Julie Christie like a shot.

3

Famous Trials: Grace Elizabeth Fox, April 1953, by Sir Charles Hamilton Morley

THE PEACEFUL AND PICTURESQUE OLD MARKET TOWN OF RICHMOND stands majestically above the River Swale in one of the most enchanting corners of the North Riding of Yorkshire, commanding a panoramic view of the meadows and hills beyond. Its character and charm are evident in its many quiet wyndes; its quaint riverside and woodland walks; the Friary Tower; its cobbled market square, with Holy Trinity Church at its center; and perhaps most of all, in its ruined castle, begun in the year of our Lord 1071. The castle dominates the town from its steep hilltop above the Swale and offers many remarkable prospects in all directions.

It was in the town of Richmond that a young doctor from Stockton-on-Tees called Ernest Arthur Fox arrived by bus on March 21, 1919, to take over the practice of the venerable Dr. MacWhirter, who, at the age of seventy-seven, had decided it was finally time to retire.

After his brilliant career at medical school, where he distinguished himself in both neurology and microbiology, Dr. Fox had recently returned from his duties at a base hospital in Flanders, where he had helped treat victims of mustard gas and other war injuries. We can no doubt be certain that many of the memories he brought with him of our gallant young wounded soldiers were the stuff that nightmares are made of, and that, perhaps as a result of these, his expressed desire to enter into general practice in a small town, while, of course, maintaining his research interests and teaching connections with local hospitals in both Newcastle and Northallerton, should not have come as a great surprise to his family and friends.

Dr. Fox presented a robust and vigorous figure possessed of that certain dignity of bearing that is indicative of good breeding. He could frequently be seen striding the many woodland and riverside footpaths, walking stick in hand, cape billowing in the wind. Though none would describe Dr. Fox as a handsome or a warm-natured man, he possessed a certain almost aristocratic charm that earned him the respect of all who came into contact with him, if not their love.

Dr. MacWhirter's thriving practice was situated on Newbiggin, a broad, cobbled, tree-lined street close to the market square. Dr. Fox was able to take as his first lodgings the apartment directly above the surgery. Dr. MacWhirter remained in Richmond for one month, during which time he acquainted his successor with the ways and customs of the local townsfolk and farmers, and with the manner in which he had found it best to manage his practice. After that, he left the district, and our story, never to return.

By all accounts, Dr. Fox proved as thrifty and industrious as he was robust. No doubt things were difficult for the young doctor at the beginning, Yorkshire folk being notoriously resistant to change and reluctant to part with their money, but it is reported that he soon won the confidence of the local people—and, perhaps more important, their purses—and before long he was running such a successful practice that, in 1923, he took on as his partner one Dr. Clifford Nelson, from the nearby market town of Bedale. Dr. Nelson's young wife, Mary, proved invaluable to the business side of the practice, with her bookkeeping and accounting skills.

In time, Dr. Fox was able to move from his cramped apartment to a small detached house overlooking the Richmond cricket ground, and his practice continued to thrive. In addition to his duties as a general practitioner, he consulted on certain surgical cases and diseases at the Royal Victoria Infirmary, in Newcastle; involved himself in various research projects around the country; assisted in a number of minor operations; and delivered lectures on various learned topics.

Dr. Fox was also among the first gentlemen in Swaledale to purchase a motor car, a Rover 8, and such a spectacle did he make as he roared along the more remote Dales roads, wearing his pilot's helmet and goggles, black bag secure on the seat beside him, that when people heard his approach, they came out on their doorstops to watch and wave.

The years passed and the practice grew, yet still Dr. Fox had not entered into the holy state of matrimony. He had not yet found the right woman to make him a suitable wife, he responded with a laugh to anyone who inquired. Such close communities as Richmond, however, have their traditions and their expectations, and that the local GP should have a wife to send him out with a hearty breakfast inside him each morning, to darn the socks he wore out on his daily rounds, and to have his slippers warming by the fire on a chilly winter's evening were certainly among them. Dr. Fox cannot but fail to have been unaware of these rumblings.

Thus it was an occasion of great joy in Richmond when Dr. Fox introduced to his partner Dr. Nelson and his wife, Mary, on June 12, 1936, seventeen years after his first arrival, a beautiful young woman of twenty-three by the name of Grace Elizabeth Hartnell, whose beauty, natural charm, domestic competence, cheerful disposition, and delicate femininity soon conquered the hearts of everyone she encountered. If Ernest was the practical and dependable rock of the family, then Grace was its warm and gentle heart.

Grace worked as a nurse at the Royal Victoria Infirmary, in Newcastle, and that was where she and Ernest began to meet more and more regularly for tea. They were already acquainted, as Dr. Fox was a friend of the Hartnell family, who hailed from Saltburn-on-Sea. In no time at all, Grace became a well-known and much-admired figure around Richmond, and the general opinion was what a wonderful doctor's wife she would make. This step was finally accomplished after she had finished her training, on a warm, sunny September 26, 1936.

OCTOBER 2010

I had hardly been out of the house all week, except to buy some more food, wine, and office supplies, when I decided to visit one of the local pubs I had found online, which was in the village of Kirby Hill, a couple of miles farther up the road at the end of my lane.

Heather Barlow had rung earlier and told me that she and her husband, Derek, would be delighted to come for dinner on Saturday. After the briefest of pauses, Heather had gone on to ask me if it was all right if she brought a friend, "to round out the numbers." I detected a whiff of matchmaking in the air, but what could I say? Her name was Charlotte, Heather told me, and she was nice. A solicitor. I would like her. We would see about that.

The piano tuner had come and gone, and he had done an excellent job. I had set up my office around the walnut escritoire, tinkered with a few ideas, themes, and chord sequences at the grand, but I didn't yet feel settled enough to immerse myself in the sonata I was hoping to write. I know that piano sonatas aren't especially popular with composers these days—most opt for shorter, more impressionistic fragments—but I like the four-part structure with its intricate themes and variations, perhaps because it is similar to the way I approach my film-score work. Schubert and Beethoven are my touchstones, but I haven't ignored everything that's happened in music over the last two hundred years, and I have great regard for Britten and Shostakovich.

At least I had been sleeping much better. Though I still awoke occasionally to the strange nighttime sounds, I became more adept at ignoring them and going back to sleep, saving my movie-watching binges for the long evenings. By the time darkness started to fall on Thursday, I felt lonely and restless and couldn't even settle down to *Peeping Tom*, one of my old favorites, so I decided to venture out.

I still found it hard to get over the sheer isolation of Kilnsgarthdale every time I drove along the bumpy one-track lane to the main road. It was only a mile and a half, but that's actually quite a long way to be from civilization. Perhaps not in the American West or the Australian outback, but in little old England it is. I couldn't even see my neighbors a mile away behind me, over the hill. Even the main road was a meandering, undulating, tree-canopied B road two miles from Richmond to the south and, in the opposite direction about the same distance from Kirby Hill, where I found the Shoulder of Mutton. The pub stood at a bend, opposite the church, where the road turned left into the village, and the view from the car park across the fields to Holmedale and across the A66 to the moorland beyond was stunning, with the last vestiges of sunset on my left, a Technicolor wasteland.

The pub was moderately crowded, and in the room to the right of the small bar, a few people sat eating dinner. I walked over to the bar and ordered a pint of Daleside bitter and a packet of cheese-and-onion crisps from the young girl, who graced me with a shy smile. One or two of the regulars paused in their conversations and gave me surreptitious glances, as if they didn't see too many strangers in there, or as if word of my presence in the area had spread around. It wasn't quite *An American Werewolf in London*, but it wasn't far off. I wasn't sure whether I would get, or wanted, any conversation. Yorkshire people are notoriously contrary when it comes to these matters. They can be as friendly as you like, and bend your ear until you've had enough, or they can simply pretend you don't exist. And you can't always be sure which course they will take. I thought it was best to be prepared for all eventualities, so I took a book along with me.

I carried my pint and crisps over to an empty table in the corner directly opposite the bar, close enough to the blazing fire to catch some of its warmth. The brass and polished wood gleamed. There were no machines or pool tables, no posters advertising quiz nights or karaoke, and, of course, no smoking. I tried to read the names of the single-malt whiskey bottles displayed on the plate racks around the room. A petite, energetic woman I took to be the landlady was dashing in and out of the bar, stopping to chat and joke with the regulars. She flashed me a quick smile and said hello as she passed my table.

It was hard to concentrate on my book, an espionage novel by Alan Furst, even though I was enjoying it. I kept overhearing snatches of conversation, or the punch line of a joke, and one of the women at a busy table nearby had a very loud laugh. As the place filled up, I watched people come in, and soon all the tables were taken. A couple about my age glanced over from the bar and came over. The man asked if the chairs were taken. I said no. I had seen them chatting with the landlady when they came in, so I guessed they were regulars, but I had no idea they knew who I was until the man opposite me said, "You're the new owner of Kilnsgate House, aren't you?"

"Yes," I said, putting my book down on the table.

"I'm sorry to disturb you," the man said. "You were reading."

"That's all right. I only brought the book because I didn't know if there'd be anyone here to talk to."

"Or anyone who would want to strike up a conversation with an incomer?"

"Well, yes . . . I suppose so."

The man leaned forward and whispered, "As a matter of fact, I'm not from around these parts. I'm an incomer, myself, a bloody southerner. Brighton."

I laughed. "Chris Lowndes," I said, holding out my hand.

He shook. "I know who you are. I'm Ted Welland, and this is my wife, Caroline." Caroline was a shy woman in a green cardigan, showing the bulge of a handkerchief over her skinny wrist. The tip of her nose looked red, and I guessed she was carrying the hankie for a purpose. She blushed and averted her eyes when we shook hands.

"It looks like an interesting book, at any rate," Ted went on, glancing at the cover.

"I'm a spy-fiction fanatic. I cried when they pulled down the Berlin Wall."

Ted laughed. "I'm afraid I'm more of a nonfiction man myself. History, biography, that sort of thing."

I noticed Caroline roll her eyes, as if she recognized the beginnings of a boring lecture. "You're a historian? You should—"

"Good lord, no! Just a curious mind, that's all. An avid reader. Especially anything about World War Two. Now that I'm retired, I find I have plenty of time on my hands, and it keeps me out of mischief. Doesn't it, darling?"

He patted his wife on the knee, and she smiled. "I'd like to think so," she said, then she blew her nose.

"Perhaps you can help me?" I said.

Ted Welland raised his eyebrows. "Perhaps."

"Do you know Kilnsgate House?"

"I've walked by it on a number of occasions. I know where it is."

"There's a funny sort of humped stone ruin on the hillside opposite, a folly or burial mound of some sort. Do you know what it is?"

"The lime kiln?"

"Is that what it is?"

"You mean you don't know why it's called Kilnsgate House?"

"Well, no, I suppose I don't."

"It means 'the way to the kiln.' That ruin is a lime kiln. They were used to make quicklime by burning limestone. See, it's got an outer layer four or five feet thick, and inside there's a kind of bowl made of brick or sandstone to withstand the heat, open at the bottom."

"I noticed a sort of arch, a crescent opening."

"That's where you put the coal in. The 'eye.' There should be one at the other side, too, though it's probably buried in the hillside by now. It formed a sort of air tunnel, you see, to keep the fire burning. Above it, inside, there should be an iron grate. You layer crushed limestone and coal up inside, then cover the top with sod, put more coal in the bottom, and set it alight. They used to burn for days. People used the quicklime to spread on the fields or for mortar in building, and maybe to get rid of a body or two." He winked. "Though I heard once that it can actually have the opposite effect and preserve a dead body. Anyway, there are a couple more kilns about two hundred yards farther along, on the same side of the dale as your house."

"When did they stop using lime kilns?"

"The 1850s, or thereabouts. Demand got too high, so the manufacturing of lime became industrialized. The smaller kilns weren't needed anymore. Pity. You can imagine what a sight they must have been in the Dales, especially at night, the plumes of smoke and the fiery eyes."

"You seem to know a lot about the area for a southerner," I said. "Do you live here in the village?"

"Yes," said Ted. "Just over the road, by the green. Been here six years now. I worked in banking. Got out early, before the whole world started to hate us." He leaned back in his chair and narrowed his eyes.

"I understand you're something to do with Hollywood, the movie business? Famous, aren't you?"

"Word gets around," I said. "Though I'd hardly call myself famous."

"I've heard of you," Caroline sounded as if it had taken her a great deal of time and courage to let the words out. "You did the music for that last Sandra Bullock film, didn't you? I liked it. I mean, the film, but the music, too. It was very romantic."

"Well, I'm grateful for that," I said. It wasn't one of my favorite efforts, but it had a pretty theme, which in one scene played well ironically against the heroine's tears of distress.

"You don't seem at all the way I pictured you," Caroline said.

"Well, my studio photo's a couple of years old now, but apart from a few more gray hairs I haven't changed all that much."

"No, I don't mean that," she said. "I've never seen any photos of you. I mean more . . . like a composer . . . . like someone who's . . . I'm sorry, I can't really express myself very well."

"Well, I don't look like Beethoven, that's for sure. Not enough hair, for a start."

Ted rushed into the awkward silence with the panacea offer of another drink.

I was thinking of saying no, that I had to go, but I thought Ted Welland might prove an interesting source of local knowledge. I still wanted to know more about the house I was living in, and the people who used to live there. "Pint of Daleside, please," I said. I didn't imagine that one more pint would put me over the limit, and I doubted that there were many police patrols on this road, anyway. I had noticed that the car park was almost full, and nobody seemed to be sitting around drinking Coke or tomato juice.

"Can I have a rum and blackcurrant?" Caroline asked. "For my cold."

Ted patted her on the shoulder. "Course you can, love." He made his way to the bar.

After a short pause, Caroline asked, "Did you like living in America?" She had a curious habit of glancing at me sideways when she asked me a question, sniffling occasionally, her hands clasped on her lap.

"Most of the time," I said.

"I've never been there. Are you working on a new film?"

"Not at the moment. I'm taking a break."

"Must be nice. Is that why you came here? For inspiration?"

It was an odd sensation, having a conversation with Caroline. I felt as if she really needed to ask her questions but had little or no interest in the answers. "Partly," I said.

"Kilnsgate's a big house for just one person, isn't it? I mean, I've never been inside, but even from the outside . . . you can tell."

"Yes, it's big," I said. "Probably too big. But I got used to having a lot of space in America. It suits me fine. I imagine it's the kind of place that used to have servants and the like?"

"It would have had once," said Caroline. "But it's been empty for a long time. It's too far off the beaten track, and nobody can afford big houses these days. Nobody from around these parts, at any rate. It's the economy, you know."

Fortunately, Ted came back with the drinks, his hands wrapped around two frothing pints, yet still managing to hold Caroline's rum and blackcurrant cordial with his fingertips. He bent to set the glasses carefully on the table and sat down again.

"Your wife was just telling me that Kilnsgate House was empty for a long time," I said, as a way of bringing him back into the conversation.

Ted glanced at Caroline, then back at me. "Yes, that's right. Interestingly enough, during the war it was used for a while by some hush-hush military unit. The Special Operations Executive would be my guess. Cloak-and-dagger boys. They were mainly involved in overseas missions, supporting resistance groups, sabotage and the like, so I imagine they used the place for briefings and training. I would love to have been a fly on the wall for that."

"And later?"

"Not so interesting, I'm afraid. In the fifties and sixties it was mostly just sitting there, going to wrack and ruin. In fact, I even think some hippie commune took it over for a few years in the early seventies. Then the owner, or his solicitor, got a rental outfit to manage the property, but they had constant trouble renting it out. It just sort of stalled, more trouble than it was worth. You must have been a godsend, old boy."

"Why did nobody want to rent it or live there?"

"Well, let's face it, the place is hardly a cottage, and it is rather remote, isn't it? Talk about *Wuthering Heights* or *Bleak House*. And it's not a great spot for farming. Then . . . Do you know much about it, yourself?"

"I know there was a murder there, if that's what you mean."

"Right. Yes. Well, perhaps people were also put off by what happened there. I mean, it's not everyone who wants to live in a house where there's been a murder, is it? I'm sorry. I didn't mean . . . you know."

"No need to apologize," I said. "I had no idea of its history when I bought it. All the negotiations were conducted from a distance, and my estate agent didn't see fit to tell me."

"Can't blame him, can you?" said Ted. "Might have put you off."

"It doesn't bother me, but it does interest me. Do you know much about the case?"

"Not a great deal. I'm afraid murder isn't my forte, so to speak. But it was back in the early fifties," Ted went on. "They lived there, I think, from about the midthirties until 1953. That was when she poisoned him. A woman's method, if ever there was one."

Caroline had been following our conversation with that sideways gaze of hers, sniffling and blowing her nose from time to time. She took a sip of rum and blackcurrant and gave a little moue as Ted spoke. "Oh, Ted," she said. "Don't be so chauvinistic."

"Well, it is! Name me one famous male poisoner."

"Dr. Crippen," said Caroline.

"He didn't do it," Ted argued. "They've proved it wasn't his wife's torso they found under the cellar floor. DNA."

"That's just a theory. Besides, it was someone's torso, wasn't it?" Caroline argued. "And it didn't get there by itself."

Ted had to concede that she had a point there.

"Will you let me carry on, woman?" he said testily. "As I said, they found traces of poison, arrested the wife, and that was that. She was hanged at Armley Jail in April 1953. Got a fair bit of notoriety at the time, but it didn't seem to linger in the national psyche like some murders do."

"Why do you think that was?"

"I don't honestly know," said Ted. "It had all the ingredients. Sex, intrigue, a mysterious beautiful woman, a nice juicy murder. A hanging. Maybe she got overshadowed by Ruth Ellis a couple of years later? And, don't forget, she also came between Bentley and Christie, too. They were both pretty controversial and sensational cases. I mean, not a week or so after she went on trial, they started finding the bodies in the walls at 10 Rillington Place. That'd blow everything off the front page, wouldn't it? Whatever the reason, the Kilnsgate poisoner has been largely forgotten by posterity. I'm afraid she got short shrift in the famous murderers department." He gave a nervous laugh.

"Do you know if there's a written account?"

"I do believe it was written up in *Famous Trials*. You might be able to find a copy in a secondhand bookshop somewhere. One of those old green-covered Penguins that turn to dust when you open them. Try that secondhand place in the market square. Richmond Books. I'd imagine it would be long out of print by now. There'd be newspaper accounts, too, somewhere."

"You mentioned Armley Jail a while back. I used to live near there. Do you remember what this woman's name was?"

"Yes. She was called Fox. Grace Fox."

I DID KNOW ABOUT GRACE FOX. OF COURSE I KNEW ABOUT HER. I'D JUST PUSHED her name to the back of my mind, like the rest of the country. Still, I had an excuse. Thirty years of Hollywood murders will do that for you. But as soon as Ted Welland told me where she had been hanged, I remembered, and I felt an odd surge of excitement, of *connection*.

You see, in a strange, oblique sort of way, I was *there*. I was a part of it. Not when it happened, of course. I was only three then. But before Kilnsgate House, before this return to England, even before Hollywood, Grace Fox was already a part of my personal mythology.

My old junior school, Castleton, which I attended between the years of 1958 and 1961, stood right next to Armley Jail, which towered over us like an old medieval fortress. One of its rough stone walls also formed the wall of our playground. We played cricket against it, chalked wickets on it, bounced tennis balls off it, kicked footballs against it. I even, on one occasion, smashed the school bully's head on it and made him bleed and run crying to the teacher.

We used to imagine murderers escaping, climbing down knotted ropes into the playground and running amok, foaming at the mouth. But the wall also stood as a warning: if we didn't behave ourselves, the headmaster told us at the beginning of each term, we would end up behind it, and we could only imagine what sort of world lay waiting there.

They used to hang people in Armley Jail, and one of the people they hanged there was Grace Fox.

I glanced at my watch. Only 9:30 P.M. It would be an hour later in Angoulême, where my brother Graham lived, but I was certain he would still be awake. Graham always was a night person. Sure enough, he answered he phone on the fourth ring.

"*Allo?*"

"Graham? It's me. Chris."

"Chris! How are you, little brother? It's been a long time."

It was true that Graham and I had not been in touch as often as we should have over the years, but we had the kind of familiar closeness that can easily survive a little time and distance. Laura and I had spent some very happy vacations at his farmhouse, enjoyed the local food and wine with him and his wife, Siobhan, and they had visited us in L.A. The last time I had seen them was at Laura's funeral eleven months ago, and I had noticed how old and tired Graham was looking. He had been pleased to hear that I was moving back to England.

"I'm well," I said. "Settling in. And Siobhan?"

"Thriving. Heard from Mother lately?"

"I dropped by to see her a couple of weeks ago. She's doing fine."

"Excellent. Something I can do for you?"

"I want to pick your brains, your memory."

"You're welcome to what's left of it. Some days I can't even remember what I had for breakfast by lunchtime."

"It's longer ago than breakfast."

"There's a much better chance, then. Fire away."

"Grace Fox."

"Grace Fox. Now, there's a blast from the past. What do you want to know about her for?"

I explained about looking into the history of Kilnsgate House and finding out there was a murder there. Then Grace Fox's name had come up. Graham listened, and when I had finished there was a brief silence. I could hear his breathing and some French voices in the background. It sounded like a news program. Television or radio.

"Well," he said finally. "I can see why you'd be interested."

"You were there that day, weren't you, at school?"

"I was. I was ten at the time."

"Do you remember it?"

"Like yesterday. Better. I told you all about it. Scared the pants off you. Don't you remember?"

"Why would I? If you were ten, I was only three. Humor me. Tell me again."

Graham sighed. "Word had got around, of course. Hanging a woman was rare then, you see, and Grace Fox was what the tabloids today would call quite a 'stunna.' She was a very beautiful woman. Long dark wavy hair, full lips, pale skin, lovely figure. Of course, that didn't mean a great deal to me at the age of ten. I was far too caught up in cricket and football to be very concerned about female pulchritude. But boys will be boys. We knew even by then that there was some mysterious thing about women's bodies we were supposed to desire, even if we'd rather collect frog spawn or keep toads in a jar. It was all a little vague and smutty. There was even a rhyme, I remember, that we used to chant in the playground. A bit of doggerel." Graham cleared his throat and recited:

> " 'Gracie Fox, poor Gracie Fox
> They stretched her neck
> And put her in a box,
> Stretched her neck
> And put her in a box.
> And now the worms eat Gracie Fox.' "

"Charming," I said.

"Children can be very cruel and insensitive. There was a lot of anticipation. It was April, I remember, not long after Easter, and a lovely morning. Breath of spring in the air. I walked to school with Kev and Barry, as usual, and we were excited, even a bit scared. We knew something terrible was going to happen that morning. It had been in all the papers, and we'd heard our parents talking about it."

"When did you find out?"

"We were in morning assembly, standing in silence. Old Masterson had just walked on the stage to begin. It would have been nine o'clock, just after, and we heard the bell toll. That's when we knew it had happened, that she was dead. Terrible fast was that Pierrepoint." Graham paused, then went on, "I can still remember the silence after the bell had tolled, as if all the air was sucked out of the room. And you could hear the fading reverberations, though I'm sure that was just fanciful on my part. I had a tight feeling in my chest. Even old Masterson seemed a bit choked. Then we sang 'To Be a Pilgrim.' I won't forget that morning in a hurry."

I felt myself give a little shiver as he told me. We moved on to talk of other things, and I promised to get over to see him and Siobhan before Christmas. Finally, I hung up the phone and made myself a cup of tea. When it was ready, I took it into the living room, where I put some logs on the fire, set my iPod in the speaker dock to Alfred Brendel's *The Farewell Concerts*, and sat down to think about everything I'd heard that night.

IN A VERY STRANGE AND ROUNDABOUT WAY, THROUGH MY OLDER BROTHER, I had become close to Grace Fox without even knowing what she looked like. Now I stood in the vestibule before the painting and realized that it must be Grace and her family. She wore a bolero jacket with puffed shoulders over a silk blouse and a long skirt, her long wavy hair done in a Veronica Lake style, with a deep side parting. She was smiling with her mouth, but her eyes looked faraway, her expression distracted. In an odd way, I was surprised to find, she reminded me of Laura, though

Laura had been a natural blonde. It was something about the lips and the eyes. The man, her husband, Ernest, I assumed, stood erect, hands clasped in front, his chest puffed out, his suit and waistcoat tight, straining at their buttons, looking very much like the proud owner of the entire scene. He was rather portly, with a ruddy complexion and a bristly mustache. The child between them seemed uncomfortable in his Little Lord Fauntleroy outfit.

I walked through to the living room and sat in my armchair. I must have remembered Grace somewhere deep in my mind, I realized, because when I grew up and cast aside childish things, such as football, cricket, and frog spawn, for the charms, wiles, and torments of the opposite sex, the mysteries of which Graham had spoken, she was still there, somewhere in the vaults of my memory, in a way that only a lovesick teenager addled with romance and chivalry and a vague grasp of Keats can understand. The idea of wantonly destroying such beauty, *any* beauty, at the end of a rope was unthinkable to me, no matter what crime she had committed.

Later, at university, when I became interested in Thomas Hardy after seeing John Schlesinger's *Far From the Madding Crowd*, I was at first shocked to find that Hardy was an aficionado of public executions, because I was very much against capital punishment. But when I read his erotic description of the hanging of a woman called Martha Browne, it was Grace Fox I pictured, a vague but beautiful dark-haired female shape hanging there on the blasted heath, the gallows creaking with the weight, her body twisting languorously in the wind. The features were blurred, of course—this was simply someone my brother had mentioned to me years ago—but my imagination had no problem in supplying the female form under the clinging wet shift. It could have come from any one of the magazines I was hiding under my mattress at the time. I won't say that the image excited me—I have never been drawn to necrophilia or sadomasochism—but I had to admit that there was a certain grim sensual and erotic aesthetic in it all, which Hardy, bless his soul, had grasped at once.

Now here I was, forty years later, living in Grace Fox's house. What of it? I asked myself. It was certainly a coincidence, though not a great one; in reality, it was more like one of those "small world" stories. But

after Ted Welland's tale and my talk with Graham, I felt a certain frisson when darkness fell upon Kilnsgate House that night. When the
wailing and creaking woke me from my sleep once again and sent me
downstairs for whiskey and forgetfulness, I found myself standing at
the top of the landing for a few extra moments, looking down the corridor in the dark, looking for Grace.

4

Famous Trials: Grace Elizabeth Fox, April 1953, by Sir Charles Hamilton Morley

GRACE ELIZABETH HARTNELL WAS THE DAUGHTER OF A SUCCESSFUL SALTburn bank manager and alderman. She was a clever girl who attended her local grammar school, where she excelled both in the arts and in the sciences, and was generally regarded as a quiet and reserved child. Grace was nonetheless possessed of an inquiring mind and a kindly disposition, and she demonstrated an inherent gentleness and compassion toward all living creatures.

Perhaps the only blot in the copybook of her youth was a broken engagement to a most suitable young man from the nearby town of Redcar, an ambitious young solicitor called Edward Cunliffe, whom her father very much admired, in favor of a far less appropriate paramour. This rejection of her father's choice of partner showed a certain early rebellious and headstrong element in young Grace's behavior, an unwillingness to bend to the will of her father, and a tendency to forsake the duty incumbent upon the daughter of a local dignitary for the fickle will-o'-the-wisp impulse of romantic love.

Much of the business still remains shrouded in mystery, as neither Grace nor her parents cared to speak of it in later times. The young man she chose, contrary to her family's wishes, was an aspiring poet by the name of Thomas Murray, who turned out to be a rake of the most unspeakable order. Thomas soon deserted Grace for another woman, leaving her so distraught that it was thought best she should retire to her aunt Ethel's house in Torquay to recover from her attack of nerves. She returned a contrite woman and soon regained her father's affection, though not that of the broken-hearted young solicitor Edward Cunliffe, who had taken flight to seek his fortune in Argentina. Thomas Murray later died fighting for the International Brigade in the Spanish Civil War.

All this took place in late 1930, when Grace was merely eighteen, and by which time her husband-to-be was already an established GP in Richmond. A short while later, Grace began her training as a nurse, a profession at which she excelled beyond all her father's misgivings.

Grace trained at the Royal Victoria Infirmary, in Newcastle, submitting to the almost nunlike existence of the nurses' home, with its strict curfews and rules against male visitors, all under the eagle eye of Matron. She soon showed evidence of the three qualities essential to a good nurse—devotion to her patients; technical proficiency; and that essential feminine quality of tenderness, or gentleness, that in no way interfered with the efficiency with which she discharged her rigorous duties. Grace qualified as a state registered nurse with flying colors in 1935, and only a year later, she met and married Dr. Ernest Fox. The couple soon moved into Kilnsgate House, where everything proceeded as normal for the following three years.

When war was declared, Dr. Fox curtailed his duties at the Royal Victoria Hospital and turned his attention toward the Friarage, in Northallerton, which had recently opened as an emergency medical services hospital to receive casualties in the event of the bombing of Teesside's civilian population.

Throughout late 1939, Grace and Ernest continued to live at Kilnsgate House, tended by loyal maidservant Hetty Larkin. At this time, they also accommodated for several weeks an evacuee from Newcastle, affectionately known as "Billy," until the air raids that had been predicted never materialized and his parents took him back home.

It was around this time that Grace joined the Queen Alexandra's Imperial Military Nursing Services and went to pursue her training at Netley, in Hampshire. There she learned of the many duties of a military nurse, including running the dispensary, a skill that was to be declared of great significance during the course of her trial. After brief stints in military hospitals around Dover, where she helped nurse survivors of the British Expeditionary Force after Dunkirk, Grace bade farewell to her husband in July 1940, and spent much of the rest of the war in service overseas. Ernest continued his work at the Friarage, in both a teaching and a practicing capacity, throughout the war, even after it became a Royal Air Force Hospital in 1943, and he was also often absent from the practice as he traveled around the country to supervise training programs and present research papers at various institutions of learning. Hetty Larkin found useful employment in a munitions factory near Darlington.

During the war years, Kilnsgate House provided the occasional brief billet for a transferred officer or two, but much of the time it was empty except for Dr. Fox and, once or twice a week, Hetty Larkin. The isolation was partly what made Kilnsgate less attractive to the armed forces, though during one period this played in the house's favor, when it was used in a top-secret capacity between August 1940 and July 1942.

Dr. Fox's own practice continued as best as it could. Dr. Nelson's wife, Mary, as usual, handled most of the administrative duties. These were quiet times for the most part in North Yorkshire, and one wonders what thoughts passed through Ernest Fox's mind as he sat puffing his pipe in front of a crackling fire during the darkest and loneliest days and nights of the war.

Grace finally returned to her husband and her family home on November 4, 1945. Once back at Kilnsgate House, she left the nursing profession forever and took up her duties as a housewife. Ernest settled into life as a country GP again, while continuing his various research projects, and almost a year later their only child was born, a son named Randolph, after Grace's own father, who had died of pneumonia during the war. Grace then appeared to devote herself to motherhood and housekeeping, with the faithful Hetty's help.

As mistress of Kilnsgate House, Grace remained outwardly gracious and courteous, the kind of woman who would do anything to help a friend in need, but close friends also marked a change in her since the war: dark moods, unpredictable outbursts, and grim silences during which she seemed to retreat into some secret place within herself. What ailed her we will never know, as she never spoke of it to anyone.

Was it in that dark, lonely place where she first hatched the plot for her husband's murder? Because according to the Crown, this was far from a crime of passion executed in the heat of the moment, but a coolly thought-out, nearly foolproof way of ridding herself of a husband she had ceased to love. Grace merely seized the opportunity of the snowstorm and the witnesses present in Kilnsgate House to put into action a plan she had been long devising. Whether Samuel Porter himself was involved in the plot must also remain within the realm of speculation, for no accusation or proof was ever brought to bear on the matter, and no charges were ever laid against him. So we move now to January 1, 1953, as cruel a winter's night as there had been in Swaledale for many a year.

OCTOBER 2010

The following morning I took my first walk around Kilnsgarthdale. I turned right outside the gate and carried on by the beck side about a couple of hundred yards, where the dale seemed to end at a drystone wall. I saw when I got closer that it was actually two walls enclosing a track, with a stile for access on my side. The track ran south over the hill, toward Richmond, and in the other direction it seemed to come to an end by the two overgrown lime kilns on the slope. After this, the track was obscured by shrubbery and grass, the remains of the wall just a pile of stones. Beyond the second wall lay the woods.

I retraced my steps and crossed the little packhorse bridge outside Kilnsgate House, then walked up the opposite daleside to the lime kiln I could see from my bedroom window. I hadn't had a really good look at it close up, and now I knew what it was I paused to do was just that. It was certainly a creepy place, like a half-buried drystone dome or egg, its eye half obscured by weeds. I bent and peered in as deep as I could, but could see no trace of the grates over which the layers of limestone and coal were laid, or the ashes of the fire below. I scrambled around the back, higher up the hillside, and saw the top was covered with sod. To think it had squatted there unused, useless, for over 150 years. What comings and goings had that fixed eye seen during that time?

I walked on through the fields and the small plantation beyond, emerging finally on the long grass of Low Moor, the site of the old Richmond racecourse. Since finding out about the lime kiln, I had bought a book at the Castle Hill Bookshop and read up a bit on local history. The Richmond racecourse had been in use from the late eighteenth to the late nineteenth centuries, until horses had become too strong and fast for its tight turns. Now it was a vast tract of open moorland above the town, its bridle path used for occasional training gallops.

I passed the derelict stone grandstand, imagining what a fine building it must have been in its heyday, and paused to admire the view in all directions. It was a clear day, and I could see as far as the North Yorkshire Moors and Sutton Bank, rising from the plain of York, in the southeast, and more directly east, Darlington and the Teesside conurbation of Middlesboro and Stockton beyond. The book said you could see as far as the east coast, but I couldn't make out the shoreline.

I hadn't seen a soul on my walk so far, but now I encountered a number of people walking their dogs. Most of them said hello and made some comment on the weather. When I remarked to one fellow what a lovely day it was, he agreed, but added, with a typical Yorkshire nose for the downside, that the sun had actually gone behind some clouds for a while not so long ago, and that it might well do so again soon.

I had been thinking about Grace Fox a lot since my talk with Ted Welland had provoked the sudden memory of my school days, and as I walked along across the grassy field that bright windy morning, shirt sleeves rolled up and jacket tied around my waist by the sleeves, I thought about her again. Had she trod this very same path? Had she enjoyed solitary walks, wondered about the magnificent ruin of the grandstand? What had she thought about? How had marriage to

Ernest Fox become so unbearable to her that she saw murder as her only way out? Where was the edge, and what had pushed her over it? Perhaps, as Ted had hinted, times were so different then that a woman seeking to escape a suffocating marriage for a young lover might have no recourse but murder. I doubted it, though. I couldn't help but think that there had to be more to it than that. The fifties might have been a more sexually uptight era than our own, but it was hardly the Victorian age. Surely the war must have shaken morality up a bit?

As I walked on, mulling over all this, a question formed in my mind, and I couldn't push it away: *What if she hadn't done it*? Innocent people got hanged all the time. Look at Timothy Evans, who was executed for the murders John Christie committed at 10 Rillington Place, or Derek Bentley, who had murdered no one, had simply shouted the famous and ambiguous words, "Let him have it, Chris." As Ted had mentioned, there was even some doubt these days that Dr. Crippen—such a monster that he'd been standing in Madame Tussauds for years—was innocent of his wife's murder. So it was certainly within the bounds of possibility.

What if Grace Fox *hadn't* done it? Why had no one considered that? Or had they? I realized how little I knew. Somehow, the idea of proving Grace's innocence excited me. I quickened my pace as the breeze whipped up, hardly pausing now to stop and gaze at the view of the town spread out below me as I carried on down the hill past the Garden Village development at the old army barracks, surrounded by its high stone wall and narrow entrance. The hill was called Gallowgate, I noticed. *Gallowgate.* What irony! There was a lot I needed to know, and the first thing I had to find out was where to look.

ONE OF THE SHOPS BUILT INTO THE SOUTH WALLS OF WHAT USED TO BE TRINITY Church, in the market square, was the secondhand bookshop Ted Welland had mentioned, Richmond Books, and it was there that I started my search. Unfortunately, the owner didn't have a copy of the edition of *Famous Trials* that dealt with Grace's case, though he said he would ask around and try to locate one for me. I left my address and telephone number with him. I thought of what Ted Welland had said of tracking down the newspaper accounts, too. They would be on micro-fiche somewhere. I decided to wait for the book and then see if I felt I needed more detail.

The owner did, however, point me in the direction of Wilf Pel-ham, a retired local schoolteacher, who had been eighteen when Grace Fox was hanged, and apparently still had the memory of an elephant. At this time of day, the bookseller said, glancing at his watch, I was as likely to find Wilf propping up the bar in the Castle Tavern as anywhere else. A free pint would go a long way toward loosening Wilf's tongue and sharpening his memory, he added.

There weren't many people in the Castle Tavern at that time of day, and only one of them was standing at the bar. I stood beside him, and as the barman pulled my pint, I asked him if he was Wilf Pelham.

"And who wants to know?" he replied.

I introduced myself and noticed him frown. His hair was greasy, he was overweight, and he had a three-day stubble, but his blue eyes were as lively and intelligent as they had probably always been.

"So you'll be the new owner of Kilnsgate House?" he said, turning toward me and showing interest.

"Word gets around."

"Especially if you've got nowt much else to do but listen to gossip," he said.

"Can I buy you a drink and ask you a few questions?" I offered.

"I don't see why not. Terry, give us another pint of bitter, will you, lad?"

While Terry poured the pint, I suggested that Wilf and I sit down. He didn't object, and we found a quiet table away from the bar. He smacked his lips and sipped his beer. "Aren't you something to do with Hollywood?" he asked me.

I told him what I did for a living, and he seemed genuinely inter-ested. He gave a little chuckle when I said I wrote the music nobody lis-tened to. "That must be hard to take sometimes," he said. "No matter how much they pay you."

"You get used to it. But, yes . . . I'd like to make something more memorable."

"Why don't you?"

"I'm giving it a try."

"Good for you, lad. Just don't be writing any of the atonal drivel or that cacophony that passes for music these days. I'm all for experiment and progress, but you've got to draw the line somewhere."

"Where would you draw it?"

Wilf thought for a moment. "Schoenberg."

"Well, that's pretty liberal," I said. "There are many would draw it a long time before him, *and* before Mahler, Bruckner, or Wagner."

"Like I said, I don't mind experimentation, up to a point, and I'm rather partial to a bit of Mahler once in a while. How do you do it, write film music?"

"What do you mean?"

"Do you watch the film first?"

"Good Lord, no. You start well before the film's finished, usually toward the end of shooting. But it all depends, really, on what sort of relationship you have with the director."

"How's that?"

"Well, if you work often with one particular director, then you'll be involved in the project right from the start,"

"Like Alfred Hitchcock and Bernard Herrmann?"

"That's right."

My eyebrows must have shot up. Wilf grinned, with a twinkle in his eye. "I'm not as thick as I look, you know. I was a music teacher once upon a time, centuries ago."

"I didn't know that," I said. I was starting to warm to Wilf Pelham. "Believe me, I knew you weren't thick when you mentioned Schoenberg."

"Is there anyone *you* work with often? Forgive my ignorance, but I don't follow the cinema as much as I used to do."

"That's all right. Can't say I blame you. There's a director I've worked with a few times. He's called David Packer." David was also my best friend and had been a rock during my period of deepest despair after Laura's death.

"I've heard the name," said Wilf. "But how do you know what it's all about, then? Do you work from the script?"

"Nope. Never even read them. You can shoot a script a million different ways. I need something visual, so I usually work from rough cuts and pray for inspiration."

"Sounds like a hell of a job. Anyway, I don't suppose you came here to be interviewed. What is it you want to know? It's about the Foxes who used to live at Kilnsgate, I should imagine, isn't it?"

"Yes. The man in the bookshop said you were around at the time of the trial and you might know something about what happened."

"Oh, I was around, all right. Ernest Fox was our family GP. Can't say as I ever took to him, mind you."

"Why not?"

"You have to understand, doctors back then, they were like bloody lords of the manor, and he played the part to the hilt. Ernest Fox, stuck up pillock. Treated his patients like pieces of meat. Didn't like the NHS. Never a kind word to say for Nye Bevan. Brought him a lower class of patient, you see." Wilf leaned forward and breathed some beery fumes in my direction. "Let me tell you, lad, I once went to him with an ingrown toenail turned septic—bastard games master at school made me play rugger in boots a size too small, and my feet have never been the same since—anyway, what he does, Dr. Fox, is he takes a pair of scissors and he cuts the nail right down the side—blood and pus everywhere. Doesn't bat an eyelid. No painkiller, no warning, no nothing. Then he gives me a dusting of boracic powder and a prescription for more and sends me home. Never once even looks me in the eye. Cold-hearted bastard. Lucky my mum was waiting in the surgery. I couldn't have walked back home by myself, I was in such agony. I was hobbling around for weeks. But doctors were gods back then, lad. Got away with murder. Well, this time it was the doctor's wife, only she didn't get away with it, did she?"

"Did you know her?"

"Grace? Yes, I knew her. I was just a baby when she first arrived in town, but she was always around while I was growing up. I suppose I was about fifteen or so before I first talked to her. Believe it or not, I was quite the classical music buff, even back then, in the late forties and early fifties, and Grace was a member of all the local musical societies. I used to see her at the subscription concerts in the King's Arms assembly rooms. Liszt played there once, you know. Before my time, of course. We were more likely to get Phyllis Sellick. Anyway, I also heard Grace sing at Operatic Society productions, and I heard her play piano a couple of times at Amateur Music Society evenings. I even worked with her when she was music director for the Richmond High School's *Dido and Aeneas*. That'd be 1949, a few years before . . . well, you know. Did you know that Purcell wrote that for a girls' school? I just helped with the sets, mind, a bit of carpentry, but once I heard Grace sing 'When I am laid in earth,' to show Wendy Flintoff, who was playing Dido and who was my girlfriend at the time, how it should be sung. I'll never forget it. You know the song, I suppose?"

"Indeed I do."

"I remember as if it were yesterday. The smell of sawdust and paint, Grace standing by the piano, her eyes closed, and that voice pouring out. I don't think I breathed throughout the whole song. Made me tingle all over, especially when she got to the 'Remember me, remember me' bit. I could never listen to it again after, you know, without thinking of her. She was very good. Even then, she sounded as if she *understood* it. The feeling. I don't know." Wilf took a long swig of beer. "She was a fine figure of a woman. Always very stylish, I remember—had her hair done at the Georgian House, bought her clothes in Harrogate. She had the walk, too, the confidence, elegance. She reminded me a bit of Audrey Hepburn or Elizabeth Taylor. One of those film stars, anyway. A lot of the women's fashion back then put an emphasis on a narrow waist, and Grace Fox had the waist to carry it off. But she had no side to her. She wasn't stuck up or cruel like her husband. I think all us lads—I was eighteen at the time it all happened—were secretly in love with her, and none of us could imagine why she'd married him. He was twenty years older than she was, to start with."

"Lots of men marry younger women."

"Oh, aye, I know that. My Valerie was ten years younger than me. And I'm not criticizing it, not as a practice, that is. It's just that when you're eighteen it seems . . . well, such a waste. Especially when it's a jumped-up arrogant wanker like Ernest Fox."

I laughed. "Jealousy, then? But Grace must have been how old, when it all happened?"

"Forty, or thereabouts, I reckon. But, as I said, she was a fine figure of a woman, any adolescent boy's wet dream."

"Did you know much about their life together?"

"No. Except what came out at the trial. Kilnsgate House suited Dr. Fox's lord of the manor status, he thought. Somewhere to look down on us all from. Could have got up to all sorts out there, for all I know, and nobody would have been any the wiser."

"Like what?"

"It was just a figure of speech."

"Were there any rumors?"

"There are always rumors. There'll be a few about you soon enough, you wait and see."

"Like what?"

"Orgies, dancing naked in the woods, black masses, sacrificing virgins . . ." He laughed and showed yellowing, crooked teeth.

"Were there any rumors like that about the Foxes?"

"I'm pulling your leg, lad. No, there weren't. Not that I heard."

"Did it surprise you when Grace was charged with murder?"

"I should say so. Shocked the whole town. See, it had been more than a week since he died, in the storm, like. First they couldn't get to Kilnsgate House to bring out the body because the snow had drifted so high, then the first postmortem turned up nothing unusual. Seemed he'd simply died of a heart attack. They'd had some friends over for dinner the night it happened, and young Hetty Larkin, the cook and maidservant, was there, too, and they all said Dr. Fox took poorly at the dinner table. Terrible indigestion. He took a powder and went to bed early. It was during the night that it happened. They all got stranded there, of course, and the telegraph wires were down. Trapped in a big old house with a dead body. Very Agatha Christie. Must have been pretty gruesome."

"Was this Hetty Larkin a regular maidservant?"

"Yes. She lived up Ravensworth way. Used to bicycle back and forth. Funny sort of lass, as I remember. Not quite all there, if you follow my drift. Worked at Kilnsgate House for quite a long time, too. I think she was there right from the start, when they came, before the war. Lost her brother at the D-day landings, poor cow. She used to stop over sometimes, too, if they had a fancy dinner or something like. The Foxes had a room set aside for her. The rest of the time she'd come for the day and take care of the washing and cooking and such. That night she had no choice. She had to stop."

"What became of her?"

"She died years ago, poor lass. Car accident, fog on the A66. Only in her forties, she was. Not much older than Grace herself was when she died."

"What made the police suspect Grace in the first place?"

"They didn't. Not at first. It was because of the boyfriend. Sam Porter. He was only nineteen, nearly the same age as me, lucky bastard."

"So Grace had been seeing this Porter for some time?"

"Apparently they'd been having secret trysts going on for six months or more by then. Somebody talked."

"Who?"

"Landlady of a guesthouse in Leyburn. She said she'd rented them a room once. According to Sam Porter, she approached him and demanded money to keep quiet. Well, Sam had no money, had he, and he'd got too much pride to go to Grace Fox and ask her for any, I'll give him that, so he told the woman to sod off. Which she did. Right to the police. That's partly what got Sam off, you see—not that he was charged, but you know what I mean. If he'd thought there was something to worry about, he'd have got Grace to pay her the money, wouldn't he? Stands to reason. She could afford it. It was because he told the woman to stuff it that the police got suspicious. I mean, when they found out Grace had a much younger lover, they started to dig a bit more deeply."

"You sound as if you knew Sam Porter."

"I did. Like I said, we were about the same age. He was part of the crowd sometimes. We'd drink in the pubs occasionally. You know what kids are like. But he was always on the fringes. The quiet one. The rebel. Bit of an innocent, really. Always had to be just a little different."

"What did he do? I heard he was an artist or a musician, and a bit of a ne'er-do-well."

Wilf raised his eyebrows. " 'Ne'er-do-well'? I wouldn't exactly describe Sam Porter that way. He might not have been rich or titled or anything, but he worked hard, and he had talent. He was an artist.

That's why he had no money. But he was no scrounger. He made a living, did odd jobs around town, a bit of drystone wall work, carpentry and the like. Lived in a small flat off the market square. He was pretty good with cars and mechanical stuff, too. I think that's how he first met Grace, when her motorbike went on the fritz. He also did a bit of painting and decorating on the side. Jack of all trades, really. Hardly a ne'er-do-well."

"Grace rode a motorcycle?"

"Learned in the war, apparently. Sometimes you'd think she had a death wish, the speed she went tearing up and down those country lanes."

"Was Porter any good as an artist?"

"Aye. Good enough to make a decent living in addition to his odd jobs. Back then he did a nice line in local watercolor landscapes for the tourists, but he got more abstract as time went on."

"What was the general consensus about Grace?"

Wilf rattled his glass on the table. I noticed it was empty. Mine was, too, but I had been so busy listening that I hadn't really been paying attention. I went to the bar and bought another two pints.

"The general consensus?" he echoed when I got back.

"Yes. What did people think about her?"

"Aye, I know what it means. I'm just trying to gather the pieces together. She was liked, well liked. Maybe envied a bit by some of the townswomen. They were jealous of her beauty and status. And your uppity moral types might have looked down on her. But there was a tenderness about her—she'd been a nurse during the war, you know—and she was always a bit of a mystery to everyone. Reserved. Sad, even. But, as I said earlier, there was a general feeling of shock. You could sense it ripple through the market square the day the verdict came down. Of course, when she was first accused of the crime, there were a few who just tut-tutted, as if they'd always suspected something like that would happen, but most of us were stunned even then."

"Did anyone believe she hadn't done it?"

"I daresay some did, yes. But as the trial went on and the evidence mounted up, they mostly kept their own counsel. I reckon in the end almost everyone believed she'd done it, maybe when her mind was unbalanced or something, but whether they thought she deserved hanging for it was another matter."

"And you?"

He gazed at me with his bright eyes. "I've never been a fan of state-sanctioned murder, let's just put it that way."

I nodded. I never had, either, and until recently I'd lived in a state where the death penalty thrived and men languished on death row for years.

"Mind if I ask you a question?" Wilf said.

"Not at all."

"Why are you digging all this up now? Why are you interested in Grace Fox?"

I could only shake my head. "I don't really know, Wilf. It's just . . . living in the house, finding out . . . I feel some sort of connection. There's a painting of her in the hall, with her husband and child. She looks sad, lost. She . . ." I was about to tell Wilf that Grace reminded me a bit of my late wife, Laura, but I stopped myself. No need to go there. "I don't really know what fascinates me about it all," I went on, "except it's not every day you buy a house that belonged to a murderess. Why do you ask?"

"It's been a long time since anyone's asked about the Foxes, that's all."

"Is there anything else you can remember?"

"Not offhand."

"What about her son? There's a young boy in the portrait. What became of him?"

"Young Randolph? He went off to live with an aunt and uncle down south after the execution, so I recollect. Grace's younger sister Felicity. She'd married, but they had no children of their own. Last thing I heard he'd taken their name and the whole lot of them had emigrated to Australia."

"When would this have been?"

"Late fifties. Ten Pound Poms."

"So this Randolph could still be alive?"

"Easily. He'd only be in his sixties by now. They say sixty's the new forty these days. I wouldn't know. I'm seventy-six, myself. He was only a little kid at the time, and he spent most of the trial with his aunt Felicity and her husband."

"Do you know Felicity's married name?"

"Sorry. I never met her."

"Was Randolph in the house on the night it happened?"

"Yes. He was in bed, apparently. I shouldn't imagine the police questioned him very thoroughly, but it seems he was asleep and didn't hear or see a thing." He swigged some more beer. "I'll tell you someone who might know something, though."

"Who's that?"

"Sam Porter."

"Grace's lover? He's still alive?"

"Alive and living in Paris."

"Under the same name?"

"Yes."

"How do you know?"

Wilf tapped the side of his nose. "I still keep an eye on the papers, and he sells a painting or two every now and then. It's still considered news in the *Sunday Times* arts section."

5

Famous Trials: Grace Elizabeth Fox, April 1953, by Sir Charles Hamilton Morley

KILNSGATE HOUSE STANDS, PROUD IN ITS ISOLATION, CLOSE TO THE END OF a rough, unfenced lane about a mile and a half from the nearest road. The house is almost hidden from the laneway by trees and long grass, and it seemed well befitting a successful local GP when Ernest Fox took his new wife to live there in 1936. By January 1953, it had been their home for over seventeen years, and their only son, Randolph, had been born there. Tragically, Ernest Fox was soon to die there.

The Yorkshire Dales is an area well known for its natural, if somewhat rugged, beauty, and in addition to the major dales, valleys carved in the landscape by the retreating glaciers many thousands of years ago, there are numerous small, hidden dales, many scarcely inhabited. Such was Kilnsgarthdale, where Kilnsgate House was built by Sir John Metcalfe in 1748, and inhabited by his family until their fortunes dwindled in the 1850s.

After that time, a succession of owners took possession, but nobody remained there for long. Perhaps the remoteness drove them away, though Richmond was easily accessible, either by road or by country footpaths. Dr. Ernest Fox certainly never let the isolation restrict his social existence. He rode with the local hunt; was an active member of the golf club; socialized regularly at the many public houses in the area; drove every day to his practice in town, where he often lunched with the mayor and other local dignitaries; and made house calls among the many Swaledale villages. Dr. Fox was a very busy man about the dale, and beyond.

Though Grace Fox was a keen member of the Richmond Operatic Society and was renowned for her sweet mezzo-soprano, she perhaps led a more lonely existence since giving up nursing, especially when Randolph was sent to boarding school at the age of five, and the strain of boredom on one whose nerves were already somewhat frayed may have been a contributing factor to her subsequent behavior.

Whatever the reason, in July of 1952, Grace Fox took as her lover a young local odd-job man and would-be artist by the name of Samuel Porter, then age nineteen, and as inappropriate a companion for his social standing as for his youth. Thus began the endless round of deception, sin, secrecy, and guilt that was to end, as such things inevitably do end, in tragedy. Grace Fox was thirty-nine then, yet there was no doubt regarding her youth and beauty. With her long dark hair, her hourglass figure, and her beguiling eyes, Grace Fox was a remarkably attractive woman, with perhaps the only blemish on her appearance being a slight coarseness of complexion, apparently the result of over-exposure to sunlight during her nursing duties overseas. This, however, was easily obscured with a little cosmetic powder.

We must not forget what part Kilnsgarthdale's isolation, and the dreadful weather of that January, played in our tragedy. On the fatal night, a winter snowstorm of such magnitude blew in so quickly from the north that the snow drifted to heights of ten feet or more. Roads soon became impassable, and going out on foot was a sure invitation to a cold and icy death.

As four people sat to eat, warm and sheltered in the dining room of Kilnsgate House, celebrating the new year, a fire crackling in the hearth, protected from the wind howling and snow blowing all about them outside, little could they know that one among their number would seize the moment to put into effect a dastardly plan that had been forming in her mind for some time now.

OCTOBER 2010

If I wanted to find out any more about Grace Fox, I realized, I could always go to Paris and talk to Sam Porter. But was I willing to go that far, to expend that much time and money for a passing interest in a long-dead murderess? Some people would probably think I was crazy, but that didn't really bother me. The money wasn't a problem, either, but what about my piano sonata and my life at Kilnsgate? Well, I thought, the one would benefit from a little travel and fermentation, and the other was a long-term matter. A brief absence would do no harm. I had already promised Graham that I would visit him and Siobhan in Angoulême before Christmas, and it would be no problem to stop off in Paris on my way. In fact, it would be a genuine pleasure. There was no reason why I shouldn't simply drop in on Sam Porter while I was there.

Bernie Wilkins, a London art dealer, had once worked as a consultant on one of the films I'd scored a few years ago about an art forgery ring. He had never been to California before, so the studio flew him over, and I showed him around Hollywood, even introduced him to a couple of minor movie starlets I knew over lunch at the Ivy, in Beverly Hills, and judging by the smile on his face the following morning, he got lucky. I thought I knew him well enough to call on him for a favor. He would know where I could find Sam Porter. But first, there was the dinner party.

On Saturday morning I drove into town and parked at the co-op because the open-air market had taken over most of the square. As it was the third Saturday in the month, the farmers' market was there, too, so I was able to buy fresh local meat, cheeses, and vegetables for the evening's dinner. There would be no mahimahi—not that I could find any in Richmond, anyway—but a hearty game pie with roasted root vegetables.

After I had picked up the fresh food, I called at the local bakery and found some crusty baguettes, then I bought my stack of newspapers at Mills's, picked up a few staples such as tea, cream, chocolate, wine, bread, and coffee at the co-op, and headed home. I was able to spend some of the afternoon sitting out in my back garden sipping chilled pinot grigio, listening to the birds in the trees. and reading through the various news and arts sections until it was time to prepare the meal.

I had everything organized and under control by the time my guests arrived at half past seven. I had dressed casually, the way I usually do, in light tan chinos and a button-down blue oxford, but Heather looked ravishing in a long, clinging, bottle green dress of some silky, flowing material, cut just low enough to reveal a hint of pale, freckled cleavage. Her hair cascaded over her shoulders and halfway down her back. Derek seemed a bit stiff in his Burton's best, striped tie and all, and Charlotte was attractive in a blond, healthy, sporty way, with short hair, simple blouse and skirt, rangy figure, and graceful, measured movements, like a dancer. She also proved to be intelligent and polite enough to have found out a bit about me and my work. She had obviously watched a couple of DVDs over the last week and was able to make informed comments on various themes and ask me why I had done certain things with the music. Heather had chosen well; Charlotte was good company.

It wasn't warm enough to sit outside by then, nor was it cold enough to light both fires. I settled on the one in the dining area for atmosphere. We first sat in the living room to enjoy the champagne, with Angela Hewitt playing Bach softly in the background. A sacrilege, really, but music has many purposes, as I, of all people, should know. I love the Who and Bob Dylan, too, but I would hardly play *Live at Leeds* or *Blonde on Blonde* at a dinner party.

The grand piano was an obvious talking point, and I let myself be bullied into picking out a theme or two from my repertoire, just to show them how good it sounded now that it had been professionally tuned. I threw in one of Satie's *Gymnopédies* to prove that I could also play music people wanted to listen to, and it sounded a lot better than it had on my previous attempt. My audience of three applauded politely, but I could see that Heather was genuinely impressed.

"That was lovely," she said. "You should have been a concert pianist."

"Not good enough," I said. "Oh, my teachers said I had the makings, but I didn't have the confidence, and I was too lazy. I didn't have the dedication or the stamina it takes to make the grade at that level, either. Besides, I was more interested in composition."

"Then maybe you should have been a composer?"

"I am."

She blushed. "You know what I mean."

Derek laughed. "There you go, darling, putting your foot in it again," he said in a haughty manner. I recognized a put-down when I heard one. Heather's lips tightened. There was definite atmosphere.

I picked up my glass, walked over to the armchair, and smiled to let her know I wasn't offended. "Yes, I do know what you mean," I said. " 'Promising young composer tempted away by the siren song of Hollywood.' That's what one of the newspapers wrote when I left."

"Was it true?" Charlotte asked. "Was it the money and the fame that lured you away from your true path?"

"No. It was a load of bollocks, really," I said, perching on the arm of my chair. "I wasn't all that promising. I'd had a couple of minor works performed, but that was as far as it went. Anyway, what was I supposed to do? Starve in a garret? Teach? I loved movies, loved the music. I knew it was something I could do well. It was a challenge."

"Well, bravo for you," Heather said, without irony. "And we're fortunate enough to have you to play for us in your living room, too."

When it was time for dinner, we adjourned to the dining area by the crackling fire at the other end of the room, where it was easy for me to slip back and forth from the kitchen whenever I needed to. I sat next to Charlotte and opposite Heather. I dimmed the lights and put candles on the table. The flames from the fireplace cast silhouettes over the walls and ceiling, creating a slightly eerie effect.

Inevitably, somewhere between the main course and the salad, conversation turned to Grace Fox. Heather knew I was interested in the case, and she was determined to tease me about it; I could tell by the mischievous glint in her eyes. I think I had just been in and out of the kitchen to deliver the roasted vegetables while people helped themselves to the game pie when she said, "Of course, in Grace Fox's day there would have been a cook or a servant to help you at a dinner like this. You wouldn't have had to do it all yourself."

"Hetty Larkin," I said.

This clearly surprised Heather. "Who?"

"Maidservant. Chief cook and bottle washer. Whatever. Hetty Larkin was her name. She was the one who helped Grace and Ernest Fox around the house."

"My, my, you're a fast worker. Who told you that?"

"Wilf Pelham."

"Wilf Pelham!" Derek exclaimed. "That old tosspot. I'd think twice about believing a word he says, mate. He's just a useless piss-artist."

"Perhaps," I said, rather coldly. "But I like him, and I don't think he was drunk when I talked to him. And it's hardly the sort of thing you'd lie about it, is it? I mean, why? Hetty Larkin worked at Kilnsgate House as a general maidservant, and sometimes she stayed overnight, when they had guests for dinner, or if she had extra work to do, and so on. She was there on the night it happened."

"Can you imagine the scene?" Charlotte said, the candlelight flickering in her lively brown eyes. "The four of them sitting at dinner, just like we are now."

"In the same spot we are," I added.

"Oh, come off it," said Derek. "How can you possibly know that?"

"It's an informed guess. I don't think that this part of the room, or the kitchen, have been structurally altered. I think this always was the dining room, though it was probably separated from the living area by a wall. There may even have been two or three large rooms at the back of the house in Grace's day, and since then someone has knocked them into one. Besides, it makes sense, with the kitchen door being here, by the dining table. It's a very old door. You can see that much. No sense walking the long way around to bring out the food."

"And the piano?" Heather asked.

"I think it was Grace's," I said. "Back then, it was probably in a room of its own. The music room. Between here and the living room. At least, that's my guess. The tuner said it was old, nineteen thirties probably. It makes sense. I know that Grace was an accomplished amateur musician. There's sheet music inside the bench with her notations on it. A woman's hand, at any rate, by the looks of it."

Heather rolled her eyes.

"All innocently eating their dinners and talking," Charlotte continued, glancing from one to the other of us with wide eyes, "just like we are, but with the snow falling outside, then all of a sudden, one of them clutches his chest and drops dead." She mimicked clutching her chest and slumping sideways.

Even I had to laugh. "I don't think it happened quite like that, Charlotte," I said, "but it's an interesting image."

"Can't you just imagine the music?"

"Discord. Crescendo. Tympani!" I said. "But seriously, you're right. They would most likely have been eating here, exactly where we are. The decor would have been a bit different, of course, wallpaper, and the table and chairs. But no doubt the fire was lit. It was a cold winter's night."

Charlotte gave a little shudder. The candles flickered in a draft and the shadows danced.

"So Grace played the piano, did she?" Heather said.

I poured more wine. Everyone had helped themselves to extra game pie, and the dish was almost empty. It was good, if I say so myself. "Yes, I think so."

"Was it an *accomplishment*?" Derek taunted. "Did women have *accomplishments* back then?" By the sound of his voice, he had already had too much to drink.

"Longer ago," I said. "A Victorian thing. But I'd imagine it was still quite an accomplishment. I should think she had more time on her hands to practice than her husband did. He was a busy doctor."

But Derek wasn't listening to my answer. His attention had wandered to the ceiling.

"But how do you *know* all this?" Heather asked, flashing her husband a withering glance.

"Wilf told me. Grace was very active in the local music societies. He'd heard her sing and play."

Heather wrinkled her nose. "Cheat."

She was a bit tipsy, too; I could tell by the way she spoke. I wondered who was going to drive. Charlotte, perhaps. I sensed a growing distance and coolness between Heather and Derek, and the general snappishness you find between married couples who aren't getting along very well. I was sure that Charlotte must have noticed it, too, if she hadn't before.

"Anyway," I added, "maybe it would also surprise you all to know that Sam Porter, Grace's young lover at the time, is still alive and living in Paris."

"Never," said Derek. "I told you, most of the time Wilf Pelham's so pissed he can't remember what day of the week it is."

"It can be checked," I said. "I'm going there next week, so I think I'll have a chat with him if I can find him, and I think I can."

Heather was quiet, looking me at me in a peculiar way, her eyes narrowed. "To Paris? You're certainly going to some lengths in this business, aren't you?" she said. "What is it all about? Have you fallen in love with a ghost?"

An awkward silence followed, then I said, "That sounds like an idea for a really bad movie."

"With terrible music," Charlotte added, then we were away from dangerous waters, laughing, imitating a bad sound track, back sailing on calmer seas. "Did you sell Chris a haunted house, Heather?" Charlotte asked. "How careless of you."

I had known from the start that Heather was trying to set me up with Charlotte, but the odd thing was that it became clear as the evening went on that the real attraction was between Heather and me. Even Charlotte could see that. Derek, I'm not too sure about. Husbands can be remarkably thick sometimes, and my feeling was that Derek was thicker than most. Besides, the impression I got was that he saw only himself.

I had to disappear into the kitchen a while later to plate the desserts, and I hadn't been there more than a minute or two before I heard the door from the dining area swing open and shut behind me.

"I thought I'd keep you company," Heather said. "They're talking about the stock market." She made a face and leaned back against the fridge. One long strand of hair trailed over the front of her dress. She'd brought her drink with her, and she sipped some wine. "Do you like Charlotte?"

"She's very nice," I said.

"You know what I mean."

"She's very nice."

"You . . ." She shook her head. "I don't understand you. This thing about Grace Fox. She isn't real, you know. She isn't a real, warm, living human being. She doesn't *need* anything from you. There's nothing you can do for *her*."

I had to get some ice cream from the freezer, and when Heather saw me coming closer, she held her ground and looked me in the eye. I could tell from her body language, the way she seemed to move, to open for me, that I could have taken her in my arms at that moment and kissed her. Our lips were that close, and I think she wanted me to. I think we both wanted it. I could smell the wine and game on her breath and feel her heat, the sparks jumping between us, the sap stirring. I was *that* close.

You could say I bottled out, but her husband was in the dining room, and I was still a grieving widower. I'm no saint, but I'm not that much of a bastard, either. Heather obviously didn't agree. When she saw that nothing was going to happen, she slipped away sideways and headed out of the kitchen in a huff, toward the toilet, I guessed, without a word or a backward glance, slamming the door behind her.

Back in the dining room with cheese and dessert, the atmosphere had changed, and I could tell that Heather was angry and embarrassed. She accepted a generous measure of cognac, as did Derek, though Charlotte turned it down, preferring coffee. Everyone was full, so most of the cheese remained uneaten. No matter; it would do tomorrow, along with the last sliver of pie. We heard the rain start pattering against the windows.

Heather checked her watch. "Is that really the time?" She knocked back the rest of her cognac and turned to her husband. "We really must be going. We've kept Chris up far too late already."

"Not at all," I said.

"Perhaps he has a tryst with his ghost?" said Derek.

Everyone ignored that.

They picked up their coats in the hall. Derek tottered a little, putting his on. I offered umbrellas, but nobody wanted one, the car they had all come in being just outside the gate, and the garden path sheltered by trees. Besides, it wasn't raining very fast. Heather stumbled slightly as she headed down the uneven path, and I heard her and Derek start arguing about who was going to drive. Sensibly, Charlotte stepped in and took the keys from Derek. I waved as she drove them away and breathed a sigh of relief. That was one group I wouldn't be hosting again for a long time. Then I shut the door behind me and leaned against the wood.

Maybe I shouldn't have turned Heather down. God knows, it had been a long time since I had felt a woman's body warm and soft against me, and it wasn't that I had no interest in her. But where would that kiss have led? A hotel room? An invitation to come with me to London and Paris? Afternoon delights here at Kilnsgate House? Either way it would mean deception, secrecy, guilt. The usual machinery of infidelity. No, I told myself firmly. I had done the right thing. If I was going to find another woman, I was going to find her on my own, and she wouldn't be married to someone else. Magnetic attraction happens all the time—it's a fact of nature, pheromones or whatever—but it can be resisted, and resist it I would. The last thing I needed right now was to be stuck in the middle of someone's marital problems.

I thought about Heather's taunt. Was I really in love with a ghost? Maybe I was, but it wasn't Grace Fox's, though perhaps somewhere in my mind I was mixing up Grace with Laura. After all, I had so little of meaning in my life—at least until this interminable cloud of grief passed and let the light in again—that my piano sonata and my "investigation" of Grace Fox's story had become the mainstays of my existence. Heather was jealous, I concluded. Simple as that. Jealous of a ghost.

PERHAPS IT WAS THE BOOZE, BUT THAT NIGHT I HAD THE MOST TERRIBLE dream I had experienced so far in Kilnsgate. When I awoke with a start at about half past two, my heart was hammering in my chest and I was covered in sweat, but I couldn't remember what I had dreamed about that was so frightening. I lay for a moment, deep breathing, trying to orient myself before getting up. I knew there was no point in lying there. I had to do something, make some tea, watch a movie, anything.

As I finally stumbled toward the stairs, I noticed that the door to the bedroom opposite mine, the guest room, was slightly ajar. I could have sworn I had closed it after my tour of the house, and I hadn't been back there since. Puzzled, I wandered over and gave it a gentle push.

I couldn't be certain that I saw it, but just for a moment I thought I glimpsed a figure reflected in the wardrobe mirror. I knew it couldn't be me because the angle was all wrong. It wasn't a frightening figure; in fact, I had the impression that it was a beautiful woman in a long satin nightgown. She was standing still, as if deep in thought, or shock, staring at something, then suddenly she dashed away, simply disappeared.

It was all over in a split second, and when I tried to piece it all together afterward, I decided it must have been a carry-over from my dream. There were shadows in the old house. The curtains weren't closed, so perhaps I had seen the reflection of a tree branch silhouetted by the moonlight? I didn't know. Whatever it was, it unnerved me enough to make me switch the landing lights on before I ventured downstairs.

I certainly didn't want any more alcohol, so I settled on a cup of cocoa, a habit I had got into with Laura when we went to our cabin in Mammoth for the skiing in winter. Though there was no snow outside, the wind was howling, and the cocoa smelled and tasted good. I settled down in my viewing chair, tried to put the strange reflection out of my mind, and started watching Diana Dors and a young George Baker in *Tread Softly Stranger*. The music was dreadful, melodramatic and instrusive, but the satanic industrial landscape more than made up for it.

On Sunday, I drove into town just before lunchtime, bought three hefty newspapers, then headed up to the Shoulder of Mutton and enjoyed my roast beef and Yorkshire pudding in the cozy dining room. The place was filled with bric-a-brac on the shelves and in recesses around the walls: an old black telephone; a pair of binoculars; ancient spectacles beside a worn leather case; a possing stick just like the one my grandmother used to use to wash clothes; empty bottles of Nuits-Saint-Georges, Beaujolais nouveau 1999, and various other wines; and a painting of a Vins de Bourgogne shop and a Chateau D'Yquem poster. The rough stone walls were covered in framed prints and local landscapes for sale. A large group took up several tables pulled together, about three generations, by the looks of them, celebrating a grandparent's birthday. The children were well behaved, but some of the older folks got a bit rambunctious after a couple of pints.

I worked at the *Sunday Times* crossword and tried not to think too much about the previous evening's social disaster, or the bad dream and its aftermath. It was possible that the former would all be forgotten when Heather sobered up this morning. But somehow, I didn't think so. She would avoid me from now on, which might be difficult to do in such a small community. I wondered what Charlotte thought of it all, if she would say anything, either to Heather or to me. She must have noticed the tension. Only time would tell.

Squalls had blown in from the North Sea by the time I got home, so I spent the afternoon sprawled on the sofa in the living room reading the newspapers, Mahler's Eighth on the iPod dock. It sounded a bit thin, and I thought I should invest in a decent stereo system. Mahler has plenty of meat on his bones, and he cries out for powerful amps and big speakers.

Mother rang at about four to ask if I was settling in all right. I told her I was and asked her when she was planning on visiting me. The only place she was going before the weather got better, she told me in no uncertain terms, was to Graham and Siobhan's for Christmas. An old woman like her, she said, had to be careful. Just one nasty fall could put her out of action forever. I told her she was tough as old shoe leather, but she would have none of it.

I read through the music, film, and book reviews then nodded off over my still unfinished crossword. When I awoke, I found myself, from out of the blue, in a deep depression. It happened sometimes. I felt listless, hollow, sad, and self-pitying. Moving around did no good; it didn't matter which room I went into, I still felt the same. I knew from experience that there was nothing to do but weather it out, which took me the best part of the following two days.

During that time, I didn't care about my piano sonata, I didn't care about Grace Fox, I didn't care about eating or drinking, and I certainly didn't care about Heather or Charlotte or Derek. All I cared about was my own all-consuming, all-enveloping sense of loss, guilt, and misery, the years I felt I'd been cheated out of by Laura's death.

Even at the best of times, I couldn't come to terms with losing Laura, with the three years of illness; the cycles of hope, remission and relapse, desperation and misery; and in the end, her death, as if it had been inevitable from the start. I couldn't rationalize it the way some people did. I envied others their religion; I had nothing like that to make me feel better. I didn't believe that we would be reunited one day and that Laura was waiting for me in heaven. I had no feeling whatsoever of any greater purpose or plan in what had happened, of any meaning in it, let alone any way in which it might be for the best, or that it had happened for a reason. I couldn't even feel, as many of my friends suggested I should, that I ought to feel blessed to have known her for as long as I had, to be grateful for the wonderful years we had together, the good times. Grateful to whom? God? And why? Just to have her arbitrarily snatched away?

Many was the day I had wished I could let go of my pain and anger, but I couldn't. I grabbed on to memories like a drowning man would grab a log wrapped in barbed wire just to stay afloat, to stay alive, and the barbs skewered into me and fueled my rage and pain.

But now I didn't even have my rage and pain, just a numb sort of nothingness.

In retrospect, I don't know what I did with my time. Probably nothing at all. I suppose I wallowed in self-pity. I saw the future, when I saw one at all, as a huge gaping emptiness, days to be got through rather than lived, survived rather than enjoyed. I could have been anywhere—Santa Monica, Bournemouth, Leeds, London, Paris. Location didn't matter. The only relief was sleep, which came fitfully and at odd times. There were no dreams to console or distract me. If the strange night noises continued through all this, I didn't hear them.

And then, on Tuesday morning, it was gone almost as suddenly and unexpectedly as it had begun. There may have been a catalyst. In my desperation, I put on *Doctor Zhivago*, which for many reasons is my favorite movie of all time. I thought it might at least relieve the despair for three hours or so.

The scene where Komarovsky takes Larissa to a posh restaurant while the revolution is brewing in the snowy streets outside has always been one of my favorites because it reminds me of the first time I ever saw Laura, and even this time my numb mind was drawn in by the images, the music and silence, the colors, the contrasts. And the memory.

I was in Milwaukee to talk at a convention, and I was staying at the lovely old Pfister Hotel, sitting in the lobby bar, all polished wood and brass, enjoying a predinner whiskey and a cigarette—you could smoke in such places back then, and I did— watching the heavy snowflakes drift down outside, when this vision suddenly spun through the revolving doors and floated toward me.

She was wearing a full-length fur coat and matching hat, and when she took the hat off and shook her hair, a few snowflakes fell on her face and started to melt. I wanted to lick them off. Her smooth cheeks were flushed red from the cold, and her eyes were bright blue. As her blond waves tumbled free around her shoulders, I found myself, without even realizing what I was doing, uttering, "Lara." I thought I had said it under my breath, but immediately she looked in my direction, smiled, and said, "No, it's Laura, actually." Then she disappeared around the corner toward the elevators. Wrong movie.

I saw her again later that evening, after I'd been to a boozy dinner with fellow conventioneers, and I felt sufficiently emboldened to approach her. I can hold my liquor as a rule, so I don't think I made an ass of myself—at least she agreed to have lunch with me the following day—but it was months before she finally admitted to me that she had known exactly what I meant when I said, "Lara." *Doctor Zhivago* was one of her favorite movies, too, and she remembered the scene, the combination of old-world luxury, dancing, polished oak, etched glass, brass, and the falling snow, then the blood, the horses, the glinting blades, the furs.

Somehow or other, the memory of that Milwaukee winter's night drove away the black dog. I won't say that I immediately started jumping for joy, but bit by bit, like when your arm's gone to sleep, or you get a cramp in your foot, life slowly started to come back into me.

First I felt hunger, so I ate some bread and cheese, then I realized I needed a shave and a shower, and after that I had a burning desire to get out of the house, go for a walk. By the time I'd been up to the racecourse and back, I was ready to take on the world. Not that the world knew or cared. Instead, I spent about three hours at the piano and sketched out a part of the adagio that had been troubling me for a week or more, a long, sad, slowly unraveling melodic line in B flat, and for the first time I didn't hate what I'd written when I played it back.

That was enough for one day, I thought, exhausted. I opened a bottle of wine and contemplated the contents of the fridge for dinner. There wasn't much. Just a little leftover game pie. Take it slowly, I told myself. Step by step.

The next thing was to ring Bernie Wilkins in London. If anybody could help me to find Sam Porter, Bernie could.

6

Famous Trials: Grace Elizabeth Fox, April 1953, by Sir Charles Hamilton Morley

THE DINNER WAS SUPPOSED TO BE A JOYOUS CELEBRATION OF THE NEW YEAR, 1953, and of the prospect of a new position for Dr. Fox at a hospital near Salisbury, a prospect that would mean moving out of Kilnsgate House and all the way south to Wiltshire. As was their custom, Grace and Ernest Fox had invited two of their closest friends to dinner on Thursday, January first: county schools inspector Jeremy Lambert and his wife, Alice. This was something they had done every New Year's Day since the war ended. Sometimes another couple, the Lynleys, joined them, but this year they were on holiday in Italy. Hetty Larkin, Grace's regular maidservant, had agreed to handle the cooking and cleaning-up duties, as usual. Though rationing was still very much in force, those who dwelt in the country had a distinct advantage over town and city folk, and no doubt Ernest's contacts with the Dales farmers from before the war years and beyond ensured that his larder was always full, and that fresh meat, fruit, butter, and vegetables were plentiful.

A plain Yorkshire lass from plain Yorkshire stock, Hetty Larkin was not an adventurous cook, but she was reliable, and that evening she produced a simple but excellent meal—a menu suggested by Grace Fox herself—of roast beef, mashed potatoes, roast parsnips and brussels sprouts, along with a dessert of rhubarb pie and custard. Dr. Fox was known to keep an excellent wine cellar, and a significant quantity of claret was enjoyed by the two men, in particular.

As was usually the case at such gatherings, young Randolph was given a light meal early and packed off to his room. Already, at the age of seven, a keen reader, Randolph there spent some time reading *William and the Tramp*, which he had bought with his Christmas book token from his aunt Felicity on a trip to Leeds with his father the previous day, then the boy fell fast asleep.

Downstairs in the music room, Grace serenaded her guests with the third Schubert *Impromptu* before dinner was served, and then the group adjourned to the dining room before a blazing fire. Alice was first to notice that it was snowing outside, but nobody thought any more of this as they sat down to dine, snow hardly being a rare winter occurrence in the Yorkshire Dales. Conversation ranged over such events of the previous year as the king's death and the new queen, whose coronation was due later in the year, and the recent atomic bomb tests in Australia.

According to Alice, Grace chatted animatedly about her favorite films of the year, *The African Queen* and *Singin' in the Rain*, and enthused over Barbara Pym's latest novel *Excellent Women*, while Ernest explained the importance of the first mechanical heart to Jeremy. In other words, it was a perfectly ordinary evening in a perfectly ordinary English household. There were no arguments witnessed between Grace and Ernest Fox, though Alice Lambert did mention later on that there seemed to be more than the usual tension and distance between them. Otherwise, all seemed harmonious and in keeping with the spirit of the season. The new job was only vaguely alluded to, and according to Alice Lambert, Grace Fox showed no reaction at its mention.

During the trial, however, the prosecution managed to get Hetty Larkin to admit to having heard Dr. and Mrs. Fox arguing twice during the course of the week leading up to the dinner. On the first occasion, a Tuesday evening, Hetty thought she had heard Mrs. Fox tell her husband that she "couldn't let him do it," which the prosecuting counsel swiftly interpreted to mean she couldn't let him leave Yorkshire for Wiltshire. Later, on Thursday afternoon, Dr. Fox had seemed angry about a letter he insisted was private, that his wife had somehow tampered with.

Meanwhile, on the evening of January first, the storm outside raged beyond the drawn curtains and blazing fire of Kilnsgate House. Bad weather had been predicted, but nobody expected such an onslaught as was now unleashed on the unfortunate north. Snow from three to six inches deep fell in a wide area of northern England. Drifts blocked roads radiating from Alston, Cumberland, to Penrith, Barnard Castle, and Stanhope. Many roads were slippery in Lancashire and the northwest Midlands. Thick ice on roads near Glossop, Derbyshire, made driving difficult. Kilnsgarthdale was soon cut off by snowdrifts up to six feet deep in places, and the wind was bitterly cold.

As the diners enjoyed their evening and their conversation, they had no idea how bad the conditions were becoming outside. All they could hear was the wind whistling down the chimneys from time to time, or the rattle of a loose window frame. Hetty Larkin had already arranged to stay over for the night, as it would be a late evening's duty for her, so she was not especially concerned about the weather outside, and she had far more to occupy her time than glancing out of the window to see how deep the snow was. Already this winter was shaping up to be as memorable as those of 1940 and 1947, the last times Kilnsgate had been cut off.

The Lamberts had parked their car by the garden gate, and when it became clear later that they would not be able to drive back down the lane to the main road in such conditions, and that the main road itself would probably be impassable anyway, they accepted Grace and Ernest's invitation to remain at Kilnsgate House for the night in the guest bedroom, which Hetty had already made up for them, rather than attempt a dangerous, perhaps impossible, return to their home in Gilling West. By that time, though, something rather odd and disturbing had occurred in the house, something that further altered the course of the evening.

OCTOBER 2010

I left the Volvo at home and took a taxi to Darlington station, then the train down to London. I had talked with Bernie Wilkins, my art dealer colleague, on the telephone the previous day, and he had given me Samuel Porter's address. He was intrigued by my interest and suggested we meet for dinner. It would be good to see him again, I thought, and he might be able to tell me a bit more about Sam. I had booked a room at Hazlitt's, on Frith Street, where I usually stay when I'm on business in London, so we arranged to meet at Arbutus, just across the street.

I have always found train travel relaxing, despite the frequent delays and general lack of sympathy toward passengers on the part of the staff, who act as if they're doing you a big favor by letting you ride on their train in the first place, and you ought to be jolly well grateful for it. But you only notice these things if you've spent a long time away. If you live here all the time, I should imagine you just think it's the norm and expect nothing better. But I still love train travel. Many's the time I've stood in the security line at LAX wishing there were a train I could take to San Francisco that took less than about twelve hours to travel 383 miles!

Still plagued by childhood memories of British Rail sandwiches curled at the edges, I bought a ham and cheese baguette at the station, and a large Costa latte. The train arrived on time. No one had the seat next to me, so I was able to spread out, eat my lunch and sip my latte and watch the world go by. It was a pleasant enough day, with only a few clouds and the occasional brief shower, but mostly with enough blue sky to make baby a new bonnet, as my mother used to say. Shadows flitted over the Vale of York and the distant hills of Wensleydale, and soon we were past York and Doncaster, well on our way out of Yorkshire. I passed the time pleasantly listening to Tchaikovsky's string quartets on my iPod and reading my Alan Furst.

There were no delays, and the train rolled into King's Cross at 2:44, as promised. I followed the signs for the taxi rank opposite St. Pancras. The London crowds came as quite a shock after my weeks of peace and relative solitude at Kilnsgate House. The sun was out, so the streets were crowded as the taxi made its slow progress along Euston Road, and became even slower in the maze of the narrow one-way streets of Soho. People stood or sat at tables outside the pubs and coffee shops drinking and smoking—Café Italiano, Caffè Nero, Bertorelli's, Nelly Dean's, the Dog and Duck—as we went up one street and down another. There were roadworks everywhere, it seemed, as men replaced the old Victorian sewers. It cost more to get from Oxford Street to the hotel than it did from King's Cross to Oxford Street.

Hazlitt's has undergone a few changes over the years I've been staying there, including the installation of air-conditioning and a library bar. Most recently they have extended the reception area and added a wing of renovated, modern rooms with showers. But I was happy to find, when I first arrived in London just a few weeks ago, that the old-fashioned charm hadn't disappeared.

My room this time was as delightfully eccentric as the others I remembered staying in over the years, with uneven creaky floors, worn rugs, heavy silk curtains, antiques, gilt-framed paintings of eighteenth- and nineteenth-century gentlemen and ladies in their finery, a marble bust of some Greek or Roman orator, and a high carved oak bed. It was hot, so I slid open the large sash window a few inches. It overlooked a small courtyard, where an imitation Greek sculpture stood. The bathtub was the old claw-foot style, with telephone-handset shower. The toilet chain hung from the overhead cistern, the way they all used to do when I was a child.

I had plenty of time to kill, so after a little shopping on Oxford Street and Charing Cross Road, I indulged in a quick pint of Timothy Taylor at the Dog and Duck. I had had no success tracking down the *Famous Trials* account of the Grace Fox case in the secondhand book-shops on Charing Cross Road, though I did pick up a recent book on Hitchcock's film music, which I browsed through as I sipped my pint.

The restaurant was only a few yards along Frith Street, and Bernie was already waiting at a table by the window watching the ebb and flow of Soho life outside when I arrived. It was dark by then, and there were a few early party seekers on the street, but the most interesting Soho types don't come out until much later. Bernie poured me a glass of wine and we clinked glasses.

"Good to see you again, Chris," he said. "It's been a while."

"Too long."

He lowered his eyes. "I was very sorry to hear about Laura."

I drank some wine. "Thanks."

"Anyway, let's have a look at the menu."

I went for the bavette steak and Bernie settled on Elwy Valley lamb. We decided to stick with the same wine that Bernie had ordered before I arrived. A group of giggling, scantily clad girls walked by outside, fanning out across the narrow street, on their way to a club or a hen party. One of them was wearing Mickey Mouse ears and another was struggling on impossibly high heels. A taxi honked at them to get out of the road, and they scattered, screaming and giggling. "Some things never change," Bernie said. "It's ages since I've been to the West End."

We worked on our wine and reminisced about old times until the food came. "I still appreciate the way you took care of me in L.A., you know," he said.

"It can be a terribly lonely place." I remembered my own first days there, around the age of twenty-five, working on the score of that low-budget horror movie. I was dreadfully shy and spent most of my free time either shut away in the studio or in my tiny Sherwood Oaks apartment tinkling the ivories of my upright piano. What saved me was playing keyboards in a covers band at various bars and clubs around town. This was around 1975, and still a fairly exciting time in rock, a sort of buffer between the end of the sixties and the punk era. It may have been all Bay City Rollers and Abba as far as the charts were concerned, but Bowie was turning into the Thin White Duke, and Dylan, Pink Floyd, and the Stones were still churning out decent albums. Playing in the band got me a date with the pretty young blond actress who played the blood-sucking monster's first victim. Her name was Fey DeWitt, and she used to practice her lines on me in bed. She had an insatiable appetite for oral sex and Chinese takeaway, though not at the same time, but not for much else.

There were more young girls walking by in the street outside the restaurant, and I felt a sudden pang in my heart—for Laura, for Fey, for others I vaguely remembered—but mostly for my own lost youth.

"You were going to tell me why you want to talk to Samuel Porter," Bernie said between mouthfuls of succulent lamb.

"It's a bit complicated." I explained what I had learned so far about the Grace Fox case.

When I had finished, Bernie asked me the same question as Wilf Pelham: Why was I interested?

"I don't really know," I answered, as truthfully as I could. "I'm curious, that's all. I feel a connection. She was actually hanged at the prison right next to my old junior school, and now I'm living in her house. I feel as if I'm looking into the place's ancestry, a family tree, though it's not my own family tree, of course. And she sounds interesting. By all accounts she was a very beautiful and interesting woman. Mysterious. Enigmatic. She rode a motorbike. She made notations in the margins of her copy of Schubert's *Impromptus* in tiny neat handwriting. And I love Schubert." I didn't tell him about the night noises and the dark shadows I had imagined, her resemblance to Laura, or the figure in the wardrobe mirror lest he think me stark raving mad.

"But what does it matter? She's dead."

I filled my wineglass. This was becoming too much like the sort of interrogation I wanted to avoid, mostly because I didn't have the right answers. Didn't have *any* answers. But at the same time, I thought, Bernie was showing a disturbing lack of imagination. "Is that any reason to simply forget her?" I said. "She might not have done it. There may still be family out there. There's Samuel Porter for a start. And she had a son. Don't you think if there's a truth that differs from the official version *someone* might be interested in knowing it?"

Bernie gave me a long, sad look. "Maybe and maybe not," he said. "You might find that people don't want the past stirred up after having spent so long getting used to what you call the 'official version.' Most people accept an explanation that works for them and get on with their lives. Besides, what makes you think she might not have done it, or that you can suddenly find out the truth after all these years?"

"Nothing, seeing as you put it like that. I've no idea what really happened. I'm just interested, that's all. I'd like to build up a better picture."

"I'd be careful if I were you, Chris."

I gave a nervous laugh. "Careful? Why? Surely there's nobody left alive who'd want to harm me if I came up with a different explanation of what happened?"

"That wasn't exactly what I meant, though you may be wrong on that score, too. No, I meant be careful for yourself, for your own peace of mind, that you don't let this . . . this thing become an obsession, take you over, damage your psyche. You're probably fragile after Laura's death and all the upheaval of moving back over here. And I must say it's a pretty remote place you've chosen to live. The isolation can't be doing you any good."

I put my knife and fork down. "Thanks for your concern, Bernie. You think I'm going crazy?"

Bernie laughed uneasily. He must have seen the angry gleam in my eye. "Steady on, old mate. I wasn't saying that. I was just offering a friendly warning, that's all. Besides, maybe there *are* people still around who don't want the truth getting out. I mean, if Grace Fox didn't do it, there's a good chance that someone else did, isn't there? What about Samuel Porter himself? Maybe he did it? Have you thought of that?"

I had to admit that I hadn't. I had so little information to go on so far that any speculation as to what might have happened if Grace *were* to prove not guilty was quite beyond me. "Sam Porter must be pushing eighty," I said. "I don't think I've got anything to fear from him. I appreciate what you're saying, Bernie, I really do. But I'm not going mad, and I'm not getting obsessed. I've moved into a big old house in the country where a murder was committed nearly sixty years ago. I'm taking a break from work, from deadlines. I've got time on my hands, enough money to live on, to do what I want. I'm interested, that's all. Nothing's ever as straightforward as it seems. Hindsight can sometimes give you an advantage. All right?"

Bernie held up his hands. "Okay. Okay. You're just interested. Fair enough. I get it. Maybe I'd feel the same way if I were in your position. Let's order the cheese plate, shall we?"

"Are you still going to tell me where to find Samuel Porter?"

"Of course I am. But you can hardly ignore *my* curiosity, given yours, can you?"

"I suppose not."

Over the cheese and more wine I told him about my conversation with Wilf Pelham, where I had learned what little I knew of the circumstances of Ernest Fox's death and Grace's trial. Bernie listened intently, a little knot of concentration between his eyebrows.

"It's not very much, is it?" he said when I'd finished.

"That's the problem. But don't you think it's fascinating? I'm living in that house, where the murder took place, maybe even sleeping in the room where it happened."

"Yes, I suppose it is intriguing, in a *Daily Mail* sort of way. She didn't happen to leave any of her stuff lying around, did she? Diaries? Letters?"

"Not that I know of. And, believe me, I've had a good look around. There's a family portrait in the vestibule, that's all, and some sheet music I think she might have made notations on. Of course, lots of people have lived there or stayed there as guests since then."

"Even so . . . People miss things. The police miss things."

"All I can say is I didn't find anything interesting. How well do you know Samuel Porter?"

"I've met him a few times, mostly at openings and exhibitions. I must say, he's remarkably well preserved for his age. You'll be surprised. Got all his faculties, or he had last time I saw him a few months ago. Still an expert stylist. Can be a bit cantankerous, mind you. Likes his drink. Stickler over money. Takes the Eurostar over to London two or three times a year. There was a big retrospective of his work three or four years ago. He made quite a pile on that. Samuel's quite a charmer, really, especially with a few glasses of wine under his belt. Still has an eye for the ladies."

"Did he ever marry?"

"Not that I know of. At least, no mention of a wife, living or dead, has ever come up."

"Where does he live?"

"Montparnasse. Lived in the same flat for years, apparently. Maybe ever since he first arrived in Paris."

"When was that?"

"Oh, before my time. Midfifties, I think. When are you planning on going over to see him?"

"Tomorrow."

"Well, best of luck. There's nothing wrong with his memory, as far as I know, so it all depends on what sort of mood you catch him in. He's very stubborn, Samuel. If he doesn't want to talk about something he won't do it."

"I'll use my charm."

Bernie smiled. "I'm sure you'll be fine, then. Coffee?"

I FELT A BIT SHAKEN AFTER MY DINNER WITH BERNIE. HE HAD QUESTIONED MY motives even more severely than Wilf Pelham or Heather had, and he had even warned of the damage such a quest could do to me and to others. I hadn't thought of that. Whatever the reason, the double espresso, the cheese, the wine, the conversation, I felt jumpy and restless, and I knew there was no point in going back to my hotel room just yet. Instead, I started to walk around Soho, almost oblivious to my surroundings, but somehow just registering the bright lights of neon signs, the knots of people standing outside pubs or sitting at the cafés, some drunk by now, others deep in private conversations, the smells of espresso coffee and cigarette smoke, marijuana, the couples holding hands.

At least I had Samuel Porter's address in my pocket, and tomorrow I would head to Paris to talk to him. The anticipation of that meeting thrilled me in a way I would never have expected. It was a step closer to Grace, who, I realized, had become a mystery I had to unravel, if for no other reason than because it seemed that no one else had tried. So far, she remained a remote and enigmatic figure, but I hoped, through talking to her ex-lover, to add some substance to fill in a few details of the faint outline I had.

I had come full circle and found myself in Frith Street again, still too wired to go to my room. The Dog and Duck was still going strong, as was the gay club next door. People were piling out of restaurants into pubs and clubs. Taxis dropped off well-dressed men and women outside anonymous doors that seemed to open magically to their touch.

I found myself drawn to Ronnie Scott's to catch a late set. I didn't recognize the advertised singer's name, but I was willing to give her a try. I remembered the greats I had seen there years ago: Stan Getz,

Ella Fitzgerald, Bill Evans, Nina Simone, Sarah Vaughan. Too many to mention. All dead now. I paid and went in, found a seat at the bar at the back, just beyond the tables clustered around the stage, and ordered a glass of wine. It was between sets and animated conversations buzzed around me, but no one was talking to me, so I was free to drift.

I thought of Kilnsgate House, as empty at this moment as it had been over the years. But not quite. At least there were signs of occupation, of new life. A coffee-making machine in the kitchen; scribbled sheet music strewn around the piano, music that had never existed before; my clothes in the bedroom wardrobe and cupboard by the door; a few bottles of choice wine on the rack in the TV room, where my DVDs almost filled the small tower. I was making it home, and I felt an odd wrench at being away for the first time, more than I ever had on leaving L.A.

Ted Welland and Wilf Pelham had given me a start, but I still had a lot of work to do if I was to find out the truth about Grace Fox—and if I knew one thing, it was that it wasn't to be found in any trial accounts, newspaper articles, or town gossip. I had to dig deeper than that, examine the little details, study Grace's character, find out what hadn't been said or what had been glossed over. Like houses, small towns and villages have their secrets, and they are often difficult to pry out. But pry I would. Until something gave.

The audience applauded and a trio of stand-up bass, soprano saxophone, and piano struck up, then a young woman in a long black gown walked into the spotlight and the applause grew louder. She was about thirty, with beautiful chocolate satin skin and glossy black curls, and she had a deep, slightly husky voice that seemed to be caressing me with each warm, undulating syllable. She started to sing Billie Holiday's "I'll Look Around" and I was hers for the rest of the set.

7

Famous Trials: Grace Elizabeth Fox, April 1953, by Sir Charles Hamilton Morley

AFTER HETTY LARKIN HAD CLEARED THE TABLE OF THE REMAINS OF THE rhubarb pie and custard, she delivered the port and Stilton. Ernest Fox and Jeremy Lambert lit cigars at the dinner table, while their wives adjourned back to the hearthside in the living room and Hetty Larkin busied herself with the clearing up. About ten minutes later, according to Jeremy Lambert, Ernest Fox complained of heartburn, a painful condition to which he was apparently no stranger, and the two of them stubbed out their cigars and went through to join the women. Dr. Fox there suffered for some time, then excused himself from the company and said he would take himself to bed. Grace promised to follow with a glass of whiskey and milk and a preparation of the stomach powder he sometimes took for relief, as she had done on previous occasions. This she did momentarily, then promptly returned to the living room, where she assured her guests that her husband was resting comfortably, and remained by the hearth chatting with the Lamberts about local matters until they, too, decided it was time to retire.

It was now close to midnight. Young Randolph was fast asleep.

Hetty Larkin had finished clearing up and taken herself off to her room near the back of the house some time ago and was also asleep, no doubt dreaming of some strapping young farmer lad. The Lamberts had just retired and were preparing themselves for bed. Ernest Fox, everyone assumed, was sleeping soundly, having taken the stomach powder his wife had prepared for him.

It was another half an hour before Alice Lambert, who lay reading, unable to fall immediately asleep, heard Grace come up the stairs to bed. What she had been doing during the interceding time we shall never know, for in her initial statement to the police, Grace said that she had simply been sitting there in front of the fire, thinking, occasionally walking over to the window to watch the snow falling outside. Who was to gainsay her?

According to Grace, it was about an hour after she had retired that she thought she heard a noise from her husband's bedroom. She had been reading, she said, finding it difficult to get to sleep, and had been a little worried by his earlier symptoms. Nobody else heard a sound, all being fast asleep by then. Grace said that she crossed the gallery to Ernest's room and found him sitting up in bed clutching his left arm and grimacing with pain. He was dripping with perspiration, she said, and he complained of a burning tightness, like a hot iron band around his chest, making it impossible for him to breathe. Grace had worked as a Queen Alexandra's nurse during the war, as we have already learned, and she understood the symptoms of a heart attack every bit as well as her doctor husband.

Loosening his clothes and leaving him there, she hurried as fast as she could to his downstairs study, where he kept his doctor's bag, the one he always carried with him on his rounds, and returned upstairs with it. Though Ernest Fox had no history of heart disease, he was, like many doctors, inclined to neglect himself the kind of rigorous regular medical checkups that he urged on all his patients, and several people had lately noticed the increased incidences of indigestion and heartburn and a certain shortness of breath in the doctor, all possible symptoms of cardiac problems.

Following her training, Grace Fox told the coroner that she searched her husband's bag for nitroglycerine—often effective in curtailing the onset of angina pectoris—and placed a tablet under her husband's tongue. By this time, though, she feared she was too late, as her husband now seemed listless, and she could find only a weak and fluttery pulse.

Loath to leave him again, she went on, she had no recourse but to dash down to the telephone, which stood on a stand in the large vestibule area. But as soon as she started to dial 999 and heard only silence, it became clear that the telegraph wires were down. Grace told the police that she then returned to her husband, where she prepared an injection of digitalis, the nitroglycerine having had no effect. She then waited and sat by him at the bedside with her finger on his pulse as the digitalis entered his system, but it was to no avail. His poor heart fluttered like a dying bird in a cage, and finally gave up the ghost.

Alice Lambert, a light sleeper at the best of times, had heard the dashing up and down stairs and left her bedroom to see what was happening. The door to Grace's room stood wide open, the covers of her bed thrown back in disarray, and Grace herself appeared in the doorway of her husband's bedroom opposite. She seemed surprised to see Alice standing there, but shook her head slowly and said, "He's gone, Alice. He's gone."

Alice knelt by Ernest Fox's bedside and felt for a pulse. She found none; nor did the small mirror Grace brought from her room mist over with breath when placed near his mouth. Alice could see the bottle of sublingual nitroglycerine quite clearly on the bedside table, and she also noticed the paper in which the stomach powder had been wrapped, along with the syringe from which Grace had administered the digitalis. These objects were not in evidence two days later when the police and the mortuary van were able to get through the snowdrifts and examine the room. They were, in fact, never seen again, and nobody thought anything more of them until the arrest and trial. The fire in the hearth burned almost constantly throughout those two days, however, as it remained bitterly cold outside, and the grate was full of ashes.

OCTOBER 2010

I made my way through the crowds at the Gare du Nord, accosted by panhandlers all the way, and jumped into a taxi. My train journey had been uneventful. I had simply sat back and watched the French land-scape roll by, listening to the beginnings of my piano sonata, which I had managed to get from my computer onto my iPod, scribbling down notes and ideas as I went along. I prefer to compose in the old-fashioned way, with a piano and music-notation paper, but I do love gadgets, and I have no objection to using one every now and then. I found the rolling green countryside and the train's rhythm conducive to such work.

Once again, the city crowds came as a shock, even after London. The taxi took a route that had me lost within minutes, zigzagging along narrow side streets, crossing vast tree-lined boulevards, cafés, and brasseries with rows of tables outside where people sat smoking and chatting, or just watched the world go by.

The receptionist at my hotel on the boulevard Raspail spoke English better than I spoke French, and she seemed quite happy to do so. I was on the sixth floor, right at the top, and the lift was tiny. You'd maybe get two people and a suitcase in it, at most. Luckily, I had it to myself.

My room turned out to be a tiny suite. Put the studio and the bed-room together and it would probably be about as big as the room I'd had in Hazlitt's, which wasn't saying much. Still, it meant that I could spread out and avoid that cooped-up feeling. Being on the top floor helped, too. The studio was fitted with French windows that opened onto to a small balcony overlooking the Métro station at the inter-section of the boulevard Raspail and the boulevard Edgar Quinet. When I glanced through the bedroom window, I noticed that it had a fine view of the Cimitière du Montparnasse, one of those large Pari-sian cemeteries with elaborate tombs, where famous people are bur-ied. Jean-Paul Sartre, Samuel Beckett, Simone de Beauvoir, Man Ray, and Camille Saint-Saëns, among others, lay just below my bedroom window. Maybe I would overhear their ghosts deep in conversation throughout the night? I decided I would try to find time to have a walk around tomorrow morning.

For the moment, though, my main objective was to track down Samuel Porter, who according to the address Bernie had given me, didn't live too far from where I was staying. I wondered if he also had a view of the cemetery, and if it made him think of Grace Fox. It made me think of Laura. I can't say that Paris was ever *our* city, but we did visit it together on more than one occasion. Laura's French was excellent, and she loved to poke around the bookstalls along the Left Bank and go for long elaborate meals at fine restaurants. We would walk for miles and sit outside at boulevard cafés watching the people walk by. I remember once we walked all the way out to Père Lachaise and saw Oscar Wilde's tombstone covered in lipstick kisses, and a crowd of kids smoking pot around Jim Morrison's grave. They were so young they were not even born when the Lizard King was in his heyday.

I wasn't hungry, but I was in Paris and I felt like a drink, so I took my map and guidebook down to the bistro next door, sat outside, and ordered a *pichet* of red wine from the waiter. It was from the Languedoc, and it tasted good. Sometimes I think French wine tastes better just because you *are* in France. I was surrounded by young people in animated conversations, the girls nervously pushing back their hair from their eyes, the boys gesticulating, all smoking. I had expected the familiar whiff of Gauloises to come my way, but from what I could smell, and see of the packets on the tables, most people were smoking Marlboro Lights these days.

I pinpointed Sam Porter's address on my map. It wasn't far away, somewhere in the narrow maze of streets on the other side of the cemetery. I hadn't wanted to phone Sam first because I knew there was a chance that it might scare him off, that he might wish to avoid talking about the past and would refuse to see me. But if I just got my foot in the door, I was certain I could convince him that I wasn't a sensation seeker, a reporter, or a true-crime writer, and maybe he would talk to me.

When I had finished my wine, it was a little after four thirty, which I thought was as good a time as any to call on an ageing artist. I cut through the cemetery on a marked path that led between family tombs, some quite ornate, with carved angels, cherubim and seraphim. At the other side, I crossed rue Froidevaux and found the narrow street of five-story tenements. Sam's building was next to a small patisserie, bicycles chained to the lampposts outside. He lived on the fourth floor, and there was no lift. I had intended to wait until someone came in or left to get in the main door, but it turned out to be unlocked. With a sigh, I started climbing. The building seemed quite grand and well appointed, but then this was hardly a run-down area of the city. Old, perhaps, but moneyed.

I made it to the fourth floor without running out of breath, paused for a moment to collect my thoughts, then knocked on Samuel Potter's door.

AT FIRST I THOUGHT HE MUST BE OUT. THE INSIDE OF THE FLAT WAS SILENT when I put my ear to the door and nobody answered my first three knocks. It wasn't the end of the world. I could come back later. But just as I turned back to the staircase, I heard the sound of footsteps, then the click of a lock turning. The door opened, and there he stood. "*Bonjour, monsieur. Que voulez-vous?*"

"Sorry," I said. "I didn't mean to disturb you."

"You're English." He stretched and rubbed his eyes. "It's all right. I was just having my little siesta. You need them at my age. It was time to get up, anyway. Do please come in."

The Samuel Porter I saw before me shattered all my preconceptions. I had supposed, in my imagination, that he was a disheveled, dissolute, shrunken, rheumy-eyed, whiskered, and disagreeable old man, but he was not at all like that. Even though I had just woken him from his slumber, he had the erect posture of a much younger man, was slim but not scrawny, was clean shaven, had a lined face, a full head of neatly cut gray hair, and curious eyes behind silver-rimmed glasses. He was dressed casually in jeans and a mauve-and-white-striped shirt, but they didn't look as if they had come from the local charity shop. No paint stains, no reek of alcohol.

The flat itself was a revelation, too. I had known by now not to expect a garret, but I hadn't expected anything quite so large—it must have covered most of the floor on that side of the building—or so immaculate, so clean, neat, and tidy. Every surface shone. Every book was in its place. There were paintings hanging on the walls, mostly large, colorful abstracts. I didn't know who the artists were, but I guessed they were all originals. I had to learn not to cling to stereotypes about artists. After all, I was a musician myself, and hardly wild haired and drug addled. A bit untidy, perhaps, but clean.

He led me to the spacious living room, which had French windows, like my hotel room, and looked out on the tops of the buildings opposite. In the distance, just behind the low-pitched rooftops, I could see the massive monolith of the Montparnasse *tour* sticking up high into the clear blue sky.

"Look at me," he said, "inviting you into my home when I don't even know who you are. I don't often get visitors from England here. You could be a burglar or a murderer, for all I know. Or worse. A *critic*."

"I'm not," I assured him. "Actually, I'm a musician. A composer."

"Would I have heard of you?"

"I don't know. Perhaps. I compose film music. My name's Christopher Lowndes."

"I've seen the name. I must say, I have always found music to be one of the most essential elements of film, so I do tend to notice these things. Of course," he went on, sitting down and bidding me do likewise, "I don't get out to the cinema quite as often as I used to do, but I occasionally watch DVDs." His English was precise and mannered, rather posh, in fact, and there was no way of guessing he was a farmer's son from North Yorkshire.

I noticed a slight grimace of pain as he bent his knees to sit and wondered if he had arthritis or rheumatism. Perhaps that was why it had taken him so long to answer the door. It was hard to believe, but I had to keep reminding myself that he was in his late seventies. "I'm so sorry," he said. "I seem to be forgetting my manners. Can I offer you something? A drink, perhaps?"

I didn't really feel like a drink, but I thought it might be the kind of thing that would break the ice.

"I usually take a small Armagnac, myself, around this time of day. Purely medicinal, of course. The French doctors are far more understanding about alcohol than their English counterparts. Would you mind? My legs aren't what they used to be." He gestured toward a cock-tail cabinet by the door.

I could see glasses and several bottles. "Of course." I went over and poured us each a small measure of Armagnac and passed him the glass.

He took a sip and smacked his lips. "Mm. I used to be a Cognac man, you know, but once I tasted this . . . nectar of the gods." I smiled and we clinked glasses. "So," he went on, a curious and suspicious glint appearing in his eye. "What brings the composer of music for films to visit the aging doodler of pictures?"

I swirled the Armagnac in my glass, inhaling its scent. "It's a rather delicate matter, I'm afraid," I said. "I'll quite understand if you don't want to talk about it."

He raised his eyebrows. "Now you do have my attention. But in order to know whether I wish to talk about it or not, I need to know what it is."

Now I was here, I felt nervous and embarrassed. I didn't know how to explain my interest in Grace Fox to him other than as a prurient one, though I remained convinced it wasn't. There was nothing for it but to take the plunge. "It's about Grace," I said. "Grace Fox."

His expression didn't change. In fact, he sat there frozen, drink halfway to his mouth, staring beyond me. I couldn't read him. I didn't know whether he was remembering the past or was simply stunned by my audacity. I shifted nervously, sipped some more Armagnac. Too much; it made me cough.

After what seemed like hours, he turned back to me and said, "It was a very long time ago, but I don't see any reason *not* to talk about Grace, so long as you are who you say you are." He paused. "You know, the day Grace died, a part of me died with her. It's still difficult."

"But you're still here, still painting, a success."

"A fluke. What was it Beckett wrote? 'I can't go on. I'll go on.' Story of my life."

"Story of most of our lives, if truth be told," I said, thinking about Laura. There was something else Beckett had written that had always stuck in my memory, too, from my student days: "They give birth bestride a grave, the light gleams an instant, then it's night once more." But, oh, I thought, that instant, and the things we do to fill it, the way we try to grasp who we are, why we are, the love we give, and the cruelties we inflict. That instant is a lifetime. For some reason, I remembered the young jazz singer at Ronnie Scott's the previous evening, how she brought "Someone to Watch Over Me" to life, how she made it new. If she had gone on singing forever, I would have been listening forever, and that would have been the instant between darkness and darkness. But life is made of many moments like that.

Sam grunted an end to the philosophy. "It's an awful long way to come just to talk about a long-forgotten incident."

"I don't quite see it like that," I said, "but I'm on my way to visit my brother in Angoulême, so I thought I'd take the opportunity of calling on you on my way."

"Well, would you at least satisfy an old man's curiosity and tell me *why* you want to know?"

I tried to explain to him as best I could about how I had been drawn into the whole Grace Fox business through moving into Kilnsgate House; how finding out about the murder and the hanging had stimulated my interest, along with the family portrait; my brother's memory of the day of Grace's execution; and my conversation with Wilf Pelham.

"Wilf Pelham? Now there's a name to conjure with. So he's still alive, is he?"

"Do you remember him?"

"Of course I do. I may be old, but I'm not senile. Besides, it's the short-term memory that goes first. I remember those days as if they were yesterday. We used to play together when we were kids during the war, then we lost touch for a few years, as you do. I spent most of my time up at the farm, and I don't think we had a book in the house if it wasn't to do with giving birth to calves. But Wilf's parents were both teachers, educated, cultured people, and they lived on Frenchgate. Much more middle class, you know. But later, when we were fifteen or sixteen, Wilf was one of the few young town lads I could talk to. He knew about art and music and literature. You've no idea how rare that was. I liked him, and I think I actually learned quite a bit from him, even though he was younger than me. I was raw, unformed. Mostly up to that point I'd been sketching cows in a field or trying to capture an interesting landscape.

Wilf wasn't as stupid or as limited in his outlook as the rest. They were just . . . well, you know, sport, sheep, and sex, and not necessarily in that order. Wilf had a good eye, but music was his real passion. He and I had the occasional pint together later. He even used to come and help out up on the farm at lambing and shearing times."

"Didn't you go to art college?"

"No. Never. Everything I learned, I learned from other artists."

"Where was the farm?"

"Up Dalton way. I grew up there, but I went to school in Richmond. Farming wasn't the life for me. I left when I was seventeen, went to live in town in a poky little flat over a hat shop on the market square, but I went back to help out occasionally." He sniffed. "That was one of the things the press held against me, what made it all so much worse. I was only a farmer's boy, see. Sort of the equivalent to Mellors in *Lady Chatterley's Lover*, had it been readily available back then. Funny, isn't it, but have you thought that the only people who seem to have made a decent movie out of *Lady Chatterley* are the French? It always seems such an *English* story."

"What about Ken Russell?"

"I was never a fan. *Women in Love*? Maybe. Anyway, I digress. So it was Wilf who told you about me?"

"Yes."

"But how does he know where I live? We haven't met in sixty years or more."

"He doesn't. Once I knew you were still alive, I tracked you down myself through an art dealer colleague. It wasn't difficult. You do have a public reputation, you know. A good one."

"Yes, I suppose I do."

"So can you tell me anything?"

"Oh, there's plenty I can tell you. It's a matter of knowing where to begin. I suppose I could start by telling you that Ernest Fox wasn't a nice man."

"Wilf Pelham said as much."

Sam nodded. "Fox was an arrogant, cold, and cruel bastard."

"Why did Grace marry him, then?"

"A man's true face is not always apparent from the start. Besides, he was a friend of the family, daddy's ultimatum, a man of substance."

"It was arranged?"

"*Advantageous.* We English don't do arranged marriages. You should know that."

"Did he abuse Grace?"

"Depends on what you mean. He didn't hit her, I'm certain of it. She wouldn't have stood for that. But he did treat her like chattel, and he was cold toward her. That was the cruelest thing you could do to someone like Grace. She needed . . . she . . . I'm sorry." He sipped some more Armagnac and cleared his throat. He wasn't crying, but it was clear that he had been rather more overcome by emotion than he was used to. I began to feel guilty for putting him through it. And what if he had a heart attack or a stroke? "What I meant to say," he went on, "was that she needed nurturing, tenderness, kindness, and passion. Romance. She was damaged. Ernest was insensitive and callous. He shouldn't have been allowed anywhere near another human being in pain."

"Grace was damaged? How?"

"The war, I think. She never spoke about it, but it was there in her silences, her black moods. It seemed to come out most of all when she was confronted with great beauty. She always used to cry when she looked at a great painting, or when she heard a superb musical performance. She was a Queen Alexandra's nurse, you know, and she was overseas a lot. Nobody says much about their heroism, but they went through much the same horrors as the fighting men."

"She never mentioned her wartime experiences?"

"No. But people don't, do they? They just want to forget, not dwell on it. It's different when you're just a kid, though."

"What sort of experience was it for you?"

"Me?" Sam laughed. "Well, in my case there's nothing *to* talk about. Oh, it was all very exciting at the time, though we tended to be quite away from it all up on the farm. I mean, we didn't get the bombing raids or anything. Mostly it was the usual stuff. Missing sheep, a foot-and-mouth scare, a bad harvest, dealing with ministry officials and government directives about how much to grow of what."

"So what did you do?"

"Lived in a world of make-believe. Pretended I was a soldier, or a spy. I had my fighter and bomber identification charts, my Mickey Mouse gas mask, and my steel helmet. My father even put an Anderson shelter in the garden. We grew vegetables on top of it. We heard a doodlebug once, miles away, and sometimes the German bombers passed overhead on Teesside raids. Once a Messerschmitt crashed in a field near Willance's Leap. That was as exciting as it got. Of course, we still got plenty of local gossip from town."

"Like what?"

"Blackout violations, bossy Home Guards, and one of the ARP slipping it to someone else's wife. That one ended in a big showdown. The whole town came out for it. We had the occasional house fire, shortages, a row about the POW camp being too close, a missing person."

"Who went missing?"

"A young lad called Nat Bunting. Bit of a local character."

"What happened?"

"Don't know. He simply disappeared off the face of the earth. Never seen again. He wasn't quite all there, if you know what I mean, but he was always going on about joining up, doing his bit. Maybe he did join up and went off to war, got killed. He could have got lost in a cave or fallen down a pothole. Anything. Or maybe he just moved on. He didn't have any family as far as anyone knew. I only remember him because he used to come by the farm sometimes and my father would give him a few scraps of food. I'd talk to him sometimes. He was about my age, mentally, when I was about six or seven."

"But Grace missed all this?"

"From what I could gather. I didn't know her then." He paused. "They called her a cradle snatcher, but she wouldn't snatch as young as an eight- or nine-year-old boy." He smiled to himself then turned to me again and sighed. "No, Grace didn't talk about the war. Look, I'm still rather tired. As I said, I have no objection to carrying on this conversation, but perhaps we could eat dinner together this evening?"

"I'd like that," I said.

"Where are you staying?"

I told him.

"Then let's meet at Le Dome. It's right on the corner of the boulevard Montparnasse and rue Delambre, just down the street from your hotel. You can't miss it. Marcel will find us a quiet corner. Mention my name. Don't worry, I'll be there. Say eight o'clock?"

I knocked back the rest of my Armagnac and stood up. "Eight o'clock it is," I said. "Don't get up. Please. I'll find my own way out."

He nodded, and I walked down the hall to the front door, then down the stairs and out into the street.

I MUST CONFESS THAT I HAD A BRIEF NAP MYSELF WHEN I GOT BACK TO MY hotel. I'm not seventy-eight, but the years are definitely catching up with me. Or perhaps it was the wine and the Armagnac. Gone were my days of two martinis and a bottle of wine lunches followed by late nights in smoky bars lingering over the fifth single-malt scotch. The bars aren't even smoky anymore.

Just before eight, feeling a little refreshed, I set off down the boulevard Raspail toward the bright lights of Montparnasse, past a couple of cafés and a fitness center, where dedicated members were still running on the treadmills and riding the exercise bikes, pouring sweat. I felt guilty. I hadn't had a good workout in ages. But not *that* guilty. When I reached the broad, busy intersection, I spotted Le Dome easily on the corner just to my left.

I could see the waiter sizing me up with a surly, truculent expression on his face as I walked in and deciding at which of the Siberian tables he should seat me. As Sam Porter had told me to, I mentioned his name, and suddenly it was all smiles and *"Oui, oui, monsieur. Suivez-moi."*

It was a large split-level restaurant that gave the impression of being divided into several distinct areas. No doubt the waiter knew the pecking order. I took in the thirties art deco ambience as I followed him up the stairs and around a corner by the bar. It was all fabric-covered light fixtures, paintings on the walls, shiny brass rails, mirrors, plush red velvet banquettes, and polished wood. Probably the kind of place where Hemingway or Scott and Zelda used to eat when they were flush. Same waiters, too.

To my surprise, Sam was waiting in a little alcove, quite sheltered from the rest of the restaurant, reading a *Special Suspense* series thriller. You could probably seat about six people at the table, in a pinch, but tonight there were only the two of us, and it seemed roomy enough. Impressionist landscapes in gilt frames hung on the walls.

Sam put his book down and half stood to shake my hand before I sat. Tonight he was wearing a white linen jacket, mauve shirt, and a tie that looked as if it had been painted by Jackson Pollock. He had a glass of milky liquid beside him. Pernod, Ricard, or some such aperitif, I guessed. I declined his offer of the same.

He helped me with the menu and I settled on langoustines to start, followed by sole meunière. Sam went for oysters and sea bream. "The bouillabaisse is magnificent here," he said, "but I'm afraid my appetite doesn't quite stretch that far these days. It's very filling." He studied the wine list and settled on a bottle of Sancerre to start. When we got our ordering out of the way—which Sam did in what sounded to me like perfect French—he raised his glass and said, "*Salut.* You've given me a lot to think about, my musical friend. I looked you up on the Internet. Quite the career. I must say, I'm impressed. I've even seen some of your films."

"So that's why you wanted to leave our talk until later? So you could check me out?"

He inclined his head slightly. "Partly," he said. "Trust doesn't always come so easily when you've lived as long as I have and experienced some of the things I've known happen. But your sudden and dramatic appearance at my door did rather take me by surprise, and it did kick me back through the years with astonishing speed. I needed a little time to collect my thoughts, too, and to focus. Sure you won't have an aperitif?"

"No," I said. "Thanks. To be honest, I've always hated the smell and taste of aniseed since my school days. I think I nearly choked on an aniseed ball one day."

Sam chuckled. "Good lord, aniseed balls. I'd forgotten all about them. Gobstoppers, too, that changed color as you sucked them, and knobbly liquorice sticks like bits of wood that you chewed."

"Probably all disappeared now," I said. "Are these paintings genuine?" I asked, nodding toward the walls.

"Most of them. They're not forgeries, if that's what you mean, though they're often 'in the style of.' Pupils' work. That sort of thing." He shrugged. "One or two are quite valuable. Most aren't."

"It's a beautiful restaurant," I said.

"Indeed. A bit of old Paris. And just wait till you taste the sole. *C'est magnifique.* Anyway, I'm sure there must be lots of questions you want to ask me, so do go ahead. What is it you want to know?"

I hadn't really sketched out an approach, unsure as to what Sam would either remember or would wish to talk about. Instead, I had envisaged a free-ranging conversation in as relaxed a tone as possible. I certainly didn't want to appear to be interrogating him in any way.

"Were you ever inside Kilnsgate?"

"On occasion," Sam said, with a sly smile. "We had to be very careful, of course, very discreet. We hardly ever exchanged notes or letters, for example, and if we did we were careful to destroy them. 'Eat this message.' That was our joke. Each time we met we would arrange a different time and place for our next meeting, with a backup plan in case one of us couldn't make it. And I only ever gave her one present—a silver cigarette case that used to belong to my grandmother. She took it, said she would manage to keep it somehow, but not to buy her anything else. It all sounds a bit cloak and dagger now, I suppose, but we felt it necessary at the time. Ernest did go out of town on occasion, sometimes overnight, or even for longer. Naturally, if Randolph was away at school and Hetty wasn't due, we'd take advantage of that if we could. I'd hide my bicycle in the garden shed at the back. I don't need to tell you how out of the way Kilnsgate House is, so I'm sure you can imagine it wasn't very difficult to be discreet there. Most of the time we were making do with barns, haystacks, fields, whatever. It was all right in summer, but when autumn came, then winter . . . well, you can imagine.

"We loved the east coast most of all in late summer and early autumn: Staithes, Whitby, Robin Hood's Bay, though we didn't have occasion to go there very often. We did have some of our most wonderful days there, though, just walking on the cliff-top paths, eating fish and chips from the newspaper. So many memories. It wasn't all mad passionate sex, you know. We spent hours just talking about art and music or walking along quietly, just happy in each other's company, hand in hand. Some days I'd paint and Grace would sit or lie on the grass watching me, dozing off, dreaming. We thought we'd gone far enough afield that day we spent at the guesthouse in Leyburn to get out of the rain in November, but that damn Bible-thumping old bitch remembered us."

"It's true, then? Is that how the investigation got started?"

"Yes. If it hadn't been for her . . . who knows?" He shook his head slowly. "One stupid mistake. Ernest was away in Salisbury at some medical institute or other for a few days, and Randolph was at boarding school. We were out walking. The plan was to stay at Kilnsgate House that night, to go there after dark, but the heavens opened and we got caught in Leyburn after the last bus had gone. We debated what to do and decided in the end to stop the night at a guesthouse, as nobody was expecting Grace at Kilnsgate anyway. Just somewhere we picked at random, out of the way, we thought. Enter Mrs. bloody Compton. I thought I recognized her from a job I'd done in Richmond, some wall repairs, but Grace said I was imagining things. It was a dreadful place. Cold, dour, plain, uncomfortable. Threadbare carpets. Inadequate blankets. Bibles and religious pamphlets all over the place. Biblical quotes in needlework framed on the walls. Methodist. All work and no play. It gave me the bloody creeps. She wasn't going to let us stay at first. Didn't believe we were married. So I paid over the odds. That made it all right. Damn foolish of us, when you think back on it. Leyburn was far too close to home. But we didn't have a lot of choice, and who knew that Ernest Fox was going to die in a little over a month's time? Oh, maybe I should have just gone to Grace and asked her for the money to pay the old witch off. It wasn't that much. Grace would have given it to me, if it meant peace for us."

"She would only have come back for more," I said. "Blackmailers usually do."

Sam rubbed his forehead. "I suppose so. It was just the damn nerve of the woman that riled me. And the hypocrisy. I'm afraid I lost my temper, and that really set her against us. She even had the gall to make up things she said she'd overheard. Outright lies."

"What were they?"

"The lies she repeated in court. That she'd overheard Grace whispering about getting rid of Ernest for his money, poisoning him, then the two of us running off together."

"And you never did talk like that, not even in private?"

"Never. We may have fantasized about what life would be like if we were free, able to be together always. Grace may even have imagined out loud how it would be if Ernest were dead and we could go away together. Paris. Rome. Perhaps we even said we'd be happy to be rid of him. But nobody ever mentioned poison or killing him. Grace and I may have both had a touch of the bohemian in us, and Lord knows we were flying in the face of conventional morality, but we had our heads screwed on the right way, and we weren't killers. Nor were we stupid enough to think that we could murder Ernest and get away with it. We never even thought about it. The best we could hope for was that he would tire of Grace and kick her out, but he enjoyed tormenting and controlling her too much."

"Do you think that's why she killed him?"

Sam gave me a stern, questioning glance. "What makes you think she killed him?" he asked.

I was dumbstruck for a second, and it must have showed. The question of Grace's guilt was one I had been deliberately avoiding. Luckily, at that moment the waiter delivered our starters, along with the Sancerre, which he opened, let Sam taste, then poured and put the bottle in an ice bucket on a stand beside the table, covered it with a white linen napkin, and left.

"I'm trying to keep an open mind," I said in response to Sam's question, once we had sampled our starters and praised them to the skies. Enough people had already accused me of setting out to prove Grace's innocence that I was trying to sound as neutral as I possibly could. I should have known that, if anyone would, Sam Porter would certainly believe her to be so.

Sam pointed his fork at me. "Good. So let me tell you something before we go any further. Neither Grace nor I ever once spoke or dreamed of murdering Ernest Fox. I mean, we just weren't killers. It's not something we ever discussed or considered. I know everyone says it was my response to the interfering old landlady that got me off, showed I wasn't guilty, that if I'd had anything to hide I wouldn't have been so foolish as to send her away with a flea in her ear—that I'd have paid her off or murdered her, too."

"Did you tell the police that she had come to blackmail you?"

"Of course I did."

"And what did they do?"

"They laughed in my face."

"What did they think of your role in general?"

"They thought I was involved, of course. Especially after the other woman came forward. Some of them knew me, and they were already a bit dubious about the farmer's boy who'd left the farm to become an artist and made his living patching up walls and fences and fixing broken-down cars or motorbikes. Questioned me for hours. Beat me about a bit. That bastard Dettering and his cronies. But they'd no evidence."

"What other woman?"

"Landlady of a pub in Barnard Castle said she'd overheard us talking about 'getting rid' of somebody."

"It wasn't true?"

"Of course it bloody wasn't true. We were nowhere near Barnard Castle that day. We were in Leyburn, all right, but we never set foot in Barnard Castle. Oh, she was discredited before it went to trial as just an attention seeker—apparently she'd done that kind of thing before—but the damage was done by then as far as the police were concerned. Besides, they were coming out of the woodwork by then."

"Who were?"

"The town gossips, rumormongers. People who said they'd seen us together or overheard us plotting. People wanting to get in the limelight. People who said they'd seen other men coming and going from Kilnsgate House when Dr. Fox was out. The Compton woman started it, spreading poison to anyone who would listen. In chapel, at Bible class, wherever the moral lanterns burned brightly. *Everything* Grace had said and done over the past six months or more came under scrutiny, And who among us could stand that? They twisted and misinterpreted everything she had said and done. If the piano tuner had been to Kilnsgate, for example, there would be someone to say she saw a man coming out of Grace's house when she was supposed to be alone there. It was all rubbish, of course, and mostly easy to shoot down, but it did do some damage. Someone saw her down on Castle Walk talking to a young man in uniform a few days before the murder, and that became a big talking point for the gossips, then someone else thought she lingered too long talking to a young shopkeeper a day or so later. It was ridiculous. They tried to make a big thing out of all that, tried to make out she was a tart and I was only one of her many conquests."

"Who said this?"

"The townsfolk. The police."

"Who was the young man in uniform? Who were they talking about? Do you know?"

"No idea. I didn't see Grace after the middle of December. Randolph was home from school, and she was busy with Christmas. I spent most of the time until Christmas Eve staying with my uncle in Leeds while I was fixing up a few local bangers to make enough money to buy presents. Then I went up to the farm for the holidays. I could never find enough work in Richmond to keep me in paint and canvas."

"Did Grace's husband know about the affair?"

"If he did, he never said anything to her, or she never said anything to me."

"I see." I paused a moment to let everything he had said sink in. "But the police didn't charge you with anything, even after all this?"

"No. They couldn't prove anything. How could they? They had nothing but innuendo. I may have had as strong a motive as Grace in their eyes, but I had neither the means nor the opportunity. I was snowed in up at the farm with my mum and dad when the murder happened. The best they could have got me on was conspiracy, and that would have been pushing it."

"Did you testify to that in court?"

"I didn't get to testify. I mean, not to say what I really wanted. I was a witness for the prosecution. What do they call that on *Perry Mason*? A hostile witness? Adverse, I think they said. I don't remember. But if they thought I was going to help them hang Grace they had another thought coming."

"What did you tell them?"

"The truth, whenever I could get a word in. But all the prosecutor wanted to know about was my affair with Grace, my young age, how could we, where did we do it, that sort of thing. To establish her motive, since they hadn't been able to charge me. It was a morality show. No matter what I said, the jury was against me. If I tried to defend Grace, they just assumed I was lying to get her off because I loved her. Admirable, but not quite good enough. But no matter what the bastard inferred, or however much he bullied me, I wouldn't speak out against Grace, so in the end they gave up on me. You know, he even suggested that I'd been very clever in arranging things so that Grace took all the blame, that I knew my denial of the old woman's demands would result in the investigation into Grace's actions and, subsequently, in her arrest. I was basically told I was lucky not to be on trial for my life, too."

"But why on earth would you do that to someone you loved?"

"Exactly what I said. The courts don't take a particularly romantic view of love. They thought she did it for the money. Grace wasn't interested in money."

"Didn't Grace's barrister question you?"

"Of course, but what he could do? The damage was already done. And what could I say, anyway? That I loved her? Yes, it was true. That we'd been having an affair? That was also true. That her husband was a misogynistic bully? That would have gone down really well coming from a farmer's son. I think even the judge belonged to the same golf club or hunt. Fox had connections, you know, worked at them. All I could tell anyone was that Grace and I were two lost souls in love, and that neither of us would ever dream of hurting anyone. And who would believe that? It just wasn't enough."

As Sam spoke, his eyes welled with tears and he had to pause to check the emotion. "I'm sorry," he said. "I had no idea, after all this time, how angry and how sad it still makes me to talk about those days. Such a waste. Grace was a gentle, loving creature. I honestly can't believe that she murdered anybody."

"So you think she was hanged in error?"

"She wouldn't be the first one. Or the last."

"Did you visit her in jail?"

Sam looked down at his plate and shook his head. "I couldn't face her, and she asked me not to come, said that she was accepting her fate and that seeing me again would be too hard for her to bear. It would tear her apart. I never saw her again after mid-December, apart from that day in court. We wrote once or twice. Even that was hard enough. She'd told them in her statement that I had nothing to do with what happened, you know, and that I had no knowledge of her husband's death. That helped with my case, too."

"But she didn't confess to murder, herself?"

"No. She never did. She always maintained that he'd had a heart attack, and she went to help him, but she was too late. And I believe her."

"It would seem an obvious conclusion. But what did happen? How was she supposed to have poisoned him?"

"Potassium. Apparently it mimics the symptoms of a heart attack."

"What did Grace say in her letter?"

"She told me to forget her, to get on with my life."

I swallowed. That was close to what Laura had said to me when she knew she was dying. "Did Grace ever actually protest her innocence to *you*, tell you that she didn't do it?" I asked.

Sam frowned at me over his fork. "She didn't need to."

"But what about the evidence?"

Sam snorted. "What evidence? Grace was convicted on her morality and on the status of her husband. That she was having an affair with a much younger man, a mere farmer's son at that, only made her husband appear more the victim and gained him more sympathy from the jury."

"Do you think you had a chip on your shoulder?"

"Damn right I did." He let himself relax for a moment, shot me a sharp glance and emphasized it by pointing his fork at me again. "I still do. You should understand, given your background. How many times have you been judged and found wanting the moment you opened your mouth? It even made you run away to America."

"Well," I said, "the girls over there certainly do love an English accent. *Any* English accent. I didn't know you could find out so much about me on the Internet."

Sam poured more wine and managed a crooked smile. "You'd be surprised."

"Did no one else know what sort of person Ernest Fox was?" I asked.

Sam sniffed. "Oh, I'm sure they did. But in that, I wouldn't say he was a lot different from anyone else of his social standing. A pretty wife was a feather in his cap, something to hang on his arm, if I can mix my metaphors. So nobody said anything. And I wasn't even given the opportunity. The prosecutor tried to lead me in that direction a couple of times, into slagging off Fox, the clever bastard, but Grace's barrister was at least sharp enough to know how much more damage it would do if I attacked the character of Ernest Fox in court. Nobody wanted to go there. It's all a game, a delicate balance. Basically they tried to make out that Grace was the cold one, that they had separate rooms because of her, because she couldn't bear her husband touching her and denied him his conjugal rights."

"And that wasn't the case?"

"No. They'd had separate rooms ever since the sixth month of Grace's pregnancy with Randolph, and after the boy's birth Ernest decided he liked it that way. She'd given him his heir. He never touched her again."

8

Famous Trials: Grace Elizabeth Fox, April 1953, by Sir Charles Hamilton Morley

THE SNOW FINALLY STOPPED FALLING, AND ON THE MORNING OF SUNDAY, January 4, 1953, over two full days after the tragic event at Kilnsgate House, a local snow removal vehicle was able to clear the lane. The telegraph wires were still down, so no communication had been possible between the house and the outside world. In no time at all, though, once the situation had been explained, an ambulance arrived, but there was nothing to be done for Ernest Fox except to remove his body to the mortuary. Grace had left him in his bed and covered him with a clean white sheet. She had let the fire burn out in his bedroom and had not relit it, so that the winter chill had provided a natural preserving effect, ensuring that no unpleasant decay occurred in the body.

It is difficult for anyone who was not there to imagine the tension, the despair, and the horror of the four people marooned in Kilnsgate House for two days while the storm raged and the snow deepened. When help, therefore, finally arrived, the Lamberts and Hetty Larkin especially were no doubt grateful to find themselves homeward bound after spending two days trapped with a corpse and a grieving widow. What the grieving widow felt, we cannot know.

There was, at this time, no possible reason to suspect foul play, and therefore there was no immediate police search of the house. Because of the amount of time that had passed between Dr. Fox's death and the "discovery" of his body, however, and the need to determine an official cause of death, a coroner's inquest was ordered. Grace Fox described the actions she had taken on discovering that her husband was suffering a heart attack. The medical evidence was presented, and the pathologist who carried out the perfunctory postmortem noted that Dr. Fox had, indeed, died of natural causes—of a myocardial infarction—and the certificate of death was duly registered to that effect. The inquest was adjourned, the doctor's loss was mourned by the whole community, and the funeral was planned for Friday, January ninth. Grace's sister Felicity and her husband, Alfred, drove up to Kilnsgate as soon as they could after hearing of Ernest Fox's death.

That should have been the end of the matter.

However, on January 8, the local superintendent of CID, Kenneth Dettering, received a disturbing message from one Mrs. Patricia Compton, who ran a boardinghouse in Leyburn, to the effect that Grace Fox had been "carrying on" there with a local artist and odd-job man by the name of Samuel Porter, that Mr. Porter was, in her own words, "nobbut a boy," and that she had overheard the two of them in her guests' lounge planning to rid themselves of Mrs. Fox's husband by poison and run away together. Samuel Porter was in financial distress, of course, and without access to Ernest Fox's money, the two lovers would soon have found themselves at a pretty pass. And Grace Fox was known to have rather extravagant and expensive tastes. She might want to run off with a younger man, Detective Superintendent Dettering concluded, but she would want to do it with her husband's money.

On making discreet inquiries in the area, Detective Superintendent Dettering learned from some of the local shopkeepers and innkeepers that Grace Fox most certainly *had* been seen with the Porter boy in Leyburn that day, and that they had also been seen together in other places. He also learned of the new job prospect to which Dr. Fox had alluded at the New Year's dinner, which would take not only the good doctor, but also his wife, Grace, away from Richmond and, more important, away from Grace's lover, Samuel Porter. Suspecting that this threat of separation was the final straw for Grace Fox, Detective Superintendent Dettering immediately informed the coroner of his suspicions, and after a brief legal skirmish, the funeral was postponed; a second postmortem was ordered; the inquest was reconvened; and a police investigation into the death, now termed "suspicious," was ordered to commence immediately.

OCTOBER 2010

After coffee and rich chocolate desserts, Sam brushed aside all my offers to pay and asked me if I would care to join him for a nightcap back at his apartment. It was still early, not much past ten, and a very pleasant evening for strolling the boulevards of Paris, so I said I would be happy to do so.

We walked up the narrow rue Delambre, past the closed *poissonerie*, where you could still catch a whiff of the day's deliveries on the wet pavement. Sam wore a panama hat and carried a stick with a lion's-head handle, which he used more as a prop than as a necessary aid to walking. He walked slowly, but with a straight back, and without any noticeable shortness of breath. We waited for the lights to change at the boulevard Edgar Quinet, by the dark cemetery.

"This may sound like an odd question," I said, "but was anything bothering Grace when you last saw her? Did she seem upset, worried, unusually depressed, anything on her mind?"

"Not when I last saw her," said Sam. "But you have to remember, that was three weeks before her husband's death, and our relationship wasn't like that. We lived in our own world, a fantasy world, if you like. Grace didn't tell me about her domestic problems, if she had any. Most of the time I didn't really know what she was thinking. She loved art, music, books, and that's what we talked about when we weren't making love. We cared nothing for money and the material world. For Grace,

I think, our relationship was an escape, time out of time. She would have tired of me before long, I'm certain. There was a restlessness to her nature. I couldn't fathom her, didn't know what she was searching for."

"Was she religious?"

"I wouldn't say so. Certainly not in the ordinary way. She said she'd lost her faith, though she never amplified on why, but I think it was something she still struggled with. I think she was a deeply spiritual person. You know, with some people, you think they can go either way, become complete atheists or Catholic converts. Grace liked Graham Greene. He was one of her favorite novelists. That tells you something about her, I think."

"Greene was a Catholic convert."

"Yes, but it always seemed a bit of a struggle for him. Grace went to church for the sake of appearances. Most people of her social standing did attend back then. But she probably thought more about God than many who professed to be believers. The only thing that made church bearable for her was the music. She sang in the choir and played organ from time to time. She loved Bach and Handel. I mean, I'm an atheist, but it doesn't mean I don't appreciate Michelangelo or Giotto."

"Did she never talk about her problems or her feelings about her husband?"

"Oh, she told me about the separate rooms. But that was because *I* got jealous and started telling her how I couldn't bear the thought of anyone else touching her, making love to her, especially him. She rushed to assure me that nobody did, not even her husband. And she mentioned her little day-to-day problems now and then, but she never overburdened me with them. They weren't part of our relationship. I wasn't there to comfort her over Randolph's scraped knee or his getting into trouble at school, that sort of thing. She was quiet sometimes, distracted, even moody, but mostly, as I said, we inhabited a kind of idealized, romantic world. Other people didn't exist for us—until one burst into our haven with a vengeance. It was a very fragile, rarefied sort of affair. No, she didn't say anything else about how her husband treated her. I only inferred his coldness and cruelty from certain moods she had and things she alluded to."

"If you loved each other so much and didn't care about money, why didn't Grace just divorce Ernest and the two of you run away together? Surely people did that, even back in the fifties?"

"Oh, yes, of course they did. Sometimes. But it was more difficult and had far more stigma attached. Ernest Fox wouldn't have allowed it, for a start. I couldn't imagine a man like him accusing his wife of adultery and being branded a cuckold in public. People like him swept these things under the carpet, came to some sort of arrangement, carried on with their private cruelties, and presented a civilized veneer to the world. He was the kind of man who would have dragged her back home if she dared to desert him, just to prove his power."

"From what I can gather, though, Grace had always been a bit of a rebel, headstrong, a bit unconventional, wasn't she? She rode a motorbike, for one thing. That must have been unusual back then?"

Sam regarded me with a sad smile. "The Vincent. Yes. It was a bit of an affectation, really. She learned to ride during the war and found she quite enjoyed it. But that hardly meant she was the kind of woman who'd just abandon her husband and child, not to mention the status and comforts of her life. She wasn't *that* much of a rebel. Oh, we might have done it eventually, run away, had the relationship lasted, but we didn't, and then it was too late. If anyone overheard us saying anything, it would have been indulging in fantasies about running away together. But whatever we felt in each other's company, perhaps we both knew, when we were apart, that it wasn't going to happen. That we didn't have the courage, or whatever it took. Sometimes dreamers are only dreamers. And there was the child, don't forget. She wouldn't have abandoned Randolph to Ernest, and we could hardly have taken him with us. There was no room for a child in our fantasy world. God knows, Ernest didn't particularly like the boy, but if we *had* taken Randolph, Ernest would have hunted us to the ends of the earth to get back his rightful heir."

The light changed and we crossed to the rue de la Gaîté and carried on toward the rue Froidevaux, off which Sam's narrow street ran. There were plenty of people sitting out at the cafés and bistros, and passing one place, I actually caught a whiff of Gauloises, which took me back to school days. We used to buy all kinds of exotic cigarettes in a little tobacconist's on Boar Lane, in Leeds city center—Sobranie Cocktails, which came in different pastel colors and had gold filters; Sobranie Black Russians, with the long black tube; the oval Passing Cloud; Pall Mall and Peter Stuyvesant from America, along with Camels, which we believed were made of genuine camel dung; and from France, Disque Bleu, those yellow Gitanes, and Gauloises. Most of them tasted awful and made us cough, but we persisted, thinking ourselves sophisticated.

"How did you meet?" I asked, as we approached the tenement building.

Sam flashed me a smile. "At a local artists' exhibition in the indoor market in summer. It was July 19, I remember, the day the Olympics started in Helsinki. There'd been all that fuss about the Russians coming back in."

"And Grace?"

"She was just browsing around the exhibits. I thought she looked stunning. If you'd only seen her . . ." He shook his head. "'Age cannot wither her, nor custom stale her infinite variety.' Age just didn't come into it. It was a warm day, and she was wearing a yellow summer frock and a wide-brimmed hat with a matching band and a feather in it. You might think it odd, but one of the first things I noticed was her feet. She was wearing light, high-heeled Italian sandals, and you didn't see them very often in Richmond. Very elegant ankles, she had, and a fine arch."

"The artist's eye?" I remarked.

He shot me a wicked grin. "Exactly." The twinkle was still in his eye, all these years later. "She also carried a fan with an oriental design, which she used to swish the humid air about now and then. A bit affected, but attractive, nonetheless. Anyway, we got talking about one of the paintings she was thinking of buying for her sewing room, a rather anemic watercolor of Easby Abbey, I thought, and I was trying to steer her toward buying one of mine. I needed the money. In the end, she realized what I was up to and laughed."

"Did she buy it?"

"Yes. We went for a cup of tea in the market square, all perfectly innocent, you understand. Like I said before, I used to fiddle about with cars and mechanical stuff a lot back then, too, made a bit of money at it. She said she had a Vincent she was having a bit of a problem with, and I said I'd have a look at it. I asked if I could sketch her portrait in return. She knew quite a lot about art, music, and poetry. She was a fan of the Pre-Raphaelites, whom I thought represented a sort of over-blown eroticism. We disagreed, argued, but it didn't matter. That's how it all started. I was smitten from the beginning."

"And Grace?"

"I rather like to believe I amused her. You have to remember, we were both very shy. This sort of thing was new to both of us."

"She told you that?"

"That she hadn't had any other lovers since her marriage? Yes. I was very jealous. I'm sure I questioned her relentlessly. She did tell me that an officer kissed her once, during the war, but that was all."

"So why then? Why you?"

Sam paused and stared into space. "God only knows. She was bored, unhappy. She'd been living a lie for too long." He shrugged.

"The painting she bought?" I asked. "Do you remember what it was?"

"Do I remember? How could I forget? It was an oil painting of the lime kiln opposite Kilnsgate House. She hung it over the fireplace in one of the upstairs rooms, at the back. That was *her* room. She used it for sewing and reading and getting away from her husband for a bit of peace and quiet, and she had a lovely antique rolltop walnut escritoire where she used to sit and write her letters. She recognized the view immediately, of course, and we both thought it odd that I'd been out there several times making preparatory sketches and she hadn't seen me. You usually do notice strangers out Kilnsgarthdale way."

"It's still there," I said. "The painting. I like it." What Sam had just said excited me in a way I couldn't explain. It was *my* study now, Grace's old sewing room. In a way, it had chosen me. Sam's painting of the lime kiln still hung on the wall, the chair where she had sat reading or sewing into the small hours still stood nearby, the rolltop escritoire where she had written her letters and dealt with household matters was now my work desk.

"Thank you," said Sam.

"Did you ever see the family portrait at Kilnsgate, in the vestibule?"

Sam made a face. "Oh, my God, yes. Vivian Mountjoy, an old pal of Ernest Fox's from the golf club. Perfectly dreadful, isn't it?"

"I think the artist caught Grace's inner turmoil quite well."

Sam gave me a stern look.

"What about the boy, Randolph?" I asked, sensing that it was probably a good idea to change the subject. "Didn't he get in the way?"

"He was away with some relatives in Devon for the summer holidays. Seaside. Then, in the autumn, he went back to boarding school."

We arrived at the flat, and I must confess that the stairs gave me more trouble than they did Sam, though his knees seemed to be giving him a bit of a gyp. He grinned at me through his pain and said, "I've been thinking of moving for years, but I probably never will. It's too much trouble. I've acquired far too many possessions. Besides, I'd never be able to afford anywhere as grand as this now. They'll probably have to carry me out in a box."

Sam led me through to the living room and poured us both a generous Armagnac before flopping down in his favorite armchair. I noticed a slight sheen of sweat on his brow. He lit a small cigar, the first I had seen him smoke. "Another little indulgence," he said. "But only after dinner, and only the one."

"It was an excellent meal," I said, raising my glass. "Thank you."

"My pleasure. As I said, I don't get many English visitors these days. How are things in old Blighty?"

"Same as ever. The taxes are too high and the standard of living is miserable. Cutbacks all over the place. I understand you still travel there quite often?"

"For sales and exhibitions sometimes. But I tend to live a life of luxury when I'm there. Nice hotels, gentlemen's clubs, high-priced escorts, expensive restaurants. It's not the same as actually being part of the fabric of life, the way I used to be, paying taxes and worrying about bills and all that. Not exactly grass roots."

"Well, you still wouldn't find too much fancy stuff in Richmond," I said. "For that, they tell me, you have to go to Northallerton or Harrogate."

"Some things never change. Grace used to love going shopping in Harrogate."

"What did you do after the trial?"

Sam paused before answering. "Nothing. Not for a while. I stayed on at the flat in town at first, but people threw stones at the windows and scrawled obscenities on the door, so the landlord chucked me out. I couldn't get any work. I went back to live with my parents for a while, up at the farm. They didn't approve of what I'd done, of course, but they were good to me. I suppose it's true that home is the place where they always have to take you in. I still hoped there'd be a reprieve or something, that it would all turn out to be just a bad dream."

"Did all the townspeople turn against you?"

"No. Not all. Some offered sympathy, some pitied me, and some pretended nothing had ever happened. Wilf always stuck by me, I'll give him that."

"Did you go to Armley?"

"Once. Just to see it. I knew where it was, of course. My uncle lived in Wortley. I just stood outside, next to the school, and stared up. It was a forbidding building, like some dank medieval fortress."

"It still is," I said, "though there are modern additions now."

"I didn't want to be anywhere near there, when they . . . you understand? Call me a coward if you like, but I simply couldn't face it. I moved to London, then traveled around the continent for a couple of years, then I came here in the summer of 1956. Grace wrote me a very nice letter just before she died. A bit stiff, perhaps, a bit formal, but considering the circumstances, she was hardly going to pour out her soul. Still, she remained affectionate and tender to the end."

"What did she say?"

He raised an eyebrow. "Now, *that* I'm not going to tell you!"

"Fair enough."

He gazed at me for a moment as if considering something, then got slowly to his feet. "Come with me," he said.

I FOLLOWED SAM DOWN THE HALL, THEN HE TURNED LEFT ALONG ANOTHER corridor. Just how large was this apartment? I wondered. After another turn, we arrived at a door, which he opened, turned on the light, and stood by to let me enter. "Sorry it's so untidy," he said.

It wasn't really untidy, just cluttered, and there wasn't a great deal of space to move around. We were standing in a small room, not much more than a storage area, really. Several shelves were piled high with sketchbooks, and stacks of canvasses leaned against the walls. He searched through a heap on one of the shelves and pulled out a large, nicely bound sketchbook and handed it to me. I opened the pages. Inside, I found sketch after sketch of the same beautiful woman I had seen on the wall at Kilnsgate. I felt my breath catch in my throat. For one absurd moment, the image of the reflection in the wardrobe mirror also flashed across my mind. It was foolish, I told myself. I hadn't seen the figure clearly enough to recognize her. My imagination was playing tricks on me again.

"Grace," I said.

Sam nodded.

Some were nudes. I could see the firmness of her breasts, the little mole just over her heart and another beside her navel, the triangle of hair between her legs rendered like a mysterious dark mist. Her tummy was slightly rounded, her thighs slim, tapering down to shapely calves, exquisite ankles, and small, delicate feet. Though her skin was pale, it wasn't without blemishes, discolored patches and perhaps rather more moles than you would expect.

Some of the sketches were close-ups of various parts of her anatomy, a hand, an arm, a torso, and some were portraits, head and shoulders. There was a challenge in her gaze, her wide mouth, lips slightly parted, her big dark eyes narrowed as if she was squinting to see something beyond the artist, the tumbling black waves of her hair falling over her straight shoulders. Some of the sketches showed her lying on her back, hands behind her head with her eyes closed, a serene expression on her face, dozing in a field of grass and wildflowers, some close up, others with cliffs and sea in the background.

I must have been holding my breath as I looked at them, for I felt a sudden need for air. I turned to the door.

"There's more," Sam said.

He reached into a stack of canvasses and handed over the first one. It was an oil painting of a pose from one of the sketches, in which Grace reclined not unlike Goya's *Nude Maja* on a chaise longue. It was a good painting, I thought, trying to be objective, the lines flowed well, curves and loops, the swell of her hips, the draped fabric, the light and shade were all evocative, mysterious, hinting at pleasure enjoyed, or yet to come.

Another canvas showed her head and shoulders from behind against a neutral background, emphasizing the contrast of her dark tresses with the pale skin of her long neck and symmetrical shoulders. It reminded me of a Dalí painting I had see in St. Petersburg, Florida, once.

Another showed her full face, head slightly inclined. She was almost pouting, sad or distracted, absorbed elsewhere. One of the dark moods, perhaps, that Sam had spoken of.

There were more: Grace in a meadow kneeling to pick a flower; Grace naked on a bed, looking playful and mischievous; Grace dipping her hand in seawater, its Impressionist surface sparkling like diamonds into the distance. Grace against a dark window, the moon outside casting a pale, ghostly light on one side of her face.

One thing they all had in common was that when you looked at her, you never thought of age. Later, I calculated that she must have been close to forty when they were painted, but it didn't show. There was no doubt that Sam had idealized her image and projected his own desire into his creations, but they gave me a definite, palpable sense of Grace, something I had been unable to grasp before, when I was chasing after whispers, searching for the motif, the theme, or the telling detail that would bring her to life. And here it was, in Sam Porter's storeroom. A cascade of images of Grace, with nothing hidden but her soul, though I even fancied I could glimpse that in certain expressions, certain poses, certain turns of the head and angles of the neck. I felt intoxicated by her, dizzy, entranced, under her spell.

Sam studied my reaction. "Still rate Vivian Mountjoy?" he asked.

I could only shake my head in wonder. "Did the police see these?" I asked, my mouth dry.

"Good Lord, no! Can you imagine their reaction? Philistines. That would certainly have added fuel to the fire."

"But surely they searched your flat?"

"My flat was the size of a water closet. I did most of my painting in Staithes, in a studio a local group of artists let me share. They were all older than me, but they sort of took me under their wing. They had connections with the Staithes group, quite collectible these days, and I picked up a bit of the Impressionist influence from them. Have you heard of Laura Knight?"

"I'm afraid not. My modern art isn't quite up to scratch."

"She was one of the few surviving members at the time. Formidable woman. Must have been about seventy-five around then, but you wouldn't have known it. And the things she'd seen. She was the official war painter at the Nuremberg trials, you know. That's when she did *The Dock, Nuremberg,* one of her most famous works. She wasn't up at Staithes often, but the times we met she and Grace got along like a house on fire, spent hours together gabbing away, God knows what about. I'd never seen Grace so animated as those times."

"Did you know any of her other female friends?"

"I don't think she really had any. Acquaintances, yes, from the various societies she belonged to, and from other social activities, but not close friends."

"Didn't she keep in touch with anyone from the war?"

"She mentioned a woman called Dorothy once or twice. They might have seen each other now and then. But other than that . . . no, I don't think she did."

"I thought I recognized the east coast in some of the backgrounds."

"Very perceptive of you, when the foreground's so absorbing."

"So you kept them at your studio?"

"One of the older artists, Len, let me use his lockup, and I kept all my nudes of Grace there. The police didn't search the Staithes studio, but even if they had, they wouldn't have found them. They would have had no reason to search Len's property."

"When did you paint them?" I asked, as Sam turned out the light and we made our way back to the living room.

"In the summer and autumn of 1952, when we were first together. As you can see, they're mostly derivative, the poses and styles, at least. There was nothing derivative about Grace's beauty. She wasn't perfect. Perfection is so boring. You probably noticed the flaws on her skin. She must have suffered badly from the sun at one time. But I couldn't imagine anyone more beautiful. She deserved much better than I could ever do. I've never . . . since. I haven't been able to, even from the sketches, haven't wanted to try. I study them sometimes, but not so often as I used to do. I sometimes wonder what my executors will make of them when I'm dead."

"Thank you," I said, "for allowing me to see them."

Sam grunted, sat down, and took a long sip of Armagnac. "You're the first person I've ever shown them to since they were painted," he said. "I don't even know why I did."

"You never thought of exhibiting them, or selling any?"

"Never."

He seemed weary now, pale and spent, as if it had all been too much for him: the day, me, dinner, our conversation, the paintings, his memories.

I was just about to take my leave when he looked at me with a desolate, almost frightened, expression on his face and said in a trembling voice, "Christ, she was so beautiful. So alive. *So alive.* Please go now, Chris. I'm sorry . . . I . . ." He waved his hand. "It's unbearable. I'm so tired. Please just go."

I went.

9

Famous Trials: Grace Elizabeth Fox, April 1953, by Sir Charles Hamilton Morley

THE FORMAL POLICE INVESTIGATION WAS AS THOROUGH AS SUCH THINGS can be over a week after an alleged crime has taken place. Unfortunately, time is frequently of the essence in these matters; evidence decays, or simply disappears; people forget; stories change. However, science does not lie, and the second postmortem uncovered both a high level of potassium in Dr. Fox's body, along with traces of chloral hydrate, a powerful sedative.

Things went badly against Grace Fox from the start, partly because of her own unwillingness to cooperate with the police. At interviews, she was evasive, distant, and frequently monosyllabic. She had had plenty of time, the Crown later argued, in the intervening days between her husband's death and the arrival of the authorities, to clean up after herself. What did she have to hide? All she was able to tell the police was that she didn't remember very clearly what she'd done, that she was acting on instinct and must have tidied up, thrown the scrap of paper on the fire and cleaned and sterilized the syringe before returning it to Dr. Fox's medical bag, along with the remaining nitroglycerine tablets and the digitalis. It was her nature to be tidy about such things, she claimed, part of her nurse's training.

She had also washed the glass Dr. Fox had used to take his stomach powder in a small amount of whiskey and milk. It was what she would normally have done, she said, and who was to prove her wrong? After all, she went on, as far as she was concerned, she was not expecting to face such a rigorous investigation, or any investigation at all, for that matter, and she was overwhelmed by shock and grief over the sudden death of her husband. She said she knew nothing about the chloral hydrate, but that her husband occasionally took a sleeping draft.

As soon as news of the police investigation spread, ugly rumors started doing the rounds: Grace had a string of lovers in addition to Samuel Porter, people whispered, and her latest was a handsome young soldier with a mysterious birthmark on his hairline, with whom she had been seen in deep conversation on Castle Walk only a few days before her husband's murder. It was left up to the police to sort out the truth from the mere baseless gossip, and in the end none of this so-called evidence of Grace Fox's promiscuity was actually allowed in court.

When it was clear that the police were quickly becoming suspicious that there may have been more to Ernest's death than the chance misfortune of a heart attack, it was Felicity who first suggested that Grace hire a solicitor, which she immediately did. After this, any police interviews were carefully monitored by Mr. Rathbone, and Grace had little of interest to add to any of her earlier statements except to maintain that she had merely done her duty and had done nothing wrong.

Grace Fox was finally arrested and formally charged with the murder of her husband, Dr. Ernest Fox, on Tuesday, January 20, 1953. She appeared before the magistrate the following day and was remanded into custody.

Even at this early stage, the evidence against her appeared damning. In the first instance, she had a clear motive. Her affair with Samuel Porter was threatened by the impending move, and they shared a mutual desire to be rid of her husband without losing access to his money. In the second instance, she had the means. Grace Fox was a trained nurse, well versed in the contents of a medical dispensary and possessed of the knowledge of how to use them. An extensive range of drugs, some of which could be fatal under certain circumstances, or under the wrong conditions, were available in Dr. Fox's medical bag, or even at his surgery, to which Grace Fox also had easy access before the dinner on January first. In the third instance, Grace Fox had ample opportunity. It was she who took him the stomach powder. Nobody saw her tend to him while he was dying; nobody actually *saw* her administer the nitroglycerine or the digitalis to him.

The two syringes in Dr. Fox's medical bag were both sterile, and though this did not preclude that one had been used and replaced after cleaning, it certainly could not be said to *prove* it, either. Digitalis and nitroglycerine were also found in his bag, but that was, of course, where one would expect them to be. Dr. Nelson confirmed that Dr. Fox usually carried two syringes, along with digitalis and nitroglycerine in case of emergencies. Sometimes, in the high dales, he said, you might be called to treat a heart attack victim, and these were usually the first lines of defense. Of course, we have only Grace Fox's word that she did all she could to save her husband's life. Alice Lambert admitted to seeing the paper in which Dr. Fox's stomach powder was folded, and which may well have contained traces of chloral hydrate, too, but this was not found in any subsequent searches of Kilnsgate House.

Whether Grace hastened her husband's demise through the introduction of poison into his system was to become a subject of much contention during the trial. While the pathologist, Dr. Masefield, on his second postmortem, did find traces of chloral hydrate in Dr. Fox's system as well as digitalis, he did not find any fatal substances. He did remark on the relatively high level of potassium, but he also admitted that this was often the case after death, especially after a heart attack, because the blood cells burst and the tissues broke down, releasing large quantities of potassium into the system. While the cold conditions under which Dr. Fox's body had been stored slowed down this process, they did not prevent it entirely. Thus, the defense, that Grace would not have preserved her husband's body under such conditions had she wanted to destroy any evidence of poisons she may have introduced into his system, was rendered void. She must have believed that she had committed the perfect crime, that there would *be no* investigation, until the Leyburn landlady's suspicions piqued the police's interest.

The case that the Crown was about to bring against Grace Elizabeth Fox had all the elements to guarantee a conviction. Sir Archibald Yorke KC would set out to argue that the accused wanted to be rid of her husband, that she had free and easy access to chloral hydrate, which she added to the victim's stomach powder to sedate him so that he would not feel the sting of a later injection of potassium (for, to be effective as an agent of death, potassium must be injected intravenously). Whether the indigestion itself was caused by some medical agent, or simply by a certain low cunning in the devising of the evening's rich menu, was never decided one way or the other.

And so the stage was set for the trial to begin at Leeds Crown Court, on March 16, 1953.

OCTOBER 2010

The evening after my dinner with Sam Porter, I took the train from Paris Montparnasse to Angoulême, and my brother Graham was waiting for me at the station. It was spotting with rain as we drove through narrow streets past the Romanesque buildings, the beautiful Cathedral of St. Pierre, high on the cone-shaped hill, a dark shadow hulking over us. Graham lived outside a village in the Charente valley, about half an hour's drive from town, not far from the river itself, and his cottage had a view of the distant meadows and vineyards. It was a beautiful rural landscape, but not at all like the Yorkshire Dales. I had spent most of the day walking around Paris, including visits to the Cimitière de Montparnasse, the riverside bookstalls Laura used to love, and the Luxembourg Gardens, which I loved, followed by a long lunch on the boulevard St. Germain at a café with a glassed-in dining area at the front, people watching.

It was well after dark when we got to the old stone farmhouse. Graham led me through to the kitchen, where Siobhan was already busy over the old Aga-style stove. She put down her oven mitts and hurried forward to give me a big hug. "You're looking good, Chris," she said, prodding my belly. "Been losing weight?"

"I doubt it. And I've been very sloppy about exercising regularly, too."

"We'll soon put a bit more meat on your bones tonight," she said, turning back to the stove.

Siobhan was a terrific cook, as Laura and I had told her on the many occasions we had dined there over the years, and tonight she said she was concocting a rabbit stew with red wine, shallots, locally picked mushrooms, and her special mix of herbs from the garden. It smelled delicious. I knew there would be a plate of wonderful cheeses after the main course, too, and perhaps a bisque or foie gras with crusty bread to start.

"Dinner won't be long," said Graham, ushering me into the living room. "In the meantime we'll leave Siobhan to work her magic and have a splash of vino."

"Honestly, you lot drink even more than the English, and that's saying something," I said.

"Now don't you go bringing your American new age Puritanism rubbish over here. It won't go down at all well, you know. Anyone would say you've been in California too long."

I laughed as he passed me the bottle. "They make wine there, too, you know, or are you lot just too snobbish to acknowledge it?"

"New World wines have their place," said Graham, and left it at that.

The bottle didn't have a label, but I knew it would be good. The first taste told me it was. Graham doesn't make his own wine—he insists that homemade wine always tastes like homemade wine—but he does know a lot of people in the business, as he was once a successful wine merchant in Oxford.

We relaxed in the well-worn armchairs by the fireplace, which was blazing away with logs, there being a bit of an autumn chill in the valley. Graham shared my love of music, classical in particular—he was quite a good pianist himself—and I recognized the Elgar violin sonata playing softly in the background. The lamps were shaded, filtering the light to a warm orange glow. A well-thumbed paperback copy of Balzac's *Lost Illusions* lay facedown on the table beside the chair, about a third read. Occasionally a log shifted and sighed, or crackled and spit out sparks onto the hearth.

I could feel the city life and the stress of travel drop away like weights from my shoulders as I sipped the wine and massaged the back of my neck with my free hand. "It's funny," I said, "how two city boys like us have both ended up living in the country."

"I suppose so," said Graham. "It was never really my intention, but . . . too good a bargain to pass up. And I must say, I don't miss the city at all."

"Me, neither, so far," I said, thinking more of Los Angeles, or Santa Monica, than of anywhere else. After all, it had been my home for over thirty years. And Santa Monica was fine in its way. Small enough, far enough from Hollywood, with plenty of excellent local restaurants and pubs, the Pacific Ocean rolling in practically at my feet, and a climate that suited my British blood perfectly, though it was too cold for many Angelinos. But it was true that I didn't miss the place, that I hardly thought about it at all, and when I did it was because I was thinking of Laura. Even then, my memories veered more toward Milwaukee, where we had met, or to our holidays in New England, where her family lived, Boston mostly, with its snowbound winters and chill winds off the Atlantic. No, I didn't miss America, but I missed my wife.

Graham's living room was no place for such mawkish reminiscence and recrimination. I soon polished off the first glass of wine, and Graham poured me a second as we continued talking about country life. I had seen the village, about half a mile down the road, many times, and it was like a cliché of French provincial life. A stretch of sere, well-trodden grass shaded by trees, where old men in berets played *boules;* a café with rickety tables outside where everyone sat and shared local gossip; the *boulangerie,* which, of course, made the best baguettes in the whole of France; a *charcuterie;* a small *epicerie* full of local seasonal produce and a few imported items; and a more modern minimart that sold everything from paper clips to wine. Then, of course, there was the ancient *église,* that other essential hub of the French village. By eight in the evening the center was usually deserted, as people watched their TVs at home, apart from a few late diners and pipe smokers outside the café, if it was a particularly warm evening, no doubt arguing the merits of Proust over Flaubert. If you wanted a night on the town, you went to Angoulême. Even Cognac wasn't that far away. If you really wanted to push the boat out, you went to Poitiers or La Rochelle.

But in Graham's little farmhouse, even the village felt distant, and all I could hear outside was the wind in the trees and the occasional call of a night bird.

Over a delicious dinner, we caught up with family gossip—Mother, my kids and theirs. The cheese plate was excellent, as expected: a runny Camembert, a rich Roquefort, and a tasty Port Salut. Graham and I cleared away the dishes and put them in the machine, then Siobhan said it was time for her to go to bed.

Graham looked at me. "Tired, little brother?"

"Not particularly," I said.

He stood up. "Come on, then," he said. "Let's you and me have a serious nightcap and a bit of man talk."

Siobhan rolled her eyes, gave us each a peck on the cheek, and said good night.

I followed Graham into the living room.

GRAHAM SELECTED A BOTTLE OF COGNAC AND A COUPLE OF CRYSTAL GLASSES from his well-stocked liquor cabinet. The fire was still crackling, and he put a couple more logs on and slipped in a Cecilia Bartoli CD. Graham might love his music, but he hasn't quite caught up with the iPod generation yet.

"So," he said, pouring a couple of large shots before we settled down in our respective armchairs. "Are you still chasing your ghosts?"

"I don't think I ever was," I said. "But if you mean am I still interested in the Grace Fox case, then the answer's yes. Perhaps even more so now than ever."

"Why would that be?"

I told him all about my conversation with Sam Porter and the conclusions I had drawn about Grace's innocence. I also mentioned the noises in Kilnsgate and the piano I thought I'd heard. Graham might dismiss these as the products of an overheated imagination, but at least he wouldn't laugh at me.

"Well, I don't suppose *he* would be biased at all, would he?" Graham said. "Plus the fact that he must be about ninety by now, and he's probably gaga."

"Very funny. He may be biased. But that's beside the point. You'd expect someone in his position to defend the woman he loves no matter what. I understand that, too. But Sam's levelheaded enough, and there's nothing wrong with his memory as far as I can tell. And, by the way, he's seventy-eight."

Graham whistled between his teeth. "Wow. A toyboy."

"He certainly was sixty years ago. But no matter what you call him, his feelings for Grace were genuine enough."

"Don't be so defensive, little brother. I wasn't saying they weren't. So you think she was innocent, too?"

"All I can say is that the more I get to know her, the less I can envisage her murdering her husband. I know it sounds vague, but . . . there it is. And Sam has no reason to lie. Especially not now, so long after the events."

"How about to protect his old lover's memory? Or he may believe he's telling the truth. It's amazing the things you can convince yourself are true over the years if you repeat them to yourself often enough. I was in New York when Woodstock happened, you know, and I used to tell the girls back in England that I'd been there. Impressed the hell out of them all the way to the bedroom. I hadn't, of course, but in the end I even sort of half-believed it myself. I could see and hear Hendrix playing the 'Star-Spangled Banner' in my sleep. Maybe Sam Porter has convinced himself over the years that Grace Fox was pure as the driven snow?"

"I don't think so. Grace had her problems. But she was certainly no slut. Or a murderess."

Graham paused and sipped some Cognac. "You know," he said, "there's one big question you're raising by refusing to believe the official version."

"I think I know where you're going."

"If Grace didn't do it, then who did?"

"I don't see why anyone had to have done it. I don't know all the details yet, but I don't see why it couldn't have been natural causes. She tried to save him, but she was too late."

"Clearly the police and the pathologist didn't think so."

"Because they were only looking for evidence to make a case against Grace. What if they were wrong?"

"But what if it *was* murder? Who could have done it but Grace?"

"Well, the Foxes had some friends over for dinner that night. I don't know how many. There was also a maidservant."

"So you're saying there *are* other suspects?"

"I'm saying there could be, that's all. If it wasn't natural causes."

"Did any of them have a motive?"

"I don't know, do I?"

"So what do you think *really* happened?"

"A miscarriage of justice. I think that after the landlady's accusation, the police started to look for evidence to fit their theory. It's hardly unusual, that sort of blinkered approach. Remember, it was only *after* she came forward that any suspicions at all were raised. Before that, everyone was quite happy to accept the verdict of a heart attack."

"But let's face it, Chris, in real life, if there's a murder, ninety-nine percent of the time it was done by someone close to the victim. The husband or the wife. The police know that. They probably even knew it in 1953. Here," Graham said, getting up and bringing the bottle over. "Have a drop more." I held out my glass. He poured me more than a drop, then some for himself, and sat down again. "I'm not saying you're wrong, Chris. Maybe I'm just playing devil's advocate. But don't you think you ought to be careful not to get obsessed by this?"

"Do *you* think I'm obsessed?"

"You're certainly letting your imagination run away with you on very little basis in fact, but then you always did. These things that go bump in the night. The piano. I've often thought that you have a degree or two more sensitivity to the twilight zone than most of us do. Ever since you were a child."

"What do mean?"

"Don't you remember what happened when you were four?"

"Obviously not."

He pointed to my hand, to the long scar in the soft flesh between my thumb and forefinger. "Don't you remember where you got that?"

I look at the curving white line. As far as I knew, I had always had it. "No," I said, feeling a little apprehensive, as if I were on the verge of a revelation from which there was no return. "I take it you remember. Care to tell me about it?"

A LOG SHIFTED IN THE GRATE. GRAHAM PUT ANOTHER ONE ON, AND IT STARTED to crackle and spit smoke. Shadows cast by the flames flickered over the walls. The curtains were open, and I could see stars in the clear night sky.

"You were four," Graham began, "and we were on our summer holidays, staying at a bed and board in Scarborough. It was a large house behind the seafront on the North Beach."

"We always stayed on the North Beach," I said. "Mum and Dad thought it was far more genteel, remember? We wanted to be near the amusements and the shops, but they said the South Beach was too common."

"That was later, when you were a bit older, but yes, we always stayed in the North Beach. You liked the open-air air swimming pool and Peasholm Park well enough."

"I don't remember it at all."

"As I said, you were only four."

"What did I do, fill the bath to overflowing?"

Graham chuckled. My childhood misadventures were well known in the family, though fortunately they hadn't followed me into adulthood. Well, not many of them. "Something like that," he said. "Anyway, as I said, we were staying at a guesthouse in Scarborough. Breakfast and evening meal, six o'clock on the dot or you went hungry. I suppose I'd have been eleven. Anyway, we had a room of our own, two single beds, adjoining Mum and Dad's. They always kept the door ajar at night so they could keep a check on us. You slept like a log, and I hid under the sheets with a torch reading Sherlock Holmes. There was no telly, but they had a wireless in the living room, and sometimes Mum and

Dad would send you off to bed and let me stay up a bit later to listen to *Appointment with Fear* or *Riders of the Range*.

"There was a huge wardrobe in our room. Oak or something. Very heavy and very old. The floors of the room were uneven, so if you didn't turn the key, the wardrobe door would swing open slowly with a creaking sound. It used to scare the living daylights out of you. Inside the door was a full-size mirror. You didn't like that wardrobe at all, even when it was secured. Am I ringing any bells?"

"I don't remember any of it," I said, puzzled by Graham's story. Was this four-year-old boy scared of a wardrobe really me? I began to feel that familiar chill of recognition, as if I not only knew what was coming but had experienced something similar recently, in the guest bedroom at Kilnsgate. It wasn't quite déjà vu, but that was what it felt like, in a strange way. "Yes, but you know what it's like when you're kids," I argued. "You imagine monsters under the bed, in the cupboards, at the bottom of the garden, God knows where."

"Yes. Well, one day—it had been a hot one, I remember—we'd been on the beach all afternoon. It was crowded. You were playing with your bucket and spade, building sand castles, making friends with some of the other kids, going for a paddle occasionally—all under Dad's eagle eye, of course—and I . . . well, I don't know, really. I'd probably been reading a western or something, wishing I was off with my mates having adventures. But the point is, you were especially tired when we got back to the guesthouse. You could hardly stay awake through dinner. Mum and Dad packed you off to bed early, and we spent a while in the living room listening to the wireless, Dad reading his paper. There weren't many other guests, and most of them seemed to have wandered off to the pub, except for one old lady who sat nodding off in the armchair. And the woman who ran the place, of course—Mrs. Gooch, I think she was called—cleaning up in the kitchen.

"It must have been shortly after eight o'clock—there was some science-fiction serial I was following on the wireless, I remember— when we all heard this almighty crash and the sound of breaking glass and someone screaming—*you* screaming—from upstairs. Dad was first to his feet, I think, shortly followed by me. We dashed up the stairs two, three, at a time, probably both of us with the same thought in our heads—the wardrobe had somehow come open or fallen over and some terrible accident had resulted, that maybe you were hurt.

"Anyway, we ran into the room, me just behind Dad, and there you were, just standing there looking terrified, blood streaming from your hand. The curtains were closed, but they were made of thin material and it was still light outside, so the room wasn't in complete darkness. The wardrobe door was swinging open and the mirror lay smashed in pieces all over the floor, as if someone had slammed the door shut too hard."

"Jesus!" I said. "Was it me?"

"You said it was an accident. We worked it out that you must have been asleep and heard it creaking open, or had a bad dream or something, and got out of bed to shut it, but you slammed it too hard and the mirror broke."

"And?"

"Well, nobody could think of any other explanation, though it must have been one hell of a push. I mean, you *were* only a little kid. We bandaged your hand and Dad took you to the hospital, where they stitched you up. Then Dad came back and calmed Mrs. Gooch down—he knew he'd have to pay for the mirror, of course—and I think you slept in their room that night. Things were a bit frosty over breakfast the next couple of days, then we went home."

"I don't remember any of this. And I don't see—"

Graham held his hand up. "Wait. I haven't finished yet."

I felt a strange kind of tightness in my chest. I didn't know what he was going to say, but I sensed that it was going to change things, make me feel differently about myself. I almost wanted to tell him to stop, but I couldn't. Cecilia Bartoli was singing *Panis Angelicus*, and I took a deep breath and let the music calm me down.

Graham went on. "We also shared a room back home in Armley, remember? I think I was twelve or thirteen before we moved to the new estate and got a room each. Anyway, the first night back after the holiday, you couldn't sleep. Your tossing and turning kept me awake. I asked what was wrong. That was when you told me what had happened in Scarborough. You said that you got up to go to the toilet—I think you'd had far too much pop that afternoon—and you noticed that the door to the wardrobe was open. As you passed it to go out to the landing, you caught a glimpse of a reflection. There was something odd about it, you said, so you stepped back and stood in front of the mirror to see. *It wasn't you.* That's what you told me. You couldn't see your own reflection but that of a young woman, and she seemed to be floating there, reaching out to you, calling you in, as if she wanted to tell you something. Drag you into the wardrobe mirror with her. That was when you slammed the door, out of pure terror, and the mirror smashed."

I held my breath. A log shifted on the fire. Cecilia sang on.

"You look pale, little brother. Have another sip of your Cognac."

I did as Graham suggested. I was starting to feel a little drunk.

"I wasn't trying to scare you," he went on. "I was only trying to tell you how you've always been overimaginative, morbidly sensitive, that's all, the same as with this Grace Fox business."

"Yeah, like you're saying I see dead people. Is that it?"

Graham laughed. "Not quite. Maybe you're sensitive to traces. I don't know."

"Sounds like a load of bollocks to me, big brother," I said, with rather more bravado than I felt. "Did I tell you what she looked like, this woman?"

"No. Just that she seemed young and sad. I think you might have mentioned that she was wearing a long nightie. Don't worry, you weren't having visions or premonitions of Grace Fox. That's not why I'm telling you all this."

"Then why? What *did* you make of it?"

"Well, naturally, I thought you'd awoken from a bad dream involving this young woman in distress, got out of bed half asleep, that somehow the door had come open and you saw your own reflection, maybe thought it was the monster coming out of the wardrobe, and you panicked."

"That would seem to be the logical conclusion," I said slowly, swirling the rest of my Cognac in the large glass.

"And that's probably exactly what happened," Graham went on. "Except . . ."

I felt a sense of panic. "Except what?"

"No, that's probably exactly how it happened."

"Tell me," I pleaded. "You can't lead me this far and then leave me stranded."

"It was just something I overheard Dad say later. I don't think I was supposed to hear it."

"What?"

"Well, the incident gave Mrs. Gooch a hell of a shock. It wasn't just the money. That's basically what she was telling Dad the next day. But she had a daughter, and that used to be her room before her mother turned the place into a bed and board."

"So? There's nothing odd about that. The daughter got married and left home, and her mother and father converted the house into a guest-house rather than move to somewhere smaller. Makes sense. Scarborough attracts a lot of visitors."

"Yes. Only that wasn't quite the way it happened."

"Oh?"

"No. The daughter had a few problems. She was a highly strung girl. She got jilted by her fiancé, a soldier, and she . . . well, she hanged herself in that room. Naturally, Mrs. Gooch would hardly tell her guests such a thing, but as I said, she was so upset by the mirror incident that she did let it slip to Dad. The wardrobe door was open at the time, and she saw the reflection of her daughter's body in the mirror first, before she saw her actual daughter hanging there. What happened to you just brought it all back, that's all."

I could think of nothing to say. An icy sensation flooded through me. "So you believe that events leave traces?"

"I never said that. I admit the whole thing puzzles me, and it would be very easy to grasp on to a supernatural explanation."

"Couldn't I have heard about what happened before? Imagined it?"

"It's possible, but I don't see how. You were only four. Even I didn't really understand what I overheard, but it stuck in my memory. Years later, when I was at grammar school, I tracked down the story in the newspaper archive. It happened in 1945. It would appear, reading between the lines, that an American GI had got the girl pregnant, promised to marry her and take her back to Kansas or wherever with him, then just abandoned her. She couldn't face the shame, life without him . . . whatever, and she snapped."

"And that's who you think I saw in the mirror? Her?"

"There's no way of knowing that," said Graham. "Maybe you imagined the whole thing in the half darkness. Maybe it was the carryover from a bad dream."

"Or places have memories and I can read them?"

"Now you *are* being fanciful. I just don't want all this Grace Fox business to drive you over the edge, that's all I'm saying. You're fragile enough already after the grief you've been through over Laura."

That was exactly what Bernie Wilkins had said, and it annoyed me. "It's not about the noises or the shadowy figures I sometimes think I glimpse," I said. "Or the piano I hear. They're all exactly what you say they are, phantoms of an overworked imagination playing on the natural sounds and shadows in an old house. Special effects. It just happens that the house has a history and they heighten it, or vice versa. They don't bother me at all. They just keep me awake sometimes. I'm not sleeping well."

"Most old houses have a history."

"Who knows? Maybe I *am* seeking something to distract me, a mystery to lose myself in. Maybe I am getting a bit obsessed. If I stand back and take stock of myself honestly, I find it hard to know how I got so drawn in, what my motives are, or how deeply I *am* in. I don't know where it's all heading, but I do want to know what happened. I'm not at all convinced, through what I've heard from Wilf Pelham and Sam Porter, that Grace Fox really did murder her husband. And even if she did, I want to *know* it for myself. Does that sound so weird?"

Graham sat up and put his empty glass down on the small round table beside his chair. "No, as long as that's how it stays. You've got time on your hands. I wish you luck, little brother. Just don't get too carried away with it, that's all. I wouldn't want you running amok and smashing up Kilnsgate House. Or this place, for that matter." He looked around at the farmhouse I knew he and Siobhan loved dearly. "This place has its history, too, you know, its memories. Not to mention its night noises."

I smiled and stood up. "I'll try not to let them drive me to destruction," I said. "Good night, Graham, and thanks for the Cognac. And the story."

Graham nodded. "See you in the morning."

I WAS DEFINITELY FEELING A LITTLE DRUNK AS I MADE MY WAY OVER THE uneven stone flags to the creaky wooden stairs. Graham was right; this was an old house, and it no doubt had a few stories to tell of its own. I wasn't in the mood for them tonight, though; all I wanted was sleep.

But, of course, sleep wouldn't come. The room I was in was the same room where I'd slept with Laura when we visited. The same bed. It felt much lonelier than the bed at Kilnsgate, in which I had never slept with anyone. Thoughts like this spiraled in my mind, the way they do when you're a bit drunk, and began to turn into thoughts about the conversation I had just had with Graham.

I thought of taking out my iPod and listening to some soothing music, or to a story. I had an unabridged audiobook of *Far from the Madding Crowd* that I was very much enjoying. But I knew I wouldn't be able to concentrate. Graham's story haunted me, though it still sounded very much like something that had happened to someone else. Still, the scar was there, on my hand, and sometimes it itched.

Had I really seen a young woman's figure in the mirror and smashed the glass out of fear? Had it really been the image of a woman who had hanged herself in that very room several years earlier, or had I simply awakened from a bad dream and imagined it all? I didn't know. And how could I ever know? It was the same with the figure I'd glimpsed in the wardrobe mirror at Kilnsgate. I'd put it down to a trick of the moonlight, but was it something else? Was it Grace? I hadn't told Graham about it. I hadn't told anyone. Why? Because I couldn't explain it rationally? Because it would make them think I was going mad?

I trusted Graham. He had no reason to lie to me about something as momentous as this, but nobody could really know what happened in that room except me, and I couldn't remember. My father was dead, so he couldn't help me, and Mrs. Gooch was no doubt long since departed, too. I supposed I could ask Mother and check the newspaper archives, as Graham himself had done later, but what was the point of that, if I believed him? It would only confirm the truth about the suicide, *not* that I had seen anything unusual in the mirror. Graham had told me everything I needed to know. Only through remembering could I be certain about what happened that night.

All these questions circled in my mind like birds of prey while I tried to get to sleep. What did it all have to do with Grace Fox and Kilnsgate House? I wondered. I had thought it was *my* choice to become interested in Grace's story, but was it? I remembered the sense I had had on first approaching Kilnsgate that the house was somehow *waiting* for me. Had I been pushed into my investigation by forces I didn't understand? I found it hard to accept that powers beyond my own will were playing me like a puppet. It all seemed a bit too *Don't Look Now*. Donald Sutherland thinks he sees his wife on the prow of a funeral boat in Venice when she's supposed to be out of town, and it turns out to be his own funeral. He was psychic but he didn't know it. Music by Pino Donaggio.

I heard creaking noises outside in the corridor, then realized that it was probably just Graham going to the toilet. A few moments later, I heard a flush and more creaking as he went back to his room. His story had got me edgy, and I found myself jumping at every little thing.

I pictured Grace again, and this time her image was calming. She appeared just as she did in one of Sam's best portraits: pensive, distant, but still sensual and alluring, her mouth downturned slightly at the edges, eyes like midnight lakes you just wanted to plunge into and drown in, the tangle of ringlets and curls framing her oval face, her shoulders pale and naked. I felt myself drifting toward sleep. Grace opened her arms to me. Then the image changed into Laura, the snowflakes melting on her cheeks, in her golden hair as she took off the fur hat, then it became someone else, someone I didn't recognize. Perhaps the girl from the mirror. I could smell cocoa and hear the wind outside scraping some fallen leaves across the courtyard. The image in my mind started to say something to me but, mercifully, oblivion came at last.

10

Famous Trials: Grace Elizabeth Fox, April 1953, by Sir Charles Hamilton Morley

A PALE GRACE FOX APPEARED IN THE DOCK WEARING A SIMPLE GRAY CARDIgan over a high-buttoned pearl blouse, her face free of makeup, her hair tied back in a tight bun. The austerity and severity of her appearance would be in similarly marked contrast to the picture that Sir Archibald Yorke KC was about to paint of her for the jury. Grace also seemed remarkably composed, or resigned, for a woman on trial for her life, and her expression, though drained of all color and joy by the dim and airless character of the prison cell, rarely showed any signs of emotion.

Sir Archibald Yorke KC hitched his capes with a flourish, adjusted his wig, and set about his opening remarks, depicting Grace Fox in no uncertain terms as the deceitful, sexually profligate wife of an elderly unsuspecting country doctor. Finding her relationship with a penniless artist young enough to be her son threatened by a potential move out of the area, Grace took the dramatic step of putting an end to her husband's life. This, Sir Archibald argued, she did with a great degree of cold-blooded cunning and premeditation. Not only did she have the necessary means at hand, but she also made certain that she had a house full of captive witnesses whom, she hoped, would all be willing and able to appear in her defense, having participated to varying degrees in the charade she had planned for the night of January 1, 1953. In his words, Grace Fox was "a very clever, manipulative, resourceful, and evil woman."

Grace knew full well that her husband suffered from stomach problems and was prone to heartburn and indigestion, especially after so rich and hearty a meal as they had enjoyed on the evening in question. She also knew that this had never curbed his enthusiasm for food and drink, which she supplied in plenty. Though Hetty Larkin had prepared the dishes, she had done so under the full supervision and instructions of Mrs. Fox, who had provided her with both the menu and the recipes. Mrs. Fox knew that she needed witnesses in order to ensure that no blame fell on her, that her husband's death appeared as if it had occurred from natural causes, and that it appeared as if she, as a trained nurse, had done everything within her powers to save him.

What Grace had, in fact, done, Sir Archibald contended, was adulterate her husband's stomach powder with chloral hydrate, thereby sedating him, then returned to the dinner party and rejoined the unsuspecting convivial gaiety of the Lamberts. Later, when her guests and her servant had all retired for the night, Grace entered her husband's room—they had been sleeping in separate bedrooms for some time now, Sir Archibald stressed—and injected Dr. Ernest Fox with enough potassium chloride to cause cardiac arrest.

When her husband had begun to show symptoms, Grace Fox had raised the hue and cry, thereby ensuring that the eminently sensible and light-sleeping Alice Lambert would be present to watch over Grace's desperate ministrations to her dying husband, the very husband she had poisoned in the first place. But Ernest Fox died even faster than Grace had imagined, and Alice Lambert arrived on the scene only *after* Grace had administered the final, futile injection of digitalis. Could ever a crime be so heinous in its machinations? Sir Archibald demanded of the jury at this point.

Afterward, in the hours and days during which the four people were snowbound and out of communication with the rest of the world,

Grace Fox had plenty of opportunity to get rid of the evidence. The paper that had contained the contaminated stomach powder could easily have been destroyed in the fire downstairs, which was burning constantly due to the excessive cold, and the syringe had been thoroughly sterilized and replaced alongside its companion in Dr. Fox's medical bag. Any traces of potassium chloride or of chloral hydrate that remained in the house could also have been easily destroyed, as none were found.

It was a shrewd but simple plan, Sir Archibald concluded. Afterward, all Grace had to do was clear up after herself, keep quiet, play the grieving widow, and forbear secret meetings with her lover for some months. They had been careful and discreet in their adulterous meetings, but then they had not bargained for Sir Archibald's first witness, Mrs. Patricia Compton of Leyburn.

OCTOBER 2010

I stayed with Graham and Siobhan for another couple of days, as I had no urgent business back in Richmond, and perhaps also because I wanted to convince Graham that I wasn't obsessed with Grace Fox, that I could relax and enjoy the scenery. It was the end of October, and though the days seemed longer in the south, at night there was a distinct autumn chill in the air. Both days started with an early mist through which the sun had usually burned by midmorning, and the afternoons were comfortably warm, usually somewhere in the midteens, rather like Santa Monica in January. At least, I didn't find it cold.

The three of us went for long walks by the river and in the woods, and we spent one day exploring the old buildings of Angoulême, lingering for dinner in one of Graham's favorite restaurants. We played *boules* in the village, and the old men laughed at us. The first evening was unexpectedly mild, and we ate outside at the café, talking and drinking wine under the stars until it was obvious that the owner wanted to put up the shutters. We didn't talk any more about Grace

Fox or the mirror incident in Scarborough, nor did Graham tell me the history of the farmhouse, though he did mention that the family who lived there during the war gave shelter to Jews and were eventually discovered and shot on the village green.

Mostly we talked about my film work—Siobhan was always keen to know the latest star gossip, and I tried not to disappoint her—and about the state of the European Union, which seemed pretty dismal with more and more members needing to be bailed out. I slept well. If there were ghostly echoes of guns shooting and frightened Jewish children whimpering in the attic, I didn't hear them.

Then, on the fourth morning, I knew it was time to go home. Much as I loved Graham and Siobhan, I realized that I missed Kilnsgate House and the life I was beginning to forge there. I missed working on the piano sonata, too, and had one or two intriguing variations I wanted to work out drifting around in my mind. Graham let me use his piano one evening, but it wasn't quite the same.

Graham and Siobhan invited me to come and spend Christmas with them, especially as Mother was honoring them with her presence this year. They usually had a big dinner at the farmhouse with their children and grandchildren, along with some members of Siobhan's family from Ireland. I said I wasn't sure, that I'd like to spend my first Christmas in Kilnsgate and assured them I would be okay. If I felt lonely, I promised, I would catch the first flight over there, then Siobhan gave me a big hug and Graham drove me to the station.

THOUGH EACH INDIVIDUAL JOURNEY WAS HARDLY MORE THAN TWO OR THREE hours, what with all the delays and hanging around at stations, it took me nearly all day to get home, and it was well after dark by the time I pulled up outside Kilnsgate House, which was waiting for me like a neglected lover, with a mingled mood of sadness and anger. No doubt I was projecting again.

Perhaps I was also projecting about the slight, hooded figure I thought I saw standing by the lime kiln, because by the time I got out of the car and hurried to the packhorse bridge, there was nobody there.

Nonetheless, the incident shook me a little, and I wondered just how vulnerable I was out here. What if it was a burglar casing the place? What if there was a gang with their eyes on Kilnsgate? I remembered the terrifying scene in *A Clockwork Orange* when Alex and his "droogs" visit a house in the country and shuddered.

I had left a couple of the lamps on timers to discourage burglars, so the house wasn't in complete darkness when I went in. I locked and bolted the door behind me and made a quick check of the rooms to see if everything was all right. It certainly didn't look as if anything had been disturbed during my absence.

I had left the heat at a low setting, which meant it wouldn't take long to warm up, especially with the fire I planned on starting in the living room. That would cheer the dear old place up a bit and take the edge off her chilliness and my jitters. Security checks finished, I picked up the post and wandered through to the living room, where I put some lights on and set about making a fire in the grate. It didn't take long—with the help of fire starters—before the logs were blazing away just as they had in Graham's house all those miles away. It was much cooler in Yorkshire, of course, and from what I could see outside, the sky was covered with clouds.

As the old wartime posters used to ask, was my journey really necessary? I didn't know. I felt that I had learned a lot from Sam Porter, but when I thought about what, it didn't really add up to much.

I had seen the drawings and paintings of Grace, of course, and they were probably worth the trip in themselves. Also, Sam had given me a personal insight into Grace that I couldn't have got from anyone else, and that was invaluable. I had seen the images, could picture her walking the coastal path at Whitby hand in hand with him, pointing out a seascape, pausing to feel the wind through her hair, her cheeks flushed. I could see her crying as she gazed on a painting or listened to a symphony. She was more vivid, more real than she had ever been to me before. I had already seen her tiny neat handwriting and Vivian Mountjoy's rather pale version of her, but now I felt I could almost imagine her voice and the feel of her skin.

I checked the phone for messages and found none, put on Liszt's *Années de Pèlerinage*, poured myself a cranberry juice to offset all the booze I'd been drinking lately, and settled down with the post. Besides the polite thank-you cards from Heather and Derek, and from Charlotte, there was nothing much else, though I was happy to receive a couple of utility bills at long last. Now I was legitimate. I could prove that I existed. I could go to one of the other banks in the market square and open an account, which would make life a lot easier. There were a couple of invitations to concerts and premieres back in L.A., which I tipped into the flames along with a request for extending the warranty on my television.

For the moment, being home in front of a warm fire with Liszt's music and the latest issues of *Gramophone* and *Sight & Sound* to browse through would suit me fine.

I WALKED ACROSS THE LITTLE PACKHORSE BRIDGE, THEN UP PAST THE LIME KILN and through the fields that led me, eventually, to the old racecourse. It was a clear enough morning, crisp but not too cold, and I certainly needed the exercise. The fine dining I had done in London and France was beginning to take its toll, and if I wanted to keep eating well and not restrict myself to a diet of rabbit food and carrot juice, then I needed to burn off a few calories. I was already discovering that the kind of health regimes one seems to adopt naturally in L.A. don't necessarily travel well to Yorkshire. I also had a few letters to post in town.

The Dales landscape always made me think of my father. We had visited the area frequently when I was a child, most often in summer, when we would walk the high moors and watch for curlews and lapwings—tewits, he called them—or wander through meadows full of buttercups and clover, where I would watch the swallows swoop and glide. I loved to watch the swallows. Sometimes I would just stand there for hours it seemed, the only still point, and feel the air from their wings as they wheeled around and above me in ever changing, ever more complex patterns, flying so close to the ground sometimes you would think they would crash and tumble over. Why was it that those summer days of my memory were always sunny, the still, honeyed air droning with insects and filled with the scents of cut grass and wildflowers?

I do remember one autumn visit, though, on a day very much like this one, when I ran down a country lane joyfully kicking up the heaps of fallen, crispy leaves, delighting in the sound and the spinning kaleidoscope of color I had created, while my father moved slowly behind me with his walking stick, that small smile no doubt on his face, taking it all in. He was a countryman at heart, forced, like so many, to move to the city for work after the war, and never so happy as when he could walk the lanes or lean on a drystone wall as he admired the view. He could name all the trees, wildflowers, and birds. I like to think I have something of his country soul in me, though I was city born and raised.

After queuing for some time in the post office—it seems that some people conduct all their business there except for buying stamps and posting packages—I turned left at the square, intending to go to the King's Head for lunch, and almost bumped into Charlotte coming the other way.

"Hello, stranger," she said. "I thought it was you."

"Hi, Charlotte. Thanks for the card."

"It was a lovely evening."

That wasn't exactly my memory, but I didn't say anything.

"Look," Charlotte gushed on, "I've been wanting to have a word . . . you know . . . if you've got a moment." She seemed to be pushing her hair back from her forehead as she spoke—it was quite windy by now— even though she didn't need to. It was an attractive pose, rather like the cover of an old *Health & Efficiency* magazine, but with clothes on, and it showed off her slim, athletic body.

I could have said no, I suppose, that I was busy and had to get back to Kilnsgate House, but I've never been a good liar, except to myself. I could probably convince myself black was white if I wanted to, but nobody else would believe me. Besides, I was intrigued, and the prospect of lunch with an attractive woman is not something you turn down so cavalierly at my age. "Fine," I said. "I was just going to have lunch. Care to join me?"

"That would be super."

Who on earth says "super" these days? Well, Charlotte does. That is the kind of woman she is, with her sporty good looks and layered blond hair. She looked as if she ought to have a tennis racquet or a golf club in her hand, but she had a Stead & Simpson bag.

"Had you anywhere in mind?"

"What? Oh, lunch. No, not really. King's Head?"

"How about Rustique? My treat."

So we went to Rustique, just off the square, on Finkle Street. We sat in the glassed-over courtyard, with its tiled floor, framed French posters, and wall mural of a nude fan dancer. I wanted some wine with lunch, but Charlotte declined, so I decided to stick with water and coffee myself. I'd been a good boy yesterday, hadn't touched a drop of anything alcoholic, so I could do the same today as well.

"So what have you been up to lately?" Charlotte asked.

I told her about my visit to Sam Porter in Paris, careful to make it sound as if my brother Graham, not Sam, was the real reason for my crossing the Channel. The waiter came and we gave him our orders. I quickly forgot my earlier resolve and ordered a glass of Costières de Nîmes. Charlotte asked for a diet bitter lemon. That's the problem. I don't like fizzy or diet drinks, coffee's for mornings, and water just doesn't quite do the trick, so it has to be wine or beer, really. At least, that's my excuse.

We talked about my Grace Fox theories for a while. When I came to mention Grace's lack of motive, Charlotte said, "And you don't believe she had a good one in this Sam Porter?"

"No. They existed in a kind of fantasy world."

"But surely a fantasy world can have its dark side?"

"I suppose it can, but that's not the impression I got. I will admit that a lot of it so far is just my take on things, my sense of Grace, the kind of woman she was."

"You certainly make her sound beguiling. Are you sure you're not a little bit in love with her?"

"It would be easy, wouldn't it?"

"What do you mean?"

"To be in love with someone who no longer exists. The perfect escape from the reality of commitment. No pressures, no tough decisions to make, no sacrifices. Like a sort of inflatable doll. No demands. Especially for someone in such a 'fragile' state as me."

Charlotte reddened. "Oh, gosh. I didn't mean that," she said. "I'm sorry. I didn't mean to upset you. I was just being flippant."

She really said "gosh" as well as "super." I wondered if she sometimes said "golly" and "brill" too. How can you be hard on someone who says "gosh" and "super"? I smiled and touched her hand to let her know it was okay. "The thing is," I said, "you're probably right in an abstract, harmless sort of way. Here I am, to all intents and purposes a sensible, reasonable, successful man, spending my time trying to prove the innocence of a woman who was hanged nearly sixty years ago. Insane, isn't it?"

"Is that what you're doing? Trying to prove her innocence?"

"I didn't think so when I set out, but I seem to be heading that way, don't I?"

"And if you succeed?"

"I haven't thought that far ahead. Tell the authorities, I suppose. Official pardon, apology, and all that. It's too late to do anyone any good, I know, but isn't that how it goes?"

"I suppose it is. All I can do is wish you good luck, then."

"Thanks. You said you wanted a word with me?"

"Yes." Charlotte gave a quick shake of her head. "It's nothing, really . . . I mean, it's not important or anything, just a bit . . . well, delicate . . ."

Our lunch arrived, and we paused while the waiter put the plates down and asked us if we needed anything else.

"You've got me interested," I said to Charlotte when he'd gone. "You might as well go on."

"Well, it's about Heather. We've been friends for a long time. Went to school together, in fact. Jolly hockey sticks and all that. We've had our ups and downs over the years, and some long periods apart, but I like to think we're still the best of friends."

"I'm happy to hear it," I said. "How can I help?"

"Oh, it's nothing like that. Well . . . perhaps it is." She gave a little laugh. "Isn't it silly? Now I'm here, I don't know what to say."

"Just say it."

"All right." She put her knife and fork down. "I just don't want her to get hurt, that's all."

Though I had an inkling of what she might be talking about, remembered the tension at the dinner party, the little charade in the kitchen, I said, "What do you mean? Why should she get hurt?"

"She might not seem it. She puts on a tough front, I know. She's got a hard exterior. Comes with the territory in her line of work. But she's really very vulnerable, not at all as sure as she likes to pretend to be about things."

We both concentrated on our food for a minute or so. I sipped some wine. I think I already knew what Charlotte had just told me about Heather.

Charlotte leaned forward and lowered her voice. "I probably shouldn't be telling you this, but Heather and Derek are going through a rather difficult patch in their marriage right now. They had a brief separation two years ago then got back together again, but it doesn't appear to be taking. Things don't look good, to be perfectly frank. All in all, it's a very tough time for Heather."

"I'm sorry to hear that. If there's anything I—"

"You can stay away from her," Charlotte said.

"I? . . . what? What has she said?"

"She hasn't said anything. And I'm sorry if that sounded so brutal, but I'm just not very good at these things. It was obvious to me at dinner the other night that you weren't interested in me, that the two of you were . . . that there was something between you."

"There's nothing between us," I said.

"Are you sure? Do you mean it?"

"Heather was a little drunk, that's all. She was flirting."

"But there seemed to be . . . I mean, I thought you were having an affair."

I put down my knife and fork. "An affair? Good Lord, no. I haven't been in town ten minutes. I'm not that fast a worker."

"Oh. I suppose I'm not very good at spotting what's going on, am I? But I know she likes you. I can tell. I've known her long enough to recognize the signs. I suppose what I'm saying is that I think she'd *like to* have an affair with you, and I'm asking you not to lead her into it. It would be bad for her. She's too fragile."

"What about me?" I said.

"Sorry? What do you mean?"

"Aren't I supposed to be fragile, too? After all, I'm the recent widower."

Charlotte put her hand to her mouth. "Oh, I didn't mean . . . I am so sorry. Forgive me. I'm putting my foot in it again. I shouldn't have . . . I mean, I was just thinking of Heather."

"I'm not some amoral predator, you know."

"But these things happen."

"Yes, they do. But I promise you I'll do nothing to encourage her. Is that good enough?"

Charlotte smiled. "That's fine. And I really am sorry. I could tell you felt you'd been set up on a blind date with me, and they can be so disastrous. I knew you didn't like me, not in that way."

"I like you well enough, Charlotte. Perhaps I'm just not ready for any sort of relationship yet?"

"Perhaps not."

I held out my hand. "Truce?"

She nodded. "Truce."

We shook hands.

"I wish I'd had that glass of wine now," said Charlotte, patting her chest.

"There's still time. Why don't you? I'll have another one with you."

"I shouldn't."

"Don't be a stick in the mud."

"I'm afraid I am, rather, aren't I? A stick in the mud."

The waiter passed by and I ordered two more glasses of red. "There, now, you can't let me drink both of them by myself."

Charlotte laughed. When the wine came, we clinked glasses. "To Heather," I said.

"To Heather. How would you like to come over on Bonfire Night? I'm having a little soirée. Drinks, just a few nibblies."

"Sounds good," I said. "Where do you live?"

"Maison Dieu. The address is on the thank-you card I sent you. Come early or you'll miss the fireworks."

It took me a moment to realize that she was speaking realistically, not figuratively. "I'll be there," I said.

11

Famous Trials: Grace Elizabeth Fox, April 1953, by Sir Charles Hamilton Morley

Mrs. Patricia Compton, the Leyburn landlady, clearly belonged to that class of person most commonly referred to as "the salt of the earth." Substantial in girth, fervently Methodist in opinion, she was observant of, but not in the least intimidated by, the rites and trappings of a Crown Court trial.

Though Mrs. Compton's appearance did provide a certain amount of inadvertent comic relief at times, her evidence established primarily—and most importantly—that Samuel Porter and Grace Fox had, indeed, spent a night "in the throes of illicit passion" at her bed and board establishment in Leyburn, and that she had heard them plotting the death of Ernest Fox. This latter remark was challenged by Mr. Montague Sewell for the defense and found to be somewhat lacking in substance, but the jury had heard it, nonetheless, and it would stick in their minds.

When it came to the ugly issue of blackmail, try as he may, Mr. Sewell could not find a chink in the formidable Mrs. Compton's armor. She was a God-fearing woman, Sir Archibald maintained, a pillar of the chapel without a stain on her character. The police had discounted Samuel Porter's story in the first place; they merely regarded it as a weak attempt to throw them off the scent. The truth remained, as the judge was to remind the jury in his summing up, that even if Mrs. Compton *had* tried to blackmail the lad, reprehensible as that was, her testimony was still damaging to Grace Fox.

Where Mr. Sewell did succeed in scoring a point or two was with the flurry of forensics specialists, who duly and dully listed their findings, or lack of them, in dry, academic terms. Much was made of the missing stomach powder paper, the chloral hydrate, the syringe and potassium chloride, but in every case, Mr. Montague Sewell was able to create seeds of doubt in the expert testimony, and to show that there was nothing sinister or amiss in any of it. It would only be natural for Grace Fox, a trained nurse, to clean and tidy up such things as a used syringe and a scrap of wrapping paper, he insisted, and there was no reason whatsoever why Dr. Fox should not, himself, have taken a dose of chloral hydrate, as he was known to have done on previous occasions. Dr. Fox had also, according to Alice Lambert, exhibited symptoms of indigestion when they had dined together over the past few months.

Even the pathologist, Dr. Laurence Masefield, who insisted that he had identified *two* superimposed needle marks, implying that Grace Fox had first injected the potassium, and then, in an attempt to cover up her crime, the digitalis into *the same spot*, was ridiculed by Mr. Sewell, and Dr. Masefield had to grudgingly admit that high levels of potassium often did occur naturally in victims of cardiac infarctions. Mr. Sewell also got the doctor to admit that Ernest Fox's heart was far from being the healthiest he had seen, to such an extent that an imminent heart attack had not been entirely out of the question.

All in all, then, it is probably fair to say that the physical evidence was proven to be rather circumstantial, if not insubstantial, and that Mr. Sewell did an excellent job of debunking said evidence and creating doubt in the minds of the jury. Yet it was not this upon which the case rested, as quickly became apparent when Samuel Porter entered the witness box.

It was not until this moment that Grace Fox betrayed any emotion.

At the sight of her young lover, though, she grasped the rail so tightly that her knuckles turned white, her breath came palpably faster, in short gasps, and an expression of such infinite sadness and loss came over her features that might melt the heart of the most unromantic soul. But it melted no hearts in the courtroom that day. Mr. Porter was half her age; he made his living by doing odd jobs and landscape painting; and the evidence very much seemed to indicate that she had murdered her respectable, highly regarded doctor husband in order to forge a life with him. His appearance did nothing to help her cause and much to hinder it. When Mr. Porter proudly admitted, without the slightest sense of shame or embarrassment, that he and Mrs. Fox had even conducted their affair on occasion in the bedroom of Kilnsgate House while Mr. Fox was away on business, the court emitted a collective gasp. This was the ultimate outrage, cuckolding the man in his own home.

There was not much Mr. Sewell could do now to reverse the damage that Sir Archibald Yorke KC had wrought. The only thing that counted, as far as the jury was concerned, was that Grace Fox, who stood accused before them, and this pale, disheveled young artist had indulged in an adulterous relationship, had committed sexual intercourse in the woman's own home, fornicating under the roof that her husband's hard labor had provided for her. When Samuel Porter was finally excused, and Grace's dark eyes sadly followed his every move as he left the courtroom, the jury's disapproval was palpable, and I would hazard a guess that it was at this point that the case for the defense was irrevocably lost.

NOVEMBER 2010

The "few nibblies" that Charlotte had mentioned turned out to be a long table groaning under the weight of local cheeses, clusters of fruit, crusty bread, crackers, hummus and salsa dips, vegetables, and various terrines and pâtés. No doubt she had a whole stock of pies, cakes,

and sticky buns hidden away in the larder, too, for dessert. I was glad
I hadn't bothered with an early dinner. The wine was a decent enough
Rioja. I took a sip and wandered outside.

Charlotte's house had a spectacular view over the castle ruins and
the river gardens. As I looked down from the flagged patio, feeling like
the lord of all I surveyed, I realized that I had seen this very row of
houses from below shortly after I had arrived in Richmond, walking
by the river one day. They were so high up, I had imagined then how
magnificent the view must be, and I wasn't wrong.

It was a cool dry evening, perfect for a fireworks display, the air
tinged with the acrid smell of smoke from a wood fire. Below me, I
could see the meandering silvery line of the River Swale, effervescing
in places as it tumbled over the low terraced falls, finally disappearing
into the darkness of the woods west of town.

Built on the cliffs by the riverside, the castle walls rose steeply to
their crumbling jagged edge; only the towering keep within the edifice
seemed untouched by the passing of the centuries. Above it all, the sky
was scattered with stars and the moon had waxed almost full.

I thought of the shadowy figure I had seen by the lime kiln and
wondered again who it could have been. I had the distinct impression
that whoever it was had been spying on Kilnsgate House, watching for
something, or someone, but I couldn't be certain. It hadn't seemed like
a walker, but I suppose they come in all shapes and sizes and outfits.
Even so, the hoodie seemed out of place. Maybe I was making too much
of it. Perhaps I had even imagined the whole thing; I had got myself
into such a state thinking about the past, about Grace Fox, murder,
things that go bump in the night, and now I was starting to imagine
mysterious figures spying on me.

Occasionally, a rocket zoomed up from beyond the woods in Hud-
swell, or from Holly Hill, just over the river. The official fireworks
were not due to start until seven, however, so Charlotte's guests, about
twenty of us in all, were mingling, chatting, wandering in and out
to the food and drinks tables, grazing at the nibblies. Most of them
seemed to know one another already, but Charlotte was a good hostess, bringing people over to introduce to me, so I was rarely alone
long enough to enjoy the view before I was drawn again into a recap

of my career, or some small talk about their favorite film music. John Williams and Ennio Morricone—or "that bloke who did the spaghetti westerns"—were the big winners by a long chalk, which came as no surprise. They asked me mine, and when I answered *Vertigo*, hardly anyone had heard of it, let alone remembered the music.

In a rare few moments alone, I was standing by the edge of the patio admiring the view and working on my wine when I felt a light touch on my arm. I turned and saw that it was Heather, her long red hair hanging over the fringed green-and-silver shawl she wore around her shoulders. "Hello, stranger," she said.

"I didn't know you were here."

"You weren't looking in the right direction."

She stood close enough to me that I could smell the freshness of her breath, and when a light breeze blew, a strand of her hair brushed against the scar on my hand. "Well, you must admit," I said, "it *is* a stunning view."

"Yes." Heather wrapped her shawl tighter around her shoulders. "Don't say I didn't try to set you up with Charlotte. Just think, all this could be yours."

"I'm happy at Kilnsgate House."

"Alone with your ghosts?"

"There may be another one," I said, and told her about the figure I had seen.

When I had finished, Heather said, "Probably just a lost tourist checking out the mysterious house, or some anorak historian studying the lime kiln. It happens sometimes."

"Perhaps," I said. I scanned the group of people out on the patio. I didn't know any of them. "But it was dark at the time. Talking about people being lost, where's Derek tonight?"

"He doesn't like parties. I'm all on my own." Her tone was clipped, and it was clear that the subject was closed.

The thought of her coming here alone both excited and frightened me. "You must know plenty of people here?"

She rested her hip against the stone wall, adjusted her shawl, and affected a bored tone. "Oh, sure, I know most of them. Tell me about Paris."

I noticed that she didn't have a glass in her hand. "Would you like a drink first?" I asked.

"How kind of you to ask. White, please."

She turned and rested her palms on the top of the rough wall to lean and gaze down on the scene below while I went inside to the drinks table. Charlotte was playing the perfect hostess. She frowned when she saw me pouring a glass of white wine after the red. She had no doubt noticed Heather arrive and knew exactly who it was for, but she was too busy talking to an elderly academic-looking man in a tweed jacket and silver-rimmed glasses to come over and warn me off. I found myself beginning to resent her interference and disapproval, evident in the angry and frustrated glance she gave me. After all, Heather and I were both adults, and Charlotte seemed to be treating us like wayward children. Was Heather some kind of man-eater, or did I have the unearned reputation of being a womanizer because I'd come from Hollywood and worked in the movie business? I was hardly Warren Beatty, after all.

I carried the drinks outside, still feeling a little resentful over Charlotte's disapproving glance. Maybe she'd been lying to me and felt that I *was* her type? Maybe that was it. Maybe she was madly in love with me and jealous of her friend. I doubted it.

Heather was where I had left her, talking to a middle-aged couple who turned out to be connected with one of the art shops in the town center. I joined them and let my thoughts drift to other things and my eyes drift over the view while I nodded in all the right places and made all the right noises. I was aware of Heather looking at me from time to time. There was an intensity to her gaze that demanded it be returned. I didn't return it. Finally, the couple drifted on. "You forgot to tell me about Paris," Heather said.

I told her, playing down the conversations I'd had with Sam Porter about Grace Fox, and instead concentrating on the sights and meals of the city. I left out any mention of the sketches and paintings Sam had shown me.

"I wish I'd been with you," she said. "Think what a time we could have had. It's been perfectly miserable back here."

"Stop it, Heather."

"But it has. You have no idea."

I went on to tell her about visiting my brother's farmhouse in Angoulême and the walks we had in the woods and by the river, the local wine we drank, the game of *boules* on the village green. But I didn't tell her about the figure in the mirror I had broken the night I got my scar. She probably thought I was crazy enough already when it came to seeing things.

"How exciting to have a brother with a farmhouse in France," she said. "My brother lives in a two-up-two-down in Scunthorpe."

I paused for a moment, not sure whether she meant it seriously, then I saw that the muscles of her face had tensed in an effort to keep from laughing. I couldn't help myself. I laughed first, and she joined me.

"You should have seen your face," she said. "It's not true, of course. Barry lives in a semi in Dorchester, but Scunthorpe just sounds so . . . desperate. Do you remember the old joke about Scunthorpe?"

"Which one?"

"If Typhoo put the *t* in Britain, who put the—"

"Heather, darling." It was Charlotte, escaped from her academic at last and worming her way between us, draping a possessive and restraining arm over Heather's shoulders. "So good to see you. I do hope Chris here isn't monopolizing you?"

"Not at all. I was just telling him that if he'd played his cards right at dinner the other night all this could have been his."

Charlotte blushed. "Heather!"

"Oh, it's all right," Heather said "Don't get your knickers in a twist. I'm not being serious. Actually, I was just telling Chris an old joke about Scunthorpe. If Typhoo—"

The first fireworks lit up the sky with bursts of red, gold, and blue. The guests all moved out onto the patio, which soon became crowded. Heather and I were pushed together close to the wall. We had a great view, and our bodies couldn't help but touch. Heather turned halfway toward me, and I felt the firmness of her breast against my arm. We just about had room to lift our drinks to our mouths. Charlotte was somewhere behind us, drawn into the crowd, chatting away to someone else, no doubt keeping a sharp eye on us, annoyed that she couldn't get close enough to intervene.

Laura had loved fireworks, and as I watched the display, a familiar melancholy made its way through my veins like a soporific. I could see her face in my mind's eye, like a child's, lit up by the fireworks, yes, but with an inner light, too, shining out of her. She had looked like that at the very end as she lay dying, holding my hand, before the light was extinguished, quoting one of her favorite poems. "Don't feel sad, my love. I am already 'half in love with easeful death.' "

From behind the castle walls, bursts of red and green fire continued to shoot high into the air and explode into shapes like dragons' tails or enormous globes, then crackle or bang, leaving wispy trails behind as they fell to earth. I tried to turn away from my melancholy, remembering the Bonfire Nights nights of my childhood. We never had anything like this, of course. All the kids in the neighborhood saved up for months to buy their meager supplies of volcanoes, rockets, jumping crackers, Catherine wheels, and threepenny bangers, while we amassed our piles of chumps, carefully guarded against raids from other gangs. On the night itself, the fire was lit in the middle of the cobbled street—there were few cars in the neighborhood then—and everyone, old and young, gathered around for parkin and treacle toffee and potatoes baked in tinfoil on the fire. We set off our own fireworks, shooting rockets from milk bottles, nailing the Catherine wheels to wooden fences.

I felt a hand rest on mine. "Penny for them," a soft voice said in my ear.

I turned, summoned back from my melancholy and nostalgia. Heather's face was close to mine, illuminated in the multicolored light from the sky. It felt like a moment from *To Catch a Thief*. Cary Grant and Grace Kelly. Unmemorable score by Lyn Murray. I could have kissed Heather right there and then, and I would have, but we were surrounded by people she knew, people who no doubt also knew her husband. She realized it, too. I gave her hand a light squeeze. She squeezed back and let go. "You seemed miles away," she said. "Were you thinking about your wife?"

"No, I was just remembering Bonfire Nights when I was a kid," I said, editing out my thoughts of Laura. "It wasn't all so organized then."

"It's always been like this for me," Heather said wistfully, glancing up at the sky. "Oh, I don't mean being here, like this, just organized. You know, you pay to go in, sometimes they have a band, you get drunk, someone's sick all over your shoes, maybe you have sex in the bushes, there's a fight . . . " She gave a slight shiver and wrapped the shawl tighter around her shoulders.

"Cold?" I said.

"No. A goose just walked over my grave."

LATER, DRIVING HER HOME IN THE CAR, I ASKED, "DO YOU THINK YOU COULD do me a small favor?"

"Depends."

"Could you try and find out who the last owner of Kilnsgate House was?"

"I'm not sure I can. He or she seemed to want to remain anonymous."

"But surely there must be records?"

"You've got the deeds."

"They only name Simak and Fletcher."

"That's the firm I dealt with."

"Maybe if I took a utility bill and asked them nicely?"

Heather laughed. "I think it would take more than a utility bill in this case."

"What about Charlotte? Could she help?"

Heather shook her head. "Family law. She doesn't do conveyancing. But why does it matter? Are you thinking this mysterious stranger you saw was the old owner come to check out the new one?"

"I don't know," I said. "That's why I'd like to find out who it is and where he or she lives. It's just another mystery I'd like to get to the bottom of, that's all."

"Anyone would think you were a private detective and not a composer." Heather remained silent for a moment, then went on. "I'll try. No promises, but I happen to know one of the partners, Michael Simak." She gave me a sidelong glance. "As a matter of fact, he rather fancies me. Tried to feel me up at a Christmas party once."

"Charming. I'm not asking you to prostitute yourself for me."

"I should hope not. Don't worry, I can handle him. Michael has a loose tongue. A couple of drinks after work one day . . ."

"I'll pay the bar bill."

"It's just here." Heather pointed ahead.

I pulled up on a street of old limestone semis up the hill about half a mile from Charlotte's house. Somehow, I couldn't see Heather living here. She didn't seem to fit in with the pebble-dash and prefab-conservatory crowd. She had said she was going to walk home, but it was dark, I told her, the hill was steep, and it was on my way. Besides, I liked to think of myself as chivalrous. I'd only had a couple of glasses of wine all evening, and I had to drive back to Kilnsgate House, anyway.

I noticed how quiet she had become as we approached the house and remembered what Charlotte had said about her marital problems. Had they had a row about going to the party? Was that why Derek hadn't been there? "Everything okay?" I asked.

Heather sighed, then nodded. "Yes. Thank you. It's been a lovely evening."

"What's wrong?"

"Nothing."

But I could see even in the streetlight's weak glow that there were tears in her eyes.

"Heather?"

"It's nothing."

I touched her cheek. It was damp. Then I put two fingers under her chin and turned her face toward me. She unbuckled her seat belt, and the next thing I knew we were kissing. It was a tender and sweet kiss, but there was no mistaking the promise, the need. Her hand curved around my neck, pulling me gently down to her mouth, her tongue flicking under my upper lip. Thinking about the kiss later, I couldn't for the life of me figure out who had initiated it.

When we moved apart, Heather just stared at me for a long moment, the tears still glistening in her sad eyes, then she got out of the car and ran a few yards down the street to one of the houses. She didn't look back. I waited until the front door had opened and closed, then I reversed out of the street and continued on my way. Whatever it was, I reflected, it had begun. But who did I think I was fooling? It had begun the moment I had first clapped eyes on her.

I PARKED OPPOSITE THE DARK EYE OF THE LIME KILN IN THE LIGHT OF THE moon, but there was nobody up there watching tonight. Inside the house, there were no mysterious figures, either, no signs of a break-in, only the chilly, empty rooms waiting for me. I turned up the thermostat and went into the living room, where I lit a log fire. It was still quite early, only around nine o'clock, and I wasn't at all tired. I sat at the piano and thought of Heather's touch, her tears and her kiss, and wished for a moment that I'd invited her back and that she was here with me now, naked on the sheepskin rug before the fire with her red hair spread out in a halo around her head.

I felt desperately lonely and horny, and, for a moment, the isolation of Kilnsgarthdale I had sought and come to love so much became oppressive and claustrophobic. I longed for America again, for the California sun and its special quality of light, its open spaces, longed for Santa Monica, the streets, the ocean, the pier with its carousel, my apartment, my friends, even for the excitement of a rough-cut viewing or a mixing session. And for Laura, always for Laura.

Foolish thoughts. I dismissed them. I had promised both Charlotte and myself that there would be no affair between Heather and me, and now here I was wavering in my resolve at the first fleeting physical contact. The problem was that I felt *right* around Heather. I couldn't really explain it to myself any better than that. Not necessarily comfortable, or even happy—she didn't drive Laura from my mind—just *right*.

I remembered Laura telling me time after time in her long and painful journey toward death that when she was gone I should get on with my life, have girlfriends, have fun, whatever, even remarry if I wanted. I had assured her tearfully that I would, but so far I hadn't had the impulse. About six months after Laura died, there had been one rather sordid drunken night with a fading B-list actress I knew vaguely, but that was all. Now this. If I were to be honest with myself, I probably felt more guilty because of Laura than because Heather was married. If Charlotte were to be believed, the marriage was on its last legs. I had seen the same thing happen to enough couples back in L.A. to know that there are some brinks you just don't come back from.

But so far it had only been a kiss, I told myself, and a kiss is just a kiss, as the man sang. The decent thing would be to stop at that before things went too far. As Charlotte had already told me, Heather was vulnerable. I could tell that myself by the games she played and by the flip, flirtatious persona she adopted to mask her pain and her insecurity. Stripping that away would only expose her to the raw pain and confusion of the failing marriage, of which I had seen some expression in her tears tonight. I had always been faithful to Laura, and even if Heather and Derek were on the outs, I was not a marriage breaker.

I had planned on doing a little work on the sonata, but it just wouldn't come tonight. I was too restless, too distracted. Instead, I put on Charlie Haden and Pat Metheny, poured myself a glass of wine, and sat in an armchair by the fire staring into the flames, haunted by memories of those long ago childhood Bonfire Nights and of Laura's face in the glow of July the Fourth fireworks. It morphed into Grace Fox's face, and I knew I was lost.

12

Famous Trials: Grace Elizabeth Fox, April 1953, by Sir Charles Hamilton Morley

DENYING THE JURY AND THE WORLD AT LARGE THE OPPORTUNITY TO HEAR at firsthand Grace Fox's account, in her own words, of what had really happened in Kilnsgate House on the night of the first of January 1953, might seem to some an oversight in the extreme, but we must bear in mind that there is no legal requirement for the plaintiff to appear in the witness box, and that the burden is on the prosecution to prove their case against the defendant beyond a reasonable doubt.

The placing of the accused in the witness box, thereby bringing the matter of her character into the proceedings and opening her to cross-examination by the Crown, has always been a matter of contention in the circles of criminal law, and perhaps the general opinion of most barristers is that the defendant should definitely not appear in his or her own defense, odd as this may sound to the layperson.

Some would argue that putting the defendant in the witness box is a strategy far more often regretted when not done than it is celebrated when done. "If only the jury had had the opportunity to see for themselves what an honest, sensitive, and upright character my client really is," the disappointed barrister may often chide himself after a failure. Yet even the most honest, sensitive, and upright among us may tremble, quail, and even crack under the strain of a relentless cross-examination by a determined Crown barrister such as Sir Archibald Yorke KC, and Mr. Sewell knew nothing if he did not know his opponent and his reputation. On the whole, Mr. Sewell put up a valiant effort in Grace's defense, and he did indeed gain much ground toward the end, but he had too little ammunition at his disposal, and he simply failed to capitalize on his competent destruction of the medical evidence, which was possibly his finest moment.

As minor facts are given major significance, as little white lies and omissions loom large as the shadow of the gallows, as our every word and deed is subject to the most detailed and merciless probing and interpretation—tell me, who among us would not quake at such a prospect?

In general principle, then, putting the accused before her accusers is frowned upon because it exposes the *character* and magnifies all blemishes. Why, then, the gentle reader may ask, would a barrister *ever* decide to put his client on the stand? Because, on occasion, there is the faintest chance that testimony from the accused may tug at the heartstrings of the jury and may thereby tip the delicate balance of mercy in her favor. The accused's testimony may create compassion on the part of certain jury members and engender seeds of reasonable doubt which, in the deliberations that follow, may result in the jury being unable to come to a unanimous verdict of twelve, as required by law. Might this have happened in the case of Grace Fox? We will never know.

Mr. Sewell had clearly decided that it was not worth the risk of finding out. If the aloofness and lack of interest exhibited by Grace Fox in court was also a feature of Mr. Sewell's private meetings with her, then one can only applaud his judgment. Juries may be willing to forgive a contrite and repentant adulteress, but not an arrogant and detached one. Juries want tears, protestations of innocence, much wailing and gnashing of teeth, but Grace Fox had not given them that, and there was no reason to assume that she would be any different in the witness box. So she remained a lonely and forlorn figure in the dock.

Mr. Justice Venable's summing up was as fair and unbiased with regard to matters of law as we have come to expect from the members of our senior judiciary. He apportioned the correct weight to each scrap of evidence presented to the court, and his summary was a model of conciseness and clarity from which we could all learn a great deal.

On the other hand, it is perhaps fair to say that the judge demonstrated little sympathy for the characters of Grace Fox and Samuel Porter. If Grace did, as the police and the prosecution contended, administer to her husband a large dose of deadly potassium chloride after first sedating him with chloral hydrate, then this, in itself, Mr. Justice Venables declared, was a devilish plot, which must have taken a great deal of planning and cunning to bring to fruition, evidence in itself of the killer's determination and cold-blooded premeditation.

According to the Crown, Grace Fox had also selected witnesses to her cleverly staged and cynical attempt to revive her husband for show, the judge said, when in fact she wanted him dead. Mr. Justice Venables also alluded to Grace's capability as a nurse, the knowledge she had gained when she had worked for a spell in a hospital dispensary during her training. She had access to her husband's surgery, and she clearly knew the properties of the various lethal substances therein.

Mr. Justice Venables also spoke at length of the night that Grace and Samuel had spent at Mrs. Compton's guesthouse in Leyburn, of the frenzied orgy of sexual intercourse they had clearly experienced there, and asked if it were not reasonable to assume that a woman under the sway of such a passion would not undertake such a desperate course of action as murder if she found herself under threat of imminent separation from the object of her ardor?

The judge also dealt with another important legal matter in his summing up. Not calling the defendant raises its own problems, not the least of which being that the jury assumes the accused, by not standing up and speaking out for herself, has something to hide and must, therefore, be guilty. The judge was careful to discount this. When it came to Grace Fox's silence, he was quick to remind the jury that, while they had not heard from the accused herself, they were not to take this as any indication whatsoever of her guilt. It was a legal matter, purely, and perfectly within her rights. He also went on to warn them that he could understand why they might have no sympathy for an immoral woman like Grace Fox, but that however much they found her character and actions abhorrent, they should lay this prejudice aside, and this serious defect in her character should not necessarily make them more ready to convict her of the crime, unless they felt compelled to do so by the evidence they had heard.

So it ended. The jury was out for one hour and seventeen minutes before returning with a verdict of guilty. Mr. Justice Venables grimaced, called for his black cap, and pronounced the sentence of death. Grace Fox gripped the rail, and one tear rolled over the lower rim of her left eye and down her cheek. Then she was taken down by the bailiffs.

NOVEMBER 2010

Over the next few days, the weather took a turn for the worse, with gale-force winds, heavy rains, and hailstones the size of cricket balls. I didn't go out much, but I did make one quick foray into town when the man from Richmond Books phoned to tell me that he had got hold of the edition of *Famous Trials* I had asked for. He recognized me straight away and brought out the rather tattered old paperback, for which he wanted £3.50, which seemed reasonable to me. I also bought a couple of other books, as my reading material was running low: Alan Sillitoe's *Saturday Night and Sunday Morning*, because I hadn't read it since I was at school, and Kazuo Ishiguro's *Nocturnes* because I was a sucker for stories with a musical context.

Back at Kilnsgate, with the rain hammering against the French windows, I sat by the fire and spent the rest of the afternoon reading Sir Charles Hamilton Morley's account of Grace's trial. When I had finished, I was not much the wiser as regards what made Grace tick, but I did know a lot more about the evidence against her and the way the trial had been conducted.

The prosecution presented a strong case based on very little evidence and a great deal of innuendo, and, to my mind, the defense was lackluster. The evidence was at best circumstantial, more a matter of absences than presences, but the prosecution made a good job of presenting it in a damning light, and the defense barrister did very little to demolish the house of cards the prosecution had built except for a few of the more outrageous scientific theories.

I put the volume aside and went up to my laptop, which I kept on the escritoire in Grace's old sewing room, and tracked down what I could about the author of the piece: Sir Charles Hamilton Morley. He was born in Edinburgh in 1891, the son of a Scottish banker and an English noblewoman. Educated at Eton and Oxford, he was called to the bar in 1913. After surviving the First World War, in which he was awarded a Military Cross, he enjoyed a distinguished legal career in which he first took silk and was then appointed to the bench in 1936. He retired due to ill health in 1947, at the age of fifty-six, then turned his talents to writing, producing several potboilers in the John Buchan mold, a three-volume history of the English legal system, and a number of volumes in the *Famous Trials* series. Ill health or not, he lived to the ripe old age of eighty-three and died peacefully at his country house in Buckinghamshire in 1974. One unusual fact about him emerged: Sir Charles was known for his strong opposition to the death penalty in his later years.

Perhaps I was typecasting Morley, but it wasn't hard to imagine what a man from such a rigorously disciplined and privileged background as his would make of a woman like Grace Fox. Still, I reminded myself, Morley wasn't the judge at her trial; he wasn't the one who sentenced her to death, he was merely the voice that brought it all to life.

OVER THE FOLLOWING COUPLE OF DAYS, I WORKED ON THE SONATA AND MADE A few minor harmonic breakthroughs, skirting the edges of atonality, but not quite crossing the borderline. Sometimes I spent a little time in the TV room watching old movies: *This Sporting Life*, *The Go-Between*, and *Whistle Down the Wind*, with its haunting theme by Malcolm Arnold. Now, there was a man who had written plenty of music people listened to. I remembered what Bernard Herrmann had said about there being no such thing as a "film composer," that you were either a composer or you were not. That made me feel a bit better about myself and more confident about the sonata. I was a composer, I told myself.

In the evenings, I lit a fire in the living room and read a story from *Nocturnes*, or reread sections of Morley. The more I read it, the more I became certain that Sam Porter was right, and that the authorities had decided in advance that Grace was guilty, then set out a case to prove it. They hadn't even bothered to investigate any other lines of inquiry, the possibility that someone else may have done it, or that Ernest Fox might have died of natural causes.

I remember talking to an acquaintance at a party once—a high-profile criminal lawyer who had defended a number of Hollywood celebrities—and he told me what a dangerous tactic it was for the defense to conduct its case by trying to implicate somebody other than the defendant. You certainly couldn't rely on the kind of witness-box confessions that Perry Mason always seemed to winkle out of some apparently innocent bystander who couldn't keep his or her mouth shut.

The main problem, my lawyer acquaintance said, was that if you tried to suggest that someone else did it, and you failed, then the jury's suspicion would inevitably fall back on the only other person involved: the accused. It is also, my acquaintance told me, practically impossible to conduct a two-pronged approach—defense of the client and the prosecution of another—without the DA's, or in this case, the Crown's, resources. Montague Sewell, Grace Fox's barrister, hadn't had such resources, so he had simply done the best job he could under the circumstances. As far as I could tell, it wasn't a very good one, and even Morley seemed to regard him as somewhat of a lightweight.

Why hadn't Grace spoken out? That was the one thing that still bothered me in all the accounts I had come across so far—Wilf Pelham's, Sam Porter's, Sir Charles Hamilton Morley's. Grace's silence. Why hadn't she stood up there, in court, in the police station, in the street, on the rooftops, and shouted it out for all to hear, "I am innocent! I didn't do it! I did not murder my husband!"

No doubt she had her reasons, but still, her silence, easily mistaken for indifference, bothered me. Maybe Grace had felt confident that the whole world would see she was innocent and set her free, at least during the early stages of the trial. She hadn't gone in pleading not guilty and expecting to be hanged, but her attempts to prove her own innocence had been halfhearted, to say the least. I understood the arguments Morley had laid out against the defendant entering the witness box and exposing herself to questions of character from the prosecution, but surely, I thought, Grace's presence in front of the jury, her honesty, directness, beauty, and tenderness, might have played on their heartstrings, helped convince the twelve people good and true that she wasn't a murderess? We would at least have heard her voice, heard her story, and not been left with only this troubling silence.

On the other hand, as Morley suggested, her appearance might have had quite the opposite effect if she had come across as either cold and detached, the way she seemed to be acting in court, or as a hard-headed seductress, libertine, corrupter of young men such as Samuel Porter. That was exactly the way she did appear to the jury, as it turned out. They were seeing a scarlet woman who had been fornicating with a young man half her age. Who can fathom human nature?

There were still a number of little things that nagged away at me, including my own mysterious visitor and the young man in uniform with whom Grace had walked and talked shortly before her husband's death. Perhaps he was as much a figment of malicious gossip as anything else.

Wilf Pelham might be worth another chat, I thought, now that I was armed with a bit more information. I decided that I would go down to town when the weather improved—I had to go shopping, anyway—and bribe him with another pint or two.

I also thought about Heather a lot during my brief self-imposed exile, but I didn't make any attempt to contact her; nor did she try to get in touch with me. I wondered if perhaps she, too, had come too close for comfort the other night and realized that she had to back off now, before it was too late. I didn't know whether she would come through with the vendor's name or not, but it probably didn't matter. It was only idle curiosity on my part, I realized. And perhaps an excuse to see her again. Why did it matter whether Grace's son had sold the house to me through a firm of solicitors? He would hardly know anything more about the events at Kilnsgate House all those years ago, when he was a mere child, and if he did, he probably wouldn't tell me. Why should he? I had no authority or power to change the past.

About a week after Bonfire Night, after the best night's sleep I'd had in ages, I awoke around nine o'clock to a misty scene, the trees still and dripping, the lime kiln like the eye of some monstrous kraken awoken from the depths. Mixed with the mist was a heavy drizzle, the sort of weather they call "mizzling" in Yorkshire, where they have a special language for all things wet and gray.

I dressed, showered, and went downstairs to make coffee. By the time I had finished my second cup and eaten my toast and marmalade, the drizzle was starting to ease off a bit. I sat at the piano and played through what I had written so far, making notes when I came to unsatisfying transitions or sagging lyric passages.

I knew that I was favoring the Schubertian long melodic line, and I tried to split up some of them, slip in more variations, tempos, and even key changes. I didn't want to sound dazzlingly contemporary, but nor did I want to sound like a pale imitation of the Master. I took out the sheet music again and studied Grace's notations on the Schubert *Impromptus*. Scanning the tiny neat hand, I remembered the paintings and drawings Sam Porter had shown me, then thought of the image Morley presented of Grace in court, her drab clothing, pale face, hair tied back in a bun. What was going through her mind? Did she realize that all was lost sooner than I imagined she did? Had she already given up?

Laura had, of course. Given up. That was why she came home from the hospital; she wanted to die at home, in familiar surroundings, with me by her side, holding her hand. And that was exactly how it happened. At least she hadn't ended her days at the end of a hangman's rope. I shuddered.

I knew that I was feeling restless when I found myself constantly checking the weather through the window. By early afternoon, the mist had gone, dispersed partly by the wind, which was also tearing gaps in the charcoal clouds for the sun to lance through. I would get nowhere hanging around here waiting for things to improve, so I got in the car and drove to Richmond.

———————

THERE WERE PLENTY OF FREE PARKING SPOTS IN THE MARKETPLACE, AND THE wind nearly took my car door off when I got out. I made a quick dash for the Castle Tavern and was surprised not to see Wilf Pelham propping up the bar. The bartender remembered me.

"Looking for Wilf again?" he said.

"Yes."

"He's poorly. Off his food. Hasn't been in for a couple of days."

"Nothing serious, I hope?"

"Shouldn't think so. Strong as an ox, is old Wilf."

"Do you know where I can find him?"

"He'll be at home, that new sheltered housing just up the road."

I knew where he meant. He gave me a street and a number. "I'd like to take him a little something," I said. "Any ideas?"

"He likes his bitter best, but when it comes to bottles, Wilf's strictly a Guinness man."

"Thanks." I bought a couple of bottles of Guinness, jumped back in the car and drove up to Wilf's house. He answered my ring after a short wait, seemed a bit surprised to see me, but stood aside and bade me enter.

"If it's not the man who writes music nobody listens to," he said.

"I'm trying to put that right," I said. I handed him the Guinness.

"Glad to hear it. Sit down. And thank you. I won't have any just now, if you don't mind." He touched his stomach. "Bit of a tummy upset. Cup of herb tea?"

"Perfect."

The small living room was spic and span, its surfaces free of dust, just a few books scattered here and there, newspapers, a half-empty mug, a couple of empty beer bottles, the place of a man of limited means comfortable living by himself. Wilf collected up most of the books and returned them to a bookcase, then went to make the tea. I studied his library while he was gone. I have always found it fascinating to discover people's tastes in music or literature. Wilf definitely favored the serious stuff, mostly classics: Dickens, George Eliot, Charlotte Brontë, Elizabeth Gaskell, Henry James, and Thomas Hardy were all accorded prominent space, many in handsome Folio Society editions, along with a few European writers in translation, Zola, Balzac, Flaubert, Dostoevsky, Chekhov, Tolstoy, and Proust, with a smattering of Mann, Camus, and Sartre. And they all looked as if they had been read. An old edition of Grove filled one shelf, and biographies and history filled up the rest of the space. Wilf also had a collection of old vinyl, mostly classical, some jazz, that would have been the envy of many an audiophile.

Wilf came back with the tea and a plate of chocolate biscuits on a tray and plonked it down on the table.

"How are you?" I asked. "What's wrong?"

"I don't know," he said, touching his lower chest. "I've been having a lot of heartburn, acid reflux the doc calls it. Probably cancer. They're going to stick a tube down my throat soon as they can arrange an appointment at the hospital. Who knows when that might be, the way the NHS is these days? In the meantime, I've got some pills. They help a bit. Sometimes. Anyway, you don't want to hear about my health problems. I suppose you came to ask me more questions?"

"I'm afraid so."

"That's all right, lad. I don't get a lot of company these days. And you did come bearing gifts." He poured the tea and glanced at me expectantly.

I gave him a précis of what I had done and found out since we had last talked, withholding any conclusions I might have come to in the meantime.

"You certainly do get around, don't you? I've been to Paris a few times, myself. Lovely city. I visited once or twice with school groups. The Louvre, Musée d'Orsay, Napoleon's tomb, Notre Dame. The cultural and historical highlights. But that's not why you were there, is it?"

"No. I was on my way to visit my brother in Cognac, and I stopped in to talk to Sam Porter on the way."

"Sam? So you found him all right? How is he?"

"I found him. It wasn't difficult. He's fine. He seems to be doing well for himself. Says hello."

"Hooked up with some pretty young artist's model, is he?"

"I don't know about that. He seems to be living alone. To be honest,

I don't think he ever got over Grace and what happened all those years ago." I sipped some tea. It was a pleasant surprise. Vanilla and black-currant, or something along those lines. "Sam said the two of you used to play together during the war. Do you remember that?"

"Course I do. We were kids. There was a gang of sorts. It was all a big game to us. Not that anything much ever happened around here."

"What about the Messerschmitt crashing?"

Wilf smiled at the memory. "Aye, now *that* was fun. You should have seen us, tiptoeing around it, and when that pilot climbed out . . . We were off like a shot. Scared the living daylights out of us. A real live German."

"He didn't die in the crash?"

"No. Funny, you know, the only thing I remember about him is that he looked like my big brother."

"What became of him?"

"No idea. He ran off into the woods. Probably more scared than we were. I suppose they caught him eventually."

"Sam said something about a POW camp."

"Aye, it was out Reeth way. We used to bicycle out there sometimes and watch them through the fence. There was a bit of fuss between the locals and the military, but guess who usually wins in wartime."

"Why the fuss?"

"Oh, people were worried about escapes and such." He laughed. "They needn't have bothered. It was mostly Italians, and they had no desire to go back to the fighting. We got a few Jerries later on, too, and they seemed happy enough to stay there as well. It was hardly Colditz or Stalag 17. I think they lived a pretty good life. Most of the prisoners used to help with the harvest. Some of them ended up marrying local lasses. The Bartolini family still lives up near Marske, and there are Schnells in Grinton. But why the interest?"

"Nothing, really. Just trying to get a broader picture of the way things were back then. I heard Kilnsgate House was requisitioned by the military for a while?"

"For a couple of years, yes. It was all very hush-hush, barbed wire, armed guards and all that."

"But Ernest Fox still lived there?"

"I suppose so. I can't really say I paid much attention to the good doctor's comings and goings. He was probably well in with them. Typical of him. Nothing he liked better than going around with a smirk on his face as if he knew something nobody else did. Old Foxy had been involved in military matters ever since the first war. Mustard gas and such. His way of doing his bit."

"Talking about doing one's bit, do you remember Nat Bunting, the man who went missing? Sam mentioned him."

Wilf frowned for a moment, then it dawned on him. "Nat. Of course. He was what you'd call a bit slow. Challenged you'd say, these days, I suppose. Nice enough lad, though. Lived rough, somewhere near Melsonby, as I remember. Did odd jobs. You'd see him walking all over the place with his tool kit slung over his shoulder, like someone out of a Thomas Hardy novel, then one day he was gone."

"Anyone ever find out why?"

"Not as I recall. I'm sure they looked for him, sent out a search party or two, but people didn't ask too many questions in wartime. The walls have ears and all that. Besides, priorities were different. The individual was rather less important than the state, and the state was the military. We had a country to protect, a war to win."

"Sam said he thought this Nat might have joined up."

"Well, he did used to go on about it, but I would have thought nobody would have him. He had a gammy leg. Not to mention the . . . you know. Nat Bunting. Haven't thought of him in years. Aye, well . . . I don't suppose you've come to pick my memory about the war?"

"Not entirely. It's just interesting, especially to those of us who missed it by a few years. But there are a couple of things I *would* like to ask you about, if you don't mind, to clear up some questions I have?"

Wilf crossed his legs. "I don't mind. I can't promise to be of any use, but I don't mind."

"I've been reading the trial account, and it seems that Dr. Fox had received a job offer from a hospital near Salisbury around the time he died."

Wilf scratched the side of his nose. "I do remember hearing something about that. I think it was a fairly recent thing, though, hadn't quite done the gossip circuit before . . . well, you know. Why? Does it matter?"

"I think so. The prosecution put it forward as another motive for Grace to get rid of her husband. The job would take him a long way from Richmond, and therefore take Grace away from Sam. But it seems to me an indication of Sam's lack of involvement."

"Come again?"

"Sam can't have known about the job offer. Not if it came as late in the day as it apparently did. He was in Leeds for a while, then up at his parents' farm over Christmas and New Year's. He hadn't seen or talked to Grace since mid-December, so he couldn't possibly have known about her moving away until it was raised at the trial."

"True," said Wilf. "But it hardly matters, does it? Sam wasn't on trial. Grace was."

"But it does mean that if Grace killed Ernest, she did it completely off her own bat, so to speak, without even any certain knowledge that Sam would go off with her. He might have been appalled by what she'd done."

"Unless they hatched the plan together earlier?"

"But they didn't know about the job then, neither of them. It seems to me that's rather an important point, especially as this job was put forward as one of the major motives, and Hetty Larkin said she'd heard Grace and Ernest arguing about a letter a few days before the dinner. Mrs. Compton's testimony has Sam and Grace talking about getting rid of Ernest in late November, long before there was any letter or hint of a job offer that would split them apart. Don't you find that a bit strange?"

"Now that you mention it, I suppose I do," said Wilf.

"The trial account mentions that Grace was seen walking and talking with a young man in uniform on Castle Walk shortly before her husband's death. Nothing more was ever said about it."

"I certainly heard nothing," Wilf said, "but you have to understand that some people were saying all sorts of things about Grace then, spreading rumors, blackening her character. I should imagine that was part of the campaign. Luckily, none of it got to court."

"But there must have been some truth in it, surely? I don't nec-

essarily agree with anything people might have read into it, but the
event itself probably happened. It could be relevant. I don't believe that
whoever she was talking to was a lover or anything like that, but the
meeting itself could have been important to Grace's state of mind, even
a trigger for her subsequent actions. Surely the police must have followed up on it? Who was he? What were they talking about?"

"The police?" Wilf snorted. "They already had their minds made
up, and they were probably no different then than they are today. They
decided Grace had done it, and that was that as far as they were concerned. Whatever evidence fit that theory went in, whatever didn't,
they ignored. And once the ball got rolling, it wasn't too hard to get
people to speak against her. These things have a habit of snowballing."

"What do you mean?"

"I hated that vicious, mean-spirited holier-than-thou attitude all
this business stirred up, the hypocrisy, the things some people said,
even people who were supposed to have been her friends. It brought
out the worst in some people. And Alice Lambert was no better than
the rest."

"Alice? What did she say?"

"Oh, she didn't say anything in court, she stuck to the facts there,
appeared for the defense, for her friend, butter wouldn't melt in her
mouth, but word soon got around about the Foxes having separate bedrooms and Grace being a bit coldhearted toward her husband. Alice
always did have a soft spot for Ernest Fox. It was him she met first,
you know, not Grace. They were old friends. And then she goes telling everyone she'd always thought Grace was a bit too free and easy in
her manner with the opposite sex, especially younger men, that sort of
thing. Innuendo, fuel for the fire they wanted to burn Grace on."

"Is this true about Alice Lambert and Ernest Fox?"

"That she had a soft spot for him?"

"Yes."

"You could see it clearly when you saw them together. Like you and
that estate agent woman."

I almost choked on my tea. "What? Heather? How do you . . . I
mean . . . ?"

Wilf laughed. "Oh, don't get so flustered. You look like a schoolboy caught with his hand over the tuckshop counter. I've seen you chatting in the market square once or twice, that's all. The body language. I've told you what small towns are like. I'd watch it, if I were you."

"We're just friends. She helped me get set up at Kilnsgate."

His eyes twinkled. "If you say so."

"Oh, knock it off, Wilf. Was there anything in it, Alice Lambert and Ernest Fox?"

"Like what?"

"You know what I'm getting at. Were they having an affair? Did Alice's husband know?"

"Surely you're not . . . ? Not Alice Lambert?"

"I was thinking more of Jeremy Lambert."

"Jeremy Lambert? You must be joking. He wouldn't say boo to a goose."

"You knew him?"

"Of course. He was the local schools inspector, even after I started teaching. Nice, cushy job in those days. Maybe not so much now, if they still have them. You'd be likely to risk getting knifed or shot. But Jeremy Lambert, a murderer?" He shook his head. "I can't see it."

"Alice?"

"Look at your own reasoning, and you'll find she doesn't have a motive."

"Sometimes it takes a lot of digging to uncover a motive."

"Even so . . ."

"Everyone focused on Grace and her affair with Sam. But what about Ernest Fox? He must have had plenty of opportunities to put it about. Were there any rumors? Anything about him bedding any of the lovely ladies of Swaledale?"

"Not as I can recall. At least, I never heard nowt about him chasing women. But he was away a lot. I mean, he could have got up to anything then, couldn't he?"

"I thought he was supposed to be a local GP?"

"He was, but he did a lot of consulting. Traveled a lot. To be honest, during the war and after, Dr. Nelson carried the practice."

"Can you think of *anyone* else who might have wanted Ernest Fox dead?"

"Plenty. But none of them were at Kilnsgate House on the night he died."

"What was Dr. Nelson like?"

"Cliff Nelson? He was a steady, dependable, dedicated sort, a bit dull, if truth be told. But he was a gentleman, and full of common sense. Lived down by the green. As I said, he practically carried the practice through the war, and after, for that matter. You never saw his wife, Mary, much. She worked behind the scenes, doing the books, keeping house, taking care of the kids."

"They had children?"

"Three boys."

"There were no rumors, no gossip?"

"Dr. Fox and Mary? No. I'm afraid you're barking up the wrong tree there."

"It wouldn't be the first time. What about Grace and Dr. Nelson?"

"What about them?"

"Their relationship."

"They got on well, as far as I know. Cliff used to play piano a little, too, so he and Grace had that musical connection. They were friends. I think she also felt she could talk to him. He and her husband weren't always on the best of terms."

"Why not?"

"I should think because most of the burden fell on Cliff Nelson's shoulders. One thing," Wilf went on. "I don't know if it would have made any difference, but Dr. Nelson told me not long after the whole business that he had offered to appear as a character reference for Grace at her trial. He was convinced she was innocent."

"What happened?"

"He was told that the defense didn't plan on using any *men* as character witnesses. That it wouldn't look good."

"I suppose they had a point. Did Grace actually have many female friends?"

"Not as I recall. There was Alice, and Mary, I suppose, and one or two ladies from the Operatic Society. But she was more of a man's woman—and I don't mean that in a bad way."

"Was she really as free and easy as people said?"

"Free and easy? Depends on what you mean, and how you construe it. Grace didn't walk around town with her nose stuck in the air like some, and maybe as some would have expected from a doctor's wife. Like I said, she'd even pass the time of day with the likes of me at a subscription concert, while the rest of them ignored anyone they felt beneath their social standing. I'm not saying Grace wasn't a snob in some ways—she certainly appreciated her place in society—but not when it came to people. She had a big heart. She'd help anyone, talk to anyone. If that's free and easy."

"Sleep with anyone?"

"No. It was nothing but scurrilous nonsense," Wilf said indignantly. "A load of bollocks. Grace Fox was not a whore. She may have been many things, including an adulteress and a murderer, but she was not a whore. Grace and Sam had an affair, okay, but that wasn't a symptom of bad character. He wasn't a notch on her bedpost. They were in love, for crying out loud."

"Did you ever have an affair with Grace, Wilf?"

"Me? Don't be ridiculous."

"Were *you* in love with her?"

Wilf turned away and fell silent. He grimaced and put his hand to his stomach. "Thanks for the Guinness," he said, "but I think you'd better leave now. I'm feeling a bit poorly."

Well done, Lowndes, I said to myself on the way out. Now you've managed to piss off the only two people you've met who actually knew Grace Fox.

13

**Extract from the *Journal of Grace Elizabeth Fox*
(ed. Louise King), July–August 1940,
Liverpool and at sea.**

MONDAY, JULY 29, 1940

WELL, HERE I AM, AT SEA FINALLY, HEADING LORD KNOWS WHERE. I SET
off from the training hospital in Netley under cover of darkness
two days ago, after being awakened and told to pack in the middle of the night. We arrived in Liverpool late the following morning. I
was billeted in a terrible hotel near the docks, sharing with a girl called
Kathleen, whom I had met during training. Kathleen is a statuesque
blonde, very beautiful, but somewhat austere. I have already heard one
of the officers call her an "ice maiden," which I do not think fair. She
has a terrific sense of humor and a most startling laugh, rather like the
braying of a horse. The hotel was so bad that we had to wedge a chair
under our door handle every night to keep out the sailors who thought
we were there for their pleasure. We could not get a wink of sleep, but
we did laugh a lot.

This afternoon we boarded the *Empress of Australia*, a luxury ocean liner converted into a troop carrier. Luckily for us, the luxury has not all been stripped away, like the fine china and crystal, to be stored safely until the end of the war. I am to share a first-class cabin with Brenda, another girl I met during training. Brenda is a great deal more untidy than I am, and it will be a hard task to get her to pick her clothes up from the floor and chairs and keep her toiletries from spreading all over the bathroom.

Brenda and Kathleen and my other friend, Doris, are all single, and they seemed most surprised to hear that I am married, and that I would leave my husband to go to war. I told them that if the men could leave their wives at home, then I could leave my husband. What use would I be back there, anyway, buried in the Yorkshire countryside, when it is out here that men are dying and there are lives to be saved? Besides, I know that Hetty will take good care of Ernest.

There are fifty-five sisters onboard and Lord knows how many officers and serving men. Lots of the sisters are thrilled at the prospect of all these handsome young men paying them attention. There will be dances, dinners, and romance, no doubt. Matron has already singled me out and has given me a stern talking-to. I am to be the responsible one. I am to set an example. I am to keep my eye on some of the flightier, more wayward girls and direct them away from any foolish courses of action they might consider in the heat of a shipboard romance. Lucky me! How boring! Already there is talk of finding a pool of talent and putting on a small concert in a few days. Doris blabbed about my playing the piano and singing, so I have already been approached and roped in by the committee. Some of the officers who play instruments are forming a small dance band.

We are sailing in darkness with an escort of destroyers because of the U-boat danger. The vast dark sea surrounds us, moonlight sparkling on its surface, the lights of England fast disappearing behind us. The motion of the ship is easy and very calming as I lie here in my soft bed and write this. I can hardly wait until tomorrow to explore the ship. Lord only knows where we are going and what awaits us at the end of our voyage!

Friday, August 2, 1940

The weather started out quite dull and cool for this time of year, the sea became rough, and some of the less hardy women and men were terribly seasick. It was also quite chilly on deck, but with every day, it has been getting warmer outside, and now the ocean is less gray, more aquamarine and turquoise, and much more placid. We have been at sea for four days now, and I still have no idea where we are. We have not been told what our course is, or where it will take us. Sometimes the other ships in the convoy seem close enough to see us wave at them; other times we can't see them at all and worry in case they have been attacked by U-boats.

Yesterday we passed a distant group of islands. Someone said it was the Azores, but I am not sure that is true. Could we have traveled that far so quickly? You would be surprised by how many rumors do the rounds every day in the close confines of a ship where nobody knows their destination! I have looked at maps and a compass, and all I can tell is that we are heading generally southwest, so it may have been the Canaries or the Madeira Islands, and we must be on our way to Africa. Last night I saw phosphorescence in the ocean, a green will-o'-the-wisp shimmering over the water's surface, like Coleridge's poem come to life, all under a canopy of sparkling stars and a sickle moon.

The days pass in a glorious haze of indolence and pleasure. We have lectures, and duties to perform in the sick bay, of course, but there are no serious cases, and we have plenty of time to ourselves. First thing every morning, a drill sergeant leads us in physical-training exercises on deck. It is remarkable how so many of the men seem to be up and around so early, pretending to stare out to sea! After breakfast and lectures, I play tennis, usually with Brenda or Kathleen, but I am quite thrilled to find myself able to beat some of the strapping young male officers. Doris, too, is enjoying herself, swimming in the large pool, reading, writing letters to her sweetheart every day. She says she feels like royalty.

We also have a small library onboard. At first I was disappointed to find nothing I have not already read by Mr. Greene, Mr. Waugh, or Mr. Maugham, and far too many books by Mrs. Christie and her ilk, but on Doris's recommendation, I have finally settled on Trollope, whom I have avoided for years, perhaps because of his unfortunate name. Anyway, I have started *Can You Forgive Her?* and I am already deeply fascinated by the Palliser family. I find Trollope perfect company for the long days at sea. He is so very English, too, and almost makes me feel homesick at times. The news we hear from home is not very encouraging. There seem to be regular bombing raids on our cities, though I am sure that Ernest will be quite safe in Kilnsgate.

NOVEMBER 2010

Heather rang me around six o'clock a couple of days after I had talked with Wilf Pelham.

"Hello, stranger," she said.

"Heather. How are you?"

"Fine. Good."

"Have you managed to get any information about the vendor?"

"Is that all you're interested in?"

"Of course not. I just thought—"

"Oh, never mind. Yes, I think I might have some information for you."

"What is it?"

"Not so fast. What's it worth?"

"Heather, stop teasing."

"Buy me dinner tonight and I'll tell you."

"What about Derek?"

Heather fell silent for a moment, then said stonily, "Golf-club dinner."

"You're not invited?"

"Golf bores me."

"Okay. Where and when?"

"Try not to sound so thrilled by the prospect. I've just about finished a viewing, in the Garrison," Heather said. "How about you meet me at the Station in half an hour?"

"Half an hour? Fine. I'll see you there."

I hadn't been out since talking to Wilf, had mostly wandered the house from room to room, task to task, the sonata, e-mails to friends in the U.S., a phone call to my mother, another to Graham and Siobhan, a chat with my director friend Dave Packer about a possible future project, that sort of thing. I had also invited Dave and his wife, Melissa, for Christmas, though I doubted they would be able to come. Even if Dave was free, which was unlikely, Melissa was a very big movie star and probably wouldn't be able to get away, or even want to come to remote, wintry Yorkshire, for that matter.

The previous evening I had watched a young Diana Dors in *Yield to the Night* and thoroughly enjoyed it every bit as much as *Tread Softly Stranger*. *Blonde Sinner*, they called *Yield to the Night* in America, where they always did have a flair for avoiding the poetic. Diana Dors never did very well over there, anyway; there were too many other blond bombshells around America in the fifties. But she was terrific in this tale of lust, jealousy, and murder, spending most of the time looking rather dowdy in a cell for the condemned, reflecting upon the events that led her there. It was a little like the Ruth Ellis case, and much too close to Grace Fox's story. It disturbed me, and I slept badly that night, troubled by vivid dreams and eerie noises. I couldn't figure out whether they were part of the dreams or part of the house.

It was, of course, pitch dark and pouring down outside when I set off to meet Heather. By habit, I glanced toward the hump of the lime kiln as I got into the Volvo, but saw no shadowy figure. It had been a while since the visitation, and I was beginning to believe that Heather was right, that it had simply been a lost tourist or a local archeologist.

The Station really had been the local railway station until Dr. Beeching's cuts in the sixties, and the branch line to Darlington had been closed in 1969. Now the small 1850s building was home to a kind of cultural center, with exhibitions of local paintings on its open upper level, on the gallery above the restaurant; occasional antiquarian book fairs; two small cinemas showing relatively new movies; and even a bakery, the smell from which was enticing.

It took me a while to find a parking spot, but I finally managed to get one down by the swimming pool and the Liberty Health Center that I had so far put off joining. I was still about five minutes early, even after I made the dash through the rain to the Station entrance, so I got a glass of wine from the bar and took a table at the back of the restaurant.

Heather was only ten minutes late. I saw her lower her umbrella and scan the area for me as she entered the building. She finally saw me through one of the gaps in the hangings that partially screen off the restaurant, waved, and headed over. She was wearing black slacks and a matching jacket, narrowed at the waist, over a plain white blouse, very businesslike. Her hair was tied back in a ponytail, which showed off the freckles over her nose and made her look about ten years younger, and she carried a leather briefcase.

"Well, hello again, you. What a day."

"Difficult?"

Heather sat down opposite me. "Just busy. Mostly on your behalf, by the way. I could murder a glass of Chardonnay."

Not one to miss my cue, I went to the counter and got her a large glass. It was an odd sort of setup for a restaurant, because you had to go over to the counter to order your meal and to get your wine. But then I had spent many years in America, where you get used to waiters or waitresses bringing you drinks, even in fake English pubs. The meals, mercifully, are delivered to the table. We browsed the menu, and Heather asked for a salmon and crayfish salad while I went for a cheese and bacon burger. When I went back to the counter to order, I also picked up a bottle of wine. It would save me any more trips. I had been drinking red, but I knew that Heather preferred white, and Chardonnay was fine with me.

"So what's this information you've got for me?" I asked after I had sat down again.

Heather flashed me with her green eyes. "Hold your horses. Don't you want to know how I'm doing first?"

I smiled. "How are you doing, Heather?"

"Not so bad, thank you for asking."

I lowered my voice. "About the other night—"

She put a finger to her lips. "Ssshhh. Let's not talk about that."

I didn't know whether she meant the tears or the kiss. I wanted to talk about both. Maybe I'd been living in America for too long and had picked up too many foreign ways, but I was quickly remembering that Yorkshiremen don't talk about things like that. About anything emotional, for that matter. Yorkshirewomen, too, it seemed. "Whatever you say."

We sipped our wine in silence for a while, not exactly tense, but not comfortable, either. Conversations and laughter ebbed and flowed around us. Heather gestured over to the movie theaters behind me. "Did you notice what's playing?"

I shook my head. It had been dark and raining, and I hadn't bothered to look.

"*Death Knows My Name*," she said.

I put my hands to my head and groaned. "Oh, my God, no." It was the most recent movie Dave and I had done together, a couple of biggish names, including Dave's wife, Melissa; a bunch of young hopefuls; and a very old-fashioned score to suit an old-fashioned atmospheric thriller. There were chases, love scenes, fear, panic, creepy moments, sudden reversals, unexpected climaxes, all mirrored in the music. It wasn't exactly done by rote, but it hadn't taken a great deal of originality or soul-searching. Which was just as well, as I hadn't been able to muster any originality or soul-searching in the months after Laura's death, when I had written it. Definitely not one of my favorites, but as it happened, it was a big hit. The American public had seemed to enjoy it, and it had done extremely well at the box office. It had only just been released in the UK.

"Maybe we can go see it after dinner?" Heather said.

"What?"

"You know. Go to the movies. Me and you. Sit in the back row and neck."

I must have blushed because she laughed and touched my arm. "Don't worry. I'm only teasing. I won't molest you. I just think it would be really cool to go and see a movie with the guy who wrote the music, that's all. Won't you indulge me? Just this once."

"I've already seen it."

"Chris, please?"

The way her green eyes were imploring me as she spoke, I couldn't find it in myself to say no. I already knew that my own opinions of my work often didn't match those of the public or the critics, or even my friends, so there was no sense in telling her it wasn't a movie I was especially proud of. I'd get through it somehow. "Sure," I said, and smiled at her. Our food arrived. "As long as you actually *listen* to the music. There'll be a test afterward. Now, tell me what you've discovered."

"I had lunch with Michael Simak," she said, wrinkling her nose. "I thought it might be easier than after-work drinks . . . you know . . . they can sometimes lead to dinner and . . ." She shrugged.

"And dinner can lead to?"

"You know what."

"Movies?"

Heather laughed and dug her fork into the salad. "That's it. Movies. Or the expectation of movies. Anyway, I managed to get away with my virtue intact, you'll be glad to hear."

I laughed. One of the things I liked about Heather, I realized, was that she made me laugh. Laura was the only other woman I had known who had been able to do that. Conventional wisdom has it that women like men who make them laugh, but I can vouch that it works the other way, too. "I didn't doubt it for a moment," I said. "But did you get any useful information? Did he give up the goods for a . . . for a what?"

"A pint of Stella? Not exactly, but he gave me enough to make one or two further inquiries of my own. That's how I spent most of my afternoon. Michael's firm has handled the Fox family's affairs forever, and I know one or two of their retired partners and associates. It's a small town, and I've been around here long enough to be a pretty good information hound, you know."

"I'm sure you have. What exactly did you dig out?"

"Ooh, look. My glass is empty and it's a long story."

So was mine. I poured us both a refill. "Did you find out who owned Kilnsgate House?" I asked.

"Yes, I did. And I think you'll find it very interesting indeed."

I pushed my almost empty plate away. "Go on."

Heather leaned forward, excited by the story she was about to tell. The childlike enthusiasm in her expression, her hand gestures and her eyes were infectious. I leaned forward, too, and it seemed as if an invisible canopy formed over us, and the rest of the world was somehow *out there* and couldn't get in. Luckily, this was Yorkshire, so we didn't have to worry about waiters coming over every five minutes to ask if everything was all right with our meals.

"Well, you know that Grace and Ernest's son was called Randolph? Randolph Fox."

I nodded.

"He'd just turned seven when his father died. He was in the house at the time but was deemed too young to give evidence in court. The police talked to him, but he had nothing to tell them. He slept through it all."

"You paid a whole pint of Stella for this?"

"No, this is what I dug out myself, later. Idiot. I'm trying to piece it all together in chronological order. I'm telling a story. Do you want to hear it or not?"

"Of course. Sorry."

"During the trial and the period leading up to Grace's execution, Randolph stayed with his aunt and uncle, Felicity and Alfred Middleton. Felicity was Grace's younger sister by seven years. They couldn't have any children of their own, and had always liked young Randolph, so after Grace was . . . well, you know . . . hanged . . . the necessary arrangements were made."

"Felicity and Alfred adopted Randolph Fox?"

"Yes. Loved him as their own. He became Randolph Middleton. They lived in Canterbury. Alfred Middleton was an architect. He made a decent living. Felicity was what they used to call a housewife. The boy had every advantage."

"I'm sure it was a good life for him. What happened?"

"Opportunity knocked. Alfred worked on a project for his firm that took him to Melbourne. He fell in love with the place and the possibilities there, and they offered him a job at the branch. This would be the late fifties, when Randolph was thirteen or fourteen."

"Aha," I said. "You really are demonstrating excellent detective skills."

"Thank you, Watson." Heather slugged back some wine. "Anyway, it must have been quite an upheaval for him. My parents moved from Harrogate to Richmond when I was twelve, and that was traumatic enough. Imagine starting a new school in another country at that age, with a funny accent."

"He got picked on, bullied?"

"Apparently he gave as good as he got, and he soon managed to fit in. The family never mentioned their lives in England, and Grace Fox was never discussed. Taboo. To all intents and purposes, Randolph put his birth parents right out of his head. Felicity and Alfred became his mum and dad. The only interruption in their new life was when a reporter found out who they were and came bothering them around the time they banned hanging over here in the sixties."

"Wait a minute. You got all this from Michael Simak?"

Heather arched her eyebrows. "I cannot reveal my sources."

"Come on, just for me."

"Oh, all right. One of the retired associates visited Ralph over in Australia several times. First on estate business, then they became close friends, so he'd go over for his holidays, take his wife along. Most of it he got from the horse's mouth, so to speak. The rest I either figured out for myself or got from Mr. G."

"Mr. G?"

"Google. You'd be surprised by what's out there, if you know where to look."

"Carry on. What did they do when someone found them?"

"They changed their name and moved out to Perth for a while. Alfred's firm had a branch there. They were very understanding and gave him a job." She took another sip of wine. "I get the impression that there are a lot of people in Australia with something to hide, whether it's something personal or a dodgy family history. Anyway, nobody objected or asked any questions. After this, the family name became Webster, and Randolph became Ralph. He'd always hated Randolph, anyway."

"Ralph Webster. I see. And Kilnsgate?"

"It was held in trust for him. When he turned twenty-one it became his. That would be in 1967. He had little interest in it, but he was dead set on not selling. Mike said he didn't know why, just that it was well known around the firm. Of course, they did what they could, used one of those cottage rental agencies, but as you know, Kilnsgate is hardly a cottage. Far too big. Much of the time it was unoccupied and in a state of disrepair. Some hippy squatters moved in for a while in the early seventies and started a commune, but they didn't last long. At least they were the peaceful kind and didn't wreck the place. Once in a while, someone would come in and have a go with it, give it a lick of paint and a bit of a face-lift, but they would never last long, either. Ralph can't have made much income from it, in fact it probably cost him money in the upkeep, but he was doing well enough himself by then. Anyway, I'm getting ahead of myself. When Ralph was eighteen, *before* he inherited Kilnsgate, the family moved back to Melbourne after a few years in Perth. Arthur and Felicity made sure Ralph got a good university education, and he ended up as a civil servant in the Victoria parliament, quickly making his way up through the ranks."

"Did he ever return to Kilnsgate?"

"Only once," Heather said. "But that was later. That part of his life was effectively over and done with. Except, he owned Kilnsgate House. As far as we know, he had no contact with anyone back in Yorkshire other than his solicitors. He got married to a woman called Mette Koenigsfeldt in 1980, a Danish immigrant. He was thirty-four at the time, and she was thirty. They bought a house in Brighton, a suburb of Melbourne by the sea. There was a daughter, Louise, born in 1986, and that was it as far as children were concerned. The couple split up in 1994, and Louise went to live with her mother, Mette, in a small town near Brisbane. Still following?"

"Just about." I poured the last of the wine. During the brief break in Heather's narrative, I once again noticed we were in a busy restaurant, people chatting all around us, music in the background. More music that nobody listens to.

"Everything's pretty much ticking along quietly after that for the next few years. Ralph gets a house in Brighton, not far from Felicity and Arthur, throws himself into his work at the legislature. Never remarries. Life goes on."

"And in the small town near Brisbane?"

"Ah. Things are a bit more interesting there. Mette marries a man who turns out to be an abusive alcoholic, and when she finds out he's also abusing Louise, she gives him his marching orders. It's the usual sad story, probably even more common in some of the isolated areas like where they lived. Court orders, restraining orders, appearances before the magistrate, but in the end, he goes out there one day and blows her head off with a twelve-gauge shotgun, then turns it on himself."

I felt a chill down the back of my neck. "And Louise?"

"At school, thank God. But she found them."

"What happened after that?"

"She went back to live with her father in Brighton, obviously traumatized. Things were apparently a bit chilly at first, but they soon grew close again. That's about it, really.

"Ralph Webster died last year in Brighton at the ripe young age of sixty-three. Lung cancer. He was a lifelong smoker. He left Kilnsgate House to his daughter, Louise. She saw no reason to keep it in the family any longer. It didn't mean anything to her, and she could use the money. She put it up for sale, then you came along, Mr. Bountiful, and paid the exorbitant asking price."

"And you told me I'd got a bargain."

"Ah, well, we know how to play you rich, gullible Americans. There's one born every minute."

I laughed. "What about Alfred and Felicity?"

"Alfred's long gone. Heart attack in the mideighties. Felicity's in an old folks' home. She must be about ninety now. Gaga."

"Did Louise know about Kilnsgate's history, about Grace?"

"Not until Ralph was on his deathbed. The poor girl must have been devastated. Think about it. First she finds her mother and stepfather dead in a pool of blood, then a few years later she discovers that her grandmother was a notorious poisoner who killed her grandfather and got hanged. What a recipe for a fucked-up life."

"And is she? A fuckup?"

"Apparently she ran a bit wild for a while in her late teens. Now? I don't know." Heather glanced at her watch. "My source tells me she's a bit of an activist. You know, anti-Iraq and Afghanistan wars, stop clubbing baby seals to death, stop global warming and the rest of it. A *Guardian* reader, no doubt. Come on, Chris, if you hurry up and pay the bill here, then we'll just have time to slip in and see *Death Knows My Name*. My treat."

"I don't know. It's not very good."

"Come on." She took me by the arm. "Don't be a spoilsport."

"WELL, *I* ENJOYED IT," SAID HEATHER AS WE MADE OUR WAY WITH THE CROWD out of the tiny cinema.

"I'm glad for you."

"Misery guts. What's wrong with it?"

"Nothing, I suppose," I said. "It's just not one of my finest. Too clichéd, too derivative."

"That scene where they kiss for the first time, the music there, it's unexpected, lush and romantic, yes, but it's also dark and foreboding, those creepy cellos and that clarinet."

"Bassoon."

"Whatever. Then you find out what happens to him, who she really is. Does your music often do that?"

"What?"

"Foreshadow."

"I suppose it does. I suppose that's part of the function of good film music. Like when you hear a certain theme, you associate it with a specific character, or you expect something to happen, and you can put different spins on it, variations, to match different moods and twists."

"You're a bloody genius, you are."

I laughed. We got into the main Station area again. "Coffee?" I suggested.

"I shouldn't, really." Heather paused. "But what the hell." She sounded edgy.

"Is something wrong?"

She shook her head. "Nothing for you to concern yourself with. Let's have that coffee."

We nursed our cappuccinos and discussed the film. Heather remained genuine in her enthusiasm, and I was just as genuine in my disdain, though I toned it down for her sake. She didn't know that I'd written most of the music by rote in a haze of alcohol, pills, and self-loathing after Laura's death, and she didn't need to know.

"Thanks very much for digging up all that information you gave me earlier," I said as we finished our coffees and prepared to leave.

"It's nothing," Heather said. "I found it a very interesting story. Tragic, but interesting. What terribly hard lives some people lead."

"What amazes me is that they survive," I said. "Not only that, but some of them never even complain. They put up with it all, the abuse, pain, poverty, humiliation, betrayal, serious illness, and they always have a kind word for everyone and a smile to face the world."

"I know. Doesn't it make you sick? My sister's like that," said Heather. "Nothing but boyfriends from hell, husbands from even worse places, thankless children, never enough money, one soul-destroying job after another, and she even lost her foot to diabetes. Never once complains and never stops bloody smiling."

"Is this like your brother in Scunthorpe?"

"Dorchester." Heather smiled. "Hell, no. Kirsty really *is* like that."

"And you?"

"Me?" We finished our coffees and walked out into the rain. "I'm a moaner."

I laughed. "There is just one more thing. You mentioned earlier on that Ralph Webster had returned to Kilnsgate just once. When was that? Why?"

"It was in 1982," said Heather. "They were building an extension at Armley Jail and they had to move all the graves. The people they'd hanged and buried there within the prison grounds."

"They moved Grace Fox's grave?"

"Yes. Reburied somewhere on the coast near where she grew up. Ralph was there for the reinterment. Now I really must go."

"Wait. Lift?"

"Not tonight. I've got my own car. See you."

Then she was off, umbrella up, slipping away into the darkness. "Good night," I whispered to the disappearing shadow. "And thank you again."

THE GARDEN GATE WAS OPEN AT KILNSGATE. I CLEARLY REMEMBERED SHUT-ting it, as I always did, and the latch was strong enough that the wind couldn't blow it open. So what, or who, had opened it? I glanced behind me but could make out no one by the lime kiln.

The house didn't look any different from the outside. The lights I had left on were still visible, and no others shone. I did a quick check around the perimeter and saw no sign of broken windows or forced doors. Once inside, I had no sense of any alien presence, either, or that someone had been there in my absence.

I shrugged it off, went upstairs, got out of my wet clothes, then dried myself, put on a dressing gown and went into the living room to light a fire. I felt unusually aware of the empty rooms above and around me. It was true that Kilnsgate was far too big for me, and the sense of space was very different from that in California. There, the space was all bright, open and airy. Here, it was dim, shadowy and claustropho-bic, full of other presences just beyond my reach. Or so it seemed. Sometimes I heard them and caught fleeting glimpses on the landing at night, but mostly I could just sense their presence. I told myself that the isolation was getting to me, or the stupid film I'd just seen, which was about a serial killer in a remote coastal village in northern Cali-fornia. A bit like Hitchcock, the way my music was a lot like Bernard Herrmann's.

I had enjoyed my visit to the cinema with Heather, I had to admit. I didn't go to the movies much these days, which must sound odd coming from someone in my profession. I used to love going when I was young—that love was what accounts for what I do today, after all—but it was a habit I had got out of over the years. There were enough private screen-ing rooms available to me in L.A. that I never needed to go to a public cinema. I did occasionally, of course—sometimes I just had to experience the big screen and the blast of *my* music with a live audience—but I became quite happy with the home theater alternatives.

All through my adolescence in Leeds, I had watched my favorite cinemas turned into bingo halls, carpet warehouses, Sikh temples, or mosques—the Lyric, Lyceum, Clifton, Clock, Western, Crown, and Palace, all gone. It seemed hardly a week went by without one of them disappearing for good. Darkened auditoriums where I had stolen my first kisses, dared to put my hand under a girl's blouse, where I'd captained missions to outer space and fought bug-eyed monsters with Flash Gordon, rode the western plains under a hot sun with Hopalong Cassidy, fought the Germans on land, air, and sea with John Mills or Jack Hawkins, the Japanese with John Wayne and Audie Murphy, and visited that gloomy castle high on its hill, lightning flashing all around, while the mad Vincent Price pursued his obsession of the moment, or Christopher Lee sought yet another victim's blood. The magic had stayed with me, but the channel of its power had changed. Still, tonight had been good.

As the fire crackled to life, I poured myself a small single malt and put on Marvin Gaye's *What's Going On*. I was in the mood for something other than classical music, and Marvin Gaye fit the bill. I even turned up the volume. There were no neighbors to hear it. Instead of going up to work in my study, which tonight seemed even more than ever filled with Grace's spirit and her absence, I brought the MacBook down with me and sat by the fire, my feet propped on a stool.

Heather was right. Mr. G knew a hell of a lot more than most of us gave him credit for, if we knew where to look for it, and as I typed up notes from what she had told me, I went on little Internet excursions here and there to fill in as much detail as I could. I didn't know what it all meant, but I certainly had a fuller picture than I'd had before at the end of a couple of hours, by which time Marvin Gaye had long finished, and my eyes were starting to close. I thought that what I had learned was leading me somewhere, but I didn't know where. I didn't even know whether I wanted to go there.

There was a small armchair in the corner of my study, and when I took the MacBook back up, I could have sworn for a moment there was a figure sitting in it, a woman. But when I looked again, I saw that it was empty.

I had been intending to go to bed, but the vision, or whatever it was, had shaken me, and I knew that sleep wouldn't come easily. Instead, I went back down to the dying fire, put on another log and poured another whiskey. This time I put on my Ella Fitzgerald playlist.

As I sat there staring into the flames, listening to "When Your Lover Has Gone," the scotch burning my lips and tongue, my imagination filled in the outline of the figure I had seen upstairs. It became the image of Grace, just sitting there dressed all in white with some sewing in her hands, the needle slowly moving in and out of the silky material, just waiting. She looked up at me expectantly with those dark eyes of hers, dark waves framing her pale oval face, then slowly turned her gaze back to her sewing. Her eyes, her expression, her demeanor, gave away nothing. That was the problem. She never gave away anything. Not a scrap. Nothing. God, how frustrated she must have made them all at the trial, sitting there day after day, enigmatic as the Sphinx, listening to all the lies. I'll bet her barrister, Montague Sewell, just wanted to shake her sometimes.

I wondered whether I would come to a dead end in my pursuit of Grace Fox and what I would do if I did. Would I realize it when I got there? Would I give up, or would I keep banging my head against the brick wall?

I wasn't finished yet, though, I thought, giving the embers a poke. There were still one or two unexplored avenues I could travel before that brick wall loomed ahead. Ralph Webster had told his daughter, Louise, about Grace on his deathbed. Much of what he had said might not have meant a lot to her, but it could mean something to me, if I could find her. I didn't even care if I had to go all the way to Australia. I had the money and I had the time.

14

Extract from the *Journal of Grace Elizabeth Fox* (ed. Louise King), August 1940, at sea.

Sunday, August 4, 1940

TONIGHT WE PUT ON OUR FIRST CONCERT! IT WAS A VERY AMATEUR AFFAIR, but it was something to do, and I think everyone enjoyed themselves. Three of the officers dressed up as women, did a funny dance and sang "Three Little Maids" from *The Mikado*. I laughed so much I nearly cried. When it was my turn, I sang some simple folk songs: "Down by the Salley Gardens," "The Ploughboy," "The Trees They Do Grow High." I ended with "Linden Lea." Everybody sang along, and I don't think there was a dry eye in the house.

The nights in the cabin are hot now, despite the electric fan, and I use my extra pillow under my knees in bed to keep me cool. It must be terrible for the poor soldiers down below. All they have is a bunk or a hammock in cramped and airless quarters. They eat from bare wooden tables, while we enjoy three-course meals in the elegant dining room, with tablecloths and proper cutlery and china. It is not fair, but so much about the army and the war is not fair. Matron says we will all be glad of the discipline if we ever see any action.

TUESDAY, AUGUST 6, 1940

As from today, we are allowed to wear our tropical uniforms. The hot weather is much more bearable in my white drill frock, with its pretty scarlet and white epaulettes. The pearl buttons up the front are a bit of a nuisance, though, and take some time to fasten. Brenda tries to help, but she is all fingers and thumbs, and I lose my patience quickly in this heat. Much of the day I wear tennis shorts, also now allowed, but I do get tired of the men whistling at me.

This morning I was sitting at the piano in the banquet hall, which for once was gloriously empty, playing through some Chopin *Nocturnes*. When I had finished, I was annoyed to hear someone applauding behind me, and I turned around to see Lieutenant Fawley leaning in the doorway. He had taken part in the concert, and we had spoken briefly on a few occasions. He walked over to me and asked if he was right in thinking the piece was by Chopin. I told him he was, and that I was surprised he recognized it. He said there were many things about him that would surprise me. I was beginning to feel uncomfortable, as Lieutenant Fawley is generally regarded as a very handsome man, with a strong jaw, straight nose, and piercing blue eyes, rather like the hero of a romantic novel. Many of the sisters, including Brenda, have swooned at the sight of him on deck more than once. When I stood up and walked to the door, he walked beside me, chatting about Chopin's piano concertos. He told me that before the war he had been a violinist in the Hallé Orchestra, which I thought must be a great honor and a marvelous occupation, and said so. We parted on the deck, but not before he told me his first name was Stephen, and I told him mine was Grace.

After dinner this evening, we had a wonderful dance band. All the officers I danced with were perfect gentlemen, including Stephen Fawley. Of course, this all took place under Matron's eagle eye, and I think the men are even more terrified of Matron than I am! I noticed Kathleen and Brenda dancing with a number of young officers, but Doris remained at the table, despite a number of requests, being cheerfully true to her young fighter pilot.

I never imagined that the sea could have so many different moods and colors. We must be quite close to land, as flocks of birds follow us, squawking after scraps from the kitchen. The food is wonderful. After rationing, it is marvelous to get dressed up in our best mufti and sit down to a grand dinner of such exotic foods as *filets de poisson au buerre, cotelettes d'agneau reformé, pommes roties,* and *pêches Melba.* For breakfast we get real bacon and eggs, mushrooms and tomatoes, with toast and marmalade to follow. The coffee is always on the boil, a cup of tea always available. Sometimes I do not even care where we are going, and I hope we will never get there. Life onboard is so luxurious, I think I could live like this forever. I miss Ernest, of course, but he will no doubt be busy with his friends and his war work.

Thursday, August 8, 1940

We had our first sight of the Dark Continent this morning, though I must admit that it is not quite what I expected. Instead of a desert, with camels and sand dunes, there are rolling green hills dotted with houses, sparkling like diamonds in the bright sun. We came into the Freetown harbor, which is not very large, so we have to lie at anchor with the destroyers and fishing boats and carry on all our refueling and restocking through lighters. Sadly, we are not permitted to go ashore. How I would love to wander among the crowds at the markets and bazaars.

The colors are like none I have seen before. Of course, there is green, and there is brown, the blue of the sky, the white of the houses, flashes of red flowers and yellow foliage, but each seems somehow more vibrant than any I have ever seen in England. It gives a very odd, quite dizzying effect, as if I am watching a color film rather than seeing the real world. The place has a unique smell, too, made up partially of sea and smoke from fires, but more subtle, with many elements I cannot name, perhaps exotic spices and flowers. Little boys and young men row out to us in boats made of hollowed-out logs and dive in the clear green water to swim like dolphins. We throw them pennies and they smile up at us.

Monday, August 12, 1940

It has been almost unbearably hot since we left Freetown, and just keeping cool is a hard enough job in itself. We still manage the morning exercises, and the swimming pool is a godsend, but there are no more afternoon games of tennis. Instead, we try to find room in the shade for our deck chairs and sip gin and Tom Collins with ice. I am still getting along well with my Trollope, and I have just started *Phineas Finn*. Sometimes I could almost swear that reading Trollope actually makes me feel cooler! None of us is sleeping well, and we feel listless all day, like wilting flowers. Stephen said it will get cooler the farther south we travel. We will arrive in South Africa in their winter, he said, though he added that it would not be as cold as ours. I certainly hope not! At night, with the fans going at full power, we eat dinner and sometimes the band plays, though fewer people have the energy to dance now. More of us have taken to strolling around the deck, where one can occasionally catch a welcome breath of breeze, and I have witnessed many stolen kisses.

Thursday, August 15, 1940

Everybody is so excited because we dock in Cape Town tomorrow! The convoy will split up because the harbor is not large enough to accommodate all of us. Some of them will be going on to Durban, and the convoy will re-form off the coast there in two days. We are promised shore leave in Cape Town, so all the sisters are queuing for the laundry to get their best clothes washed and ironed in time.

NOVEMBER 2010

It was a late afternoon near the end of November, and already getting dark, the time of year when people start to wonder whether they will ever see the sun again and begin to think about heading south after the swallows, already long gone.

I made some tea and wandered up to my bedroom for a sweater. The central heating was patchy, hot spots here, cold spots there, and it could not possibly keep such a big old drafty house at a constant and comfortable temperature. I couldn't keep a log fire lit all the time, either, so I had taken to wearing layers of clothing. As I rifled through my dresser drawer, I glanced out of the front window through the drizzle across the valley and thought I saw a figure lurking by the lime kiln. I couldn't be certain, but I thought it was the same hooded stranger I had seen watching the house once before.

I wasted no time. More angry than afraid, I dashed downstairs. This time he wasn't going to get away. I flung the door open, determined to set off in pursuit and not to give up until I had caught him, but I had no sooner got to the garden gate when I stopped in my tracks. As I stood at the gate, I watched him cross the old stone bridge over Kilnsgarthdale Beck and walk straight toward me.

"What do you want?" I asked when he got near enough. "Why have you been watching this house?"

"I'm sorry," the stranger said. "I've been trying to pluck up the courage." Then he pushed back his hood, and when I saw his face and hair clearly for the first time, I realized it wasn't a he, but a *she*.

"Who are you?" I asked, though I thought I already had a pretty good idea.

"I'm Louise," she said. "Louise King. You bought this house from me. I just wanted to come and see it, that's all. I've never been to England before."

I stood aside and gestured toward the path and the front door. "You'd better come inside, then."

She hesitated for a moment and studied me with a serious and guarded expression on her face, then she walked ahead of me up the flagged path.

WHEN WE WERE COMFORTABLY ESTABLISHED IN THE LIVING ROOM AND I HAD LIT a fire and made a pot of tea, I was able to get my first good look at Louise King. She was slight, which was perhaps why I had first taken her for a boy under the hooded anorak she had been wearing against the rain, but there was no doubt now that she was a young woman in her midtwenties, wearing jeans and a pale blue jumper. She had what I imagined to be her Danish mother's high Nordic cheekbones, though her short, layered hair was the glossy coal black of her grandmother's. She also had Grace's eyes, unnerving in their darkness and unwavering gaze, especially in contrast to her overly pale complexion. She wore no makeup and had made no attempt to cover up the pits and blemishes of old acne or chicken pox. Perhaps no one would call her pretty or beautiful, but she was certainly striking, and the studs and rings she wore in her nose, lip, eyebrow, and ears also made her look a little intimidating.

Louise held her mug of tea, with milk and three sugars, in both hands, close to her heart, as if using it partly to keep her warm. Her fingers were long and tapered, the nails bitten low, the flesh around them chewed and red. She wore no rings or jewelry of any kind except on her face. Her legs were folded beneath her in a way that I had only ever seen women sit and still manage to seem comfortable and relaxed. I had put on one of my most recent loves, Imogen Cooper's third set of live Schubert piano works, the second disc of which was as close to sublime as it gets for me. Louise had already asked about the *Impromptus*, which she recognized, said she liked them but that she knew very little of classical music. She had, however, she admitted, taken piano lessons as a little girl and had proved rather better than she, or anyone else, had expected. But she had let them lapse. I offered her biscuits with the tea, but she said she wasn't hungry.

"You've come a long way just to see an old house," I said.

"You've no idea." She had a funny way of looking at me, as if always trying to make her mind up about whether I was being sarcastic or having her on in some way.

"Where are you staying?"

"I've rented a holiday flat in Staithes. It's pretty cheap at this time of year."

"I should imagine so. A bit nippy, too, I'll bet."

"Yes, but I love it when the sea gets wild and lashes at the harbor walls."

"Why Staithes?"

She glanced down, into her tea. "I don't know. It was the first one I saw advertised."

For some reason, I thought, she was lying, but I didn't challenge her. It didn't matter. Samuel Porter had shared an artists' studio in Staithes many years ago, had kept his paintings and sketches of Grace there. But surely Louise couldn't know that? Staithes could mean nothing to her. Maybe she wasn't lying, after all. Maybe I was trying to find connections where none existed.

"How long do you plan on staying there?"

"Not long. I'm moving to Cambridge soon."

"Is that your home now?"

"It's going to be. Why, do you know it?"

I smiled. "Cambridge? Yes. I was a student there. I lived there for five years, 1968 to 1973. A fine time to be in Cambridge. Good memories."

"Why?"

"It was exciting. There was a great music scene for a start. Classical, jazz, rock, whatever you wanted. Pubs, social life, pretty girls, brilliant professors, punting on the Cam."

"Did you study music? Somebody told me you're a composer. Is that true?"

I told her that it was, and what I composed. Naturally, she had seen some of the movies I had scored but couldn't remember any melodies. I told her that meant I had done my job, but that the films wouldn't have been half as effective without the music.

"*The Birds* worked," she said. "Without a musical score, I mean."

I raised my eyebrows. It was true that *The Birds* had no music, but most people didn't even notice. It made a good trivia question, a way of separating the bluffers from people who knew what they were talking about. "Yes," I said. "But that was the point of it, really, wasn't it? The lack of music *was* the sound track, in a way. Or the birds, themselves, were, the sounds they made."

She thought about that for a moment. "Who are your favorites?" she asked.

"The classics. Erich Korngold. Max Steiner. Bernard Herrmann. Franz Waxman. And maybe some of the more avant-garde composers who worked with great foreign directors. Toru Takemitsu. Nino Rota."

"*La Dolce Vita*," said Louise. "I love that movie. And the music."

I raised an eyebrow. "You seem to know a lot about the subject."

She turned away, as if embarrassed by her own enthusiasm, and looked at me sideways again. "There was a time when I went to the movies nearly every day," she said. "Classics. Hollywood blockbusters. Art house. Foreign movies. The lot. I had no discrimination. It was pretty much my life those days."

"Escapism?"

"I had a lot to escape from. But tell me more about you, how you work. It must be very exciting."

As we continued with our small talk, I found myself wondering whether Louise was aware of what I knew about her. I imagined that perhaps one of the family solicitors Heather had talked to might have mentioned my name.

Louise gestured toward the grand piano. "Is that where you work?" she asked. She had an Australian accent, but it wasn't as strident as some I had heard, and she didn't effect the kind of slang you usually get on TV. Louise was far more soft-spoken, and there was a definite English cadence in her educated speech. Her early, formative years with her father, I imagined, along with her own education, perhaps.

"Sometimes," I said. "I'm working on a piano sonata." I don't know why I told her that.

"Like this?"

She meant the Schubert B-flat, which had just started. "I'm not quite up to that standard."

"It's a beautiful piano."

"It was your grandmother's," I said, and held my breath. I had no idea what her reaction would be, whether she would be angry or upset, how much she knew, or even whether she cared at all. She was silent for a few moments, thoughtful, sipping her sweet tea. It crossed my mind that she was a very serious young woman. There were frown lines on her brow. I hadn't seen her smile once yet. "You are Louise *Webster*, aren't you?"

She glared at me defiantly. "I'm Louise *King*. I changed my name. It's all legal."

"That's a version of your mother's name, isn't it? There's been a lot of name changing in your family."

"Yes," she said. "Someone told me you'd been asking questions about my grandmother. Why are you so interested in her?"

The family solicitors again, I guessed. "I don't know. Maybe because I live in what used to be her house."

"Is her ghost haunting it?"

"Why does everybody ask me that?"

"It seems the obvious question, I suppose. Though she wasn't killed here, so there's no reason why her ghost should linger, is there?"

"None," I said. "And I don't think it is. I hear a lot of noises, that's all. Old-house noises. See things in the shadows."

"Have you ever seen *her*?"

I thought of the figure I fancied I saw in the wardrobe mirror and in the sewing room chair the other night. "No," I said. "I don't believe in ghosts."

"Me, neither. Only the ones inside my head."

"You're haunted?"

She nodded, as if it were a simple answer to an everyday question. "What about my grandfather?" she asked. "After all, he's the one who died here."

"I haven't seen him, either. What made you sell the place?"

"I need the money. Well, that's not strictly true. Daddy left me plenty of money. But I didn't want an old house. I didn't want it hanging around my neck. It seemed to make the most sense to sell it. I hope you're happy here."

"I'm doing all right."

She put her cup down on the table beside her.

"More?"

"No, thanks. I should go."

"You're welcome to stay for something to eat if you want. It's nothing special. I was just going to cook up some salmon."

"Did you catch it yourself?"

"No, not exactly. Supermarket special. There isn't any around here."

"I don't know much about nature, except that we need to respect it more."

"Me, neither." But I'm learning, I might have added. "Anyway, what about it? Tea?"

"Okay. Thanks. That's nice of you. No rush. I'm not starving or anything."

"How did you get here from Staithes?"

"I drove. I'm parked in the Richmond market square. I walked up here."

"Quite a way back. I'll drive you to town later, after tea, if you want."

"Cool. Can I use your toilet?"

I showed her the way to the one at the top of the stairs. While she was gone, I took the salmon out of the fridge and started to prepare it. She must have heard me puttering around in the kitchen, because when she came back down she joined me there and sat at the table, gazing out of the window toward the drystone wall and the woods at the end of the dale. "That's quite the bathroom," she said.

It was one of the old kind, with a claw-foot bathtub, gold-plated fittings, high ceiling, and blue and white tiles, after the Portuguese fashion. "Yes," I said. "I should imagine it's been that way for years, probably since the days your grandparents lived here."

"It's very remote," she went on. "How do you put up with it? I think I'd go batty."

"I do go batty sometimes," I said, wrapping the mustard-smeared salmon fillets in prosciutto. I glanced up at her. "Perhaps that explains why I'm so interested in your grandmother's story. It helps me put up with being so isolated here." I realized as I said this that in an odd way, Grace was *company* for me, but I didn't say it out loud because I knew how crazy it sounded.

Louise was watching me work now, as if fascinated by the simple kitchen techniques. I wondered just what kind of life she had lived. I remembered what Heather had told me, and I knew that this slight young girl sitting before me had found her mother and stepfather dead from point-blank shotgun wounds. What kind of damage that inflicts on the psyche I could hardly imagine. She had run wild, so Heather had told me, and that could mean anything—drugs, crime, alcohol, bad company, maybe all of them.

I put on some rice and began to chop vegetables. Louise still watched me, fascinated. When I had done that, I unscrewed a bottle of red wine and offered her some.

"I don't drink," she said, shrinking in on herself, as if every cell in her body wanted to reach out and accept. I had seen the signs of alcoholism before, but not in one so young.

"I suppose I don't need to, either," I said, and put the bottle away, out of sight.

"I don't care if you do," she said. "I mean, I'm not against it or anything."

"It's okay," I said. "No skin off my nose. It'll do me good to abstain. At least, I'll wait and have some later with the meal. In the meantime, you said you came to have a look around the old place, so would you like the guided tour? There's nothing for me to do here while the food's cooking."

"Please," she said, and stood up.

LOUISE PAUSED IN THE VESTIBULE AND STOOD BEFORE THE FAMILY PORTRAIT, at which she had glanced on her way in. "That's my family, isn't it?" she said.

"Yes. Your grandmother and grandfather, and your father."

Louise nodded. We continued with the tour. The kitchen and living/dining room she had already seen, so all there was left downstairs, apart from cupboards, was my TV room. She enthused over the large screen, scanned a few of the DVD titles, and said, "Do you play them just for the music, or do you like the movies?"

"What a funny question," I said, though on reflection it wasn't, really. "Like anyone else, I watch the films, but maybe I'm a bit more aware of the music."

"Have you ever gone to see a movie only for the music?"

"*Star Wars*," I said. "I'm not a big science-fiction fan, but everybody was talking about it."

I wasn't going to show her the empty cellar, so we went upstairs next. When we got to the guest bedroom at the front, over the gallery from mine, she stood and said, almost to herself, "This is where it happened."

I didn't know whether this was true or not, so I said nothing. If it was true, then it meant I was sleeping in what had been Grace's bedroom as well as working in her sewing room, and that the room where I thought I had seen a woman's—Grace's—figure reflected in the wardrobe mirror had been Ernest's room, the room where he had died.

We moved on. Louise seemed awed most of all by the sewing room, sitting for a moment in the small armchair. Then she sat at the escritoire. Her hand disappeared underneath it and felt around. A few seconds later, a small hidden drawer sprang open on the bottom left. It was empty.

"How did you know about that?" I asked. I had searched for ages and found nothing.

"Granny Felicity told Dad about it."

Louise pulled out an Everyman edition of Shelley's poetry and turned to Grace's name, written neatly on the first page: *Grace Elizabeth Hartnell, 1928.* Then she examined the oil painting of the lime kiln beside which she had stood to observe the house. The signature "S. Porter" was just about visible once you knew where to look for it. She found it, ran her fingers over it, then stood back and took the whole thing in. "Her lover," she whispered.

"He's still alive," I said. "I've met him."

She raised an eyebrow. "I know his work. I'm a painter myself. Not terribly good, but I dabble."

"We'd better go down and check on the food," I said. "There's nothing else up here, and the attic's empty."

Louise followed me out of the door, with one backward glance at the painting, along the corridor and down the stairs. "Thank you," she said when we went back into the kitchen.

After a few moments, dinner was ready. I thought the kitchen might be a more relaxed and informal setting than the large dining area, so I set a couple of places at the pine table. I put some coffee on for later and served up the food, then dimmed the lights.

"What kind of music do you like?" I asked.

"I don't know. All sorts, really. I don't listen to anything much. I liked what you were playing before. And I like violins. Anything with a violin. And cellos. They sound so melancholy."

I poured myself a glass of wine, put the iPod in the kitchen dock, and turned to Sol Gabetta's recording of the Elgar cello concerto—you couldn't get much more melancholy than that—and we settled down to eat.

"THAT WAS DELICIOUS," SAID LOUISE AS SHE RESTED HER KNIFE AND FORK ON the empty plate.

"Thank you. I'm sorry, but there's no pudding."

"That's all right. I'm quite full enough. I don't eat very much as a rule. Can we sit in the other room by the fire again?"

"Of course." I put the dinner things in the dishwasher and poured us both a cup of coffee, then we went through to the living room. It was pitch black outside. I threw a few more logs on the fire and closed the curtains before sitting down.

The Elgar had finished, and Louise didn't seem to care one way or another about having anything in the background, so I didn't put on any more music. She settled into the armchair and crossed her legs under her. It was a still evening, and the deep silence enveloped and permeated Kilnsgate House. It pushed against my ears like noise-canceling headphones. All we could hear was the soughing of ashes and knotty logs crackling in the fireplace, the scraping of blown leaves against the flagged patio out back. After a long pause, during which Louise stared into the flames, which reflected in her dark eyes, she looked up at me and said, "This is all very new to me, you know. Meeting people, having dinner and all like real folks do. It's not easy."

"I don't suppose it is," I said. "You haven't had an easy life."

She shot me a defensive glance. "My father was kind to me."

"I'm sure he was."

"He never talked about it, you know, about his background, his mother, where he came from, about his family over here. Not until the very end."

"I'd heard," I said. "Do you want to tell me about it?"

"I didn't. Not at first. They told me you were interested, asking questions. That was why I just stood outside and watched. But I wanted to come in. I wanted to see the inside, where she lived, where it happened. I think maybe I can talk to you about it now, if you're willing to bear with me and listen."

"I'm willing. You know I'm interested."

"You can have another glass of wine if you want. It doesn't bother me." She smiled for the first time. "You might need one."

I held up my cup of coffee. "I'm fine with this for the moment."

She nodded. "Then I'll begin."

15

Extract from the *Journal of Grace Elizabeth* Fox (ed. Louise King), August 1940, Cape Town.

Friday, August 16, 1940

WHAT A THRILL IT WAS TO SET FOOT ON AFRICAN SOIL AT LAST! THE FIRST thing we saw on the quayside was a row of shiny, expensive cars, all sent by British firms operating in South Africa. They were at our disposal, we were told. The business community here wants to show true South African hospitality to the fighting men, and to us sisters, too, of course!

A group of us piled giggling into one large car, which happened to be a spacious and elegant Bentley, the kind that Ernest would just love to own. Our driver Julian was a representative of a diamond mine, but sadly, he had brought no gifts of diamonds for us. Kathleen and Doris were with me, along with Stephen and two of his fellow officers, but we lost Brenda somewhere along the way. No doubt she was in another car and being well taken care of, too.

Stephen had brought his Leica camera and wanted to keep stopping to take photographs. Julian wanted to show us the Cape Peninsula first, and then he said we could go wherever we wished. He drove overland to the coast and followed the road down, hugging the hills on one side and overlooking the rocky and sandy coastline below. We passed through Simon's Town and saw some navy corvettes and destroyers at anchor there, then we carried on until the road became too rough to drive any farther.

We all piled out of the car, and the wind almost took our breath away. Stephen snapped away with his camera, taking a picture of me standing on a rock, trying to hold my hair out of my eyes. The sea below was a beautiful shade of blue, and waves pounded against the rocks, making a deep booming sound and showers of brilliant white foam. Farther out, little whitecaps flittered across the surface.

Julian gave us some time to explore the immediate area, and we all wandered hither and thither, seeking good vantage points. I found myself in the shelter of some rocks, and suddenly I was alone, everything quiet and still. Before I knew it, Stephen was standing beside me. Gently, he took me in his arms and kissed me. At least he tried to. I pulled back. I could not do it. So much of me wanted to, and I still wonder as I write now with a trembling hand if that makes me a bad person. Ernest need never have known, I tell myself, but it does no good. I could not give myself to Stephen. He was disappointed, but he is gentleman enough to understand.

We heard a noise and noticed a group of baboons on the rocks above us. They were looking down at us in quite a threatening way. Julian had warned us that they can be dangerous, so we backed away, out of our little hollow. They seemed not to care, and they turned their backs on us and make a rude gesture. Stephen and I almost collapsed with laughter and relief as we dashed back to join the others. Kathleen gave me a questioning glance, to which I did not respond.

Throughout the rest of the day, I could not help thinking of that almost kiss and how young, handsome, and charming Stephen is. Ernest seems so far away, and in my memory, so dour and preoccupied. Sometimes I wonder if he loves me at all.

We drove back to Cape Town and visited a busy market full of exotic bolts of material in vivid colors and patterns, unusual dried roots and herbs, and heaps of brilliant yellow, red, and golden spices. I bought some white handmade sandals and several yards of silky material in an orange, green, and brown pattern to make a dress. I also bought a colorful bead necklace, which I will probably never wear, but which will always remind me of this beautiful and troubling day. After that we visited some Western-style shops where we could stock up on lipstick, powder, and accessories such as handbags. Everybody was so warm and friendly, but they all stared at Kathleen, with her blond hair, long legs, and statuesque figure. She is over six feet tall.

After the shopping, Julian took us for a special dinner at the home of one of the important government officials, and we ate so much food that we could hardly dance. There was lobster and langoustines and meats that I had never heard of, such as springbok and kudu, all delicious.

After dinner we had a concert of local music, the men in colorful native costumes beating drums and chanting in a most exotic and charming way, and the ladies dancing, and then the orchestra played in the ballroom, and we danced until late. I danced with Stephen toward the end of the evening, and he apologized for the incident on the rocks. I forgave him. It is wartime. People do impulsive things. It made me realize how careful I must be, that not even I am invincible to the romance of the sea, the war, or a handsome young man.

Now, as I lie here writing this, with Brenda snoring away gently across the cabin, I still remember the strength and warmth of Stephen's arms around me, and I wonder if I will dream of him tonight. When I remember our stolen moment, I let myself believe I may be falling in love with him, but it is a love that can never be. I am starting to behave like a silly schoolgirl, though I remind myself that I have done nothing wrong.

SATURDAY, AUGUST 24, 1940

Now we are sailing on the Indian Ocean, and at times the water is so still and clear I can see the bright-colored fish in its depths. Porpoises and dolphins follow in our wake and play for us, twisting and turning through the air, slipping back into the water without a splash.

The days are hot and humid, and a sort of languid spell seems to have fallen over everyone. Brenda hardly moves from her bed unless she has to work a shift in the sick bay. She just lies there completely still, with the electric fan pointing at her until evening, when the sun has gone down. Even then, it is not much cooler, though it is a blessing to be away from the heat of the sun. There seems to be no respite. I have not seen much of Stephen lately, though I think of him often, especially when I see the couples hand in hand walking around the deck under the light of a huge golden moon. Everyone seems to have fallen in love. It must be the magic of the east, the ocean, the stars and moonlight, and the sultry nights. I would like to fall in love, too, perhaps with Stephen, but I cannot allow myself to do so. The voyage will soon be over, and the veil of secrecy has finally been lifted. We have discovered where we are headed. Five sisters, including Kathleen and Doris, are to land in Hong Kong, the lucky beggars, and the rest of us, equally lucky, I think, are bound for Singapore, where we are to help start up the brand-new Alexandra Hospital!

NOVEMBER 2010

"I don't know how much Uncle Rolly told your friend," Louise said, "so if I'm going over familiar ground just stop me."

"Uncle Rolly?"

"Don't you know him? Roland Everett. He was Dad's solicitor in Northallerton, and they became close friends. I just call him Uncle Rolly. He isn't really my uncle. I've known him ever since I was a little girl."

Uncle Rolly must have been Heather's source, I realized, or one of them. I poked the fire and the logs split. Flames and smoke spiraled up the chimney. "Go on," I said. "What was your childhood like?"

She seemed surprised by the question, as if anybody should be interested. "Very happy," she said. "At least the first eight or nine years were. We had a nice house by the sea, Dad was making a good living, and Mum co-owned a catering business. Then it all went wrong. I suppose it must have crept up on them very slowly, but it hit me like an express train. I mean, I remember late-night arguments, tears, hushed conversations, consultations with my grandparents, the Middletons, I mean, but really, the first time I knew there was something serious in the wind was when Mum told me to pack a bag and go with her."

"Why?"

"I had no idea. I think I managed to piece it together a bit later. You see, Dad suffered from depression—fits, bouts, whatever you call them. He managed to function, go to work and all, and the doctor gave him pills, which seemed to help, but Mum was more outgoing, a social butterfly, and it just dragged her down, like he was sick all the time but there was nothing physically wrong. You know what some people are like. They can't stand being around illness of any kind, they think everyone should stop malingering and just get on with life? Mum was like that, and she just couldn't take it anymore. Don't get me wrong, she had a good heart. But she didn't want to be a nursemaid, a carer. She wanted to go to dances and parties and meet people. She was always laughing and she loved gossip. She didn't want to be stuck with an invalid for the rest of her life, so she bolted. And she took me with her." Here, Louise paused and stared back into the fire. She had been right, I could have done with another drink, but I restrained myself.

"You don't have to talk about it if you don't want," I said. "I mean, the details. Heather—Rolly's friend—told me some of it. I know what happened."

"Now I've come this far . . . Anyway, the next thing I knew we were in Brisbane. Suburbs, really."

"It must have been a wrench for you."

"Oh, Brisy's all right. Plenty to do, nice weather, and lots of beaches nearby, even better than Brighton. The weather, anyway."

"But no father."

"No. That hurt. I missed Dad a lot, and I worried about him. He wrote, of course, phoned, and I visited him for holidays and stuff. But it's not the same."

"And your mother?"

"Mum started hanging out with the party crowd, mostly divorced.

She drank a bit too much, talked a bit too loudly, wore short skirts, embarrassed me in front of my school friends once or twice. She was becoming a bit of a burden, but she was my mum. You couldn't help but love her. There was no harm in her, do anything for anyone except take care of the sick."

"So you stuck with her?"

"Yes. What else could I do? Pretty soon I was entering my teens, and she was seeing Gray regularly. He seemed okay at first. Not the fullest bottle in the row, you know, but okay. It was only after they got married that he really started to show his true colors. I remember the first time clear as day. I was there, sitting at the table doing my home-work. Mum was fixing dinner, and he came home late from an after-noon in the pub with his mates, pissed as usual. Mum said something, made some sarcastic comment, and he just punched her in the face, quick as lightning. No warning, nothing. Just turned and, smack. Not a slap, but a real punch. Meaty. Mum swayed then she just stood there, horrified, blood running down her chin, dripping on her white cot-ton blouse, then she put her hands to her face and ran to the bedroom, crying. I felt my skin crawling, my heart in my throat. I thought it was going to be me next."

"But it wasn't?"

"Not that time. He just held my chin in his hands tight, so it hurt, breathed alcohol fumes all over me, and said, 'Let that be a warning, young lady.' Then he laughed and went back to the pub."

She was starting to fidget with her hands, and once or twice she put her fingers to her mouth to chew on. "Are you okay?" I asked. "Because you don't have to go on."

"I wouldn't mind a smoke."

I'd given up years ago, and smoking is practically illegal in Cali-fornia, but I just nodded. "Go ahead."

"Thanks." Louise lit a Marlboro Light and blew out the smoke with a sigh. "There's not much more to tell, really. A couple of nights later the midnight visits to my room started. There was nothing I could do. He was much too strong. Believe me, more than once I thought of kill-ing him myself."

"Did you tell your mother?"

"No. There wouldn't have been much point. She wouldn't have wanted to believe it, and it would only have added to her burden. He kept on hitting her, and in the end it was all she could do to gather what little strength and dignity she had left and move us out of there."

"Where did you go?"

"Not far enough. Another suburb farther inland, on the river. A small apartment. Just the two of us. I had some of the happiest days of my life since my childhood there. Mum would help me with my homework—she was clever—and she'd cook really beautiful meals. Moreton Bay bugs. Delicious. On weekends we'd pretend we were tourists and take a drive along the Sunshine Coast or the Gold Coast. We'd even go to the Big Pineapple and the Australia Zoo." She seemed lost in her memories for a moment, and a ghost of a smile passed across her features. "Then I came home one day from school," she said in a flat tone. "I was sixteen. Mum was on the floor, that good heart of hers blown all over her favorite Axminster carpet. Gray was sitting on the sofa, the shotgun still in his hands. Most of his head was gone. That was eight years ago."

I didn't know what to say, so I swallowed and kept silent.

Louise looked at me. "I'm sorry," she said. "It is a bit gruesome, isn't it? Not at all like movies or TV."

I wanted to tell her about Laura, that I had sat with someone I loved and held her hand as she died, took her in my arms as her last breath fluttered from her exhausted body, but I didn't. What good would it do? Was it supposed to trump her story, create a bond of sympathy between us? I just shook my head slowly.

"After that, things were a bit of a blur for a while," Louise rushed on. "I went back to live with my dad in Brighton. He was still getting those bouts of depression, but he was seeing a shrink and learning how to cope better. And I didn't mind taking care of him when he was down. I guess I didn't inherit Mum's gene on that one." She flicked her cigarette end into the fireplace.

"Maybe your grandmother's?" I said. "She was a nurse."

"I know. But she was a murderer, too, wasn't she?"

"I don't know about that," I said.

She gave me a sideways glance through narrowed eyes. "Uncle Rolly said you were on some campaign to clear her name."

"I'm not on any campaign, I just have my doubts about what happened, that's all. Would it make any difference to you?"

"If my grandmother wasn't a murderer?" Louise contemplated the idea for a moment. "Yeah. Yeah, I suppose it would."

"When did you hear about Grace?"

"When Dad knew he was dying. He was trying to explain his depressions and let me know that he had some understanding about how I felt when my mum was killed. I don't know if that was the cause, or if the depressions were just a clinical thing, but it seemed important to him to talk about it. To be honest, he didn't know that much. Just shared a few of his childhood memories. He was too young to follow the trial, and then his aunt and uncle took him to Australia. He got on with his life and didn't ask too many questions about his past, like most people who end up there. It's a very long way from Pommyland, and most of us prefer it that way."

"How did it make you feel?"

"How did it make me feel? You sound like my shrink." She gave me a disappointed glance, then went on. "Oh, I suppose I was angry with Dad at first, for not telling me all those years, because he'd never talked about her before. But when I thought about it, I realized he couldn't, really, could he? I mean, what do you say? And I was a bit sad, too, but more about losing my illusions than anything else. I had always thought of the Websters as my grandparents. Granny Felicity and Granddad Alf. We'd always been really close. But suddenly they weren't who I thought they were anymore. That hurt. I still loved them the same, of course, as they loved me, but it just felt different."

"What did your father actually tell you?"

"Not much. Just what she'd done, you know, and what happened to her. He told me that his mother had been hanged for murdering his father back in England when he was seven, and he told me about the lover and all. Sam Porter. He said he didn't remember much about it. Well, you wouldn't, would you? Not at that age. But it's like a cancer growing in me. I can't forget."

"Not even now?"

Louise shook her head. "I don't mean I think about it all the time or have nightmares or anything. I don't. I sleep fine. I just feel blighted, heavy, cursed. I can't really explain it. First Mum and Gray, then finding out about Grandmother and Grandfather. Maybe it would make a difference if my grandmother turned out not to be a murderer, though I never even met her. I do feel I know her a little bit. Maybe he did pass on some of her genes. I have to say she doesn't strike me as the murdering kind. But what do I know? I didn't even spot Gray for what he was at first. I'm taken in by surfaces just as much as everyone else. I couldn't even help my own mother."

"It wasn't your fault."

She glared at me. "Everyone says that. But I should have been there, been with her. I had a tummy ache that morning, and I so wanted the day off school, but it wasn't long from exam time, and she made me go, thought I was malingering. I was sick as a dingo. I should have been at home. I should have saved her."

"Or died with her," I said.

"Even that would have been better, I think, sometimes."

"What happened when you went back to live with your dad?"

"What happened? Dad did his best. I had everything money could buy. He was only in his fifties then, at the peak of his career, making good money. But I blew it."

"How did you do that?"

"It was easy. It's amazing what a few snorts of coke and a bottle of vodka will do. I suppose I didn't much care for myself, or my life, so I just kind of drifted with the flow, took whatever pills or powders were handed me, ended up with the rest of the flotsam and jetsam. I dropped out of uni after my first year, lived in Sydney for a while, in Kings Cross, with a bloke twice my age, a dealer. Hitchhiked to Perth with a few long stops on the way. It's the usual story. I did heroin, gave twenty-dollar blow jobs to pervs for a fix. I drank until I couldn't feel the pain or see the images in my mind anymore. Woke up in more strangers' beds than you've had hot dinners. Spent a few months in jail. You must know the story. It's common enough. Pathetic."

"I've had a few friends whose kids have gone off the rails like that," I said. "And not always with as much reason as you had."

"There's never a reason," she said. "Only an excuse."

"I don't know. Don't be so hard on yourself. I guess I was lucky with my own kids."

"Luck has nothing to do with it."

I could see that there was no point in arguing this matter with Louise. She had come to her own unshakable conclusions, and a certain vehemence, almost evangelical, had crept into her voice. I could hear the unmistakable tone of self-blame, and wondered whether, along with the piercings, she also went in for self-harm. I had known kids back in L.A. who had done exactly that, slashed themselves with knives, burned themselves with cigarettes. I wanted to cool Louise down, not fan the flames of her self-hatred. "But you came out the other side," I said.

She nodded. "When Dad first got sick with cancer—oh, three or four years before he finally died—I went back home and cared for him. I was about twenty-one then, and I was a mess. But I quit drugs and booze, stayed away from men, got some professional help from a colleague of Dad's shrink."

"Is that when you went to the movies nearly every day?"

She gave me a surprised glance. "You remembered. Yes. It was my escape, just like you said. Granny Felicity was a great help, too, though she was in her eighties by then and starting to show Alzheimer's symptoms. She's in a home now. I go and see her sometimes, but she doesn't know me. It's too sad. Anyway, I got into a computer course and it turned out I was quite good at it. I'm not saying life wasn't tough, and there weren't times I thought of giving up, or even ending it all, but for some reason I held on. I guess Dad being sick gave me a reason to stay alive. Isn't that weird? Then, last January, he died."

"And now you're here."

"Yes. As it happens, I've got a job offer here through some contacts I had in Melbourne. Down in Cambridge. Computers. I start next week."

"Congratulations. I thought the brain drain usually went the other way."

"I was headhunted."

"I see. So what else did your father tell you about his life here?"

"Very little." Louise surveyed the room. "He told me about this house, described growing up here, what he remembered of his mother—her kindness, her gentleness, her smile, the sound of her laughter, her lovely singing voice, her love for him. All so cruelly taken away. But he didn't understand what was happening, the trial, the execution. He was only seven, eight when he left, and he somehow got stuck with the impression that she must have been evil."

"Did he talk much about Sam Porter?"

"Not much. He didn't know him. They never met. At least he doesn't remember that they did. I think my grandmother must have been very discreet in her affairs."

"Affair," I said. "As far as I know, she only had the one."

"Perhaps."

"And one indiscretion was enough."

"Yes."

"Have you read the trial account?"

"I didn't know there was one."

"Want to?"

She paused. "Please."

"I'll lend you the book. So what else did your father tell you about Grace?"

"It wasn't so much what he told me that impressed me," said Louise. "It was the stuff in the box he gave me."

I felt a little frisson of excitement run through me. "What do you mean?" I asked. "'Stuff'?"

"Her things. What was left. The box of stuff they brought over from England. Granny Felicity told Dad that when she went to stay with my grandmother when the police started asking questions, my grandmother gave her some odds and ends and asked her to keep them for her in case things didn't turn out well. She had a bad feeling, and she didn't want the police going through her private stuff. What do you call it, a foreboding? Anyway, when Granny Felicity started to get ill, she passed the box on to Dad, to keep the memory in the family. There's not much. But it was enough for me. It brought my grandmother to life."

I felt my pulse quicken, but I didn't wish to appear overeager in front of Louise, lest she think me ghoulish. After all, this was her grandmother we were talking about. "What are these things?" I asked. "Photos?"

"Some, yes, mostly from the war."

"Letters?"

"There aren't any letters. They must have got lost somewhere, or somebody must have destroyed them."

I tried to hide my disappointment.

"There's the journal," Louise said.

"Journal?"

"Yes, an old leather-bound thing. Grandmother's journal. Granny Felicity told Dad that Grandmother kept it in a secret drawer in the escritoire, and she took her up one day and got it out for her. That's how I knew about the drawer. Granny Felicity told Dad, and he told me."

"Good Lord. Does it say . . . I mean, is there any . . . ?"

"It blew me away. Maybe you'd like to read it?"

"You know I would. You brought it with you all this way from Australia?"

"Like I said, there's not much. But I think she wanted it preserved. Maybe it was her legacy. Or maybe she was just trying to keep it from public scrutiny. She probably knew what was going to happen, the arrest and trial and all. I'm planning on staying here, so I brought all my worldly goods with me, all I cared about, at any rate, and my grand-mother's stuff is among my most valuable possessions, the only ones, really, apart from a few mementos of Mum and Dad. If you want to see it, you'll have to come to Staithes in the next couple of days, though, before I head down south."

"There's nothing I'd like more than a day at the seaside."

16

Extract from the *Journal of Grace Elizabeth Fox* (ed. Louise King), December 1941–January 1942, Singapore.

MONDAY, DECEMBER 8, 1941

IT IS HARD TO BELIEVE THAT OUR CAREFREE YEAR OF GOLF, TENNIS, TEA DANCES, afternoon siestas, and Singapore slings at the Raffles Hotel may soon be over, but today the war has come to our little island. The Japanese have bombed us. There were no warnings, and the casualties have been pouring in all day. Major Schofield said at lunchtime that we still should not worry. We have our guns pointed at the sea, and a land invasion is impossible. At worst, he allowed, we may undergo a minor siege, but even that, he felt, was unlikely. Happily, tonight's dinner dance at the Cricket Club has not been canceled, and my shift will soon be over!

THURSDAY, DECEMBER 11, 1941

The HMS *Repulse* and HMS *Prince of Wales* have both been sunk off the Malay coast. We are told to expect more casualties in the coming hours, mostly burn victims, which are most difficult and heartbreaking to deal with. I fear poor Brenda will be worked off her feet after her experience with the burns hospital at Bangor, and she is already suffering so much with the heat and humidity here, not to mention the mosquitoes!

THURSDAY, DECEMBER 18, 1941

Life goes on much as normal, apart from the air raid precautions. We did not get as many survivors of the naval disasters as we expected, and one of the VADs told me she had heard nearly one thousand men were killed. The Japanese are advancing south and west from Kota Bharu. There is now fierce fighting across the Straits of Johor, and many people are fleeing south to safety in Singapore. According to one of our casualties from the Suffolk Regiment, the refugees are blocking the roads with their cars, rickshaws, and bicycles, and the relief troops cannot get through. The Japanese planes are constantly strafing and dive-bombing them. He also told me that the jungle is proving no barrier to the Japanese. They are running rings around us. They can shoot straight, too, he says, contrary to the rumors that went around. The Alor Star Hospital, in the far north, has already been evacuated. They loaded all their patients onto an ambulance train and headed south. We can only try to carry on as if all will be well. After all, the north is still a long way away, and we have strong defenses.

THURSDAY, DECEMBER 25, 1941

We had a fine Christmas dinner at Raffles Hotel with the civilians and the surgical staff. It was all rather depressing for a while because of the news of the Japanese advance, which shows no signs of halting or slowing down, but in the end we decided it was Christmas, so we ought to try to forget our troubles for a while and enjoy ourselves. Naturally, there was dancing afterward, though I spent much of the time sitting it out. Whenever I see people dance, I think of Stephen Fawley, who disembarked from the *Empress of Australia* at Hong Kong with the rest of his regiment. It seems so long ago now. I am troubled by rumors I have heard about the behavior of Japanese troops in Hong Kong. It is so hard to get any reliable information here. Even if people do know something, they are more than likely to keep it a secret, as if information were some kind of currency. I am almost certain that Hong Kong has surrendered to the Japanese, but I have no idea of the fates of those sisters and military personnel there. We can find no news of Kathleen or Doris, or of Stephen and the others. For Christmas, Brenda very thoughtfully gave me a waterproof oilskin bag for my journal. I can hang it around my neck under my clothing, complete with pencil stubs! I gave her a lovely hand-painted Chinese fan I found at the Sungei Road market to help her keep cool.

THURSDAY, JANUARY 1, 1942

Today we evacuated over a hundred convalescent Australian patients to free more beds here. It was a sad day for me, as I had come to know some of them, and the sisters who accompanied them, quite well over the past year. I waved good-bye to Amelia, to Gillian, to Florence, Jimmy, Mick, and Kenny. We have only one hospital ship now, a decrepit old riverboat called the *Wu Sueh*, and we are making arrangements to ship more patients to Sumatra when they are well enough to travel. The fighting up north is getting fiercer and closer, and we are receiving a steady stream of wounded coming in daily. The air raids continue, and we also have many civilian casualties to contend with. We are all so rushed off our feet I barely have time to scribble this before bed. The blackout is annoying. Last night, crossing the grounds after my shift, I tripped over a root and almost sprained my ankle.

SATURDAY, JANUARY 3, 1942

Our bright new hospital is no longer what it was. It used to be a nice place to work. The wards are filled with casualties from the fighting, and there are drip stands and oxygen cylinders everywhere. We also have some cases of battle fatigue, which I have never witnessed before. They are most unnerving. They want to do nothing except lie around and sleep all the time, but as soon as the bombs start to fall, or the artillery fire begins, they jump out of bed and hide underneath it, or try to dig holes in the earth or hide themselves under the sheets. It is very upsetting because there is so very little you can do but try to comfort them and talk to them. Their fear is terrifying to watch. Everything seems to be happening at once, and we are still rushed off our feet, filling in the forms, giving transfusions, sending patients off to the theaters. When we get back to our quarters after a long shift, all we want to do is take our uniforms off, lie down, and fall asleep in the blissfully cool blast of an electric fan. That is all there is now. Work. Sleep. Work. Sleep.

Monday, January 12, 1942

I heard that Kuala Lumpur fell yesterday. It can only be a matter of time now. Guns facing the sea are not much use when the enemy invades by land, which everyone said could never be done. We can turn them around, of course, but everyone says they are no use in this kind of battle. We would only end up shelling ourselves. The talk among all the European women in the Raffles Hotel and the Cricket Club is whether to stay or go. They are frightened, and they would like to leave Singapore before it falls into the hands of the Japanese, but they do not want to leave their husbands and be perceived as cowards or deserters. The news coming out of Hong Kong is deeply disturbing. We hear of medical staff and patients alike tortured and killed, sisters subjected to the most degrading ordeals. It seems the Japanese have no respect for the Red Cross, for medical staff, for the wounded, or for women. Major Schofield told me they did not sign the Geneva Convention, so they do not play by our rules. I worry constantly about what has become of Stephen, Kathleen, and Doris, and I shudder to think what that will mean for us when the Japanese arrive here, for arrive soon they surely must.

DECEMBER 2010

On the day following Louise's visit, I got two phone calls that gladdened my heart. The first was from my daughter, Jane, in Baltimore. She was ringing to ask me if she could visit me for Christmas and bring her fiancé, Mohammed, with her. *Fiancé!* It was the first I had heard of this. Of course, I told her she could.

A short while later my director and best friend Dave Packer phoned to remind me of the offer I had made the last time we talked, and to ask if he and Melissa could take me up on it and come over for Christmas. They were planning a short tour of Europe and would love to include Richmond. Melissa had a break in her filming schedule, and Dave was mulling over a few scripts for his—he hoped *our*—next project. Again, I said yes, delighted. Dave was Jane's godfather, and Melissa would certainly raise a few eyebrows around Richmond, I was sure of that.

So there *was* going to be a Christmas, after all. Though it was only early December, I would have to get busy soon, order the turkey, get a case of decent champagne delivered. Crackers. Presents. A tree. Tinsel. Lights. Ornaments. I started making a list and was about halfway through when the phone rang again.

It was Heather. "Look, I'm still at the office. It's been a really, really bad day, and I could do with a drink before I head home. Any chance of you joining me?"

Her voice took some of the wind out of my sails. She sounded sad, tired. I looked at my watch. It was seven o'clock. I had plenty I wanted to tell Heather—and I certainly owed her a lot after all she'd done to help me. The only thing that held me back from jumping at the chance was that I still fancied her, and something like this would only serve to fuel my desire. Even so, I paused for only a few seconds before answering, "Sure. Black Lion, half an hour?"

"Perfect," she said. "See you there."

THE BLACK LION WAS FAIRLY QUIET AT THAT TIME ON A WEEKDAY EVENING IN December. There was no live music, no pub quiz. A few late-season tourists sat at the tables in the dining room, finishing their meals. I hadn't eaten yet, so I thought I might order fish pie or something. The reason I had chosen this particular pub was the little snug beyond the dining room, which fortunately was empty. I bought a drink at the bar and went to sit in there and wait. Five minutes later, Heather arrived and popped her head around the door.

"I thought you might be in here," she said. "Very cozy."

"If you think it's likely to do your reputation any harm being alone with me like this, we can go back into the public bar."

"What, and listen to regulars talk about football and last night's television? You must be joking. No, I'll risk my reputation, such as it is, thank you very much."

She asked for a vodka and tonic, and I went to get it for her, casting my eyes over the menu chalked on the blackboard.

"Eaten?" I asked Heather when I got back.

"I'm not hungry."

I ordered fish pie at the bar and went back to join Heather in the tiny wood-paneled snug. The room was so small that if two people were in there and someone checked it out, they most likely wouldn't come in. You could hear voices from the dining room and the public bar, but you couldn't really make out what people were saying.

Heather downed her vodka and tonic with the speed of someone determined to get drunk. She looked fraught, frazzled, and there were bags under her eyes from lack of sleep. I wondered if it was just work, or if there was something else. When I brought her the second vodka and tonic, still working on my first pint of Tetley's Cask, before I could ask her what was wrong, she said, "You might as well know, Derek's leaving. We're separating."

I just stared at her, speechless.

She stared back. I couldn't read her expression. "Come on, Chris," she said. "Don't act so surprised. You must have known it was in the cards?"

"I might have had the impression that things weren't going too well," I said, "after Bonfire Night. But . . . What are you going to do?"

"One of the perks of being in the estate agent business. I've picked up a sublet on a nice little flat in the Convent development down on Reeth Road. That's why I'm so late tonight. Been wheeling and dealing. Very fitting, don't you think? Me in a convent."

I laughed. "Very."

"I suppose this puts an end to any interest you might have had in me?" she said, one eyebrow raised.

"What do you mean?"

"Oh, don't be so thick. It doesn't suit you. It's one thing flirting or having a fling with a married woman, and the way things were going, we might well have done that. But a single woman? Doesn't that reek too much of entrapment, commitment?"

"You're far too cynical for one so young," I said.

"I'm not that young. I'm forty-five."

"That still makes you fifteen years younger than me."

"Just think. When you were a thirty-year-old whiz kid taking Hollywood by storm, I was a gawky fifteen-year-old schoolgirl with freckles, glasses, and ginger hair madly in love with Geoff Johnson, who didn't even notice my existence. You wouldn't have fancied me at all then."

I couldn't help but laugh. "I should hope not. But look how far you've come since those days."

She sat silently for a moment, then wiped her eyes with the backs of her hands, smearing a little mascara. She stared down at the table when the girl delivered my fish pie, then excused herself and went to the ladies'. While she was away, I thought about the implications of what she had said. She was wrong in saying that her separating from her husband would cause her to lose her appeal to me. It was the opposite, really. I had been resisting an affair, not strictly on moral grounds, but because they are, in my experience, messy, disappointing, and ultimately painful to some, or all, concerned. Though I had never been unfaithful to Laura, I had had a brief fling with a married woman before we met, and it had ended badly and messily. If Heather were free, it would be another matter. But I wasn't going to tell her that. Not before she'd made the move, at any rate, no more than I was going to offer to help her move—and it wasn't for lack of gallantry or willingness. I didn't want to appear to influence or encourage her in any way. Not that I had, but people don't always see things in the same light. I had learned that long before I encountered either Heather, Charlotte, or the Grace Fox case.

When Heather came back, she was composed. She also had another drink in her hand. "I hope you're not driving," I said.

"Walking up the hill."

"Sure you don't want anything to eat?"

She reached for my fork and helped herself to some fish pie. "No," she said, when she'd finished it. "That's enough for me." She pushed her drink away. "I don't even want this, either, truth be told. I thought it would be a good idea to get drunk, but . . ."

"When did you and Derek make this decision?"

"It's been brewing for a long time. You may or may not know it, but we separated once before. Anyway, it all came to a head again on the night of your dinner party."

"That's why you were so . . . ?"

"Pissed and at each other's throats?"

"Well, not quite that, but I did notice some tension."

"You're so kind, Chris, but we were awful."

"And between now and then?"

"Fights, excuses, evasions, recriminations. Last night he finally came out with it. He's got another woman, and he wants to start a new life with her. Which is exactly what I suspected."

I almost choked on my beer. "Derek?"

"Why not? Don't look so surprised. Still waters run deep and all that. Besides, he's an attractive man in his way. Was when I married him, anyway. A lot more fun, too." She sighed. "All the joy's gone out of it, Chris. All the passion. All the laughter. It's someone from work. She's only thirty-two. *Bitch*." Heather dabbed her eyes again, then patted my arm. "Sorry for unloading all this on you. I couldn't think of anyone else I wanted to talk to."

"That's all right," I said. I noticed she had left her hand resting on my arm. "When do you move in?"

"Whenever I want. The flat's empty right now, owner's abroad, key's in the office. Maybe tonight or first thing tomorrow. I find these things don't get any better for being dragged out. To be honest, I don't think I can stand the bloody sight of him anymore. I'm afraid if I stay any longer I'll murder the bastard."

"I'm sorry, Heather."

She moved her hand. "Don't be. I'm not. It's time for a fresh start. I'm looking forward to it. Want to help me shop for furniture, put together a few things from Ikea? Only joking."

"No, but you can come for Christmas dinner, if you want." I told her about my phone calls, and then I went on to tell her about Louise King's visit. She seemed interested, but was distracted, naturally, and when we had exhausted that, she said she had to go. She wouldn't accept a lift, said she needed the exercise, so I gave her a light peck and a hug and she was gone. I sat awhile over another half of Tetley's Cask, then I headed back to Kilnsgate House and *A Kind of Loving*.

17

Extract from the *Journal of Grace Elizabeth Fox* (ed. Louise King), January–February 1942, Singapore.

SUNDAY, FEBRUARY 1, 1942

WE JUST HEARD THAT THE LAST OF OUR TROOPS, THE REMAINS OF THE Argyll and Sutherland Highlanders, retreated across the Johor causeway and blew it up behind them. Witnesses say there are only about ninety men left out of over eight hundred. The Japanese have set up their heavy artillery directly across the Straits. There are rumors that the Tan Tock Seng civilian hospital was the first place to be hit. More frightening stories about the Japanese atrocities against sisters and medical staff in Hong Kong appear daily. We understand that those who survived are now in prison camps, and I can only hope that Kathleen, Doris, and Stephen are among them. We are all feeling very frightened lest we meet the same fate, but we have to carry on with our work as long as there are patients to care for.

Wednesday, February 4, 1942

We try to keep our spirits up with visits to the cinema and dances at Raffles Hotel, but it is difficult. Everyone still maintains that we can survive a siege. They argue that Tobruk held out for seven months with almost nothing, and we have two good reservoirs and lots of food. I am not sure that I can endure seven more months of this. We have started a "dig for victory" campaign, though I can hardly see us planting sprouts and spuds in this climate!

Friday, February 6, 1942

The casualties keep pouring in, and the injuries get worse, mostly burns and gangrene. Some of the boys have been blinded by fire, and many have lost limbs. Sometimes there is nothing you can do but mop their brows with a cold cloth and mutter endearments as they beg for their mothers and die slowly in agony. We can hardly keep up with the casualties, and we work such long hours we are dead on our feet most of the time. Every day now the Japanese bomb us. Sometimes we have to operate in candle and lantern light because the power fails.

Monday, February 9, 1942

Yesterday we managed to get four more ships of women and children away. Not long after they sailed, we had the worst bombardment ever. The earth was shaking fit to break in pieces, and I thought the world was coming to an end. The explosions were so loud and frightening that I crouched in a corner with my hands over my ears until Matron came and told me to pull myself together. She is right. There is no use in falling apart now, not when we are most needed. The wounded are flowing in, and the ones who can speak all tell us that the Japanese have rebuilt the causeway and crossed the Straits of Johor. They have landed on our northwest coast and are on their way to the city. It seems funny, but I remember the Straits as a peaceful place, near the reservoir, where we used to go for picnics when the weather was bearable enough, and look out on Malaya across the water. It was so romantic, especially in the twilight.

Last night, the navy fired the dockyards and abandoned them. I could not believe the clouds of thick black smoke that rose from the burning oil reserves. There are still hundreds of nurses left on the island, and I do not think there are any more ships for us. General Percival promises that he will not allow one nurse to fall into enemy hands, but I do not know what he can do to stop it. I do not know what will become of us. We work until we drop. It is all we can do. We are at full capacity now. All the hospitals are. The bombs fall, the bullets ricochet, the shells burst, and we change dressings, give transfusions, assist in surgery, then, when we can no longer stand up, we sleep for a few short hours, if we can sleep through the noise. Then we start all over again. Some nights Brenda and I huddle together for comfort on our mattresses on the canteen floor, despite the heat. At least the Alexandra Hospital has not been hit yet. The Indian General at Tyersall was bombed today, with two hundred patients and staff killed.

TUESDAY, FEBRUARY 10, 1942

Today I heard rifle fire in the distance. They are very close now. Even the RAF has abandoned us. The last squadron left this morning for Sumatra. There was nothing they could do against the modern Japanese planes, as they had not much more than obsolete Wildebeests to fight back with. We carry on. The floors and staircases are sticky with blood, but we have no time to clean them. All the servants have gone, so we have to do everything else ourselves now in addition to our nursing duties—cook the food, wash the bedsheets, scrub the floors. We evacuated twenty civilian nurses, VADs, and over three hundred casualties on the *Wu Sueh* for Java, so now even our little hospital ship has deserted us.

WEDNESDAY, FEBRUARY 11, 1942

More gunfire, even closer now. Snipers are a big problem, and three orderlies have been killed here already. We have to be very careful whenever we go outside, or even stand by a window. Matron gathered us together this morning and asked for volunteers to leave on the

Empire Star tonight, but nobody volunteered. We do not want to leave our patients, and we know that if we leave, we might never see our friends again.

Matron then chose names at random. Brenda's and mine were not among them, but half the sisters left. Last night, I sat up late with a young private from the Norfolk Regiment. He had no sooner got off the troopship than he found himself in the jungle fighting the Japanese. He never stood a chance. There was nothing we could do for him. He had lost both legs and the gangrene was too advanced. He had a high fever, and in his hallucinations, he believed I was his mother. He would not let go of my hand. All I could do was mop his brow with a damp cloth, tell him I loved him and that he was going to be all right, though I knew that he was not. He died in my arms at five o'clock in the morning, and tired as I was, I could not get to sleep for crying. I truly felt as if I had lost my own son

THURSDAY, FEBRUARY 12, 1942

The authorities here have assembled a fleet of eighty vessels at the abandoned Naval Dockyard. The Australian nurses left today on the *Vyner Brooke*. It was another sad farewell. The Japanese are getting closer. We must be next.

DECEMBER 2010

The drive to Staithes the following morning was pleasant enough. At one point, I saw a sign for Saltburn and almost took the turning, but I didn't think I would be able to learn anything there. Saltburn was where Grace Fox, or Grace Hartnell, as she was then known, had grown up, and that was one reason why I thought a quick look around the place might be interesting. But Grace had left Saltburn in the thirties, so it was highly unlikely that there was anyone left who remembered her, or if there was, that I could find them. Grace had lived the last half of her short life at Kilnsgate. So I continued on to Staithes for my appointment with Louise King. My excitement at the thought of reading Grace's journal had been mounting over the last couple of days, only slightly distracted by Heather's problems and my plans for Christmas.

Though the landscape was bleak and sere for the most part, it was an unusually sunny day for December in Yorkshire, and when the coast came into view near Boulby, below the high cliffs to my left, I could almost imagine that it was a summer's day. The choppy water was bluish-gray, dotted with whitecaps and long curving lines of breaking waves. A couple of tankers sailed out on the horizon, and six fluffy clouds rode almost in formation, like giant white chariots overhead, on the stiff breeze.

As Louise had given me directions while I drove her to her car in Richmond market square the other evening, I left the Volvo in the car park at the top of the hill and started to walk down. It was very steep, with magnificent views of the bay, the seascape, and the cliffs, and I didn't relish the climb back up. The sun belied how cold it actually was, mostly thanks to the strong winds off the North Sea, and I was glad I had brought the fleece-lined winter jacket I had picked up at Yorkshire Trading.

It was around half past eleven when I turned down the snicket Louise had told me about between the jeweler's and the baker's. The cottage was at the far end of the short narrow passage. Louise answered my knock and asked me in. I had to stoop to avoid banging my head on the lintel. I found myself in a small living room, very cozy, with a low ceiling and French windows leading out to a small patio. A table and two chairs stood outside, but I doubted that anyone would be sitting on them until spring. The view was stunning, across the harbor to the lifeboat station, and out to sea. But that was not what I had come for.

On the low table in front of the sofa lay strewn an array of objects that I took to be Grace's legacy. I could hardly contain the excitement I felt, and it made me vaguely ashamed of myself for letting Grace Fox become such an obsession. Here I was, like a gourmet in front of his meal, or an alcoholic in front of a bottle, barely able to wait for permission to tuck in.

Louise was looking far healthier and more attractive than she had the first time we met. Her hair shone with gel, and she had applied a little makeup, which improved her complexion no end. Wearing jeans and a scallop-neck red top, she still had that gaunt, haunted quality; the facial metal; and a deep, damaged seriousness that guaranteed she would be difficult to know and love, should anybody get close enough to try. She could also stand to put a bit more flesh on her bones. It was impossible for most people to begin to imagine what she had been through, and what reserves of strength, courage, and perseverance she had had to draw on in order simply to survive intact. She seemed relaxed enough at the moment, and even chatted for a while about the history of the cottage and the Staithes fishing traditions. She could no doubt see me eyeing the table greedily, practically salivating at the prospect before me, but she talked on.

"Help yourself," she said finally, gesturing to the table. "I'll make some tea."

"Okay." I didn't need telling twice. She was no sooner at the sink filling the kettle than I had a wad of photographs in my hand. Black and white with deckled edges. Some had faded corners or traces of stickiness on the back, as if they had been removed from albums. Most of them featured Grace and her fellow nurses posing with wounded soldiers, many of whom had their arms in slings, bandaged heads, or legs missing. The nurses were often dressed in tropical uniforms of flattering white dresses, veils, and shoes, and sometimes in plain shirts and slacks, or even battle dress.

It was easy to pick out Grace, though the only images of her I had seen so far were the family portrait in Kilnsgate and those painted by Sam Porter. Her dark wavy hair fell only as far as her neckline, and she wore it mostly tucked behind her ears.

There was one photograph of her that pierced my heart. She was in some sort of makeshift medical tent in her white dress and veil, stooping as she handed an emaciated patient a mug of tea, trying to place it carefully in his outstretched hands. His face was completely covered in bandages, with a small gap for the mouth and breath holes by the nostrils. I guessed that he had probably suffered serious burns, perhaps lost his eyesight. It was so real that I could almost *see* his hands shaking. Grace had an expression of such mixed concentration and compassion on her features, lips compressed, eyes tender, a small furrow in her brow. In the background, outside the tent stood an army truck with a big cross on its side. It was clear she hadn't known she was being photographed, and I guessed that a colleague must have taken it and given it to her later.

There was another photograph of Grace with a group of friends, and they seemed to be having fun, all wearing bathing costumes, laughing and frolicking on a beach. In another she stood holding her hair back from the wind on a rocky promontory against a backdrop of rolling waves. It could have been Cornwall, I suppose, but she was wearing a white dress with epaulettes and little buttons up the front. In another, she posed astride a large motorcycle in full army battle dress, tin hat cocked at a jaunty angle, a lopsided grin on her face.

There were two photographs of Grace standing outside Kilnsgate House, her hair longer, wearing a pale dress that came in tight at the waist and flared out below, buttons up the front, like her white nurse's uniform. She was shielding her eyes from the sun and smiling at the photographer. Another showed her with her arm around the shoulder of a young boy in the garden at Kilnsgate, near the gate, pointing toward the lime kiln. He was about Randolph's age at the time of the murder, so I wondered if it had been taken close to that time. But Grace was wearing a summer frock, and the boy wore only short trousers and a shirt. I couldn't see his face because he was in profile. I asked Louise about it when she brought the cups and teapot over on a tray.

She shook her head and said, "No, that's not my dad. I don't know who it is."

Another puzzle. I had a vague idea of who it might be, but I would need to do a lot of research before I could find out whether I was right. And even if I was, it was still puzzling that the photograph had so obviously been taken *at Kilnsgate House.*

There were no wedding photographs, in fact no images of Ernest Fox at all, and only a few of Randolph ranging from age two or three to five and six. There was one photo of Grace and a female friend in Richmond market square that showed an old tenement building by Trinity Church and the obelisk. It certainly wasn't there now. I didn't know who the friend was. Could it have been Alice Lambert? Grace had other female friends in town, too, I assumed, women she had met through the operatic and dramatic societies, for example, or from the subscription concerts she went to, but I hadn't heard anything about them. Clearly, none of them had played a relevant role in the events of January 1953, though I couldn't help but wonder if she'd had a friend close enough to be a confidante, someone to whom she had told all her troubles and indiscretions. I realized it wouldn't help me if she had, though. If the friend was Grace's age, she would be pushing a century now and most likely dead.

That thought made my whole endeavor seem suddenly futile, and a wave of tiredness and depression surged through me. What was I trying to prove? Why? What did it matter? I glanced at Louise and wondered how much the truth would really mean to her, assuming I found it and it differed from the official version. Would the truth make Louise any happier, or would it damage what fragile balance she had worked so hard to achieve? Maybe Bernie had been right all those weeks ago in Soho when he told me it was sometimes best to leave the past well alone. Was I doing this all for myself? Was it about Grace, or was it really about me? Was it only me who needed the explanation to be different from the official verdict? I didn't know the answer to any of these questions.

I shook off the melancholy, put the photos back down on the table, and picked up the small leather-bound journal. The cover was soft and scuffed. Some of the pages were stained. Blood, tea, water, wine, I had no idea. In the front flyleaf Grace had written, "If lost, please return to Grace Fox, Kilnsgate House, Kilnsgate Lane, Kilnsgarthdale, near Richmond, North Riding, of Yorkshire, England."

When I opened the volume to the first entry and saw Grace's tiny, precise hand, just like the notations on the Schubert, I felt a shiver run up my spine. I also realized that there was no possible way I could read this in the short length of time I would be spending in Staithes, and I felt a sense of panic creep up inside me. Most of it seemed to have been written in pencil, with the occasional entry clearly in fountain pen. Ballpoint pens hadn't been invented then, I supposed, and a fountain pen would have been too difficult to maintain in some of the conditions Grace had had to endure.

It was with slight disappointment that I found the journal covered only the years 1940 to 1945 and did not stretch as far as 1952 or 1953. Even so, I knew it would make fascinating reading, and it might contain a hidden gem of information or two, some missing pieces. Also, from what I could see on a brief perusal, she had skipped over whole periods, months sometimes. Most of the entries were brief, almost in note form, but some were quite lengthy, and there were only three or four empty pages at the end. She had just made it. Some pages were smudged and unreadable.

I put the journal down, sipped some tea, and examined some of the other things. There was a copy of Graham Greene's *The End of the Affair*—perhaps the last novel Grace had ever read—along with a small collection of jewelry in a black velvet pouch from a Richmond jeweler's. From what I could see, it was tasteful and of good quality, but not very expensive: earrings, a heart-shaped pendant with no photographs or locks of hair inside, a simple chain bracelet, semiprecious stones, a necklace of Whitby jet. There were no wedding or engagement rings. There was also a medal, a Maltese cross with red arms and a circular gold center. On the arms were written FAITH, HOPE, AND CHARITY, and, on the bottom one, the date 1883. The ribbon was dark blue with crimson edging.

"It's a Royal Red Cross," said Louise. "I looked it up. It was given for special exertion in nursing sick and wounded soldiers or sailors. Florence Nightingale was the first woman to get one. It's the highest honor a military nurse can earn. There were only two hundred and sixteen given in the whole war."

"Nobody I've talked to has mentioned it to me. Not Wilf, not Sam."

Louise shrugged. "Maybe she didn't tell anyone."

There remained one more object, an engraved silver cigarette case. When I studied it more closely, I could see that the engraving was of a pastoral scene showing a young man playing panpipes and a young woman nearby languishing against a tree. There was a small town or village in the distance, along a winding path. It was difficult to make out because the silver was tarnished and worn. There was some sort of inscription, so I took out the drugstore reading glasses I always carry for such occasions—like CD covers and crossword puzzles—and read: "Forever wilt though love, and she be fair!" It was Keats, "Ode on a Grecian Urn," one of the poems I had been forced to memorize at school. No names, no dedication. Sam's only present to Grace. The one she dared risk keeping. I remembered the Everyman editions in the sewing room. Shelley. Keats. Grace had clearly loved Keats, as had Laura, who had quoted him with almost her last breath. I opened the box. It was empty, but I fancied I could still smell tobacco in it. On the bottom was written:

> *Beauty is truth, truth beauty, — that is all*
> *Ye know on earth, and all ye need to know.*

Louise was watching me with a peculiar half smile on her face. "What?" I asked, looking up.

"Nothing. You look like a detective poring over clues, that's all."

"The journal. Would it be possible to—"

"No," she said. "I can't let it out of my possession. I won't let any of this out of my possession. Surely you can understand that?"

"I can. It's just that I was hoping . . ."

Louise held up her hand and stood. "Just a minute," she said, and left the room. I could hear the wooden stairs creaking as she went up them. When she came back, she was carrying my copy of *Famous Trials* and a computer disc. "I finished the book, thank you," she said, "and I thought you might be interested in this."

"What is it?"

"When I got this stuff"—she gestured at the table—"I realized how fragile it was, and how unique. The journal and the photos especially. As you can see, some of them are already in poor condition. It seemed sensible to get it all scanned and put it in the computer." She handed me the disc. "That's a DVD. A copy. It's got everything on it. Photos, journal, digital photographs of the other objects. You can print it all out for yourself."

I held the disc in my hand, astonished. "Go on, then," Louise said. "Take it. It's yours. To keep."

"I . . . thank you," I managed to stammer, putting the disc and book in the battered leather briefcase I always carried, my "man bag" as Laura had teasingly called it. "Look," I said, "can I buy you lunch somewhere?"

"I thought you'd never ask. I'm starving."

"I passed a pub on my way. Is that okay?"

"No problem. Not much else here, especially at this time of year. And maybe after that you'd like me to show you my grandmother's grave?"

LOUISE SLUNG HER FUR-HOODED PARKA ON THE BENCH BESIDE HER WHILE I bought her a diet bitter lemon, contemplated joining her, then decided on a pint of Black Sheep instead. In my excitement over Grace's legacy, I had forgotten about her alcoholism, but it seemed that being around drinkers didn't bother her. I picked up a couple of lunch menus at the bar. No fresh-caught seafood, but Louise assured me that the Cumberland sausage and mashed potatoes was usually pretty good, so I went for that. She ordered a beef burger and chips.

The pub was quite empty at the moment, but I could imagine what a popular spot it would be for tourists during the season. A few locals in fishermen's jerseys stood chatting around the bar, the landlord throwing in the occasional comment, and two elderly couples, retirees by the looks of them, sat eating at other tables. There were old framed pictures of groups of fishermen on the walls, and some photographs of a storm that had hit Staithes badly. I could hardly imagine what sort of hell that must have been. Even today's wind was bad enough for me. If I'd been out at sea I would have been throwing up over the side.

February 1953, I saw on the caption of one of the photos. That stopped me in my tracks. Grace would have been in custody then, awaiting her trial. She must surely have heard about the storm. It had no doubt hit Saltburn, too, maybe the whole coastline, and she would probably have been worried about her family and friends there. What about Sam Porter? Had he been in Staithes with his artist friends, trying to come to terms with the terrible cost of his affair with Grace?

I pointed the photo out to Louise, and she seemed also to realize its significance immediately.

"As I said, I read that book you lent me," she said as we sat down. "I mean, just the account of my grandmother's case, of course."

"What did you think?"

Louise snorted. "Typical men," she said. "I honestly don't know whether she did it or not, but it sounds to me as if they made a meal out of her morality, or lack of it. If it hadn't been for that bloody woman from Leyburn blabbing, making it clear they'd had a good shag in her B and B, I'll bet it would never have come to trial. The forensic evidence was a joke. Apart from the chloral hydrate, which Ernest Fox could easily have taken himself, there was nothing to show that my grandmother had done anything wrong at all except try to save his life." She shook her head.

"My opinion exactly," I said. "Though the prosecution did make a very convincing case out of what little they had, and the defense was a bit lackluster, I thought."

"*Lackluster?* Bloody spineless, if you ask me. It was just a bloody game to them. I suppose the jury was all male, too? They probably had a good wank thinking about her every night and hated themselves for it, so they had her strung up."

I shouldn't have been, given Louise's history, but I was shocked by her angry outburst. "It reflected the morality of the times," I said.

" 'Morality of the times.' Now there's a phrase that covers many evils. So did the Roman bloody empire chucking Christians to the lions reflect the morality of the times?" Louise argued. "And what about slavery and concentration camps, too? Were they all right because of the morality of the times? Hiroshima? Nagasaki? How about sending convicts to Australia in chains in cramped conditions in stinking, disease-ridden, overcrowded ships? Was that just the morality of the times, too? If it was, it doesn't excuse them, it doesn't mean they were *good* things. And if you really think this 'morality of the times' has really progressed that much, then look at Zimbabwe, North Korea, Iran, Afghanistan. I could go on."

"I'm not saying they were right," I argued. Why did I suddenly feel like a defender of fifties morality? Especially when I'd spent the last thirty years in the relatively footloose and fancy-free world of Southern California? I might not be a revolutionary, but I was no reactionary, either. I thought of myself as fairly liberal, a liberal humanist, in U.S. terms, a Democrat, over here . . . well, certainly not procoalition.

"Sorry," Louise said, seeing my frustration. "I know it's not your fault. It just makes me so bloody angry, that's all. I'm just letting off steam."

The food came, and we ate in silence for a few minutes. I could hear the waves crashing against the harbor wall and the buzz of conversations around us, occasional laughter.

"One of the things Morley mentioned in his account of the trial grabbed my attention," I said. "It wasn't part of the evidence in the case. It came quite early on."

"Yes, I noticed he gave a bit of background on Grandma and Granddad. Those were the most interesting bits. I don't know where he got them from."

The words still sounded odd coming from Louise in reference to Grace. *Grandma and Granddad.* But it was true. She was Randolph Fox's daughter, after all, no matter how many name changes and tragedies the family had been through. Grace and Ernest's granddaughter.

"No doubt the police did thorough background checks on all concerned," I said. "Talked to Grace's parents, people who had known her in Saltburn. And Morley probably did a bit of research, too. Anyway, he mentioned a broken engagement when Grace was just eighteen. To a man called Edward Cunliffe."

"I remember that bit."

"Apparently, Grace threw him over and went off with a budding poet called Thomas Murray. He ended up dying in the Spanish Civil War, but that's probably beside the point.'

"What *is* the point?" Louise asked.

"The way Morley puts it was that Thomas Murray was a rake, a libertine, a bad boy, no doubt consumed with admiration for Byron and the romantics, who ran off with another woman soon after, leaving Grace with an abandoned and wronged fiancé and a bad case of shattered nerves. She was so ill she was sent to her aunt Ethel's in Torquay to recover."

"So?"

"Well, it was pretty obvious what he meant, don't you think? This was often the way people referred to unfortunate girls who got pregnant out of wedlock and disappeared to the country for a while to have their babies, then came home without them. It was a means of hiding a serious transgression, something that could have devastating effects on the rest of the girl's life, especially if she came from a good family."

Louise stared at me. "You mean you think my grandmother got pregnant by this Thomas Murray?"

"Not only that," I said, "but I believe she had a baby. Someone saw her talking with a young man in uniform on Castle Walk a few days before her husband's death. Whoever saw them didn't know who he was. It went nowhere. The fling with Murray took place in 1930, when Grace was eighteen. In late 1952, her son would have been twenty-two, about the right age. What if that *was* him? Grace's son? What if his reappearance had something to do with what happened afterward, or with her inability to defend herself?"

We had both finished our meals now, and a young man came and collected the plates. Louise put her chin in her hands, elbows resting on the table. "Her son?"

"You have to admit that it's a possibility."

"But you can't know this for certain."

"Of course not. It's just speculation."

Louise frowned. "I don't know. It's just so confusing. I wasn't ready for all this detective stuff."

"Okay. Maybe I *am* going too fast. But I know you're interested. I know you care about your grandmother's memory."

"Of course I do. If I can help . . . I just . . . You're so far ahead of me. I know so little."

"I've been thinking about it and studying it for longer than you. I don't have the blood connection you have, but I think I have some sense of what a remarkable woman your grandmother was and what an injustice was done to her. You'll have to trust me."

Louise contemplated me through narrowed eyes. "That's a big ask."

"Maybe, but give it a try. You never know. All I'm saying is that we both think the police and the courts did a wretched job. Maybe they missed something, some essential connection or event? Let's face it, they looked in one direction and one direction only—Grace Fox. They crucified her. Even Sam Porter was dismissed as a serious suspect pretty quickly."

"You don't think he was involved, do you?"

"No," I said. "I've talked to him. He's an old man now, still painting, as you know, full of memories and sadness, but his mind's still sharp. I think he really loved your grandmother, if you want my opinion, and he never got over her and what happened. He's as mystified as the rest of us, but he doesn't believe she did it, either."

"You talked to him?"

"Yes. In Paris."

"You went all the way to Paris to talk to Samuel Porter?"

"Yes. It's not that far. Not from here."

"But why?"

"I wanted to meet him, to know what he thought, what he remembered."

"Was it worth it?"

I remembered the paintings and sketches. "Oh, yes." One day I would tell her about them. Perhaps we would even visit Sam together, if he would admit me again, and she could see them for herself. Meeting Grace's granddaughter. Sam would like that. An artist herself, too. But not yet. She still felt a certain mistrust toward me, and I didn't blame her. I also wasn't entirely sure how stable she was after the terrible experiences she'd been through. And I didn't know how far I could trust her, either. But showing me Grace's things and giving me the DVD was a strong start. I was hoping we would be able to help each other and build up trust as we went along.

"Anyway," I went on. "What do you think about my theory?"

"I really don't know," she said slowly. "I mean, I've heard of such things, like you say. But wouldn't somebody have said something?"

"Morley did. As much as was needed. Everybody who read that would have known exactly what he was inferring."

"But at the trial?"

"It wasn't relevant. It happened over twenty years before the crime they were trying. And it was a matter of character. It was the sort of thing that might have come up if Grace had entered the witness box, perhaps, but she didn't. Her barrister wouldn't let her. He had that much sense, at least."

"I wondered about that. Wouldn't it have been better if she could speak for herself, tell them the truth? I couldn't really understand that part of the account."

"Read it again," I said. "It's one of the things Morley is remarkably clear on."

Louise chewed her fingernails and thought for a moment. "Let's assume you're right, then. Or that you *may* be right. What do we do about it?"

Here, I must admit, she had me stumped. Whatever my talents, trolling through records in dusty registrars' offices, or wherever they were kept, was certainly not one of them. I had neither the knowledge to know where to look, nor the patience to look when I did find out. "There has to be a way," I said.

Louise leaned forward. "I might just be able to help you there."

"Oh?"

"Yeah. I was never really into it, myself, but some of my friends back in Oz were really keen on compiling family trees. There's software for it, books, guides, all kinds of stuff. The information's there, all over the place. I know where to find it. We even did some of it on the computer course, just for exercises."

"So you know where to go, how to do it?"

"Hold on a minute. I know some of the basics, have a few ideas. I'm not making any promises. This was in Oz, remember, but a few of the people were digging for family roots back here. With a bit of legwork and an Internet connection you can dig up quite a lot."

"And you'd be willing to do that?"

"I've got a few days before my new job starts, though I'm heading down to Cambridge the day after tomorrow to take up my new digs. But yeah, I think I'd be able to get something going in the meantime."

"Terrific. I'll pay any expenses, of course."

She gave me a stern glance. "You don't need to do that. I've got money. Particularly since I sold you the house. Besides, if I'm doing this, I'm working *with* you, not for you."

I held my hands up. "Sorry," I said. "I didn't mean to offend you."

She gave me another long look, then nodded. "None taken," she said.

"THIS IS WHY I CHOSE STAITHES," LOUISE SAID AS WE MADE OUR WAY THROUGH the small cliff-top cemetery. "I wanted to see where Grandma was buried, and it was the closest place with a decent cottage for rent."

We were somewhere between Staithes and Redcar. The graveyard lay at the end of a rough track a couple of miles from the road. There was nothing else around except the tiny church and a cleared area for parking beside it. Louise and I walked along the overgrown path, the wind off the North Sea howling around our exposed ears. It reminded me of St. Mary's graveyard in Whitby, where Dracula had landed, though this one was much smaller and more isolated. There were no 199 steps, and the church wasn't open to visitors. The door was padlocked against vandals.

Many of the tombstones were eighteenth or nineteenth century, and over the years the salt wind had stripped the names from those facing the sea. They were dark monoliths overgrown with moss and lichen. The newer ones were easier to read, though they were overgrown, too, and Grace's simple stone stood angled slightly away from the sea. There were windblown flowers on the grave, no doubt from one of Louise's previous visits, but nothing else. The inscription was simple: GRACE ELIZABETH FOX, NOVEMBER 15, 1912 TO APRIL 23, 1953. RIP. Underneath was written OH FOR THE TOUCH OF A VANISHED HAND / AND THE SOUND OF A VOICE THAT IS STILL. Tennyson. It brought a lump to my throat and the wind made my eyes water.

"Who chose this particular cemetery?" I asked

"No idea," said Louise. "I wasn't even born in 1982. I imagine Dad made inquiries, found out where she came from, and this is what they offered. Maybe it wasn't every churchyard would take a body transplanted from a prison cemetery?"

"I suppose not," I said. I looked at the squat stone church and wondered if Grace had ever had any connection with the place. Nobody had mentioned that she had been religious at all, though I assumed the Fox family went to church in Richmond, like most prominent local families did back then. Grace was hardly that much of a rebel that she would fly in the face of that convention. She would probably have paid lip service, at least.

I pulled my collar tight around my throat. The wind was sharp and seemed to get in between every seam and button. "Want to go?" Louise asked.

I looked again at the simple stone, then out to sea, the churning gray waters, the dark clouds of a storm massing on the horizon, and nodded.

18

FRIDAY, FEBRUARY 13, 1942

TODAY THE ORDER CAME DOWN FOR ALL THE REMAINING SISTERS TO EVACU-
ate the hospital. I could not believe that we were being asked to
abandon our patients, though I know the civilian nurses and the
VADs will do their best to care for them until the Japanese arrive.
Then, who knows? Perhaps they will be killed. I tried to do my rounds
one last time, mopping brows, stroking hands, administering morphia, but it was too hard in the end, and I could not go on.

We were collected at midday, allowed only one small suitcase each,
and taken to the Cricket Club. Most of the senior members of the services were there, the Matrons, and our Home Sister from the Alexandra. There were about fifty of us in all, including some Indian nurses.
At four o'clock, we were taken by ambulances to the Naval Dockyard.
The smell of untreated sewage was all around us. Near the docks, I saw
a man drive a Hispano-Suiza into the sea so the Japanese could not

take it. I made sure my journal was secure and waterproofed in its oilskin around my neck. I would hate to lose it now. It has become like another friend to me.

There was an air raid at the docks while we were in the launches heading for our ships, and the Japanese machine-gunned us. They carried on attacking us even after we had boarded the ship, with wave after wave of aircraft. Several people were killed or wounded, and bomb splinters killed two civilian nurses and destroyed one of the lifeboats. I have never experienced anything as terrible or as terrifying as this before, but there was no time to dwell on it. We had work to do. Even before we left the harbor, we were already up to our elbows in blood, bandaging wounds while the children cried and the injured groaned in agony around us in the mingled smells of burning oil, cordite, and sewage.

We finally set sail at about seven o'clock. As I look back from our ship, the SS *Kuala*, I can see Singapore in ruins and flames. Singapore, the city that had seemed so beautiful only months ago, with its endless sunshine, blue skies, palm trees, busy markets, beautiful green parks and golf courses, and the white wedding-cake elegance of its buildings. Now filthy black smoke from the burning oil reserves fills the air, and artillery flashes light up the evening sky. There are hundreds of us crowded together on this small ship, mostly women and children. We are dirty, frightened, bedraggled, and heartbroken, and we have no idea what will become of us.

SATURDAY, FEBRUARY 14, 1942

St. Valentine's Day. Hard to believe it could be such a harbinger of doom. We awoke at dawn to find ourselves at anchor next to the *Tien Kwang* in the lea of a small island, having sailed through the night to avoid detection. I knew we could not be far away from Singapore, as this old ship does not move very fast. One of the officers we had nursed in the Alexandra Hospital offered Brenda and me a camp bed on the officers' deck, so we passed a reasonably comfortable night, though it was terribly hot and humid. We have little but the clothes we are wearing, and they are constantly soaked with sweat. Fresh water is strictly rationed.

At about eight o'clock this morning, the Japanese aircraft appeared, and suddenly there was an almighty explosion, and smoke and fire burst out everywhere. People were running around the deck screaming, mothers trying to find their children amidst the smoke and chaos, the wounded writhing and screaming in agony, the decks slippery with blood.

The SS *Kuala* was sinking fast, listing to the stern, and I heard a distant voice coming through the chaos, giving the order to abandon ship. I could not find Brenda in the crowds and the oily smoke, so I jumped. We were close to an island, but the currents were flowing in the opposite direction, and I could see people being swept out to sea, helplessly waving their arms and screaming for help, then going under the waves. There was nothing I could do for them. I knew that Brenda was a strong swimmer, and that if she made it off the ship she would have a good chance.

The crew tossed life belts and everything that would float over the side, and people were clinging to whatever bits and pieces they could find. The lifeboats were full. I swam as strongly as I could against the current. Severed arms and legs bobbed on the water's surface, along with dead fish, and kept bumping into me as I swam by. Once I saw a woman's head floating, its eyes bulging. I worried that the sharks might get me, but I realized that they had probably been scared away for the moment by the bombs.

The Japanese aircraft attacked again and strafed us in the water with their machine guns. I could never have imagined that anyone could be so cruel. I do not think I have ever hated anyone as much in my life as I hated them at that moment. Didn't they know we were just defenseless women and children, the wounded and the sick? We were struggling for our lives in shark-infested waters, against strong currents, and they were firing their machine guns at us.

I was lucky. Like Brenda, I am a strong swimmer. I struggled on and found space in a lifeboat. We rowed hard against the current to the shore. Behind us, we could just see the last of the SS *Kuala* sinking under the waves. The *Tien Kwang* was already gone. The shore was too steep and rocky for us to land, so we continued around the island until we were lucky enough to find a beach on the other side.

When we got there, I staggered out of the boat and onto the sand and collapsed, exhausted. My legs were wobbly, my arms ached, and I felt dizzy. I just lay there for a while staring into the burning sky, gasping for breath. It had all happened so quickly, yet it had felt like an eternity, too.

I quickly realized that I was half naked. I had shed most of my outer clothing when I was swimming, to prevent the weight of it from adding to the current's pull, but I was relieved to feel my oilskin still around my neck. The others from the lifeboat flopped on the sand all around me, many of them bleeding from bullet or shrapnel wounds. There had been about nine hundred people altogether on those two ships, I thought, and I wondered how many were left. I could hear the aircraft continuing to strafe the survivors, but we were on the other side of the island, and I could not see them.

That situation did not last long. It was a small island, and the Japanese decided to give us one more bombing before they left. Some of the bombs exploded quite close to us, and afterward my ears were ringing, and I noticed that I was bleeding from a deep cut on my arm. I tore a strip from what was left of my underwear and used it as a bandage.

As soon as I had got my breath back and listened to make sure the aircraft had gone, I got to work and started examining the other survivors around me. One or two were beyond help, but many just had minor wounds or concussions. The poor babies were crying, and some of the little children were wandering around calling for their mothers.

After ten or fifteen minutes of trying to create some order out of the chaos, I found Brenda. She was stunned and had a nasty gash on her forehead, which would require stitches, but otherwise she was all right. I hugged her, and she revived quickly enough. She told me that she had clung to a mattress until she came close enough to one of the lifeboats to climb onboard.

So here we are, marooned on Pompong Island, as one of the Malayan women tells us. With Brenda's help, I found some more sisters and two doctors, and together we did the best we could for the injured and dying. Brenda thinks there are about five hundred of us here altogether, which means that we lost almost half our number in the attacks.

All we want now is for the Japanese to stay away and let us sleep, but there is still much to be done while the daylight is still with us. Those who have searched already say there is no food on the island and only one small freshwater spring. We are still managing to salvage quite a lot from the ships, including a chest containing some of the crew's work clothes, though I do not find the seaman's uniform someone gave me very becoming, and it is far too large for me. Still, it covers up what needs to be covered up, I suppose, and it is better than running around in my knickers, which were all I had left to wear!

As far as food is concerned, there is not much but a few tins of bully beef, which will not go far when shared by five hundred people. We have one barrel of water. Short of Jesus coming to perform one of his magic tricks, we do not stand much of a chance of surviving more than a few days. And the Japanese know we are here. As regards medicine and medical equipment, we found a few basic first-aid kits, and that is all. At least I have been able to stitch Brenda's wound. I read *Robinson Crusoe* as a child, but I never thought I would find myself in such a situation as he did! I must stop now. There is much to do.

DECEMBER 2010

There were two numbered music files on the DVD Louise had given me, and I was curious as to what they could be. Assuming my old Mac-Book had the software necessary to play them, I selected the first one. I heard tinny, distant piano chords that sounded only vaguely familiar, as if from a tune I recognized but was not used to hearing played on a piano. Even though it had probably been cleaned up by the computer software, the recording was still scratchy and sounded faraway, recorded at some distance from the piano.

Then, all of a sudden, came the voice, sounding closer, more intimate, and surprisingly pure. Immediately I knew what it was: "*Vissi d'arte, vissi d'amore . . .* ," the famous aria from Puccini's *Tosca*. It was Grace singing. It had to be, I knew, even though I had never heard her voice before. She must have gone into one of those make-your-own-recording places, the sort Elvis Presley had used to record "My Happiness" for his mother's birthday. It would have been acetate, or a 78 rpm pressing, I supposed, and Louise must somehow have transferred it to her computer, then onto to the DVD.

When the aria had finished, I played it again and concentrated on the voice. Grace wasn't a great technical singer. Good, but not great. Her voice was strong and certainly had timbre and character, but "Vissi d'arte" has some tough dramatic moments, some powerful high notes to be hit and held. While Grace didn't always hit them from above—she was a natural mezzo, not a soprano, which the role called for—and while her voice sometimes seemed to strain and tremble over a phrase, she handled most of the song in its dramatic context with great sensitivity and skill, I thought. Interpretation was her forte, along with emotion: "I never harmed a living soul. / With secret hand / I helped relieve as much misfortune as I could."

The second song was less taxing and much simpler, but it drove straight to the heart. It was "Dido's Lament" from Purcell's *Dido and Aeneas*, the aria Queen Dido sings when Aeneas leaves her, with its keening call of "Remember me, Remember me," lingering long after the music has finished. I remembered Wilf telling me about the school production, of his hearing Grace sing it live to a similar piano accompaniment. The performance was everything it should be: simple and moving. I found that I had goose bumps all over me and tears in my eyes when it was over, and I didn't want to play it again. Not that night. It was time for a film, something light years away from Dido's or Grace's tragic tale—*Here We Go Round the Mulberry Bush*, perhaps—then to bed.

IT WAS NOW OVER A WEEK SINCE HEATHER HAD DROPPED HER BOMBSHELL, AND I hadn't heard a thing from her. I had tried to phone her a couple of times at work and on her mobile, but she never answered, and she didn't return my messages. I wondered if she'd gone away for a while, or if, perhaps, she was deliberately avoiding me while she extricated herself from her marriage to Derek. Maybe she was just plain busy.

Moving house was a hell of a job, even without the emotional upheaval Heather must be going through. Perhaps she just needed to be left alone for a while. I felt for her, but there was nothing I could do. I hoped she would join us for Christmas—my invitation had been only half in jest, but the way things were going, I might not get the chance before then to invite her properly.

Two days after my visit to Staithes and to Grace's graveside, late in the afternoon while I was in the living room reading my printout of Grace's war journal as the darkness drew in on Kilnsgate, my telephone rang. Thinking it was Louise with some news about Grace's illegitimate child, I snatched it up immediately, without even a glance at the caller ID, but, to my surprise, it was Heather.

"Chris," she said. "How are things?" Her voice sounded weary and slightly husky.

"I'm fine. It's you I was worried about. I was just thinking about you."

"That's sweet of you. It's all done."

"What?"

"Gone. Moved. All my worldly goods. There's nothing of interest to me back at the old homestead now."

"So how are you, really?"

"Really? You expect me to tell you over the telephone?"

"I'm not doing anything."

"Me, neither. I took the week off work."

"So come by, if you like. I've got wine in the fridge."

She paused. "Okay," she said finally. "That might be just the ticket. See you soon."

I wondered if I had made a mistake in inviting her to the house as I did a quick tidy up of the living room, made sure I had a decent Chablis chilling, and opened an Aussie Shiraz for myself. Of course, being November, it was dark by teatime when I heard Heather's car pull up. I already had a nice fire burning in the living room, and after hanging up her winter coat and long scarf, I took her through and brought the wine. She certainly looked as if she had been through the wringer, though I could tell that she had made an effort to cover the pain and lack of sleep with a little makeup. I could have no idea how much it hurt to have your husband run off with a younger woman, but I was determined not to appear oversolicitous or pitying. We were grown-ups. These things happen. They'd happened to me, too, before Laura. We got through them somehow, anyhow, and we kept on going. I very much doubted that Heather was here because she wanted tea and sympathy, or someone to sit and talk to about her failed marriage. And if she wanted to brood alone, she could easily have stayed at her Convent apartment and done that. She had no doubt had plenty of opportunity over the past week.

Heather quickly made herself at home, kicking her shoes off and stretching out on the sofa, swirling her wine. I had put on a Tony Bennett CD of Christmas songs, and it seemed to harmonize well with the log fire and the winter dark beyond the windows. No snow, yet, though.

"How's the convent?" I asked.

Heather wrinkled her nose. "Strict. I've got a curfew."

"No, seriously."

"It's comfortable enough. A nice apartment, plenty of room. You must come and see it. Charlotte's been clucking around me like a mother hen. She even brought a casserole over the other evening. She's driving me crazy. What have you been up to?"

I told her a little about Louise, the journal, and the box of Grace's stuff.

"Should I be jealous?" she asked. "Of Louise King, I mean, not the ghost."

"There's nothing to be jealous of."

She was half-lying, propped at a rather precarious angle, and when she shifted position, she spilled a little wine on her dress. Luckily it was white wine. I brought a serviette over to her, which she took and dabbed at the spot. When she handed it back to me, I held on to her hand, and when I felt a gentle tug, I leaned down and kissed her. It was tender at first, like the kiss in the car that night after the Bonfire Night party at Charlotte's, but as it continued, it grew more passionate, more probing. We let the crumpled serviette drop and I took her wineglass from her hand and set it on the table beside the sofa. Then I knelt and we continued kissing. I touched her cheek, her hair, ran my hand over her breasts, her stomach; she moved beneath my touch, hooked her hand around my neck, and pulled me to her fiercely.

I don't know how it all happened; everything was a bit of a blur. There was no more thinking, flirting, just a flurry of urgent need and desire that left a trail of clothes across the hall and up the stairs, where we lay in my bed, sweaty, breathless, entangled, sometime later, the mutual need satisfied for the moment, the thinking returning.

Heather spoke first. "I suppose that was a recipe for disaster," she said.

"Oh, come on, it wasn't that bad."

She nudged me in the ribs. "You know what I mean."

"Yes," I said. "So what do we do now?"

"We don't have to do anything," Heather said. "We could just lie here."

"And after that?"

"We can do it again. I've never been one to tremble in the jaws of disaster."

I ran my hand over her bare arm and shoulder, so smooth, so warm. She had freckles there, too. "You know," I said, "I almost hate to say it, but I'm glad we're not having an affair. I mean, technically."

"Me, too," she said, turning to prop herself up on one elbow and face me. "Far too sordid and messy." She pushed her hair out of her face. "Chris, I'm not stupid. I know you're not looking for commitment. Neither am I. Can't we just let it be what it is?"

I stroked her hair. "Of course. Whatever it is. I'm not making any demands. I'm not running away, either." It was silly talk, the kind of thing you say to justify what you've just done, when you realize you've fallen off the edge of a cliff and your legs and arms are spinning useless circles in the air. Call me a fatalist, but we had as little choice about where we went now as we'd had when we first met. But somehow it helps to say things like, "Let's see where it leads us" or "Let it be what it is." It gives the illusion of control, or at least of understanding. There were only two things we could do: one was to stop seeing each other, and we obviously weren't going to do that; and the other was to continue to let ourselves get more and more entangled in each other's needs and desires until one of us had had enough. To fall in love. Oh, we could play it cool, only see each other on Wednesdays, see other people, all the usual evasions, but that was really what it came down to for me. Love or flight.

Heather lay on her back and put her hands behind her head. "It's been so strange these past few days. I've been mostly on my own for the first time in years, and enjoying it. No dinner to get ready. No household responsibilities. I'm afraid the Convent flat is already a tip. I haven't done anything in the way of housework. No vacuuming, no dishes, no washing. I'm down to my last pair of knickers and I'm not sure I even know where they are right now."

I laughed. "I think you're entitled to let things go. For a while, at least. Till you can't find your way around the place anymore for the piles of old newspapers."

She slapped my chest. "It won't get that bad. I couldn't live like that. I don't even read newspapers at the flat. And I can always wash out a pair of knickers. But you know what I mean. Really. I'd forgotten how much I used to enjoy watching what I wanted on TV, not doing something if I didn't feel like it, or just sitting and reading with my legs curled up and no distractions. I read my first whole book in years, Christina Jones, a real guilty pleasure, and I even had a pizza delivered the other night. I ate most of it, too."

"Ah, the joys of single life. Is it official yet?"

"It is as far as I'm concerned. Charlotte's handling the legal details. I haven't been out telling the world, though, yet, if that's what you mean. Not even my closest friends. It's not exactly something I'd want to employ a skywriter to advertise. They'll find out soon enough, anyway, and the sympathetic phone calls will start coming in, even though I don't want sympathy. Derek and I were finished a long time ago, long before I even met you, so you needn't even think of getting big headed enough to blame yourself for any of this. It turns out he's been having this affair for a couple of years, made quite a fool of me, really, and it'll be all over town soon enough. Last week was my honeymoon period with myself, and I think I'll be happy with me. I'm sorry I didn't return your calls. I wanted to. I thought about you a lot. But somehow I knew we'd end up like this. Who did we think we were fooling? It's not that I didn't want it, but it just seemed too soon, and I . . . Besides, there was too much turmoil, so much to organize. Does that sound weird?"

"Not at all. I'm just glad you're here now."

She smiled. "Unlike you, I do have one demand, though." Her hand started to move down under the sheet. "I know you're an old man and all that, but do you think you could manage to get it up just one more time, then we can go downstairs, and you can make me dinner, pour me another large glass of wine, and tell me everything about Louise King and Grace Fox's box of goodies?"

"I might be able to manage all that, despite my advanced years," I said, and leaned over toward her.

"So let me get this straight," Heather said much later, almost lost in the folds of my dressing gown, back by the fireside with another glass of wine, her legs curled under her. "You've got Grace Fox's granddaughter running around the country trying to find out whether Grace had an illegitimate child who would be . . . what would he be?"

"Louise's uncle."

"That's creepy."

"A bit."

"And this is because . . . ?"

"It could have something to do with the murder. If it was a boy. If he was the one in uniform she was with the week before it happened."

"That's a lot of ifs. Why should it be him, and what could it have to do with the murder?"

"I don't know. One thing at a time."

"Gee," she said. "You detectives. I don't know how you do it. Have you heard anything from her yet?"

"No. These things take time. Besides, she's got her new job to deal with." I poured myself more Shiraz. The pasta sauce was simmering in the kitchen and I had just put the penne on. We were both starving. David Fray was playing Schubert in the background.

"You really *don't* believe Grace did it, do you?" Heather said.

I shook my head.

"And what if you find out she did?"

"Then I hope I'll accept the truth if I have to. But at least, by then, I'll have made damn sure I know it *is* the truth. Right now, I don't believe it."

Heather looked at me as one might regard an exasperating child. "Come here," she said eventually, smiling and reaching out her hand.

I went. As I bent to kiss her, she ducked sideways and whispered in my ear. "Is that bloody pasta you promised ready yet? My stomach thinks my throat's been cut."

"Message received loud and clear," I said, and went through to the kitchen.

HEATHER DIDN'T STAY THE NIGHT. I THINK SHE WAS STILL ENJOYING HER NEW home and her own company, and I was certainly getting used to mine. Let things develop as they would, I thought, wincing at my own clichés, at their own pace. I liked Heather a lot, enjoyed her company, and she had also turned out to be a compatible partner in bed, but neither of us wanted to give up our freedom or our solitude yet. And both of us were still carrying too much pain around with us, however we might try to mask it.

I felt that I was only just getting over losing Laura. The first few months I had been far too consumed by grief and guilt to think in terms of being "single" or enjoying my "freedom," but over my time at Kilnsgate, I was coming to see what these things meant, that there was a future without Laura. It didn't mean that I loved her memory any the less, or that I didn't miss her as much, but she had told me herself that my life had to go on without her and move in new directions, and of course, it did. Laura was right, as usual.

I cleared away the dinner plates, put the dishes in the dishwasher, poured another glass of Shiraz, and went back to Grace's journal, the fire crackling, the wind rattling the panes, bare branches scraping against the upstairs windows. I angled the standing light as best I could and put on my drugstore glasses. Grace's handwriting, tiny as it was, was neat and for the most part legible, though I stumbled on one or two of the place names. She certainly had hit all the high spots.

The bare details of her account said very little about the terrible ordeal she had been through. That was the stuff of nightmares. She described most events, however terrible, in a straightforward style, showing about as much emotion as she had at her trial, simply detailing what happened, what she did and what she saw—though I could tell how affected she was by the horror of it all. At several points in her narrative, I will admit without shame that I had to pause to wipe away my tears, and perhaps that was due all the more to her sense of restraint and lack of graphic detail. For someone gifted, or cursed, with an imagination like mine, it wasn't too difficult to fill in the spaces between the lines with pictures. My movie-obsessed mind couldn't help but flesh out the brief, fleeting images, search for the structure, the narrative arc, the musical score, even.

To say that I was stunned and surprised by Grace's account of her wartime experiences is a grave understatement. Like most people, I suppose I knew there were nurses in the war, but I never really thought about the horrors of their job, what they experienced. I never gave them much thought at all. Grace's story made me realize how we have simply overlooked the courage and suffering of women during wartime. There are exceptions, celebrated heroines, such as Florence Nightingale, Gladys Aylward, and Edith Cavell, but on the whole they are a forgotten army. They suffered many of the same hardships as their male counterparts, the same fears of being blown to bits by a stray shell or a bomb, or hit by a sniper's bullet, the same fear of capture and imprisonment, as many were. And, for women, there was also the deep-rooted fear of what traditionally happens at the hands of male conquerors. Grace had seen it all, horrors I could barely begin to imagine, and throughout it all she had kept her humanity.

No wonder she never spoke of it to anyone. No wonder she hid her Royal Red Cross. No wonder she often seemed distracted and haunted. No wonder she liked to ride her motorbike like the clappers down the country lanes and make love in the open air with a penniless young artist.

But where did Ernest Fox come into all this? Did he know about it? Did Grace ever tell him or show him her journal? And if so, what did he do or say? Did he offer her comfort and sympathy? Was he jealous of Stephen's kiss? It was my opinion that she hadn't told him the details because she couldn't, and that he hadn't read the journal, that no one had except Grace, her sister, Louise, and me. Grace had kept it hidden in the secret drawer in her escritoire until she handed it over to Felicity.

It remained my strong impression from everything I had heard about him from Wilf and Sam that Ernest Fox was something of a cold fish, and that Grace knew she could find no solace or sympathy in his arms. His coldness, his preoccupation with his job and his status in the eyes of the community had driven Grace to Sam Porter as sure as anything. It was my guess that Ernest wouldn't want a woman who had the stink of the battlefield on her hands. He wanted a pretty, elegant companion in a fine hat hanging on his arm, who could be brought out and admired at functions and balls, but not heard. Never heard. Grace had tried to be that person, but it hadn't worked for her. Nature has a way of making itself known.

The journal kept me up most of the night. I read and reread pages, turned to my favorite composers for relief—to Schubert, Elgar, Shostakovich, Tchaikovsky, Brahms. At one time, I remember getting up and opening a second bottle of Shiraz, which went the way of the first, and slowly my eyes grew heavy from reading and crying behind the inadequate spectacles. I hadn't found any of the answers I'd been looking for in Grace's words—there was little or nothing of a personal nature— only a record of great courage and suffering told with incredible forbearance and self-possession. I knew that I could never have borne a fraction of what Grace had seen, touched, and tried to heal, and it made me think how easy my own life had been, apart from Laura's death, of course. But I had found no answers. Or at least, if I had, I couldn't interpret them.

I finished my wine, took off my glasses, and settled back in the armchair, almost imagining I could hear Grace's laughter as she splashed with her friends on a rare day off in the waves of the South China Sea, while chaos reigned all around. I massaged the bridge of my nose. Fischer-Dieskau was singing "Irrlicht" from Schubert's *Win-*

terreise. Had it been summer, rosy-fingered dawn would have been spreading her array of color across the morning sky when I finally fell asleep, but it was bleak midwinter, and there was nothing outside but the darkness of the night and the coldness of the stars as the last charred log dimmed in the grate and the fire died.

19

Extract from the *Journal of Grace Elizabeth Fox* (ed. Louise King), February 1942, Pompong Island.

SUNDAY, FEBRUARY 15, 1942

THE ONE THING THAT ROBINSON CRUSOE DID NOT HAVE TO CONTEND WITH on his island was the presence of a few hundred other starving, thirsty souls. There have already been several unpleasant skirmishes, and what little order there is appears soon likely to break down as individual needs overcome the needs of the group. The Malayan police officers who survived the shipwreck are doing the best they can to keep order, and one of them has a revolver, which he has already fired into the air, but we cannot go on like this for very long. Surely someone will discover where we are and rescue us before the Japanese return in force and kill us all?

MONDAY, FEBRUARY 16, 1942

At least someone knows we are here now! This morning a small boat came from a neighboring island and brought us fruit and water.

Things have become a little more organized. There are quite a few sisters here, and with the help of some of the men, we have built some makeshift beds and put together a small hospital, roofed with palm leaves for shade. We have also drawn up a duty rota. There is talk of escape to Sumatra, where we can possibly find a British ship to take us home, but it still seems a very long way away. First, someone must let the Dutch authorities know that we are here, and that we are still alive, and all the time the Japanese must be getting closer to conquering the whole South China Sea. The heat and humidity are quite debilitating, and during the sunlight hours we spend as much time in the shade as possible. Now the sun is setting in the ocean, and it is a beautiful sight in bands of vermillion, purple, gold, and burnt orange. I remember how I loved the way the twilight lingers in Singapore, the soft balmy evening air. It was my favorite time of day, and I liked to sit outside on the veranda with my Singapore sling, if I could, listening to the cicadas as the glow of the light slowly faded to darkness and the stars came out. Under other circumstances, people might regard this place as an island paradise.

TUESDAY, FEBRUARY 17, 1942

We are rescued! Last night, under cover of darkness, a small cargo ship called the *Tanjong Pinang* came to rescue us. They already had some survivors picked up from another island, but the captain said they could take all our walking wounded, along with as many women and children and sisters as they had room for. The off-duty sisters were the lucky ones, and those who were on duty were to stay behind with the seriously wounded until more ships came. Brenda and I were both off duty, and while it was sad to leave our patients and our friends on the island, we knew that they would be all right, and this seemed to be the fairest way of organizing things. It was very difficult moving the patients onto the *Tanjong Pinang* in complete darkness, though the moonlight did help. With rafts, small boats, and pulleys, we managed to get them all onboard before dawn and sailed off while it was still dark. I think, in all, there must be about two hundred of us. Brenda and I waved farewell to Pompong as we set sail toward Java, and freedom!

DECEMBER 2010

I realized that Christmas was fast approaching, and my guests would be arriving soon. I still had presents to buy. The rest was done—tree, lights, tinsel, decorations, turkey—and I was expecting a large delivery of Champagne and other fine wines within the next couple of days. But there remained the dreaded Christmas shopping. The weather forecast called for a major snowstorm within the next twenty-four hours, so taking advantage of the first clear day since I'd driven to see Louise in Staithes, I decided to head for York and get it over and done with.

The roads were busy with other people who had the same idea, and I hit a long line of traffic at the approach to the York ring road. I still hadn't heard from Louise since my visit, I thought as I edged forward inch by inch, and I wondered if she had even had the time or inclination to do the background digging she had offered to do. I knew that she was moving to Cambridge and starting a new job, so life would be busy for her. There was no sense in pushing her. She would call in her own good time. I could hardly go to Cambridge and chase her down. Maybe I would send an e-mail, though, if I didn't hear from her before my guests arrived. I was anxious to know whether I was right about Grace's illegitimate child, and there wouldn't be much time to busy myself with such things during the holiday season. I made it to the Park & Ride at last and caught the bendy bus just before it pulled out.

If I had thought the roads were busy, the streets of York were even more so. It was only a Tuesday, but the Christmas shoppers were out in force. The whole city center was strung with lights and drenched in seasonal atmosphere. Here and there a Salvation Army band collected money, a Santa Claus rang his bell and ho-ho-hoed, or a choir of singers dressed in Victorian garb collected for various other charities. After a short while, I began to realize there was nowhere you could stand in the whole city center and not hear Christmas music.

Every time I go to York, I make a point of visiting the Minster, not because I'm religious, but because it's a beautiful building. I have done the full guided tour once, but it's not the crypt, the sacristy, the rose window, or the carvings of the kings of England that draw me back time after time, magnificent as they all are, but a very simple little thing that hardly anybody ever notices.

It is hard to spot, way up on the ceiling above the nave, but if you look hard enough, you can just make out the soles of two feet. That is how the Ascension would appear to someone from below, of course, so that is how the artist painted it, Christ's feet disappearing in the sky. Something about it tickled my fancy, so I always went to see it.

As good fortune would have it, today the choir was practicing for a Christmas concert, so I stayed and listened to "Once in Royal David's City" and "O Little Town of Bethlehem." The harmonies in that vast Gothic space of stone and shadows were exquisite. Goethe spoke of architecture as "frozen music," and I think I know what he meant. It was with an even lighter heart that I lit a candle for Laura, out of pure superstition, just because I was there and I was thinking of her, then I went back out to face the throng.

Even with the crowds, I had finished most of my shopping by lunchtime, just a few small presents for my guests from Molton Brown, HMV, Lakeland, Waterstones, and one of the secondhand bookshops down Fossgate. Feeling hungry, I found a table in Plunkets on High Petergate, between the Minster and the old Roman wall, and ordered a gourmet burger with wild mushrooms and Brie, and a glass of red wine. Piped Christmas songs played, and a fire crackled in the hearth. Sometimes in York, with its narrow streets, Roman walls, and ancient stone buildings, you could easily fancy yourself thrown back to Victorian times, or even earlier, medieval days. Looking out of the window fringed with fake snow, I almost expected Tiny Tim to come wobbling down the street on his crutches.

As I sat sipping my wine, basking in the glow of my visit to the Minster and a successful shopping expedition, I realized that this odd feeling I was experiencing was happiness. Simple happiness at being alive. It was something I hadn't experienced in a long time, certainly not since Laura's death, and it came for no special reason, and definitely not from any sense of accomplishment or achievement. After all, I hadn't finished my piano sonata, hadn't found out the truth about Grace Fox, hadn't just completed the best film score I had ever written, hadn't won another Oscar and given a brilliant acceptance speech.

Nothing. I had simply walked around a crowded historic city, stood for a while listening to a choir sing in the old Minster, and had a couple of sips of wine, but I felt like Ebenezer Scrooge on Christmas morning, when he realizes he's still alive—the Alastair Sim version, of course. I managed to stop myself from cackling and dancing a mad jig, but that was how I felt.

After a short walk on the Roman wall, I made my way back to the bus stop. As I waited in the long queue for my bus back to the Park & Ride, I checked the e-mails on my iPhone. There was one from Louise, and with mounting excitement, I opened it. I was disappointed when it simply read "Call me" and listed her phone number in Cambridge. The bus was coming, so I decided I would call her as soon as I got home.

"So what you're telling me is that there was no child, and this mysterious young soldier is just as mysterious now as he was before?"

"I suppose that's it, yes," said Louise. "Sorry."

I had been so sure of it, the evasion, the "nervous disorder," the visit to the distant aunt. It was so typical of its time. Grace had clearly been a romantic and headstrong girl, had committed an indiscretion, and her parents had married her off to Ernest, an older family friend, in the hopes of settling her down. "So Grace really did have a nervous breakdown?"

"A minor one, yes. Of course, the term covered any number of disorders in those days. I don't know any details. It was a miracle I found out at all, but—"

"Yes, you said. Her aunt's neighbor's son is still living next door. Was he able to tell you anything else?"

"He was only a child at the time. He just remembered being told to play quietly because there was a lady who was poorly staying next door."

"So he wouldn't have been old enough to know whether she was pregnant or not?"

"She wasn't. I checked all the records, and there was no record of a baby born to anyone living in that house at that time. I also checked up on my grandmother's home address in Saltburn and, just for good luck, Thomas Murray's. Nothing."

"Maybe they sent her somewhere else to have the child. Maybe they didn't register the birth under her name. Maybe—"

"Chris," she said with long-suffering patience. "Why can't you just accept it? Grace Fox did *not* bear Thomas Murray's child. There would be *some* record of it somewhere, and believe me, I've spent a lot of time combing the records. Time I should have been spending settling in at work, I might add."

"I'm sorry, Louise. Really. I do appreciate all you've done. Thanks. It's just so . . . frustrating. Now I'm back to square one." I couldn't hide the disappointment in my voice. All my speculations had come to nothing, my house of cards fallen before it was built. The pure happiness I had felt earlier in the day was fast becoming a distant memory.

"Not quite," Louise said. "You know now that he wasn't her son. Who does that leave?"

"It could be anyone. A stranger."

"No. It was someone she knew. He was an acquaintance, perhaps someone she hadn't seen in a while. Grandmother might have been many things, but she was at least discreet, no matter what some of those gossips tried to insinuate. She would not have gone walking in public in the town center with a young man if she didn't know him, and she certainly wouldn't have done it if it had been anything other than an innocent acquaintance. Think about it, Chris. You're letting your disappointment skewer your better judgment."

She was right, of course. And it wouldn't have been the first time. "I know," I said. "Sorry. Thanks for everything you've done."

"Think nothing of it. I want to know the truth as much as you do. I haven't finished with all this yet. She was *my grandmother.* Remember, *I've* read her journal, too, and I don't believe a woman like she was could have done what they said she did. Good-bye, Chris. Got to go now. Keep in touch."

I hung up the phone and glanced over at the Christmas tree by the window. Louise had been out the first time I rang, so I had busied myself by decorating it instead of pacing up and down and wearing out the carpet. The lights twinkled, and the tinsel sparkled as it fluttered in the draft from the window frame. I didn't have many ornaments, but for next year I would get the old ones out of storage in Los Angeles, if I could bear to see them again by then. Laura and I had collected them over the years on our travels, and each one held a particular memory.

I noticed that it was snowing outside and checked the time. Heather would be arriving in half an hour, and I hadn't started on dinner yet. Still, it wouldn't take long to throw something together. As I salted the water and put it on to boil, I wondered why I hadn't waited until later to trim the tree. It was something Heather and I could have done together. Then I realized it was far too soon for something as intimate as that, something Laura and I had shared every year we'd been together. I always complained about fixing the tree in the stand—they never seemed to be quite adequate for the job—and she always carefully unwrapped each decoration, all our memories. What kind of person was I? I could take the woman to bed, but I couldn't decorate a Christmas tree with her. Goddamn it, I wondered, my eyes stinging, when would the bloody pain go away. I only half-blamed my tears on the onions I was chopping.

20

Extract from the *Journal of Grace Elizabeth Fox* (ed. Louise King), February 1942, at sea.

WEDNESDAY, FEBRUARY 18, 1942

I AM NOW IN SUCH DESPAIR THAT I CAN HARDLY BRING MYSELF TO WRITE. I doubt that anybody will ever read this journal, anyway, as I am sure it will soon be at the bottom of the sea along with its writer.

I had thought things had been as bad as they could get, but I was wrong. We spent all day yesterday sailing toward Java, tending the wounded, as usual, changing dressings, handing out rations, trying to ease the pain with what little morphia we have whenever we could. It was a tiring day, and by sundown we were ready for sleep. The *Tanjong Pinang* is a small ship, and all the passengers had to go down in the hold, but in reward for our hard work, the captain let the sisters sleep on deck, where it was cooler and less crowded.

Just as we were settling down to sleep, at about half past nine, we were blinded by searchlights, followed by two almighty explosions. After that it was chaos. I seemed to be unscathed, but all around me, people were dead or dying. Brenda could walk, but she had a ragged wound down her right side, and she was losing a lot of blood. I bound it up as best I could with strips of torn clothing.

The smoke was making breathing difficult, and we could hardly see more than a few inches in front of our eyes. Everywhere we went, we tripped over bodies. I headed for the hold to see what I could do for the women and children down there, but a VAD emerged, covered in blood, and told me it was no use, everybody down there was dead. They had received a direct hit. Nobody knew whether it was a submarine or a gunboat that had attacked us, but it did not matter. The damage was done.

The ship was now listing and sinking so quickly that the only sensible thing to do was jump. I took Brenda by the hand, and together we stepped over the side. The sound of the screams in the dark was terrible, and I thought we would either be sucked down by the ship's sinking, or that we would simply drown before we found any form of flotation.

I kept an eye on Brenda. Even in her weakened state, she was a strong swimmer, and we were far enough away when the ship went down that the suction did not drag us under with it.

The crew had thrown a number of life rafts overboard. Brenda and I managed to get hold of two of these and fasten them together. After that, we went around searching for survivors and managed to get enough to fill the tethered rafts. When there was no room for any more, people clung to the sides, and we drifted away into the night.

I do not know what happened to the others on the ship. I can only believe that most of them are dead. Now it is just after dawn on the following day, and it feels already as if it is going to be a hot one. We have no protection from the sun. We lost two people during the night, both of whom had been clinging to the side of our raft. By morning they had simply disappeared. The children are hungry and crying already, their poor mothers trying in vain to comfort them. There is no comfort. We have no food or water. Brenda has a fever, and the wound in her side looks angry. She will need stitches and antibiotics soon, though, or infection will surely set in. When I look around, I see only the ocean, which, thank heaven, is calm today, and a few small islands dotted about. All we can do is keep trying to head west to Sumatra and hope a friendly ship rescues us before the Japanese find us.

THURSDAY, FEBRUARY 19, 1942

Today the children all went mad.

FRIDAY, FEBRUARY 20, 1942

There was nothing to be done for the children. Heatstroke, festering wounds, starvation, and dehydration took them. We lost them all, toddlers, babes in arms, all of them, and Brenda and I committed their little bodies to the sea in tears. One mother would not let go of her dead baby boy, and there was nothing we could do to make her. Later in the day, when nobody was looking, she slipped overboard with him and they both went under. By the end of the day we had lost three more civilians who had been clinging to the side. Whether they had died, weakened so much, or simply given up the ghost and let go, I do not know, but none of us left had the strength to search for them.

The sun is merciless. We try to cover ourselves as best we can with what scraps of clothing we have left, but it is useless. There is no way to deflect the heat. My head aches and I feel sick most of the time. My skin is hot and dry. I am so thirsty that I think seriously about scooping up a palm full of seawater. Surely a small amount could not do any harm? The daylight also exposes us to any Japanese aircraft that might pass overhead, so we have many reasons to embrace the darkness, though it is in the dark that my fears are at their worst. We have not seen any sharks yet, but they are surely nearby. They would not miss the opportunity of gorging themselves on the excess of food. I have not seen any other rafts or boats. We are alone, a painted ship upon a painted sea.

SATURDAY, FEBRUARY 21, 1942

Brenda went over last night. She was sleeping beside me, but this morning her place was bare. She slipped beneath the waves during the night, and I did not even awaken. Maybe I rolled over and pushed her off? I feel so guilty and so responsible. I should have taken better care of her. I should have held on to her. Why Brenda? Why Brenda and not me?

There are only five of us left alive now, and one of them may not survive until the end of the day. I cannot think that any of us will survive much longer. I wonder why I am still writing this, but I always find some comfort in my oilskin tied securely around my neck.

I am becoming too weak to think clearly. There really is nothing more to say. We are all dying. It is simply a matter of time. Perhaps it would be best for me to follow Brenda. How easy it would be. Some moments, I even wish the Japanese aircraft would come and bomb us. Just one quick bomb would solve everything. When I close my eyes, I am back at Kilnsgate, and there is snow all around. I am building a snowman with Billy, but all of a sudden, it starts to move and melt, and a Japanese soldier comes out of it, snarling, with his bayonet aimed at me. Sometimes I do not know which are worse, the hallucinations or the reality. Sometimes I do not know which is which.

DECEMBER 2010

Just before Christmas, we got a serious dose of winter. Schools, roads, and airports closed, including Heathrow, and the train services came to a standstill. At Kilnsgate, I was cut off from the outside world for a couple of days, though the telephone and Internet still worked. When the snow stopped falling, I was able to persuade a local farmer with a snowplow to come over and dig me out, for a small fortune. I was still worried that my guests wouldn't be able to fly in, though, as Heathrow seemed quite unable to cope with the amount of snow.

The Volvo did okay. I had driven in similar conditions many times in New England, the Midwest, or to Mammoth Lakes, in California, where we had our chalet for the skiing, but there I had winter tires, and somehow things never seemed quite as bad. I was glad I'd already done my Christmas shopping and had bought pretty much everything

I needed. I was a little worried about the wine order, but when I phoned to check, they assured me it would arrive within a day or two, and they proved to be right.

Christmas came and went without any sign of Heather. She had told me on the night she came for dinner before the snow that she didn't think it was a good idea, our spending Christmas together, and that she would visit her parents this year. I suspected that her decision may have had something to do with the tree I had decorated by myself, perhaps making her feel excluded, though I soon realized that was probably fanciful on my part. It was clearly something she had thought about and decided *before* she came over and saw the tree, on which she complimented me.

We had a good dinner that evening before the storms came, laughed a lot, talked about Christmas memories, then made love. I told her I understood her decision to spend Christmas with her family, that she was right. It was too early in our relationship and too soon after her separation for her to be meeting my family and friends. The only regret she had, she told me with characteristic Heather directness, was that she would miss meeting the famous Melissa Wilde. I said we might be able to arrange something after Christmas, depending on everyone's exact schedule, and we left it at that. She didn't stay the night, claiming she wanted to get away before the snow got too deep.

Luckily, Jane and Mohammed and Dave and Melissa all managed to get in okay, though the L.A. flight was delayed nearly ten hours. They had a few days to relax and get over it before Christmas itself, but the weather grew even colder, and any ice that might have melted during the day froze again at night. Even the hot water bottles didn't help. My American guests complained constantly. Except for Mohammed. He had lived in London for a while when he was younger and had got used to the cold. I say "younger," though he was only in his midtwenties now, an intern at Johns Hopkins with, my daughter Jane assured me, "amazing" prospects.

I have to confess that when I first heard Mohammed's name, and that he was a doctor, I expected a rather earnest and disapproving young teetotaller, but he turned out to be a Goons fan with a keen, off-the-wall sense of humor and was not averse to the occasional glass of wine, or to celebrating Christmas with us heathens, for that matter. He was, however, still a member of the medical profession, and I always feel a bit guilty being around doctors when I've had a few drinks. I always imagine that they're ticking off another year with every sip as they look at me. But Mohammed put on a silly hat and pulled crackers with the rest of us. He also ate everything I put in front of him and didn't say no when I pulled out the single malt at the end of the meal. Jane helped me with the dinner, and I was glad of both her help and her company in the kitchen. It made me realize how much I missed her. And Laura. She had her mother's good looks, that was for certain. Jane and Mohammed slept in the big guest bedroom, and neither mentioned anything to me about strange reflections in the mirror.

Mother rang from Graham's on Christmas Day. She'd had a terrible journey, she said, but she was all right now, except there were too many noisy children around. I reminded her that some of them were her own great-grandchildren, but she went on to complain about not understanding the television programs because they were all in French. I gave up on conversation then and just listened. My son, Martin, called later from his in-laws' home in San Francisco and wished us all a Merry Christmas, and the rest of the time the phone remained silent.

We didn't stay in the house all the time, of course. Despite the weather, my guests still insisted on seeing Yorkshire, so I took them to Hawes, Reeth, Castle Bolton, and York. I also wanted to show them the Buttertubs Pass between Wensleydale and Swaledale, and drive them up to Tan Hill for a pub lunch, but that was out of the question. The road conditions were too icy and dangerous, with sheep wandering the unfenced tracks and the occasional chasm on one side or the other. The weather also ruled out the coast, but I think everyone had a good time.

Whenever we went out, say to the Shoulder of Mutton for Sunday lunch, I began to feel like an outsider in Yorkshire all over again. Apart from me, they all had American accents, even Mohammed, and I hadn't so much noticed while I was living over there, but Americans tend to speak rather loudly in public. The whole subject of foreigners abroad is, I know, a contentious one, and in my experience there's not much worse than the Yorkshireman abroad, where nothing is ever quite as good as it is "back 'ome," except the weather, of course. Still, people would stare at us, and it was hard to ignore their occasional expressions of disapproval, such as when Dave questioned why the Brits couldn't even deal with a simple snowstorm, as if someone in the group had told an off-color joke or farted too loudly. I realized that they saw me as part of the offending group. Even my old acquaintances the Wellands smiled thinly and kept their distance.

Melissa certainly put an interesting spin on things, though. Plenty of people had teased Dave when he married her—both had a couple of divorces behind them, and at thirty-five she was quite a few years younger than he was—but it was a true love match. In private, Melissa Packer was an intelligent, down-to-earth, funny, slightly clumsy, and sensible woman, but most people knew her only as Melissa Wilde, from the action films or the sexy siren roles she played on the big screen. She was also gorgeous, and it was all natural, from the pearly white teeth to the firm breasts, glossy back hair, curves, full lips, and long legs. She worked out every day, of course, but there was no surgery involved in Melissa's beauty. She also did her own stunts and had a black belt in karate. Naturally, a lot of people recognized her in public—some had, of course, recently seen her in *Death Knows My Name* at the Station, in which she played the femme fatale—and quite a few jaws dropped. One or two people even came to ask for her autograph, which she obligingly gave.

Perhaps our most interesting evening, though, and the one that spun me off in a whole unforeseen direction on the Grace Fox business, was the evening of our Richmond pub crawl.

"This woman you're obsessing about," said Dave quietly, while we were wedged into a corner of the tiny snug of the Black Lion along with what seemed like a team of rugby players. An acoustic folk group was playing in the dining area, and they had charmed Melissa into singing a number with them. She had made a couple of alt. country albums before the movies took over her life, and she hadn't lost her touch. The audience was rapt. "Love Is Teasin'" had never sounded so good. Even the rugby players were listening. Jane and Mohammed had opted for a quiet evening at home, as they hadn't had much time for themselves lately, and neither was particularly fond of pubs.

I took a long swig of Black Sheep. "Grace Fox," I said. "And I'm not obsessing. I'm just interested, that's all."

"Whatever. Do you think there's a story in it?"

"Do I think there's a story *in* it? It *is* a story, Dave. A terrific one. A fantastic tale. I just don't know the end yet."

"But you know what I mean. Is it a *movie*?"

I did know what he meant. Ever since I had read Grace's journal and seen the photographs, I had been hearing fragments of music that were beginning to coalesce in my mind—I hadn't written anything down yet—and I had come to call it "Grace's Theme." It meant that I was thinking in movie terms, although I knew without even playing it that "Grace's Theme" was also the missing part of my piano sonata, the part that would give it coherence, dimension, and meaning. And if Grace had me thinking about movies, which was totally arse backward, as I'm usually among the last to get involved, then I should have known that Dave, with his cinematic and narrative instincts, wouldn't take long to cotton on.

We had already been to the Turf, the Fleece, and the Buck, and we were slowly making our way toward the market square. Though it was only a few days after Christmas, it was a Thursday night, and the town was jumping, the holiday spirit still in top gear. We left the Black Lion, much to the chagrin of the band, and headed for the Castle Tavern.

"Jesus," said Melissa as we entered the cobbled market square, still strung with Christmas lights. "Those girls are hardly wearing anything at all and it's freezing out here. Look at those heels!" She glanced at me. "Are they hookers, Chris? You never told me Richmond was full of hookers."

"Shush," I said, putting my fingers to my lips. The girls might well be slight and scarcely clad, tottering about on the icy cobbles in high heels, but their boyfriends were big strapping lads, squaddies from Catterick camp, some of them. Still, I'd have backed Melissa in a fight with any one of them. I had got used to the groups of young girls who went around most of the winter in short skirts, skimpy tops, and high heels, but I could see how they might confuse a visitor. "It's an old English tradition," I said. That covered a multitude of eccentricities.

Melissa shivered. "An unhealthy one, I'd say. Are we nearly there yet? I keep thinking I'm going to slip any moment and break my neck."

"We are."

Word must have spread about the group of crazy Americans, because as soon as we entered the pub, the conversations quieted down and people glanced in our direction. It was a mixed crowd, some kids, but quite a few pensioners and middle-aged couples, too. I saw Wilf Pelham sitting with a group of cronies down at the far end, and he waved at me. Forgiven, then. I waved back. I wanted a chat with him, anyway. There was no band, and the piped-in music wasn't too loud to drown out conversations, which soon began to pick up again all around us.

"My shout, I think," said Melissa, with a glance toward the crowded bar and a mischievous smile. "Isn't that what you Brits say?" In only a few days, with a true actor's ability to mimic, she had picked up plenty of British terms and could even manage a fair imitation of the northern accent. Geordie, which you heard a fair bit around Richmond, still defeated her.

"You don't have to," I said. "I'll go if you want."

"Why? It looks like fun. Is it unladylike?" She mocked me, putting her hand on my arm. Then she sloughed off her coat, handed it to Dave, and plunged forward into the crowd. Dave laughed, and we managed to squeeze ourselves on a bench and cadge a stool for Melissa from the next table. If she needed one, that was. She seemed to be in more of a mood to play the house, and I saw her already engaging the people next to her at the bar in conversation. They were clearing a way for her to get served before them as if she were royalty. Such is the magic of the Hollywood star. Or Melissa's charm. Pretty soon she would be playing darts with them. And winning.

She soon came back with the drinks—I'm not sure what kind of beer mine was, but it was in a pint glass and it tasted all right—and perched on the stool. Heather had said she would try to join us at some point in the evening, and I had given her a rough plan of our route. I kept checking for her from the corner of my eye, hoping she would make it. I knew she wanted to meet Melissa, and I was looking forward to seeing *her* again.

As it turned out, she walked into the Castle not long after we'd got there, with that way she had, slinky but not overdone, picking me out almost immediately and smiling at me. She obviously knew some of the people at the bar, because she stopped here and there to say hello or wish them a happy New Year before she joined us. I suppose in her job you got to know the locals.

There wasn't much room, so I jumped up, gave her a quick kiss, and let her have my spot. I introduced her to Melissa and Dave, then said I'd be back in a minute and went to have a word with Wilf. When Heather saw where I was going, she rolled her eyes, but it was an indulgent roll. Then she leaned forward and started chatting animatedly with Melissa, and I was forgotten. Even before I got to Wilf's table, the two of them had gotten up, Heather leading Melissa over to some people clustered around the far end of the bar. In seconds, they were all chatting away like old friends. Pretty soon Melissa would be best friends with everyone in the pub. She was good like that. Dave, left to his own devices, was talking to the middle-aged couple sitting next to him.

"Hello, lad," said Wilf. "Sit yourself down."

I sat and rested the pint on the table. "How are you, Wilf?"

"Fair to middling. When you get to my age you think every little ache and pain's a herald of the end."

"So you haven't got cancer?"

"Not as I know of. Just what they call acid reflux. They stuck that tube down my throat and had a shufti, then gave me a new prescription. Them new pills do the trick."

"I'm glad to hear it."

"Isn't that Melissa Wilde with your friend over there?"

"I'm surprised you recognize her."

"I keep my eyes open and my ears to the ground. " He gave me a mischievous glance. "I went to see *Death Knows My Name* at the Station a while back."

I groaned and put my head in my hands.

"Nay, lad, it weren't so bad. Tha's no Bernard Herrmann, mind you." He studied Melissa, who was talking animatedly with the people Heather had introduced her to. "Good Lord, if I was twenty years younger . . ."

I laughed. "More like fifty, Wilf."

"Hey! None of your lip. I could tell you tales would make your toes curl."

"I'll bet you could. And by the way." I pointed to Dave. "That's her husband over there."

"Then he'd better keep an eye on her, little bloke like that. Some of those lads up there, their reach exceeds their grasp when they've had a few, if you follow my drift."

"I don't think he's got anything to worry about. Dave can take care of himself." So can Melissa, for that matter, I might have added.

"They'll be friends of yours, then, from the movie business?"

"Yes." I told Wilf how I had come to know Dave and Melissa through my work, then we made small talk about Christmas for a while. Wilf had spent the holidays with his daughter and son-in-law in Blackpool until their constant bickering had driven him back home. "I wouldn't bother going at all if it wasn't for the little 'uns," he said. "But a man can't ignore his own grandchildren, can he?"

"No," I said, feeling a bit guilty about not seeing my own grandchild this Christmas.

Someone brought Wilf another pint, and he took a long swig and wiped his lips with the back of his gnarly hand. "So how's your investigation going?"

"It's not really an investigation," I said, feeling rather silly. "Anyway, whatever it is, it seems to have stalled."

"So where do you go now?" Wilf asked.

I shook my head. "I've been reading her journal."

"Journal?"

"Yes." I told him about Louise and Grace's scant possessions. "It's amazing, what she saw, what she did. She was everywhere."

"Aye," said Wilf. "We often forget what role the women played while the men were busy trying to maim and kill each other."

"It makes her seem less likely to have killed anyone as far as I'm concerned."

"Maybe it was a disgruntled patient," Wilf said. "I've told you what a sadistic bastard Old Foxy was."

"So he lacked a good bedside manner. That's not unusual in a doctor, and it's hardly a motive for murder."

"Depends what he did and to whom."

"I'll take it under advisement." I sipped some more beer. "I'm still interested in that young lad in uniform who was with Grace shortly before it happened." I explained about how my original theory had been shot down by Louise King's discoveries.

Wilf scratched his stubbly chin. "All this raking up the past has had me feeling quite nostalgic these past few weeks. You said you got the impression this was an old friend and that he would have been a young lad when the war started?"

"Yes. If she'd had a child in, say, 1931, he would have been about eight then and twenty-one in 1952."

"But she didn't."

"No. I was wrong about that."

"Well, there were lots of young men in uniform then. What with National Service, and the garrison, being so close by."

"Someone from her past? Someone she met during the war, perhaps? The person who saw them mentioned that he had an odd sort of birthmark on his hairline."

Wilf gave me sharp glance. "Are you sure about that? You didn't mention that before."

"Is it important?"

Wilf nodded over toward Heather and Melissa. "I'd keep an eye on them two, if I were you. Yon Frankie Marshall's well over the limit, and he's moving in a bit close to Miss Wilde for comfort."

"They can take care of themselves. What did you mean by asking me if I was sure?"

"Billy," Wilf said

"The evacuee?"

"That's the one. They took him in just after the war started. The government started shipping them down from Tyneside pretty soon that September. He'd have been about seven or eight then. Stopped with the Foxes until around Christmas, then his parents took him back home again."

"Why?"

"No reason. It was the 'Bore War.' Not much happening. Lots of parents took their kids back. Then, of course, after April 1940, when the Germans marched on Norway and Denmark, well . . . things heated up again. Then there was Dunkirk. Anyway, I remember Billy because he came to our school for a while and we used to play with him sometimes. Nice enough lad, but a fish out of water. City boy. Couldn't seem to get a grasp on our country ways. I think his dad managed a shoe shop in Newcastle High Street or something. I remember he had a Geordie accent, and most of us couldn't understand him. Some of the kids used to tease him mercilessly, but he took it all in good sport. He was well enough built, so if he'd wanted to, he could have given one or two of the worst a good thumping, but it wasn't as if they tried to bully him or anything. He was a quiet kid, mostly, as I remember, a bit passive. Very nice lad, though. Nicely dressed. Clean. He must have been very unhappy underneath it all."

"Why?"

"The teasing, the strangeness, being so far from home—or so it must have felt—missing his mum and dad. Not that he let his feelings show. Besides, I can't see that being stuck out at Kilnsgate with old misery-guts Fox could have been a lot of fun, can you?"

"Surely Grace would have been there? And Hetty?"

"I suppose so. Some of the time. Still . . ."

"What happened at Kilnsgate during the war? I seem to be picking up all kinds of bits and pieces, and I can't help but find myself wondering if it had anything to do with what happened later."

"What do you mean?"

"Just the way things seem to connect. Grace meeting this Billy shortly before her husband's death. I mean, she probably hadn't seen him since 1939, when he was only seven, Grace being away overseas for quite a while. You said before that the house was taken over by the military for a while, very hush-hush."

"Oh, aye. Off-limits. You couldn't even get through Kilnsgarthdale from one end to the other. They were tough, surly buggers, too."

"How do you know?"

Wilf grinned. "Well, you don't think we didn't try, do you? Most of the time if kids went prowling around, they understood it was a harmless enough game. I mean, most of the soldiers weren't that much older. It wasn't so long ago they'd been up to the same mischief themselves. They'd usually send you off with a few choice words and a smile on their faces. But not this lot. They were older. And harder. We found a weak spot in the barbed wire once and the sentry found us and pretty much marched us off at gunpoint. I don't think he would have actually shot us, but it was frightening enough."

"Any idea who it was?"

"No. A lot of these units were top secret. They'd come and go, and no one even knew their names, or acronyms, if they had any. As far as I know, none of them came into town to socialize like the regular troops billeted up here."

"But there must have been some speculation?"

"Oh, aye. We all assumed it was Special Operations Executive. A bit James Bond. In fact, I think Ian Fleming even had something to do with them."

That was what Ted Welland had told me, I remembered. "But nobody actually *knew*, or said that was what it was?"

"No."

"And what were they doing here?"

Wilf shrugged. "No idea. Training. Planning. Like I said, you couldn't get near the place."

"Would Billy know anything about it?"

"I can't imagine why. It was after Billy's time. Tell you what, have a word with old Bert Brotherton. No, sorry, he can't help you, he's long gone now, along with his son Fred. Sometimes I forget. Talk to his grandson. He might know something."

"What are you talking about, Wilf?"

"Your neighbors, the farm down the lane, over the hill. It's still in the family, far as I know."

I realized with a guilty start that I hadn't even gone and introduced myself to my neighbors yet. Still, they hadn't come to see me, either.

"What do they know?"

"I've no idea, but it was their farm that had an outbreak of foot-and-mouth in 1942, and old Bert always blamed the folks at Kilnsgate. Still, he was a bit of a cantankerous old devil. Always going on about them. Blamed them for Nat Bunting's disappearance, too, apparently. But that's Bert for you."

Nat Bunting, I remembered, was the mentally challenged young man who had disappeared from the area during the war. What on earth could he have to do with anything? "Did he say how or when?"

"No. He tended to ramble a bit, even then, did old Bert Brotherton."

"Do you happen to know Billy's second name?"

"Can't say as I remember. We just called him Billy. But I do remember the birthmark. Most of the time he kept his hair in a fringe so nobody could see it, but the first week of school—clean or not—there was an outbreak of nits, maybe from some of the rougher evacuees in the area, so we all had to have our heads shaved, and the school nurse rubbed lethane on to get rid of them. Smelled something vile, it did. Anyway, with his hair short, you could see the birthmark, like when he had a military haircut years later, I suppose, when someone saw him with Grace. But Billy was really embarrassed by it and took to wearing a cap most of the time, till the nits had gone and his hair grew back. I'll bet it was Billy, all right."

I reached into my inside pocket for my iPhone. I had managed to download the photos and text Louise had given me, and I turned to the photo of Grace and the young boy standing in the garden of Kilnsgate. I showed it to Wilf. "Is that Billy?"

He stared at the iPhone in admiration. "That's a clever gadget," he said. "Aye, that's Billy, all right. By the looks of the weather and all it must have been taken shortly after he got there, before school started. September 1939. Lovely long summer. That's Billy. And that's Grace. But you know that already."

"What would Billy want with Grace after all those years?"

"I've no idea. Maybe he was just in the area and dropped by to say hello and happy New Year? He was in uniform, you say, so the odds are he was at Catterick, maybe doing his National Service. Perhaps they were sending him off to war and he came to say good-bye."

"What war?"

"There's always a war. Korea. Kenya. I was in Cyprus, myself."

"Will there be records? You know, official records?"

"Probably. It was quite a major operation, the evacuation, but it was a bit chaotic, too. It was supposed to be organized, and they had local 'dispersal centers,' where they tried to keep friends, brothers and sisters and school parties together, but it didn't always work out that way." Wilf sipped some beer. "Someone said it was a bit like an old Roman slave market in some places. You know, the farmers would come along and pick the strong, sturdy lads who could help out on the land, and the town families picked young girls who could give a hand around the house. The local bigwigs opted for the clean, nicely dressed kids, of course. Records? I don't know. There'd have been a local billeting officer, for example. But I think you'd have a job on your hands tracking any records down after all this time, don't you?"

"I know someone who could help," I said, almost to myself. I noticed Heather glance over at me and frown. Was she annoyed that I had been talking to Wilf for so long, or were things getting a bit difficult over there? I smiled at her. She made a face and went back to talking with Melissa and the crowd that surrounded them.

"You know, you could do a lot worse than the local papers," Wilf said.

"What do you mean?"

"As it happened, Billy was the area's first evacuee. I don't mean he came by himself or anything, there was a trainload or more, but it was just announced that way, officially, like, to make a bit of a story. Dr. Fox and his wife wanted to set an example, see, be the first to take in a city evacuee. I think Old Foxy saw it as a mark of his status, or something like that, and of course the billeting officer was a patient of his. I'd imagine he could have found himself on the receiving end of a big nasty needle if he hadn't gone along with it. Needless to say, they could have taken twenty or more, that big house of theirs, or yours, now, but the good doctor only wanted the one. A nice one, of course. And the first. He got Billy. Anyway, it wasn't such a terrible mismatch, as so many were. If Old Foxy hadn't had a bit of influence, he might have got stuck with half a dozen slum kids, and who knows what would have happened to Billy? Anyway, there was a story about Billy in one of the papers. Photo and everything. It might be of some help."

"Which paper?"

"Can't say for certain, but it would have the *Northern Despatch* or the *Northern Echo*, most likely. Those were the papers we took back then."

"What was the date?"

"I don't know, do I? It was seventy years ago, for Christ's sake. It was early September, though, I remember that, not long after war was declared. That doesn't give you a lot of ground to cover."

I heard a grunt of pain and a glass break over by the bar.

"I told you there'd be trouble," Wilf said.

I turned in time to see Melissa twisting Frankie Marshall's tattooed arm up his back, his face pressed down on the wet bar towel. A glass had tipped over and rolled to the floor. The young barman was torn between doing something and fear of getting involved. Melissa leaned forward and whispered something in Frankie's ear. He nodded as best he could for a man in his position, and she let him go. He shook himself off, scowled, picked up his jacket, and stormed out of the pub. One or two of his mates laughed when the door closed behind him. Before anything else was said, Dave hauled himself over to the bar and bought a round of drinks for the house. That brought cheers, and the incident was quickly forgotten, the glass swept up, and everyone returned to their evening of fun. Nobody bothered Melissa or Heather again, and some of the lads even started to regard her with a certain expression of awe. She broke a few hearts that night, and Dave was probably the envy of the town. I remember him once asking me, not so long ago, "What on earth does she see in a short, fat, balding Jewish guy like me?" I couldn't answer him then, and I can't now. Put it down to the mysteries of love.

We didn't stay much longer. The incident took some of the wind out of our sails, and we'd all had more than enough to drink. The pub-crawl idea quickly lost much of its appeal, as I had suspected it would. I thanked Wilf for our little chat, wished him a happy New Year, and set off with Dave, Heather, and Melissa to get a taxi outside the Green Howards Museum.

"What was all that about?" I asked Melissa as we walked carefully up the cobbled square, keeping an eye out, just in case Frankie Marshall had gone to seek reinforcements.

"He grabbed my tit," she said. "Wanted to know if it was real."

"He wouldn't be the first," said Dave.

Melissa shoved him playfully. "Yeah, but he didn't do it in a *nice* way." She linked arms with Heather and they started singing "Love Is Teasin'" as we got into the waiting taxi. Dave and I quieted them down, though the taxi driver was one of those types who has seen it all. As long as we don't vomit all over his upholstery, which the sign said would cost us a £50 soiling fee, he didn't much care what we did or said. "Most of your friends were real gentlemen," Melissa said to Heather. "I had a really good time."

"I'm glad," said Heather, clearly thrilled by Melissa's approval. But Heather didn't want to come back to Kilnsgate, not with Jane and Mohammed staying there. I could understand that. We made arrangements to meet in a couple of days and dropped her off at the Convent. As the taxi headed for Kilnsgate, Melissa dozed on Dave's shoulder, and I thought about what Wilf Pelham had just told me. I should have a chat with my neighbor, for one thing. Then there was the evacuee. Billy. I couldn't see how yet, but maybe he was the missing piece in all this. If he had met with Grace shortly before her husband's death, I prayed he was still alive and able to tell me why.

21

**Extract from the *Journal of Grace Elizabeth Fox*
(ed. Louise King), February–March 1942,
Singkep Island, Sumatra.**

SATURDAY, FEBRUARY 28, 1942

T HEY TOLD ME LATER THAT A FISHING BOAT FOUND US, THE THREE OF US
who were left. They thought we were dead, but they took us
onboard anyway. I have only very hazy memories of what followed,
but I now know we are in a Dutch hospital in the town of Daboh on
Singkep Island, just off the east coast of Sumatra.

The doctor visited me yesterday morning, as usual, and he said
the Japanese would be here very soon, and if I wanted to have any hope
of escaping, I must make the journey to Padang, on the west coast of
Sumatra, where I might possibly find a British ship. He told me that
he thought I was well enough to travel, as my heatstroke was not too
severe. I must keep out of the sun, he told me, and keep myself covered
at all times, as I had suffered terrible sunburn, and even now my skin
is peeling.

Though I was loath to leave my fellow survivors, the doctor insisted that it would be foolish to wait any longer, and so, feeling as guilty as a deserter, I slinked off, traveling with some Dutch and Australian nurses who were also anxious to escape the Japanese atrocities we had been hearing so much about back in Singapore.

It was a long journey, over three hundred miles, and we traveled mostly by road and riverboat. Some members of the Dutch Home Guard, who were bravely on their way to face the invading Japanese forces, gave us a lift over the final range of mountains.

When we finally got to Padang, the harbor was crowded with troops and civilians, the whole scene so chaotic that my heart sank. There was not a ship in sight. We slept on the docks that night, and I had terrible nightmares of rolling into the water.

SUNDAY, MARCH 1, 1942

Amidst rumors of Japanese landings in Java, and even as close as the east coast of Sumatra, this morning I saw three ships come sailing in, and of course, I could not keep the song out of my head, though it was not Christmas, and I am no longer a Christian. Some may have taken the arrival of the three ships as a miracle, but for me it was pure luck, or good timing. At any rate, they were able to take the entire harborful of refugees. I was fortunate enough to be one of the small company of women on one of the Royal Navy vessels, here to refuel and replenish its stocks of food and water after a big battle in the Java Sea. We sailed as soon as darkness fell. She is heading for Bombay, where I can report to a hospital unit and arrange to be shipped home.

TUESDAY, MARCH 3, 1942

Though water is still rationed, at least we have some, and we eat very well. When I told the captain I was a QA, he put me to work immediately in the sick bay. There are many wounded soldiers from the recent sea battle, with dressings to be changed and drips to be attended to, and one or two with severe infections. We also have onboard a num-

ber of civilians suffering from dehydration, heatstroke, or exhaustion.
I am happy to be working again, even though I tire easily and often feel
far from well myself.

The Australian nurses I work with are wonderful girls. They have
all suffered so much, like me, shipwreck and near capture, but they
manage to maintain a devil-may-care spirit and hold their heads high
in the face of tragedy. I wish I could be more like them. Some were
in Hong Kong just before it fell, and they have terrible stories to tell
of Japanese atrocities. I fear even more for Kathleen and Doris, and
worry that the Japanese probably slaughtered Stephen along with the
other men.

I am also happy to be reunited with several acquaintances from
the ill-fated *Kuala*, and in the long evenings we sit out on deck and tell
each other our stories. The best moments, though, are the ones I spend
alone leaning over the railings staring at the moon reflected on the
water. I can lose myself in that beauty, and for a few moments at least,
let go of my thoughts of poor Brenda, Kathleen, Doris, and Stephen,
and whatever may have become of them, and let my mind simply float
there, like a lily on the moonlit water.

JANUARY 2011

The bad weather returned in January, after a brief thaw, and when it
snows in Kilnsgarthdale, as I had learned in December, nothing much
has changed since Grace Fox's day. Again, schools closed, vehicles were
abandoned, and the local authorities ran out of grit after the first day.
Train and bus services came to a halt. My lane was blocked for a second
time, and I couldn't leave the house for three days. I couldn't even get
in touch with my friendly farmer, who had gone to the Maldives for a
holiday, or so the person who answered the phone told me. Luckily, I
had plenty of supplies left over from the holidays, so I wasn't likely to
starve or go thirsty, and there was nowhere I had to be. My guests had

all left before the New Year, which I had celebrated by a quiet evening at home with Heather. Melissa had told me she liked her, I was pleased to hear, and Jane had said she was glad to see me looking much happier and more relaxed than I had been in a long time.

It had been wonderful having Dave and Melissa and Jane and Mohammed to stay, but I enjoyed having the house to myself again after they had gone, the silence, the late-night movie marathons, not shaving every morning, wandering around in my dressing gown and slippers, Heather stopping over for the night. I didn't think Jane would have disapproved of our sleeping together, though these things can be hard to predict, but Heather had said she would have felt uncomfortable, and I didn't blame her. It meant we had a lot of making up to do on New Year's Eve.

On the second day of my incarceration, I stood by the French windows at the back of the house and looked out. The branches of the trees were heavy with snow, bent under its weight, the woods a bare, tangled, black-and-white world. As darkness fell and the shadows deepened, I thought of that night fifty-eight years ago, when Grace, Ernest, Alice, and Jeremy had sat down to dinner and noticed that it would be impossible for anyone to go home. I also thought of the days following the dreadful event, the four of them stuck in the house, *this* house, with a corpse upstairs.

As the days drifted into one another and the snow drifted against the French windows, I lost track of the time, sleeping when I felt tired, eating when I was hungry. I kept the log fire burning most of the time, and my supplies of wood grew dangerously low. Mostly I worked on my sonata. "Grace's Theme," as I suspected, became its emotional and melodic heart, its motif, and the basis of variations in all four movements. It still needed a lot more work, especially the final movement, the "allegro," where I was having a lot of trouble with the tempo. But on the whole, I was very happy with what I had done so far.

The rest of the time, I watched old movies in my den: *Sunset Boulevard*, *The Bridge on the River Kwai*, *Peeping Tom*, *The Fallen Idol*. The telephone and Internet connections still worked, as they had last time, so I wasn't completely cut off from the outside world the way Grace and the others had been. I talked to Heather, to Louise, and to Jane in Bal-

timore and to Dave, back safely in L.A. Louise said she would help me
track down Billy when I came up with a bit more information. I tried
the Internet and, while I found out a great deal about evacuees in general, including one or two interesting personal stories that backed up
some of the vague ideas I had been entertaining, I could find nothing about Billy. I did, however, discover that Darlington Library had
a large collection of newspaper holdings, including the *Northern Despatch*, the *Northern Echo*, and the *Darlington and Stockton Times*. I would
have to wait until the weather improved, of course, but I would get to
Darlington as soon as I could.

Try as I might, I could find out nothing else about Kilnsgate House
during the war, the Special Operations Executive or any other group
that might have commandeered the place. Neither Nat Bunting nor the
foot-and-mouth outbreak were mentioned anywhere. I did find a book
about the SOE called *Forgotten Voices of the Secret War*, though, which I
ordered from the Castle Hill Bookshop. I doubted that it would contain any revelations. Wartime was the perfect cover for any number of
shabby, secret operations, and the worst of them left no traces in any of
the record books. The best you could hope for was an eyewitness with a
believable story. I reminded myself that this was a distraction from the
main theory I had been forming about Grace and Billy's meeting, a side
street off the main route, however interesting it was.

Eventually, the snow stopped and the sun came out. The view from
my bedroom window over the dale was almost too bright to bear. The
little stone bridge and the lime kiln were completely buried, mere
bumps in the undulating stretches of snow. As far as I could see, in
both directions, the landscape was blindingly white.

Even then, it was another day before I heard the sound of the
snowplow making its way down Kilnsgarthdale Lane. Of course, that
was only the beginning, I still had to dig out my front path and my
car, and that took me the best part of an afternoon, after which I was
too exhausted to go anywhere. I phoned Heather, and she came by for
dinner with the Indian takeaway I had been craving, and the previous
weekend's papers. She told me that the roads in and around town were
still awful, and cars were slipping and sliding all over the place. The
police were inundated with accidents, including a huge pileup on the

A1 near Scotch Corner. The A66, the main east-west artery in this part of the world, was, of course, closed.

For the next few days, the temperature fluctuated around the freezing point, which made things even worse, as it had around Christmas. The snow would melt to slush during the day, and then freeze at night into miniature mountain ranges of ice. People slipped on the unshoveled pavements and broke arms and legs. Most stayed at home if they possibly could. Many of the services remained closed, including the libraries.

I made my way carefully into Richmond for the first time two days after Heather's visit. I was stir crazy by then, and willing to risk even the roads for the cheer of a pint and a noisy pub. Not to mention Heather's company for lunch.

I bought a newspaper and settled down to wait for Heather with my pint of Black Sheep at a table in the dining area of the Black Lion, where a fire crackled in the hearth. It was quieter than I had expected. No tourists, no walkers. Most of the news was still taken up by stories of the weather, an English obsession, I had come to realize, and the rest with the economy—poor pre-Christmas sales, because of the weather, of course—as well as the occasional skirmish or massacre on a distant continent. Nothing newsworthy had happened in the USA, it seemed, except for a major snowstorm on the eastern seaboard, nothing new to Bostonians or New Yorkers.

Heather came in shivering and warmed herself by the fire before shucking off her long winter coat. Her cheeks had a healthy glow, though I knew she wouldn't thank me for saying so. She was sensitive about her complexion. She didn't even like me admiring her freckles. So I said nothing. I went to the bar and got her a vodka and tonic while she studied the menu on the blackboard over the fireplace. In the end she went for the venison sausage, and I decided on lamb chops.

"So how does it feel to be a member of the human race again?" she asked.

"I was seriously in danger of going crazy up there."

"A man reverting to his primitive roots. Yes. A frightening thing, indeed. But you're all right now?"

"Nothing a decent pint couldn't cure."

"Have you found your evacuee yet?"

"Billy? No. The library's still closed. This bloody weather."

"I still don't see what you think he'll be able to tell you."

"I've been working on a theory."

"Another one?"

"Say Grace did it. Say she killed her husband."

"Then I don't see any point in going any further. I thought your aim was to prove your precious Grace innocent? I thought you'd already decided that she *didn't* do it."

"I had. It was. It is. But maybe even more so it's to get at the *truth*."

"You don't think that came out at the trial?"

"Of course it didn't. I think Louise put it best when she said the jurors all fantasized about Grace and hated themselves for it, so they found her guilty. But I can't prove it. I can't prove that Ernest Fox died of natural causes."

"Then what? The next best thing? Her motives were noble?"

"In a way." I lowered my voice. I hardly needed to, as there was nobody else in the dining room and the television was on over the bar, but it wasn't the kind of thought you voiced out loud. I paused, trying to weigh the words before I said them. "What if Ernest Fox had abused the evacuee?" I said. "What if he was a pedophile?"

Heather looked aghast at me. "What?"

"It doesn't sound so strange, does it? This evacuee, Billy. He might have remembered years later. People do bury such secrets, you know, even from themselves. He found himself training in Catterick, close enough that he just had to tell Grace what he had remembered."

"And she believed him? Just like that?"

"I've thought about that, too. If Grace believed him," I said, "it was because she already had an inkling, but she didn't want to admit it to herself, that she'd been living with a pervert all those years. And they had a son. He was seven—"

"You're not saying Ernest Fox abused his own son, too?"

"I'm saying it's possible. Or that Grace had noticed the way he was starting to treat the boy, or look at him, and it worried her."

Heather shook her head. "I don't know, Chris," she said. "You've lost me on this one, I'm afraid. You're grasping at straws. This is just wild imagination. There's no evidence at all."

"Why would there be? But won't you at least admit it's possible, as a theory?"

Our food arrived and we started eating. Heather pushed back her hair. "Lots of things are possible," she said. "It doesn't mean they happened. I mean, if you're after way-out theories, you don't even have to go that far."

"What do you mean?"

"Maybe she killed him because he was abusing *her*. Have you thought of that? Or maybe he committed suicide?"

"But communities covered up things like pedophiles back then. And nobody would suspect a doctor. Ernest Fox was a pillar of the community. They'd had separate bedrooms since Randolph was born."

"If you're right, then why didn't Grace just tell the police?"

"Because they'd never believe her, for a start, because she couldn't prove it, and even if she succeeded, the shame she'd bring on herself and her son would have been too much to bear."

"More than the shame of having a father murdered and a mother hanged for his murder? I'm sorry, Chris, but that comes pretty high on my list of shameful things to live with."

"I doubt she was acting entirely rationally. And she *didn't expect to get caught*!"

"Either she was irrational, or she was calculating. You can't have it both ways."

"Of course you can. Some people are perfectly rational in their actions when they're angry or upset."

"Even so, I think that if you're coming to the conclusion that Grace Fox did it, anyway, then you should start trying to accept that the jury was right all along and give up on it. It's been obsessing you, taking over your life."

"Not really. I just want to know. There are one or two more things I can do before the whole thing dries up on me, and I'm going to do them, starting with finding Billy."

Heather gave me a look she no doubt kept in reserve for hopeless cases, then she smiled. "Well, you've certainly got staying power, I'll give you that. How about another drink?"

IT WAS BUSINESS AS USUAL ON THE A1 TWO DAYS LATER WHEN I DROVE TO DARlington, but some of the country and residential roads were still covered in snow and ice and tough to negotiate. It was a gray day with a pale, haloed disk of sunlight trying to burn through from the south, without much success. When I got to the city, there were few people on the streets, and the pavements were still covered in slush over patches of ice. I hadn't visited Darlington often, and the parking confused me, so I headed for the large, open lot in the city center. Even there, they hadn't done a great job of clearing away the deluge, and it was tricky to back my way into a parking spot without slipping.

The library was an old redbrick building, reminiscent of the provincial schools of the late Victorian era, at the back of the CornHill Center. I had phoned ahead the day before and managed to book a microfilm reader. Normally, I was told, there would be a longer waiting period, but things were a little slow due to the weather. I was glad I had something to thank the weather for.

Libraries these days are very different places from the ones of my childhood. I used to go nearly every day to the children's library in Armley, where I grew up, mostly because I was in love with Yvonne, the librarian with the beehive hairdo. There was a special smell about the place, probably a mixture of paper, glue, polish, ink, and Yvonne, that I found irresistible. She had a lovely, gentle way of stamping the books out. Today, though, it's called a One Stop Center, and more people go there to get advice about housing or benefits, pay their council tax, or play games on the Internet than to borrow books. As libraries go, Darlington wasn't bad. There was plenty of old wood; a pleasant, distinctive smell; and Jean, one of the librarians, was very helpful, though she didn't have a beehive. She showed me to the readers and got me all set up with the *Northern Despatch* and *Northern Echo* microfilms.

I was lucky that I already knew Billy had arrived in Richmond in September 1939, and it took me no more than about ten minutes to find the little story tucked away in the *Northern Despatch* between a report on the post office coating the tops of its pillar boxes with yellowish gas-detecting paint, and warnings of stiffer penalties for blackout violations. Even better, there was a photograph, poor quality black and white, but it was the same boy Grace had been photographed with in the garden of Kilnsgate, the same pinched, suspicious features and blond fringe.

> There's a new addition to the household of Dr. Ernest Fox at Kilnsgate House, near Richmond. This is seven-year-old Charles "Billy" Strang, officially the first evacuee to be billeted in the charming Yorkshire town. At Kilnsgate, Billy will take up residence with Dr. and Mrs. Fox and will no doubt enjoy the attentions, not to mention the famous pies and cakes, of maidservant and cook Hetty Larkin, of nearby Ravensworth. "He's a lovely lad," said young Hetty. "The poor mite misses his mum and dad something cruel already, but Dr. and Mrs. Fox do their best to make him feel at home. We all do."
>
> "We're only doing our duty," said Dr. Fox, with characteristic modesty. "It's nothing to make a fuss about. If we can do anything to save these poor children from the bombing that is sure to be directed against Tyneside and the nation's other industrial and shipbuilding regions, then we should do so."
>
> The doctor's wife, Mrs. Grace Fox, added, "We're more than happy to have him. He's a delightful child. Polite, well mannered, and no bother at all."
>
> As for young Billy himself, what does he have to say about all this upheaval? When asked by our reporter, he remarked that he found the countryside interesting, full of all sorts of flowers and animals he had never seen before, and that if by stopping away from home for a short while he was helping the soldiers to fight that monster Hitler, then he was pleased to do his bit. That's the spirit, Billy!

And that was it. I have to confess, I was more than a little disappointed. Apart from the fact that his name was Charles Strang and that he came from Newcastle, the article gave me little more information to go on than I already had. It wasn't much more than a propaganda piece, really. Still, I could add to that what Wilf had told me about the boy's father managing a shoe shop in Newcastle High Street, and it might get me somewhere. Strang also sounded like a reasonably unusual name.

I browsed through a few more stories but found nothing else related to Billy. I wondered if the *Echo* or the *Despatch* had done a follow-up when he left, so I checked the newspapers around Christmas and early January 1940, but again I came up empty-handed. It appeared that it was only his arrival as the first evacuee in the area that was deemed newsworthy. I had to hope that, little as it was, it would be enough for Louise to work her magic.

While I was there, I also had a quick scan through the microfiches for 1941 and 1942 for anything related to an outbreak of foot-and-mouth or the disappearance of Nat Bunting. Perhaps I scanned too quickly and missed something, but it seemed to me as if neither incident had made it even as far as the local newspaper. I thought again of trying to find the newspaper accounts of Grace's trial, which would probably be in the Leeds reference library, but I decided I didn't really need them after reading Morley's account. Besides, it wasn't really the trial I was interested in anymore, it was Grace herself.

ON MY WAY BACK FROM DARLINGTON, I DECIDED TO PAY A CALL ON MY NEIGHbors the Brothertons. Wilf had said they might know something about Kilnsgate during the war, and they were hardly out of my way. I pulled up at the end of their short drive and made my way across the frozen mud of the farmyard to the house. Two collies stood barking at me, their tails wagging. It wasn't a large farmhouse, but there were quite a few outbuildings, barns, byres, and the like, along with a chicken coop. I could hear cows mooing and smell that farmyard smell.

A man of about forty or so opened the door the moment I started to knock. He had clearly heard the dogs announce me. He was wearing a thick crew-neck sweater and jeans and had a mop of dark curly hair and black eyebrows that met in the middle. He looked at me quizzically, and I introduced myself. He smiled, shook hands, and invited me in.

I had no sooner got inside than another dog came and started rearing up at me. It looked like a mongrel of some kind. I stroked it, let it lick my hand, and it calmed down. I could see a few cats gliding around, too, and two small children stared up at me wide-eyed from a floor covered in building bricks and various other toys. One of them looked about two; the other was perhaps four. A woman came in drying her hands on a towel. "Excuse the mess," she said, "only we weren't expecting company."

I smiled. "I'm sorry to drop by unannounced, but it was a spur of the moment thing. I've been meaning to say hello for a while. Mrs. Brotherton, I assume?"

"Jill, please. And my husband's Tony. Come on through to the living room and sit down. Can I get you a cup of tea or something?"

"That would be great," I said. "Milk, please, no sugar." I followed her through to a tidy living room with its maroon three-piece suite, TV in the corner, and a low glass coffee table. The dog followed me, then settled down on the carpet to lick itself. Tony Brotherton sat down and Jill disappeared to make tea.

"I'm sorry I haven't called earlier," I said. "I'm not used to the isolation up here. I can't even *see* your house from mine."

Tony Brotherton laughed. "You get used to it. And you must forgive us, too. The rumors that you have to winter out for ten years here before your neighbors will talk to you are not true at all. It's been a busy time, Christmas and everything. Then there was the weather."

"Ah, yes. The weather."

We talked about that for a while, until Jill returned with the tea in mugs on a tray, along with an assortment of biscuits. She was a strong-looking woman with short auburn hair and a weathered complexion, also wearing jeans and a sweater, and almost as tall as her husband. She looked capable enough of handling anything that came up on a farm.

I wanted to get to the point and return to Kilnsgate to phone Louise and set her on the trail of Charles Strang, but I knew it was important to make polite conversation for a while, and to answer Jill and Tony's questions about my work and such like. I couldn't really find a natural way to bring the conversation around to the war, so instead I asked about the history of the farm, who it had belonged to over the years.

"It's been in the family as far back as we can trace it," said Tony. "I know it seems old-fashioned these days, but it seemed important not to break the continuity. There was a time when I felt like selling up and moving to the city, but Jilly here talked me out of it." He glanced toward the children playing in the other room. "It'll be little Gary's one day, too."

"What about his brother?"

"It's the eldest son who inherits," said Tony.

I wanted to comment that this seemed a little unfair, especially if the eldest didn't want to be a farmer and the youngest did, but I sensed that would only close doors, not open them.

Jill handed us each a mug of tea and came to sit on the chair arm beside Tony. She took his hand and smiled down at him.

"There must have been some very hard times," I said.

"I'll say. It's not an easy life, farming. Probably the worst was about ten years ago, just after Dad died and we were struggling to keep going. I suppose you remember the foot-and-mouth outbreak of 2001? It brought the whole country to a halt. We lost pretty much everything, just as we were starting out. Every cow and sheep slaughtered. Those were the darkest days, I'd say." He looked up at Jill, who nodded and squeezed his hand.

"I suppose it must have been tough during the war, too, with quotas and rationing and everything?" I said. "Not that you'd remember it, of course."

Tony laughed. "Believe me, I've heard all about it. It was one of Granddad's hobbyhorses, wasn't it, love?"

Jill smiled.

"We all had it easy, according to him. You hadn't lived until you'd lived through the war, as if we should all somehow go back in time and do it, just to toughen ourselves up to his standards."

I laughed. "Yes. I was reading up on a bit of history about Kilnsgate," I said. "The Foxes were living there then, weren't they?"

"That's the woman who got hanged, isn't it?" said Jill, instinctively touching her neck.

"That's right."

"Come to think of it," Tony said, narrowing his eyes, "I've heard somewhere that you've become interested in Grace Fox's story, asking questions all over the place."

"Mea culpa," I said. "Not much else to do around here."

"You can come up here and give us a hand whenever you feel like it," Jill said, with a smile to soften the implied criticism. Talk to farmers, and you'd think they're the only ones who ever do any hard work; the rest of us are soft and lazy. Still, it was a silly thing to say, and I regretted it the minute it was out. I just smiled.

"I can't for the life of me remember who told me," said Tony.

"Wilf Pelham, perhaps?"

"Perhaps. He was a friend of Granddad's. We bump into each other now and then in town."

"Did your grandfather know the Foxes?"

"I suppose he must have," said Tony, "but he never said much about them. They weren't farmers."

"What about the trial?"

"It never really interested him much. He was far too busy on the farm to pay attention to things like that. And I wasn't even born."

"Of course," I said. "Wilf was telling me how your granddad blamed the military at Kilnsgate for everything, even the foot-and-mouth outbreak."

Tony laughed. "It was one of the many bees in his bonnet, yes. He used to go on about them years after, mostly I think because they blocked off the dale with barbed wire and put out sentries, so he couldn't go for his usual morning constitutional, or graze his cattle down there. Once you got Granddad started on the war, there was no stopping him. He didn't like the folks at Kilnsgate, it's true. Even blamed them for the disappearance of some disabled local chappie."

"Nat Bunting?"

Tony's eyes widened. "You *have* done your research, haven't you."

"His name's cropped up once or twice. What did your grandfather say?"

Tony shrugged. "He said he'd seen this Bunting fellow *inside* the Kilnsgate compound, beyond the barbed wire. As I said, Granddad was annoyed most of all because he used to have free access to that land himself. To see someone else there . . . well, it naturally annoyed him."

"What did he do about it?"

"Do? Nothing. What could you do? This was wartime. The military could do whatever they wanted and shoot you if you got in their way. No, he just grumbled, and eventually people got tired of listening to him."

"Any idea what Nat Bunting might have been doing in there? I mean, from what I've heard, it was well guarded, and he was hardly a fifth columnist."

"No idea. I never heard any more about it."

"Do you remember your granddad saying *when* this happened?"

"I'm afraid I don't. I'm not even sure that he did. I mean, when he went into his rants, they were hardly dated and timed."

"Of course not. What about the foot-and-mouth outbreak?"

"Now that I do know. It was April 1942. Things like that tend to be etched in the family's collective memory. Granddad lost his whole herd. I don't even know if he got much compensation. And, of course, he blamed the military for that, too." Tony frowned. "But from what I can piece together, he ought to have thanked them. It was them that saved our bacon." He laughed. "Well, beef, I suppose I should say."

"How?"

"He had to destroy all his livestock, true enough, but that's as far as it went. The military acted fast and put a stop to the outbreak before it spread around the county, or the country—and you know how fast foot-and-mouth can spread. If that had happened, a lot more people would have lost their livelihoods, and nobody would have been in a position to help Granddad get back on his feet again, which is what they did. Whatever the military were doing, they acted quickly and decisively, and we were lucky they were there. It's not often you can say that."

"I'll say. Did no one else do medical checks? The Ministry of Agriculture? The local vet?"

"From what I could gather between Granddad's rants, we were quarantined immediately, and the people from Kilnsgate took care of everything. Slaughter, disposal, the lot."

"How did they dispose of the bodies? Fire?"

"Apparently they put them in pits and scattered quicklime over them. Of course, they didn't have all those European Union rules and regulations to deal with back then. You saw a problem, you dealt with it."

"Now, darling . . . ," said Jill, giving him a playful tap on the arm. "Don't you get on *your* hobbyhorse. I'm sure Mr. Lowndes doesn't want to hear your opinions on the EU."

I smiled. "Well, I wouldn't mind," I said, glancing at my watch, "but I'm afraid I do have to be going."

We all stood up, and Jill said we would have to get together again, for a longer and more leisurely chat next time, perhaps over dinner. I said that would be a wonderful idea, then, after saying good-bye to them both, the dog, and the children, I made it past the barking collies to my car without slipping and breaking my neck, and headed back to Kilnsgate.

22

Extract from the *Journal of Grace Elizabeth Fox* (ed. Louise King), June 1944, Normandy.

FRIDAY, JUNE 30, 1944

A CURIOUS THING HAPPENED TODAY. LIEUTENANT MADDOX, ONE OF THE surgeons, chose Dorothy and me to accompany him on a special mission. In charge was a man introduced to us only as Meers, and a couple of strong, silent corporals I can only describe as thugs. I did not like Meers. I did not even recognize the uniform he was wearing. He was cold and had a cruel twist to his mouth. I could tell by the way he acted toward Dorothy and me that he does not like women and would not have taken us with him if he'd had his way. He hardly spoke, and when he did, he only talked to Lieutenant Maddox. He did not even look at Dorothy or me. I made certain he never spotted my journal. He was the kind of man who would have confiscated and destroyed it with great pleasure.

We could see the devastation of the beautiful French countryside from the jeep. Roofless farmhouses, fields full of bomb and shell craters, dead livestock scattered everywhere. How the poor French people must hate us all, Allies and Germans alike. Even in freeing them we are destroying their homes and livelihoods. Still, I suppose these can be rebuilt, whereas a future of Nazi rule is not something to be contemplated with equanimity.

We arrived at a grand chateau, which reminded me of one of our English stately homes, surrounded by a high wall with wrought-iron gates, an arched entrance, and acres of grounds. Here and there lay a dead cow, and someone had dug a pit in which more bodies of livestock were burning. The smell was terrible. There was some bomb damage to one of the wings, and the ruins were still smoldering. Meers spoke to the officer at the gate, who scrutinized all our identity cards before letting us through. Dot and I had butterflies in our stomachs.

There were a number of military vehicles in the grounds, and groups of soldiers standing around smoking, as if detailed to be there simply to keep an eye on things. Without a word, Meers jumped out of the jeep the moment it came to a halt. Lieutenant Maddox shrugged, and we all followed Meers and the corporals inside. We were issued face masks and surgical gloves as we entered. It was a grand place, full of vast echoing halls, wainscoting, gold leaf, ornate cornices and chandeliers, broad, curving staircases with thick patterned carpets. The one odd thing I noticed was that there were no paintings on the walls. It was clear that there had once been some by the discoloration in certain areas, so perhaps the owners had hidden them in the cellar to prevent them from being damaged.

In many of the rooms and halls were rows of empty makeshift cots and beds, which made me think the place had been used as a hospital of some kind. Meers led us through a maze of imposing corridors, down some stone stairs, and we ended up at a reinforced door with a black skull and crossbones, like the Jolly Roger, on it, and a sign that read EINTRAG VERBOTEN. Even I knew enough German to realize that meant no entry.

As Meers started to open the door, he turned to Lieutenant Maddox and told him there were some men inside the room, and if anything could be done for them, especially anything that might make them capable of talking, we should do it. That was why we had been brought here. Lieutenant Maddox looked at us and nodded. This was our job, after all, no matter who they were.

It soon became obvious, however, that there was nothing to be done for anyone in that room. It was large and cool, with damp stone walls, and had perhaps once been a wine cellar or some sort of storage area, but now it was a makeshift hospital ward, with rows of beds full of dead patients, about thirty or more of them, all men, and all emaciated. Some lay half out of bed, some completely on the floor. We checked them all, and not one showed signs of life.

It was not immediately clear what had killed them. There were no signs of bullet wounds or the usual battlefield injuries. Many had terrible rashes and what looked like scald marks or electrode burns on their skin, sores and pustules, but nothing that appeared serious enough to have caused death. Still, we were not there to perform autopsies; we were there to see what could be done, and clearly nothing could.

While we were doing this, I noticed that the corporals had turned up with a handcart, and Meers was tossing the contents of the filing cabinets into it. Some of the files lay strewn on the floor, some partially burned, so it looked as if the Germans had tried to destroy them before deciding that a quick flight was the better option. Meers also forced open the medicine cabinets and added their contents to the cart. I noticed a bottle labeled SARIN, another TABUN. I had never heard of these medicines, but then my German was not that good. Meers was very careful in his handling of them, though, and he managed to find a compartmented wooden box of the kind used for shipping wine, and slotted each bottle in an individual compartment. When he had finished, he sent the corporals away and came over to us.

After a brief consultation with Lieutenant Maddox about the hopeless state of the patients, he called over one of the corporals to take us back to the hospital. That was all. We were dismissed.

Lieutenant Maddox said something about finding a cause of death, but Meers told him that was not his problem. As long as no one could be saved, then we had done our jobs and we could go. Lieutenant Maddox insisted that we should at least try to identify the men, so that we could inform their next of kin. Meers said that was not important,

that they were probably just Jews or Polish slave laborers. The lieutenant argued that he would have to conduct more extensive tests to be
sure they were not the victims of infectious diseases, but Meers would
have none of it. He said that the bodies would be burned and gave the
corporal a brisk nod. I felt that if we did not do as we were told, and
leave now, the corporal would pull out his sidearms. Things were that
tense. So we left. When we got back to the hospital, they were packing
up for a move, so we all got stuck into it and the incident was briefly
forgotten.

JANUARY 2011

I thought I had mastered the art of sleeping on planes, but that night
as we droned somewhere over the Sahara Desert, I just couldn't do it,
despite the dimmed lights and the spacious business-class seat. I had
dozed just long enough to miss the end of the movie I was watching,
and the flight attendant had surreptitiously removed my half-full glass
of wine from the tray. Now I was wide awake again. I reached for the
touch screen, desperately seeking something else to watch, but there
was nothing that interested me, especially not *Death Knows My Name*,
and though my eyes weren't heavy enough to close in sleep, they were
too tired to read. Instead, I plugged the headphones into my iPhone
and went back to the late Beethoven string quartets I'd been listening
to earlier.

Even then, my mind wasn't so much on the music as it was thinking forward to the meeting I was hoping for. Louise had done a great
job, though it had taken her a couple of weeks, and it was now the end
of January. She had tracked Billy Strang through his father, the shoe-
shop manager, finding an address and birth details. Then she had gone
on to work her magic and, after a short period of despair, when the trail
seemed simply to end, she found that he had done his National Service between 1952 and 1954, then emigrated to Rhodesia in 1956 and
moved to South Africa in 1980. He now lived near Cape Town. It was

simply the outline of a life story, and though I could imagine some of the details myself, given the dates, it would be interesting to get Billy himself and hear his story to fill in the blanks.

After talking to Louise, I had booked a flight as quickly as possible, but I had deliberately not tried to get in touch with Billy for the same reason I hadn't phoned Sam Porter before my trip to Paris. It's a lot easier to say no to someone from a few thousand miles away, over the telephone, than it is if he's standing on your doorstep. Again, I knew this was a risk. He could be out of town, could even be dead—though Louise assured me the public records showed he was still alive and paying taxes—but the risk of alerting him and of having him simply refuse to talk to me at all was too much to contemplate, so I decided to play it by ear.

The odds were good. I calculated that Billy would be close to eighty now, much the same age as Wilf and Sam, so he probably didn't get out and about all that much. And I could also think of no reason why Billy should *not* want to tell me his story. If nothing else came of my trip, I would at least get a few days' holiday in Cape Town. It was summer there, too, another reason I might find Billy Strang at home.

Because it's an overnight flight, about twelve hours or so, and there's only a two-hour time difference, I had hoped to arrive well rested and ready to go, but it didn't seem to be turning out that way. After breakfast, we began our descent and landed without incident. I looked out of the window and saw that the sun was shining on the lush green hills, the light possessing that ineffable quality I had only ever seen in parts of Africa.

I could feel the heat as soon as the doors opened and I stepped onto the Jetway. Cape Town is a busy airport, but the formalities didn't take too long, and in no time I was in the Hertz office signing my life away for a cheap Japanese compact and asking for directions out of the airport.

It turned out not to be too difficult to get on the N2 and then head northwest toward the city center and the waterfront, where I was staying. It was still the morning rush hour, and there was plenty of traffic going both ways. Before long, I came to that stretch of highway, several kilometers long, which appears to the American or northern European eye to be one enormous shantytown, with row after row of flat-roofed leaning shacks of corrugated iron and cardboard and hardly a gap between them. The kind of place you see straggling on hillsides in Caracas, Rio, or Buenos Aires. But people who knew better had assured me that there is some level of organization within the communities, schools and health facilities, and the government is also building some decent brick houses to move families into.

Soon I could see Table Mountain ahead of me, and I began concentrating on the road as it neared the city. I could stay on the highway most of the way, the woman at Hertz had assured me, but I would have to negotiate one or two city streets at the end. It wasn't so hard. At least they drove on the left, and I had got accustomed to that since moving back to Yorkshire. Soon I was telling the guard at the gate that I was a guest at the hotel, and he was waving me through. I parked by the waterfront, took my small travel bag and computer case from the backseat and went to check in.

I had booked two nights at the Cape Grace, both because its name sounded appropriate, and because I'd heard it was one of the best hotels in the city. That became pretty evident right from the start, when I was invited to sit down and enjoy a cup of tea as I checked in. In no time, I was in my room on the top floor, opening the French windows to the balcony and gazing out on Table Mountain to my left and Signal Hill straight ahead of me, across the marina and the downtown core. Though the rest of the sky was clear, there was a hint of cloud and mist on Table Mountain, which really did resemble a long, flat table, or anvil.

I leaned on the railings, breathed in the warm air, and sighed. Laura and I had come here for our "second" honeymoon in the late nineties, not long after apartheid was overthrown. I remembered South Africa then as a beautiful, blighted, haunted, hopeful, exciting country. It had fascinated us, from the tensions of Johannesburg to the beauty of the Cape Winelands and a three-day safari at a private game reserve near Kruger Park. I had so many memories, but that was over ten years ago, and the country had changed a great deal since then.

Laura had loved the markets, the crafts shops and clothes stores with their unusual patterns and bright colors, colors that seemed to exist only here, greens or browns that somehow never looked the same anywhere else in the world. I also remembered a large record shop where I had bought a lot of CDs of South African jazz, and I wondered if it was still in business.

But I wasn't here to get maudlin over my loss, I told myself. I was here to find Billy Strang, and after a shower, over an early lunch on the waterfront, I would take out the road map the Hertz lady had given me and plot a route to Simon's Town, where he was living.

I DROVE MORE OR LESS STRAIGHT SOUTH. YEARS AGO, WITH LAURA, I HAD driven down the peninsula as far as Cape Point, but I didn't remember much very clearly, except for the rolling waves and the penguins and baboons. Simon's Town wasn't quite as far, but it was a good ways down, and it seemed like a beautiful place to retire.

The house I was searching for stood high above the town, overlooking the harbor and the purplish-blue and green Indian Ocean beyond. Though the sun shone brightly and the sky was pure blue, a strong wind had sprung up, and I had to struggle to get out of the car. Below me, I could see thousands of whitecaps and larger waves crashing on the beach and the big rocks that reared out of the waters of the bay.

I turned and gazed at the house. It was a boxy sort of place, a modern design, all white stucco, large picture windows, and hacienda-style open verandas. There were three stories, each a different-size cube stuck asymmetrically on top of the one below. It wouldn't have been out of place in Southern California. Laguna Niguel, say, or Huntington Beach. Whatever Billy Strang had done since he had left England, he had done very well for himself.

When I found what I thought to be the front door, I rang the bell. Nothing happened. I knocked, then rang it again. Still nothing. He was out, and I had no idea where or for how long. I only had myself to blame for coming on spec like this, assuming an eighty-year-old man would be pretty much housebound. Maybe he was off surfing somewhere, or having a tryst with his twenty-year-old lover. The only thing I could do was keep trying.

I drove down to Boulders Beach, parked, and walked out to see the penguins. The wind was howling, blowing up sand everywhere and raising tears in my eyes. Even the penguins could barely stand up straight. I could hear the waves crashing and smell salt spray in the air, feel it in my hair, on my exposed skin. I hurried back to the car and drove farther down the coast as far as Castle Rock. The wind wasn't so bad there, so I got out at a viewing point and took a few photographs to show Heather. She had wanted to come with me, but decided in the end it wasn't worth it for just three days. I promised I would take her for a proper holiday somewhere when all this was over. Before I left, I had given her a copy of Grace's journal to read, and as I stood in the lonely spot at Castle Rock, it was an entry from that journal that came into my mind. I couldn't help but think of Grace standing here that day in 1940 on her way to Singapore, of that stolen kiss with Stephen Fawley. It looked very much as if this was where one of the photographs had been taken, the one in which she was trying to hold her hair in place, not Cornwall, after all.

A number of baboons appeared on the rocks over to my right, eyeing me curiously. I knew to be careful around them, so I started heading slowly back to the car. They watched me as I went, then turned their backs and mooned me, as they must have done Grace and Stephen, though she had been too delicate to describe it in her journal. I drove back to Simon's Town and tried Billy's house again. Still nothing.

I decided I would give it one more try today, then come back again tomorrow. I would have one more whole day after that, as my flight didn't leave until after ten the following evening. This time I found a sheltered café by the harbor and sat in a window seat sipping an espresso, reading *Saturday Night and Sunday Morning* and watching the dance of the spray through the window. I seemed to be pinning a lot of hopes on this visit, I thought, not to mention spending a lot of money. But the money wasn't a problem, nor was my time at the moment. I just hoped I wouldn't leave empty-handed. I had come this far, and I needed to know the full story.

After about an hour and two strong coffees, I drove back up the hill to the white cubist house. The first thing that raised my spirits was the silver BMW in the driveway. The front door was also slightly ajar, and I could hear the sound of radio voices coming from inside. I rang the bell, the door opened, and a head as brown and bald as a varnished banister knob and as pitted as a walnut shell peered out at me, a birth-mark like a teardrop where his hairline used to be, a bristly gray goatee around his mouth.

"Charles?" I asked. "Charles Strang?"

He eyed me with suspicion. "Who wants to know?"

"My name's Chris Lowndes," I told him. "You don't know me, but I live in Kilnsgate House."

"Then you're a long way from home, aren't you?" he said, but his manner softened. "You'd better come in. Never let it be said that Billy Strang doesn't know how to treat a visitor from the old country. And Billy's the name. Always has been, always will be." There was little, if any, Geordie left in his accent, which had also taken on a hint of South African cadence. It wasn't strong, though the result was a very unusual mix. Even Henry Higgins would have been hard pressed to guess where Billy Strang came from. He was a couple of inches shorter than me and seemed in good shape, whippet thin, sinewy and economic in his movements, as if he used just as much energy as he needed and was keeping plenty in reserve.

I followed him through a hall with a high white ceiling and a par-quet floor. "I called earlier, but you were out," I said.

"Tennis club."

"Do you play?"

"Of course I play. Why shouldn't I?"

"No reason."

"Just because I'm eighty doesn't mean I can't still give these young whippersnappers of seventy or so a good run for their money." He grinned. "Besides, the widow Cholmondeley's always there on a Tues-day, and I fancy my chances there. Lovely arse on her. Come on. Sit down." He pointed toward a huge sofa with matching armchairs uphol-stered in zebra skin. I thought that was probably as illegal as it was tasteless, but maybe it was fake. A tiger-skin rug lay on the hardwood floor in front of the huge fireplace. No fire burned. Instead, I heard the hum of a central air conditioner and felt the artificial chill. A ceiling fan whirred above, distributing the coolness. "Drink?" he offered. "I don't indulge anymore, myself, but there's pretty much anything you want."

"I'd better not," I said. "I've got to drive back to Cape Town later."

"Suit yourself." He went to the cocktail cabinet and poured himself a squirt of soda. "I suppose you'd better tell me why you're here, then," he said. "But first you can tell me how Kilnsgate is. It's been a bloody long time."

As I told him, I saw a wistful expression pass across his lined and tanned face, and his eyes seemed fixed on a point somewhere way beyond me.

"I haven't really thought about those days in years," he said.

"Why did you leave?"

"England? Because it was fucked. They sent me off to kill Mau-Maus in Kenya for two years, and when I got back I couldn't think of a thing I wanted to do in the old country. Not a thing. Kenya gave me a yen for adventure, for Africa. There were a lot of opportunities for private soldiering back then, if you weren't too fussy who you worked for. I did a few things I'm not proud of, then I met a bloke from Southampton who ran a tobacco farm in Rhodesia, as it then was. Hard work, but what a life. All there for the taking. Until the troubles started, of course. He said I was welcome to come and work for him anytime, so I did. Twenty pounds in my pocket. I soon had a few acres of my own and a well-bred English lady for a wife. I lasted until 1980 through sheer stubbornness, but it was clear long before then the way things were going, and that the stubbornness would be the death of me if I didn't get out soon. I'd already seen my neighbors butchered. It was a bad situation all round. And a dangerous one. Luckily, I'd been smart with my money, put most of it in bank accounts in Jo'burg or London. It wasn't hard to arrange a quick move over the border before the natives came and hacked us to pieces like they did my friends and neighbors. My well-bred English lady had already left me by then and gone back to her family in England. Didn't have the stomach for it. I got involved in the wine business here on the Cape. Did very well at it, too. Retired ten years ago. That's it. Potted life story so far. And now you're here. But I'm sure you didn't come all this way just to hear about me."

"Partly. It's an interesting story. I went to America. Los Angeles. It was a bit safer there."

He laughed. "That's arguable. Still . . . we're both alive to tell the tale."

"Yes. Look, I'll get to the point. When you were seven, you were evacuated to Richmond, and you spent some time up at Kilnsgate House, didn't you?"

"That's right. About four months in all. Some of the happiest days of my childhood. It was a funny time, though. As if the earth was standing still. People were expecting bombing raids and poison gas attacks every day, but nothing happened."

Now that I was approaching the true purpose of my visit, I was beginning to feel apprehensive about broaching the subject. After all, perhaps at the age of eighty, after a successful life, a man might not appreciate talking about being abused at the age of seven, might not even remember it, if he believed that those same months were the best of his childhood. I would have to edge my way there gently, if I possibly could. "How did you take to it? It must have made quite a change for you?"

"Oh, yes. I was a city boy through and through. Not a slum kid, mind you, my dad had a decent job in a shoe shop, then later in a department store, but I certainly wasn't well versed in the ways of country life, outside of a few books I'd read. Still, I wasn't as daft as some of the kids who thought apples grew in boxes and cows were no bigger than dogs."

"So how was your time at Kilnsgate?"

Billy thought for a moment. "Happy, as I told you, for the most part. That first month the weather was marvelous, and school was out till late September because of the war, so I got to explore the area. It was like an extended holiday. Are the lime kilns still there?"

"Indeed they are."

"I used to hide in them if I wanted to disappear for a while."

"Why would you want to disappear?"

"I was a kid. Playing. It was a bit lonely up there, so I lived in my own world. Maybe I was hatching my famous plans to defeat Hitler. Or maybe I was on the run from the Gestapo."

"What about school?"

"It was okay. I got teased a bit because of my accent. But there were some good kids there, too. It was certainly no worse than the school in Newcastle."

"And the Foxes?" I ventured.

"I got lucky there," he said. "They wanted to set an example, but they also wanted someone who knew how to use a toilet and wash behind his ears. I fit the bill. Rationing or no, we always had plenty of food—Hetty Larkin made wonderful cakes and pies—and Mrs. Fox used to play the piano for me and sing of an evening. Voice of an angel. I'd never heard anything like it before. Not that she couldn't manage the occasional popular song, mind you. We'd have a good knees up, every now and then. Usually when she had her girlfriends up and old misery guts was away somewhere."

I paused, remembering Grace's exquisite but untrained voice on the recordings Louise had given to me. "Misery guts?" I said.

Billy wrinkled his nose. "That's what I called him. Dr. Fox. Ungrateful of me, I suppose, but he was bit of a tartar, really. Luckily, like I said, he was away a lot. Important war business, don't you know. Or so he implied. Now I come to think of it, he was probably telling the truth, even that far back. But I didn't like him right from the start."

"Why not?"

"It's hard to say, really. I just sensed something . . . cold, maybe even a bit cruel about him. He frightened me. I remember once I had a nasty boil on the back of my neck and he lanced it. Hurt like hell. Didn't bother to be gentle or give me anything to ease the pain. It was almost as if he enjoyed it."

"Causing pain?"

"Yes. But that's probably being fanciful, in retrospect. I didn't know so much at the time."

"What didn't you know?"

"He never hit me or anything, if that's what you mean."

"And you liked Grace?"

"I adored her." He paused to remember for a moment, then frowned. "I often wonder what became of her. Do you know?"

I stared at him, openmouthed. "You mean, you don't . . . you haven't . . . ?"

"What? No. Nothing. I lost touch completely after . . . oh, it must have been near Christmas 1952, just before I got sent to Kenya. I never went back. Never heard anything again. You tend to lose touch with the rest of the world out here."

I could see the waves crashing on the rocks way below through his picture window, the rolling hills stretching all along the bay. How was I going to play this? There was no way I could avoid giving Billy an unpleasant shock. I studied him closely and decided that he was the kind who took life straight up, as it came at him. He had to be to survive the kind of life he'd lived. But I still just couldn't simply blurt it out. "Maybe I will have that drink, after all, if you don't mind?"

He gave me a knowing smile. "Of course. What'll it be?"

"Red wine, if you have any."

He went over to the cocktail cabinet and poured me a glass from a decanter. It was silky smooth and had an aroma of blackcurrant, and a hint of tobacco. "I take it you have something difficult to tell me, or you wouldn't be procrastinating in this way," he said, tilting his head to one side, birdlike.

"Am I so transparent?"

"I've had a lot of practice."

"Grace Fox died in April 1953," I said.

"So soon," he whispered. "So young. That wasn't long after I saw her. She seemed fit and well enough. How did it happen? Accident?"

Now came the hard part. I took a swallow of wine. When I was sure it had all gone down the right way, I said, "She was hanged for poisoning her husband."

Billy's eyes opened wide in astonishment. "No. She can't have . . ."

I leaned forward. "I've been thinking the same thing," I hurried on. "That she didn't do it. Can't have done it. But I'm not so sure now. It could have been natural causes, but we'll never know that for certain one way or the other. I think she might have done it, but not for the reasons everyone assumed, not for reasons that got her hanged, and if they'd known the truth they might have gone a bit easier on her. That's really why I came to see you. I think you can help me shed some light on it."

"I can't believe . . ." Billy just shook his head. "She just *couldn't* have."

"You visited her in Richmond between Christmas and New Year's in late 1952, didn't you?"

"Yes. I was finishing my training at Catterick. I found her telephone number and she agreed to meet me. We went for a walk around the castle walls. It was a lovely day for the time of year, I remember."

"You were seen together by several people. It came out in the police investigation, though it was never mentioned at her trial."

Billy frowned. "Why would it be? I mean, I don't understand."

"As evidence that she was promiscuous, a loose woman. That's what the prosecution worked so hard to prove. She had a lover, a young artist. They said that was why she plotted to kill her husband."

"I find that hard to believe," Billy said. "But the alternative is . . . surely it can't have been because of me?"

"I think it might have been," I said. It was time to take the plunge. "I know it must be difficult for you to talk about it, but I think you arranged to meet Grace that day to tell her that Ernest Fox had abused you while you were an evacuee at Kilnsgate House, didn't you? Maybe you'd only just remembered, or maybe it had been bothering you for a while, and this was your opportunity to unload the burden before you went off to war. The mind plays strange tricks. But I think when you told her, she believed you. She must have had her own suspicions by then, noticed little things, and I think she also did it partly to protect her own son. He was seven at the time, your age when you were there in 1939. People didn't talk about those sorts of things back then. Nobody would have believed her, anyway. She couldn't live with it, with him and what he'd done, what he was no doubt going to do again, so she poisoned him."

Billy sat staring at me, openmouthed. He was amazed, I supposed, that somebody had worked it out after all these years. I drank the last of the wine, and he reached for his soda. His hand was trembling slightly. The silence stretched until he finally said, "That's a very interesting theory, Mr. Lowndes, very interesting indeed, but I have to tell you that it's nothing more than a load of bollocks. Quite frankly, you're not much of a detective. You're so far off target they'd have to send out a search party for the truth."

23

Extract from the *Journal of Grace Elizabeth Fox*
(ed. Louise King), July 1944, Normandy.

TUESDAY, JULY 4, 1944

WE HAVE MOVED TO A STRETCH OF APPLE ORCHARD BETWEEN CAEN AND Bayeux that is known as Harley Street because of the concentration of hospitals and medical staff. The accommodation is not much better than before, though, and we are still in tents. With all the confusion of the move, I did not see Lieutenant Maddox for two days after the incident at the chateau, though I puzzled and puzzled about what could possibly have been going on there. Dorothy and I discussed it, too, and we came to the conclusion that poison of some kind—possibly this "sarin"—had been used on those poor men. There had been plenty of rumors of biological warfare, and we still carry gas masks, though fortunately we have not had cause to use them. Anyway, I was determined to find out what Lieutenant Maddox knows. He is a good doctor, and something of an intellectual, always with his nose in a book, if he isn't repairing some poor boy's spleen or sewing up a chest cavity.

I found him beside his tent, leaning against a tree and smoking his pipe, and when he saw me, he stiffened and asked me what I wanted. I said I would like him to tell me what his thoughts were about the other day. He did not want to talk about it at first, but I could tell that he had been dwelling on the incident, just as Dorothy and I had been.

He took me by the arm and led me away from the tent, toward the trees. Normally I would have been wary of such an action, but I knew that he simply wanted to avoid being overheard.

He did not know who Meers was, he said, but suspected he was connected with Porton Down. When I asked what that was, he told me it was a top-secret military establishment in Wiltshire where they do experiments with chemical and biological weapons. So at least part of what Dorothy and I had worked out was true, I thought.

Lieutenant Maddox told me that the chateau had clearly been used for such experiments. Sarin and tabun, he told me, were nerve agents that the Germans had developed but had not used yet. Meers was clearly looking for evidence of any further experiments and inventions, or refinements they might have come up with more recently. When I asked if this was because he wanted to put a stop to it or find an antidote, Lieutenant Maddox just stared at me, then laughed harshly. He said that was very unlikely. Far more likely, he said, was that Meers wanted as much information as he could get in order to duplicate the experiments at Porton Down, to develop something just as powerful, or more so, to be used against the Germans. We wanted the same capabilities they had. Then he told me that it would be best if I said nothing more about this business to anyone, and walked off, leaving a trail of sweet pipe smoke to vanish in the night air.

Sunday, July 23, 1944

After Caen fell two weeks ago, we started to get many more German casualties. Most of the ordinary soldiers are glad that the war seems almost over, and happy to be still alive as POWs. We have enough problems, though, that we have had to increase the number of armed guards and sentries around the hospital. The SS officers are especially difficult. They are still devoted to Hitler and cannot accept the possibility of a German defeat. Then there is the Hitler Youth. Because the German army is running short of able-bodied men, so Major Tanner explained to me, it has drafted in a lot of old men and boys to make up the numbers. The old men are quite passive and glad to be cared for, but the boys can be a nuisance. We try to treat them the same as everyone else, and most of the time we succeed, but sometimes our patience wears exceedingly thin.

There was one boy called Dieter who arrived about two days ago. He had been shot in the upper thigh, had lost a lot of blood from the femoral, and was also suffering from some form of infection. He cannot have been more than fifteen or sixteen years old. Right from the start he made it clear he was going to be a nuisance.

In his livelier moments, he would urinate and defecate on the floor near his bed, knock the kidney bowl out of my hands when I approached him, pull out his intravenous lines, and take great delight in telling me what the victorious German soldiers would do to English pig women like me when they had won the war.

I grew to hate Dieter, and I dreaded having to approach him, but he was on my ward, and there was no way around it. Dorothy helped me as best she could, but he made her even more nervous. She shook so much around him that she could not administer an injection.

Last night, while I was on duty, I heard Dieter cry out, and I went over to his bed to see what was the matter. He was burning up with fever, his breath an ominous rattle in his throat. We had known that he had an infection, but we had not known how serious it was, how long he had lain unattended before the stretcher bearers took him to the field dressing station.

His brow was hot and dry, his eyes unfocused. I made a move to go and get a cool cloth but he grabbed my wrist with a remarkably strong hand and begged me not to leave him. His English was quite good. I explained what I was going to do, and he relaxed his grasp but begged me to come back.

I brought the cloth and sat on a canvas chair beside his bed. It was dark, and the only light came from the few hurricane lamps placed around the marquee tent. The wind was flapping the canvas and making shadows, like hand-puppet shows, all over the place. Dieter seemed to be hallucinating, lost in a world of memory, or imagination, as I mopped his feverish brow and whispered endearments. I heard the word "mutter" several times and knew he was calling for his mother. So many do when they are dying. All the time he was gripping my wrist like a drowning man hanging on to a raft. Occasionally, his body would go into spasms, and he would cry out, waking some of the other patients and bringing forth a few groans and requests to be quiet.

This seemed to go on for hours. Dorothy took care of the rest of my duties for the night, and I stayed where I was, mopping Dieter's brow, telling him all would be well in the morning and he would soon be reunited with his mother. Soon, I could see faint daylight breaking through the canvas, the air outside turning slowly from black to gray. Dieter clung on. I had done all I could for him in the way of medicines and care, though perhaps if we had given him penicillin from the start, instead of the sulfonamides the Germans carry with them, it would have helped. The problem is that penicillin is so expensive, and we have so little of it, that we must save it for our own wounded. At least, that is the rule at this hospital.

Dieter's pulse fluttered under my searching finger, then it slowed down and became so weak that I could no longer feel it. He had one more spasm, then I heard the death rattle in his chest, an unmistakable sound, and he was gone.

I managed to uncurl his fingers from my wrist and gently close his staring blue eyes. I cried and cursed the war then, in that tent in the half dark with the dead German boy lying before me, made fists and banged them against the mattress impotently. I had hated Dieter, feared him, even, but I hated and feared what had killed him even more.

Now I sit outside my tent exhausted and drink hot coffee and smoke a cigarette in the dismal morning light, the day's activity starting up all around me. I hear the lonely whistle of the first train leaving Caen for Bayeux. If I do not sleep soon, there will be no sleep for me today. But how am I supposed to sleep after all this?

————

JANUARY 2011

It was my turn to look gobsmacked, and no doubt I did. I certainly felt as if the earth had shifted underneath my feet, and I couldn't find purchase anymore. *I was wrong.* The knowledge left me dizzy and empty, treading space the way you tread water in the deep end. All these months I had believed that Grace Fox *couldn't* have murdered her husband, then I had reluctantly accepted that she *might* have done, but that if she had, she had a very good reason, a reason that, for me, at any rate, partly exonerated her. Now all this had been swept away by a couple of sentences out of Billy Strang's mouth. I had been *so sure.*

I could see Billy's lips moving, but I couldn't hear a word he was saying. It was like looking down on the waves and not hearing them. I had the sensation that my ears were blocked, the way I used to feel every time in a plane at takeoff or landing. Finally, I heard his words as if from a great distance. "Are you all right? You've turned very pale. Would you like a drop of brandy or something?"

I shook my head. I was still vaguely aware that I had to get back to my hotel somehow, and the last thing I wanted was to get lost in Khayelitsha or fall afoul of the South African police over a drunk-driving charge. "No," I managed. "I'm all right. Just a bit of jet lag, I suppose. I wouldn't mind a cup of tea or something."

"I gave up tea years ago, but I can do you a decent cup of coffee."

"Thanks. Just black. No sugar."

While he went to make it, I stood by the window staring down at the silent waves, the rocks, the beach, the cars speeding by on the main coast road. It all suddenly seemed so alien, and the searing ache of missing Laura cramped my heart so hard I thought I was going to collapse. Was this what my life had become? The pursuit of an illusion? Ghosts and whispers and shadows. It was as close to fainting as I had ever come. I was wrong. Wrong about Grace. Wrong about everything. What would I say to Louise? To Heather? To Wilf? To Sam? I began to feel as if Grace herself had somehow let me down, taken me in with her heroic, enigmatic beauty and silence.

Billy came back with the coffee. "You certainly seem to have had a bit of a shock," he said. "Why don't you sit down again? Do you want to know the real story? I guarantee you'll find it even more interesting than the one you made up."

I found that hard to believe, but I took the coffee and sat. "Yes. I'm sorry," I said. "I don't usually behave so foolishly. You must think I'm crazy."

"Not at all. I don't know if it will help, but let me tell you the truth. Let me tell you why I really went to talk to Grace Fox that day."

"HAVE YOU EVER HEARD OF AN ESTABLISHMENT CALLED PORTON DOWN?"

Indeed I had, many times over the years, and I had also seen it mentioned quite recently, in Grace's war journal. "Yes," I said, frowning.

"Well, then," said Billy, "you'll know it's not exactly on a par with Watership Down. It's a collection of ugly buildings near Salisbury, owned by the military, by the Ministry of Defense, actually. Been around since about 1916, probably at first as a response to the Germans using chemical warfare in World War One, mustard gas and the like. A top-secret scientific research establishment. It kept pace with the times. It was the secret everybody knew, though nobody outside really knew what went on in there, not even the government, if we're to believe what they say. But it's also the sort of place most people have heard of, these days, and most know it's a pretty sinister establishment connected with chemical warfare, nerve gas, anthrax and the like, and not without a few skeletons in its cupboards. The sort of secret we'd rather have swept under the carpet. The sort of things other countries do, and we react with moral outrage."

"I've heard of it a number of times over the years," I told him. "And Grace mentioned it in her journal."

Billy gave me a sharp glance. "Did she now? She never told me that."

I told him about the visit to the mysterious chateau with Meers and Maddox and Dorothy and the corporals. "It's not surprising she didn't say anything to you, though," I added. "Apparently she didn't talk about her war service at all. If you read the journal, you can understand why."

"My God," said Billy. "I never knew. Poor Grace." He looked at me with new understanding. "So when I mentioned it to her . . ."

"It would have rung a bell, yes. A loud one. According to the journal, the whole incident distressed her. But I still don't understand."

Billy got up and walked over to the window, stared down at the ocean for a while in silence, then came back. His expression was grim. "I never knew, believe me. I had no idea what she did during the war, that she'd come across such things."

"Like I said, she never talked about it. She was a Queen Alexandra's nurse. Served in Singapore when it fell and in Europe right up to the end."

"How terrible it must have been for her. She had such a sweet nature when I knew her. I must admit, later she seemed sadder, more distant, but I put that down to the times, to age, and to life with that miserable husband of hers."

"You were telling your story. Porton Down."

"Yes, sorry. I . . . well, it was a few weeks earlier, actually, around the end of November 1952. Word had got around camp that if you volunteered for a week at this special place—we were told it was a common-cold unit, and they were doing research into curing colds—then you'd be given two bob a day and a three-day pass. I knew I'd be going overseas soon, so I thought I'd volunteer."

"What happened?"

"I was one of the lucky ones. At that time, I found out later, they were mostly researching nerve agents, like VX, biological agents, anthrax and the like, and riot-control tactics, like CS gas. Mostly, I just lay around in bed and had various tests, just a lot of needles, really, but one day they took me to another hut, full of little chambers, like showers. But it wasn't water that came out, it was a stream of gas. I must have passed out, because when I woke up I was back in bed and when I tried to breathe I felt as if my lungs were on fire. My throat was raw, as if I had a coil of barbed wire caught in it, and my face was stinging like I'd been whipped with nettles."

"And you say you were lucky?"

"Oh, yes. For that I got my two bob a day and a three-day pass. I had no idea what it was at the time, but looking back, it was probably some form of CS gas, the stuff the French used against the students in the '68 riots. The effects were temporary, and there was no permanent damage to my respiratory system. Other poor sods weren't so fortunate. Some got given LSD and felt their bodies crawling with spiders, and ended up in padded cells, or they got injected with bubonic plague, anthrax, smallpox, and what have you. Plenty of people who volunteered like I did ended up with chronic bronchitis, various cancers, paralysis, nervous disorders, brain tumors, you name it. Not long after I was there, there were rumors of a man, Ronald Maddison, I found out much later, who was tested with sarin in 1953 and died. They covered it up, of course, until his relatives and friends got a second inquest granted in 2004, which found his death to be unlawful. Sarin was one of the nerve agents we took from the Germans late in the war. They'd been testing that and others like it for years on prisoners in the research hospitals, concentration camps, and POW camps. Our scientists didn't even know they existed at that time. That would probably be what the man Grace mentioned in her journal would have been after."

"Meers. Yes. Grace mentioned sarin and tabun. You seem to know quite a bit about it."

"I made it my business to find out."

"And Grace? How does she fit into all this?"

Billy sighed and turned away. He picked up his glass, noticed it was empty, and went to refill it. I took a refill of wine, too. This afternoon was turning out to be far more traumatic than I had expected. If the worst came to the worst, I'd leave the car parked at Billy's and get a hotel in Simon's Town for the night.

"I told her all about it. See, I saw *him* there. Her husband. Dr. Fox. He didn't recognize me, of course. Wouldn't have, even if he'd noticed me, which he didn't. I'd grown up a bit since I was seven. But he hadn't changed much. I saw him wandering around with one of the head honchos, a reptile of a man called Smeaton, and he seemed quite at home. Very much at home, in fact. He didn't seem like part of the staff—he never wore a white coat, for one thing—but he knew his way around, like he'd been there before. I only overheard one snippet, but I'm sure Smeaton said to him, 'Of course, when you come to work here . . .'"

Suddenly it became clear to me. The new job. A hospital near Salisbury. The wartime absences, the secrecy surrounding Kilnsgate in the early 1940s, barbed wire and sentries, Fox's qualifications in neurology and microbiology, his neglect of the general practice later. All the little bits and pieces that meant nothing in themselves until the magnet underneath made a pattern of the iron filings. Ernest Fox was deeply involved with whatever went on at Porton Down, had probably been connected ever since his World War One experience with mustard gas, but certainly since the Second World War. It wasn't the Special Operations Executive at Kilnsgate, or if it was, they were working hand in glove with the Porton Down boffins. Ernest Fox had consulted, worked on special projects, kept it all secret, of course, and finally they had offered him a permanent, full-time position. His reward? Or perhaps they really needed his experience and knowledge. It was the beginning of the Cold War, and chemical warfare research and development were really coming into their own, a hot commodity at Porton Down.

"So you arranged to talk to Grace?" I said.

"Yes. I just thought she should know, that's all, so I got in touch with her. I didn't know anything about her lover or her war experiences. I must admit, I was surprised by what a profound effect what I had to say had on her, much more than I would have expected. She didn't lose control or anything, but there were tears in her eyes when she left me. Then two days later she rang me at the barracks and asked to meet again."

"You met for a *second* time?"

"Yes. In Darlington. The day before New Year's Eve. We met for a cup of tea at a café in town, and she showed me a letter. I think she partly wanted me to verify that it was to do with what I'd told her, and partly to show me I was right."

"What was in it?"

"It was from the Ministry of Defense. I can't remember all the details, but it seemed very formal. It thanked Ernest for all his work on special projects and research over the years, for a liftetime of dedication and invaluable experience. It made some special mention of Kilnsgate House in 1941, and invited him to become a member of the permanent staff at Porton Down. There was a passing reference to his having already signed the Official Secrets Act, and a reminder that the establishment's work was still of a highly top-secret nature and that he should not discuss either it, or the job offer, with anyone."

"A hospital near Salisbury," I said.

"Come again?"

"Oh, sorry. It's what he told everyone, where he was going. The police thought it was Grace's real motive for poisoning Ernest, because he'd got a job at a hospital near Salisbury, and it meant she would have to leave her lover."

"Good God," said Billy.

"What on earth made you tell her in the first place? I mean, you hardly knew her. You'd only spent four months at Kilnsgate nearly fourteen years before."

Billy paused for a moment, then said, "I suppose I was young and foolhardy, a bit zealous perhaps, once I found out what was going on. I asked around a bit, picked up a few rumors about the place and what went on there. Mrs. Fox had always been good to me. It was a difficult time in my life, the first time away from home, and I remembered her kindness. You do. Like I said, my time at Kilnsgate was a happy time. The sun shone every day. I didn't want her to have to have anything to do with what went on at Porton Down. I suppose you could say I was being protective. I also hoped that she might be able to dissuade her husband from working there. I never imagined for a moment there could be such tragic consequences."

"You couldn't know," I said. "What did Grace say?"

"She was quiet for a while, deep in thought, then she folded the letter carefully, put it away, and thanked me. She gave me a present. She must have got it that very day in Darlington, before we met."

"What was it?"

He held up his index finger then disappeared into another room for a few moments, returning with a silver pocket watch and chain, which he handed to me. GO SAFELY WHEREVER YOU MAY GO was inscribed on the back, along with REMEMBER ME and Grace's name. There was a dent near the edge on one side. "What's that?" I asked.

Billy smiled. "I had it with me in Kenya. Top pocket. It deflected a Mau-Mau bullet. Doc told me it would have entered my heart for certain, but I got off lucky. I must admit, it didn't feel that way at the time. I was laid up for a month with infections and drains and what have you, nearly lost my arm, but even so . . ."

"Now there's a story," I said. "Did Grace say anything more?"

"Yes. Just before we parted company, she touched my arm and assured me that she would do whatever she could to talk Ernest out of going to work at Porton Down. I assumed she was going to lay down the law to him. You know, once they get their feet dug in, in my experience, certain women usually get their way, and I thought Grace was probably one of them. Seems I was wrong about that, too."

"They rowed about it," I told him, remembering Hetty Larkin's testimony, "but I don't think he listened to her. She certainly didn't get her way." The letter that Hetty referred to could only have been the one Billy had just mentioned. Ernest must have discovered it was missing while Grace was in Darlington talking to Billy and showing it to him, and when she got back, he confronted her. She told him what she thought of his plans, that she wasn't going, and probably that if he had any conscience and humanity left in him, he wouldn't go, either, but he no doubt laughed in her face and brushed aside all her objections.

"So what I told her destroyed her," Billy said.

"No, Billy," I said. "What her husband *was* destroyed her. She put up with him for years, made excuses, perhaps even turned a blind eye. But when she had to face the truth, she wasn't going to go and live in Salisbury with a man who worked at a place like Porton Down. That wasn't Grace. It was against all her sense of humanity. She'd seen what those people did. Meers. The Germans. That wasn't the world she subscribed to, the life she wanted."

"But I set things in motion."

"Ernest himself did that with all the help he gave them over the years. No doubt he invited them to commandeer Kilnsgate House for a while during the war, too, and Grace may have known something about that. Or maybe it started earlier. He treated mustard-gas victims in the first war. Who knows? It doesn't really matter. One way or another, you were only a catalyst. I'd guess Grace already had her suspicions that something wasn't quite right. She wasn't stupid. And she'd have found out soon enough if they had gone to Salisbury."

As it happened, I didn't have to leave my car and stay in Simon's Town. After a couple of hours of more conversation and a cup or two more of Billy's strong coffee, I felt that I was perfectly fit to drive. I wanted to get away, needed to get back to the anonymous grandeur of the Cape Grace and think.

I was hungry, but I went up to my room first to shower and change. I'd caught enough heat to bring me out in a sweat, despite all the air-conditioning, and after my walk down by the sea earlier, I felt as if I still had sand in my hair. There were no phone messages waiting for me and no one I wanted to call right now. All I had was an e-mail from Heather saying she missed me. I fired off a quick reply telling her all was well, that I had found Billy and would tell her everything when I got back.

After I had dried myself off, I put on my bathrobe and stood on the balcony for a while in the warm evening air looking out over the harbor, the city center lights, the reflections rippling in the water, and the massed shapes of Signal Hill and Table Mountain against the darkening, crimson-streaked sky. The expensive boats in the marina creaked as they bobbed up and down, and their cables rattled and rang. Seagulls squealed as they searched for shoals of fish. I went back inside, put on some fresh clothes, and took the elevator down to the hotel dining room.

My head was still in a whirl from my talk with Billy, my emotions unsettled, so I ordered a Beefeater martini, straight up, with olives, and picked a bottle of a Glen Carlou estate red blend to drink later with dinner. If I didn't finish it, I could take the rest of the bottle up to my room and get quietly pissed on the balcony. I wasn't going anywhere tonight. I ordered fresh oysters to start and springbok loin for my main.

The restaurant was hushed and dim. I didn't have much of a view, only the other diners and a mural of Signal Hill on the wall, but that was fine with me. I was in the mood for thinking, for contemplation, not for sightseeing. After the shock of Billy Strang's tale, I had a lot of broken pieces to rearrange into some sort of new order. Perhaps I had been wrong about Grace's innocence, but I was convinced that the court had been wrong about her motives. It might not have mattered to them, had they even known. They could well have taken the establishment's side against Grace and treated her more like some sort of foreign agitator than the humanitarian she was. I thought that perhaps if they had known her real reasons, though, and learned something of what she had experienced during the war, the judge, at least, might have shown some mercy.

I tried to picture that final argument in my mind's eye, what was said. Kilnsgate on a wintry day, with the wind howling in the chimney and sparks spitting from the fire, snowflakes slithering down the windows as they melted. There was a job offer at a hospital near Salisbury, Ernest had said. He had decided to take it, and that was that. After her talk with Billy, Grace must have told Ernest that she knew the truth about this job, and they weren't going anywhere. Ernest had probably told her to mind her own business and not pry into his affairs. Perhaps he knew about Sam and taunted her about having to leave her lover, whether she liked it or not. Perhaps he threatened her, hit her, even. But that wasn't her motive. Ernest was dragging her to the monsters, to the dark side, whether he saw it that way or not.

Of course, Grace wouldn't have to do the work he was going to do, but how could she stand at his side and be his loyal wife when she knew what he was doing? And who would their friends be? Others who did the same work, no doubt, having nice dinner parties and pretending all was well while they injected people with anthrax and sprayed them with VX nerve agent and tried to concoct even more gruesome ways of debilitating and disposing of their fellow men. Never admitting what they *really* did, that they were seeking methods of mass murder. A life of lies, evasions. How could she let him do it after all she had been through in Southeast Asia, seen at the chateau in Normandy, after the things Billy had told her about? Perhaps she already suspected that her husband was a monster because of his coldness, his absences, his research, his secret war work? Perhaps she knew it had been building up to something like this. Maybe people had even told her what had gone on at Kilnsgate during the war, while she was in Singapore. All I knew was that what had seemed to me earlier to be an interesting side street off the main route—Kilnsgate's war history, the foot-and-mouth outbreak, Nat Bunting's disappearance—had now become the main route. After the letter and Grace's talk with Billy, she had reached a watershed. She couldn't go on any longer the way things were, whether she had harbored earlier suspicions or not. Now she *knew*. Things had reached the breaking point. She had to do something.

Ernest wouldn't have listened to her. He would have dismissed her as a foolish romantic woman, told her she didn't understand the necessities of modern life, that sometimes you had to do things that were unpleasant. For your country. For a way of life you believed in. He would have said she was an idealist, a dreamer. Well, perhaps she was, she argued back, but it was better than being a monster. Ernest had scolded her for taking the letter. Grace had realized that all her protests were falling on deaf ears, and in the meantime, Billy went off to fight the Mau-Mau, unaware of the storm he had unleashed back at Kilnsgate.

Dinner arrived shortly after I had finished the half dozen excellent Namibian oysters, the springbok perfectly pink and tender to the knife. I poured a glass of red and started to eat, gazing around. A young couple, on their honeymoon by the looks of them, sat to my left. Opposite was an elderly colonial type, complete with brick-red complexion and white handlebar mustache, who was probably complaining to his stout wife about the natives. One rather noisy group was celebrating a birthday or anniversary at the far end, and the only other person within my field of vision was another lone diner, like myself, reading a book on his iPad.

Perhaps Grace *had* poisoned her husband. I had to accept that I might have been wrong about that. I was certainly way off beam with my pedophile theory. Everything she had experienced and had been told to forget had no doubt burst back into her consciousness after her talk with Billy and her discovery of the letter offering a job at Porton Down. She couldn't be a party to any of that. She was a nurse, Ernest was a doctor; they were supposed to save lives, not take them. Besides, she would have remembered the sinister Meers and his thuggish corporals; rightly or wrongly, they were the kind of people she associated with Porton Down.

In a way, if Grace had been responsible for her husband's death, that made us birds of a feather. Perhaps I had wanted to prove her innocent because I wanted, in some odd, vicarious way, to partake of that innocence myself? But it had turned out all wrong. My plan had backfired on me.

Oh, there were plenty of differences, certainly. Ernest probably had a few good years left in him, despite his dicky heart, whereas Laura wasn't dying quickly enough, and her agony increased with every moment. Grace had done humanity a favor; I had done Laura a favor. She had begged me and begged me, and every time I refused, my heart broke a little more. In the end, I could stand neither her pain nor my own any longer. A little extra morphine wasn't such a difficult thing to manage at home, and if our doctor suspected, as he probably did, then he clearly thought it as much of a mercy as I did. I held her hand and watched her die, looked into her eyes and saw the life go out of them, took her in my arms, felt the spirit leave like the silence at the end of a magnificent symphony. The only difference was, you could play the music again and again; a life plays only once.

I told myself that I had done Laura a favor, and I knew in my heart that it was true, but I had still killed her. Did that make me a murderer? Did it make me a monster? Grace, too? I don't know. Sometimes I think so. Sometimes I feel that the guilty knowledge of what I have done, my shabby, heartbreaking secret, separates me from the rest of humanity, from the others here in the dining room tonight. Maybe that is why I sought such solitude at Kilnsgate. But there I met Grace Fox, and if I had ever wondered why on earth I became obsessed with her, as I had many times on my quest, then I knew now.

Taking another look around the room, I finished my glass of wine and carried the rest of the bottle back up to my room, where I sat outside and drank on the balcony in the warm African night, listening to the cables thrumming in the marina and the breeze rustling the palms below until the birds began to sing and the sun began to rise and its tentative rays silhouetted Signal Hill and Table Mountain.

24

**Extract from the *Journal of Grace Elizabeth Fox*
(ed. Louise King), October 1945, Indian Ocean.**

WEDNESDAY, OCTOBER 10, 1945

T HE DOLPHINS PLAY ALONGSIDE US NEARLY EVERY DAY NOW. WE ARE IN
that still, hot, humid world where the ocean is a blue mirror and
everything seems to move slowly, as if through thickened air. I am
going home again.

I am still not clear on why I volunteered to travel out to Singapore
again, except perhaps that I needed some sense of coming full circle,
of finding some sort of peace with myself. And for all these years,
no matter what, I have never been able to get rid of the feeling that it
should have been me who died out on that raft, not Brenda. I have carried the guilt of survival around with me through France and Belgium,
through a defeated Germany, among the mass graves, the unbearable
stench of the huts, and the walking shadows of Belsen, a ruined Berlin
full of liberating Russians. Hell on earth. I still have my guilt, and I
have not yet found peace.

Now I sit on deck after midnight, smoking, and strands of my hair stick to the sweat on my brow and cheeks and neck. Was it a mistake to come back here on the hospital ship after we had won the war in Europe? I don't think so. Deep inside, I knew it was always Singapore where I really came of age, where I lost what innocence I had. Not to men. I do not mean that kind of innocence. It was remarkably easy to remain the faithful, responsible married woman while all around me lost their hearts for a night, or a week, despite Stephen's kiss. I would be lying if I did not admit there were times when I would have liked to shed my inhibitions and everything else and joined in, and I came close to that with Stephen. The innocence I lost was of a different sort.

Everyone on this hospital ship is from the "liberated" Japanese prison camps on Sumatra; or from Changi, in Singapore; or Stanley, in Hong Kong. Some were among the hordes who arrived after us at Padang, when there were no more ships. They could do nothing but wait there until the Japanese came and took them prisoner. Others had simply been found wandering in the jungle, abandoned by their defeated guards after the bombs were dropped on Hiroshima and Nagasaki and Japan surrendered. Nobody knew what camps they were from. They have all been nursed and given nutrition in local hospitals and are now on their way home. There are no battlefield wounds, no missing limbs, but there are infections. Luckily, we have penicillin. Most are men, but there are also many civilian women and children, and sisters.

Most evenings I spend with Kathleen. She never smiles now and does not speak—I suspect as much as anything else that she must be embarrassed by the change in her voice the missing teeth have caused. I should also imagine that her surprising laugh is all but gone now. Our former statuesque beauty is a string bean, weighing only six stone, legs like matchsticks, knees like cricket balls. Her beautiful blond hair is stringy and lusterless, torn away in patches, her scalp raw.

At first, I did not recognize her, nor she me. It took one of the other sisters who had seen how inseparable we were on our first journey all those years ago to reintroduce us. It is hard. Kathleen does not remember very much. She has no passion for life. At night she has frightening dreams—they all do—and she cries out a lot. In the daytime heat she is listless and inert. She has no interest in anything. I try to talk to her about ordinary daily matters, the routine, who is causing trouble, where we are, the dolphins, but it means nothing to her. Kathleen is broken. She hums rambling melodies to herself a lot.

I managed to learn from the other sister, whose name is Mary, that Doris died of dysentery in the Stanley camp. She need not have died, but the Japanese withheld all medicines the Red Cross sent, so she could not be treated. Kathleen nursed her until the end.

Mary also told me what happened at the hospital in Hong Kong on Christmas Day, 1941. We had heard rumors before, back in Singapore, but the reality was even worse, the sisters subjected to the most vile degradations, then killed, and the men, doctors and patients alike, bayonetted.

Stories had also started making the rounds about the Bangka Island massacre. Some Australian nurses I had known and watched sail out of Singapore just before us on the *Vyner Brooke*, were bombed and shipwrecked, as we were, but managed to get to Bangka Island, where they tried to surrender to the Japanese.

When the Japanese patrol came to the beach, they first took all the men around the headland and shot them, then they forced the women to walk out into the sea and machine-gunned them all. One Australian nurse survived—the bullet went straight through her leg without causing any major damage—played dead, and eventually went on to survive a prison camp and tell her story.

I asked a number of the officers about Stephen Fawley, but they knew nothing. One thought he had probably been killed in the fighting. Either way, nobody had seen him later, in the camps.

But for the few patients who can, and do, talk, the rest are like Kathleen. They have lost their will to live. They are frightened of their own shadows, frightened of what is to come; they live in a perpetual state of fear. Though they have been half starved, they can hardly eat, as their digestive systems have weakened and suffered permanent damage from starvation at the hands of their captors. We feed them as best we can, but for the nightmares we can do nothing at all.

Even as I sit here now, in the sultry beauty of the tropical night, the peaceful motion of the ship, the gentle slapping of water against the sides, I cannot fail to be aware of the sound rising up from the depths of the ship's wards. It is a sound like no other I have ever heard on earth, made up of a thousand nightmares, the dying boys calling for their mothers, the endless wailing from the completely unhinged, and hovering around it all, the terrible silence of those who have lost everything; their voices, even themselves.

FEBRUARY 2011

Kilnsgate House was waiting for me like an old friend when I got out of the taxi I'd taken from the Darlington railway station. A pile of mail awaited me inside, scattered over the floor below the letter box. It was mostly bills and junk. Nobody writes letters anymore in these days of e-mails and texts. I wondered if the collected e-mails of John Keats would have been half as interesting as his letters. I doubted it. The medium does make a difference.

I dumped my bag in the hall, turned up the central heating, and went into the kitchen to make a cup of tea. It was late afternoon, and I had been awake all night on the plane from Cape Town and spent most of the day getting home from Heathrow, my patience with the train system definitely wearing thin. There was no excuse. It hadn't even been snowing.

I had spent my last day in Cape Town wandering the waterfront cafés and shops. I had bought a wraparound summer dress of beautiful patterned material at the market for Heather. I didn't know whether it was the kind of thing she would wear or not, but at least she might appreciate the design and the African colors and use it as a wall hanging. I thought she would look good in it, at any rate. I had also bought a few CDs of local musicians for myself—Judith Sephuma, Abdullah Ibrahim, Wanda Baloyi, Pops Mohamed—finding that the record shop I had discovered on my previous visit was still thriving.

When my tea was ready, I carried it through to the living-dining room and sat by the fire. I would probably light it later. It was early

February, and the snow had all gone, but that all-permeating York-shire chill was in the air, making it seem colder, especially after the South African sun. The temperature outside was six degrees Celsius, and the sky was gray and threatening rain. The woods beyond my back garden seemed dreary and forbidding. I put some Abdullah Ibrahim jazz piano on, then settled in my comfortable armchair to sort out the post. As I had thought, it turned out to be bills and circulars. The only letter of any interest was an invitation to speak at a film festival at London's South Bank Center in May. I decided I would probably go. It could be fun.

Next I checked the messages on my phone. There were two sales calls—BT and double glazing—and a welcome-home message from Heather. She said to give her a ring. I checked my watch. It was ten to four and already getting dark. I was too tired for company tonight, too tired for anything, really, except a final bit of research I needed to do online.

There was also a message from Mother, asking me in her inimitable way, if I was still alive. I immediately felt guilty. With all the excitement of finding Louise and then Billy Strang, I had forgotten about Mother. I rang back and listened to her complain about the weather for about fifteen minutes, then promised to come and visit her as soon as I could, and hung up.

Next I phoned Heather and we agreed to meet in a couple of days, when I had caught up on my sleep. Next, I had a couple of important phone calls to make. I had had plenty of time since my afternoon with Billy Strang to think things over, and I believed that after all my floundering around in the dark I now knew the truth about what had happened on that first of January 1953, here at Kilnsgate. Louise King and Samuel Porter deserved to know before anyone else, so I picked up the phone.

THE FOLLOWING MORNING, STILL DRAGGING MY FEET A LITTLE, I CARRIED A spade up the hill to the lime kiln and surveyed the tangled mess of weeds inside. I attempted a couple of thrusts, but soon realized it was no good; I couldn't do this by myself. I didn't feel confident enough to call in the authorities at this stage, but there was only one way to find out if I was right, and that was to dig.

I went back to the house and phoned Tony Brotherton. When I explained my theory, he clearly thought I was crazy, but I reminded him of his grandfather's concerns, and in less than half an hour he arrived with Jill and two strong farm laborers.

Feeling useless, I stood by, leaned on a tree, and watched them work. Though it was a chilly February morning, they soon broke a sweat as the pile of sod and earth grew beside the kiln. I had no idea how far down they would have to dig, and it was almost an hour later when Jill bent over and said, "Good Lord, Chris. You'd better come over here and have a look at this."

I walked over, and my gaze followed her pointing finger. There, in the bed of soil, was what looked like the skeleton of a human hand. I had no idea of anatomy, of course, and I will admit it could easily have been from a cow or a sheep, but as Jill carefully brushed away the rest of the clinging soil, the form slowly took shape, and by the time she had done the best she could, there was not one of us standing there who was not convinced that we were looking at a human skeleton.

I HAD JUST PUT THE LASAGNE IN THE OVEN ABOUT A QUARTER OF AN HOUR before Heather arrived for dinner two days later. Across from Kilnsgate, the lime kiln was still mysteriously screened off by canvas, though it was deserted at the moment. After our grim discovery, I had called the police, of course, and they had removed the remains for forensic examination. Their preliminary findings, communicated to me that afternoon by the detective assigned to the case, had borne out my suspicions, but had not determined the cause of death. Perhaps that was too much to ask after all this time.

I had planned a simple meal, entirely homemade, accompanied by a Caesar salad—a genuine one, not the kind they serve with cucumber and tomatoes at the local Italian restaurant—topped off by a dish of fruit and a plate of local cheeses from Ken Warne.

Heather looked as lovely as ever, dressed simply in black tights and a roll-neck rust-colored dress that came to just above her knees, her hair tied back with a green ribbon at the nape of her neck.

"My God," she said as I led her through to the living room. "You've got a suntan and you were only away three days."

"I tan quickly," I said. Nobody ever noticed in L.A. I had, however, developed a distinct Yorkshire pallor since I had been over here, and the tan wouldn't last long. I gave Heather the dress I had bought her, and she made excited sounds about the colors and the pattern, wrapping it around herself, trying to figure out how she could wear it decently. "Maybe we can try a few variations later," I suggested.

By the fire, which I had lit before preparing dinner, I poured us each a glass of wine, and we sat down. "From what you told me on the phone there's been more than a little excitement around here," Heather said.

"You could say that."

"It all sounds rather gruesome. Bodies in the lime kiln."

"One body," I said. "And it was a skeleton."

"Even so." She gave a little shiver. "To think it's been out there all that time."

"Since 1941 or 1942, to be exact," I said. "Nat Bunting."

"But how do they know?"

"He had a club foot. It shows on the skeleton."

"And what happened to him?"

"That we don't know."

"What do you think?"

"I have plenty of theories, but I can't be certain. At first I thought it was because he might have seen something, found out too much. Tony Brotherton's grandfather saw Nat *inside* the wired-off compound at Kilnsgate during the war."

"You only thought that at first?"

"Nat was . . . challenged," I said. "He wouldn't have known it if he had seen something he wasn't supposed to see."

"But they probably didn't know that."

"Ernest Fox did."

"So, what then?"

"I know it sounds far-fetched, but I think he may have died as a result of the experiments they were doing there at Kilnsgate, most likely infected by accident. I did a bit of research, and not much of it is public, but what we do know is that in World War Two the Porton Down people were doing a lot of experiments with biological weapons. Not so long ago, some War Cabinet committee files were released to the National Archive, and it turns out that they were particularly interested in bacteriological diseases such as typhoid, dysentery, and cholera in humans, and anthrax, swine fever, and foot-and-mouth in animals."

"Animals?"

"Yes. They produced cattle cakes doctored with anthrax. They were going to drop them over Germany to poison the food supply."

"Who are they?"

"Us, I mean."

"Good Lord. That's crazy. And terrible."

"As it turned out, we discovered that cattle are suspicious of new types of food and unlikely to take the bait, so we scrapped that plan. Anyway, there *was* an outbreak of foot-and-mouth at the Brotherton farm. It was dealt with very quickly by the military and hushed up. It never spread beyond the one farm, which is almost unheard of in foot-and-mouth."

"How could they get to it that quickly?"

"They couldn't unless they knew it had happened."

"So you think they caused it?"

"It seems a logical explanation. And I'm not even sure it was foot-and-mouth. It could have been anthrax. That could also have been what killed Nat Bunting. But that's just speculation on my part."

"What else could have happened to him?"

I shrugged. "Who knows? Maybe they actually injected him with anthrax or dysentery and he died, like Ronald Maddison did in 1953 in the sarin experiments? They may even have been playing around with antidotes, vaccinations against these diseases they thought the Nazis were going to unleash. Or maybe, as I said, he came into contact with something by accident, got too close, and they simply buried the body under the lime kiln."

"And put quicklime on it?"

"There wouldn't be much point. Most people have the wrong idea about using quicklime to get rid of bodies. Quicklime burns the skin it comes into contact with, yes, if you add water, but afterward it tends to dry out the tissues and cause mummification. Hardly getting rid of the evidence! Anyway, they used it on Brotherton's cows, mostly because it would kill anthrax spores or foot-and-mouth, but I should imagine the lime kiln was just a handy place to hide a body. As for the full story, what Nat was doing up there, what really happened to him, I doubt we'll ever know. I do know that Nat was apparently obsessed with joining up, but no one would have him because of his physical and mental handicaps. Maybe he saw the unit at Kilnsgate and went to ask if he could join up with them? Maybe they had a place for him? I don't like to think they simply plucked people out of the landscape and shot them full of dysentery or typhus, but if they did, then Nat Bunting was probably a safe bet. There wouldn't be much of a hue and cry over him. It didn't even make the papers."

"But that's terrible."

"Terrible things happen in war. Look at what Grace witnessed at the chateau in Normandy and later, in the camps. Look at some of the stories that have come out about Japanese and German medical experiments on POWs and concentration camp victims. Do you think we were that much better?"

"I do like to think so. Yes. To be honest, it's sickening to think we were brought down to that level, too. I mean, trying to give cows anthrax or foot-and-mouth is one thing, but . . ."

"I'm not saying that was the case. Just that it's possible. I certainly think they were responsible for the foot-and-mouth outbreak, or whatever it was, at Brotherton's farm—it doesn't make any sense otherwise—and however he met his end, Nat Bunting certainly didn't bury himself. I suppose it's possible that he got sick and crawled off to die there and his body just got covered up by the elements over time."

"Surely there must have been others involved in these experiments?"

"Probably. Volunteers, or prisoners from the nearby POW camp. But Nat was the one who died, and for whatever reasons nobody else spoke out."

"Couldn't it just have been some wandering maniac?"

"How many of those are there? Realistically? Besides, Kilnsgate, including the lime kiln, was cordoned off by barbed wire and armed guards when it happened. Wilf said the kids found a gap, which may have been how Nat got in, too, but a wandering maniac as well?"

Heather ran her finger around the rim of her wineglass. "Does this have anything to do with what happened later? With Grace Fox and her husband?"

"I think it does," I said.

"Tell me."

"Over dinner." I got up to check on the lasagne. It was done and only needed to rest for ten minutes while I made the salad.

"Bastard," Heather said, following me into the kitchen. "Making me wait like this."

She leaned back against the fridge, and I had to open the door to take out the lettuce. As I approached, she didn't move, just cocked her head sideways and pouted at me. I flashed back on that first dinner here, with Derek and Charlotte, how Heather had got drunk and almost made a pass in exactly the same place. This time I leaned forward and kissed her, and she responded. A lot had changed. I gently eased her out of the way and opened the fridge. "You don't have to bug me while I'm putting dinner together, you know," I said "You're perfectly welcome to go sit in front of the fire, sip your wine, listen to the music, and contemplate life."

"Well, I can see exactly how much *you* missed *me*," Heather said, with a mock pout, and left the kitchen.

IT DIDN'T TAKE ME LONG TO THROW THE SALAD TOGETHER, AND BY THEN THE lasagne was ready to cut and serve. I carried the plates through to the dining room table and Heather came to join me. The wine and fresh glasses were already there. I poured us each another glass. Susan Graham was singing "Les Nuits d'Eté" in the background. It all made for a very sensual atmosphere.

"Now will you *please* tell me what you found out?" Heather said. "I promise I'll just eat my dinner and I won't interrupt. Promise." She cut off a corner of lasagne and put it in her mouth.

"I found Billy Strang easily enough," I said. "Fit as a fiddle, he seems. As a matter of fact, he'd just come back from playing tennis. Apparently there's a young widow at the club he's chasing."

"A dirty old man, then?"

"No more than I am. Much older, though."

Heather laughed. "And was it all worthwhile? Leaving me here in freezing Yorkshire while you went gallivanting off to parts exotic? And warm."

I thought for a moment, then nodded. "I wasn't sure for a while—it seemed to knock all my theories for six—but yes, I think it was." I told her about the Porton Down connection and what Billy had said about seeing Ernest Fox there, the letter, the job offer and all.

When I had come to the end of that part of the story, Heather paused and said, "I see what you mean about it all tying together with Kilnsgate during the war, in a way, though there was no real practical connection, was there?"

"Except for Ernest's involvement," I said. "I should imagine Grace heard rumors, had her suspicions. She was very strong on war crimes. I remember Sam Porter telling me how she got along with Laura Knight like a house on fire. That was the artist who painted a series of scenes from the Nuremberg trials. Anyway, Grace would probably have heard about Nat Bunting and the foot-and-mouth, most likely from Hetty, though she probably didn't put two and two together until she talked to Billy."

"So not only does she have to leave her lover, but her husband's going off to make nerve gas and give people anthrax. Is that why she did it?"

"That was the first thing I thought when I heard Billy's story. It changed all my suppositions."

"Yes, I remember that crazy theory you dreamed up about Ernest Fox being a pedophile."

I recalled how I had felt the moment after I had expounded my pedophile theory to Billy Strang, and he had told me how far off beam it was. The ground had opened up under my feet. "Even though I was wrong, it wasn't any more crazy than the story about Ernest Fox going to Porton Down to work on chemical weapons," I said. "It was certainly a possibility worth considering. I knew there was something. I was just searching for some sort of revelation about Ernest Fox, something that would make Grace *need* to kill him and not end up being entirely unsympathetic. You have to admit, if he were a pedophile, that would certainly be the case. Perhaps if he were going to be a merchant of death, it would be, too. It made sense that Billy had come back to see Grace and tell her something important like that."

"Is it enough, though?"

"Enough for what?"

"A motive."

"You've read the journal, haven't you?"

Heather shook her head slowly. "It's . . . unbelievable . . . incredible. That anyone can go through all that."

"Well, given what Grace saw at the chateau, and given her reaction to finding out what her husband was *really* going to be doing in this 'hospital near Salisbury,' and that because of this she would have to leave Sam and spend her mornings sipping coffee with women whose husbands did much the same thing as hers, I'd say it probably is, yes."

"So you now think that's why she did it? The job, Sam, everything?"

We'd finished our main course, so I took away the plates and replenished our wineglasses. The cheeses had been sitting on the table for a while, so they had come to room temperature. Neither of us was particularly hungry at the moment, though, so we took a break and just worked on the wine. Susan Graham had finished, and Annie Fischer's Beethoven piano sonatas played in the background. "Remember at first," I said, "when I got interested in the whole story and got to know a little about Grace, I became convinced that she couldn't have done it?"

"Yes. Then you changed your mind. Then you changed it again. You were back and forth like a yo-yo. In the end, you believed that she probably *had* done it, but that she had a more noble motive than toy-boys and money. Well, isn't what you've just told me more noble? Grace obviously couldn't persuade her husband against taking the chemical warfare job, and it would have done no good her telling the authorities. Who would she tell? Maybe some people, like Grace herself, were against that sort of thing, but Ernest Fox was just going to do valuable top-secret government work as far as most people were concerned, and the less they knew about it, the better. Nothing wrong in that."

"Unless, like Grace, you've come across a cellar full of dead people as a result of Nazi experiments with nerve agents, no. But you're right. He was only doing his patriotic duty. It's just that it's the kind of duty the government likes to keep quiet about, and whenever any-one blows the whistle, they say we're only defending ourselves. And Ernest Fox was only one man. By stopping him, Grace couldn't hope to have achieved very much. She must have known that. She wasn't even a political or environmental activist. She probably voted Conserva-tive. That's why it would have made more sense if he was a pedophile, and then she could certainly have stopped him from getting his hands on any more children. At Porton Down, he would have been part of a team, and they could go on without him. He was expendable. But kill just one pedophile, and you make a whole lot of children's lives safer."

"Do you believe Grace actually thought that way?"

"Not in so many words, no, but I'll bet it went through her mind. She couldn't stop Porton Down, but it was personal for her. It wouldn't only damage lives, it would change hers for the worse."

"And she could do her little bit for good?"

"Something like that." I hadn't told Heather about the reflection in the wardrobe mirror. Nor had I told her Graham's story about the similar incident in the Scarborough boardinghouse. I hadn't wanted her to think I was crazy. It was bad enough having her worried about me being obsessed by Grace Fox, in love with a ghost, as she put it. Per-haps one day I would tell her all of it, along with the truth about what I had done to Laura, but not yet. We hadn't reached that level of confi-dence yet. Somehow, I had to find a way of telling Heather that I *knew* what had happened on the night of Ernest Fox's death without telling her exactly why or how I knew.

"What about now? Do you still believe she didn't do it?"

"Yes and no."

"That's no answer."

"Hear me out. I still thought she did it when I heard Billy's story. Billy, too, when I told him what happened to Grace. He blamed himself.

I thought she *had* done it for exactly the motives we were just talking about, to stop Ernest from taking the job at Porton Down. But the truth dawned on me during the flight home, and I've been thinking about it ever since. I couldn't sleep, couldn't get it out of my head. It was going round and round and round, then it suddenly all fell into place, the pattern I'd been looking for."

"Just like that?"

"Nothing happens just like that when you've already been working at it for months. Not a musical composition, not a theory about a past crime. It only seems that way sometimes. That's what people call inspiration, the result of weeks or months of confusion, hard slog, and sweat. But it's the only *logical* way I can make all the elements fit."

Heather frowned and swirled the wine in her glass. "Do tell."

"First off, you have to realize that Ernest Fox was ill. His heart was in poor condition. The pathologist admitted as much, and Alice Lambert mentioned that he'd been taken poorly on previous occasions."

"With indigestion."

"But the symptoms of indigestion are very similar to those of a heart attack. Any doctor will tell you that."

"And the potassium?"

"Dr. Masefield, the pathologist, also admitted that the body releases a lot of potassium into the system when a person dies of a heart attack, and he certainly didn't convince me that there was any evidence that Grace injected Ernest with potassium chloride. None was found in the house. Dr. Fox didn't carry it in his bag."

"Yes, but she could have got hold of some and destroyed the remains later."

"There's no proof. It all depended on the jury believing what the pathologist said. No trace of potassium was ever found. The only potassium discovered was in Ernest Fox's body, and that could easily have been explained by the heart attack. It was present naturally. But the jury believed Dr. Masefield. Why reach for a more complicated explanation when the simplest one's the most likely?"

"Because of Sam and Grace."

"That's exactly right. The only reason Grace Fox went to trial was because of her affair with Samuel Porter. That's the one constant, and the thing I've believed all along. Everything else that happened, all the evidence against Grace, stemmed from that affair, from the discovery of that night in Leyburn. Take her young lover out of the equation, and it soon becomes clear that it was fifties morality that killed Grace Fox, pure and simple. The defense was right about a lot of things; there was just no passion in it and not a great deal of skill. And I don't think calling Grace herself to the box would have made a scrap of difference. She wasn't the kind of person to appeal to a jury of middle-class morally self-righteous men. You could see from Morley's account how much damage Sam Porter did just by appearing in the witness box. Christ, even ten years later you had the judge in the *Lady Chatterley* trial asking the jury if it was the kind of book they would like to find their wives or servants reading. We're talking about class here, too, with a throwback to Victorian morals. Judge Venables, the doddering, old, privileged, fox-hunting upholder of tradition and morality. To judge and jury alike, Grace Fox was a loose woman, a slut, a tart, a trollop. A hundred years earlier she should have had a red *A* branded on her forehead, and a hundred years before that she would have been burned at the stake as a witch."

"Okay," said Heather, holding up her hand. "I get the outrage and the working-class angst. But what *happened*? What about the chloral hydrate? They found that in his system, all right, and it wasn't produced naturally."

"He took it himself. Why not? He'd taken it before when he had problems sleeping. If his heartburn was bothering him that much, he might have thought sleep would be a blessing."

"But they didn't find any in the house."

"So what? That doesn't prove that Grace got rid of it. Maybe it was his last dose. If it had been wrapped in paper, it could have got cleaned up along with the paper from the stomach powder. Either way, it would have ended up on the fire. Or it could have been in tablet form. It could have been loose in his pocket. The point is, again, that there is *no evidence* that Grace dosed her husband with chloral hydrate. It's all highly circumstantial."

"So what *did* she do?"

I paused. "I think it's what she *didn't* do that matters."

"I don't understand. You're talking in riddles."

"Not at all. Grace was a trained nurse. Don't forget that. More than that, even, she was a Queen Alexandra's nurse, and they were the cream of the crop. I've read a bit about them. I imagine they drove some of the doctors crazy with their set ways of doing things, but they were damn good. When faced with an emergency, any emergency, Grace would revert to her training. All this stuff about her knowing her way around poisons because she was a nurse was smoke and mirrors. The main thing, the thing that everyone forgot, or ignored, is that nurses are trained to help the sick. To bring comfort. You've read her journal. She sat up all night comforting a dying German boy she hated, for crying out loud. But it wasn't just her job; it was *who she was*. That was what I missed before. Grace herself. *Who* she was, beyond the lover, before the poison."

"But there are nurses who've been convicted of murder."

"I'm not saying that nurses never kill. Of course they do. But I think that if you examine the evidence you'll find they usually do it out of some mental imbalance or delusion. There's no evidence that Grace was unbalanced or delusional in any way. Far from it. Even if she *had* done what the prosecution claimed she did, her acts were represented as cold and premeditated by the prosecution and the judge, the products of a clever and calculating mind. That wasn't Grace. She didn't have a cold, clever, calculating mind. And Grace may have been angry and concerned, but she wasn't mentally ill, either."

"You still haven't answered my question."

I poured the last of the wine. "Okay. I believe that Ernest Fox had a heart attack that night. A massive one. The pain woke him, even from his drugged sleep, and he called out for help." I pointed toward the hall. "Grace went across the landing, just up there, and into his room. That's where I think things get a bit murky. I'll not deny that relations were bad between Grace and Ernest. Maybe she hated him. There were years of neglect and coldness, perhaps even cruelty. They hadn't shared a room or a bed since Randolph was born. Then there was their argument about the Porton Down job. And there was Sam."

"So what did she do in the room?"

"What I think happened is that she *hesitated*. Simple as that. All this went through her mind as she stood in the doorway, all the reasons she might have had for wanting Ernest dead, and I'll bet she contemplated, just for a moment, how easy it would be to stand there and do nothing and let him die. It would be the perfect solution to all her problems. And for a while, I thought that was exactly what she had done, then I realized that the missing factor in all of this was Grace herself, her character."

"How do you mean?"

"When I read her journal, I think I understood some of it. As the woman she was, she *couldn't* just stand there and watch Ernest die. Much as she would have liked to, it went against her every impulse, every aspect of her being. So she stood there watching him for a few seconds, perhaps fully intending to let him die. But she couldn't. She snapped to her senses and acted with her instincts, her compassion. It was not so much *that* she was a nurse, but it was *why* she was a nurse. She dashed downstairs and got his medical bag. Treatments for heart attacks were pretty limited back then. There was no CPR or defibrillators or anything. It was pretty much nitroglycerine, which she gave him first, or digitalis, which she gave him later when the nitro didn't work. That didn't work, either, and he died. I'll never be able to prove it, but I know it now as sure as I know day is day that Ernest Fox died of natural causes."

"What if she'd reacted sooner?"

"Maybe," I agreed. "Maybe those few seconds would have made all the difference. Maybe it was her hesitation that killed him, and as I said, she probably wanted him dead. But she *didn't* kill him. She *couldn't.* I'm convinced of that."

"So you don't believe that given the right circumstances we're all capable of murder?"

I couldn't answer that question. I had killed Laura. I didn't know whether that technically made me a murderer or not, but that didn't matter. I had killed. It was what I'd done and why I'd done it that counted for me, and how I came to live with it. I felt that I knew Grace now. Fanciful or not, imagination or supernatural, she had called to me as soon as I entered Kilnsgate House, drawn me in, chosen me, willed me to tell her story, to find the truth. I had heard her playing the piano. I had seen her in the mirror, hesitating, then moving swiftly away to do what had to be done, just as I had seen the young woman who had hanged herself in the mirror at Scarborough. Even if all these things were inventions of my mind, I had still experienced them.

What I saw in the mirror was what I *believed* happened that night at Kilnsgate in 1953, a re-creation of what had happened when Ernest had his heart attack. But that sounded crazy. Perhaps Graham would understand, but I wasn't going to repeat it to Heather. Grace had nursed dying Germans, dressed suppurating wounds, sat up all night cooling the brows of those men who had done such terrible things to her sisters and to the officers she had laughed and danced with. Heather had read about that, too. A woman who had done those things wasn't going to plan the cold-blooded murder of her husband, as the prosecution had argued, and the judge and jury had believed. Perhaps I needed Grace to be innocent so that I could partake of that innocence, too, as I had realized in Cape Town. But I didn't believe that Grace could have stood by and watched Ernest die any more than I could have stood by and watched Laura live and suffer any longer. I couldn't tell Heather that, either.

Heather tossed back the last of her wine. "Supposing you're right?" she said. "What happens now?"

"Nothing," I said. "It's all over now."

"Really?"

"What else is there to do? None of it can be proved. The cause of Nat Bunting's death. What Grace did that night. Besides, it happened nearly sixty years ago. The only people who care, apart from me and you, are Louise, Sam, and Wilf, and I've already talked to them."

"How did they react?"

"I think they saw the logic of it. Louise sees her grandmother as a heroine now, a martyr, and not as a murderess or a scarlet woman. That can't be a bad thing after all she's been through. Wilf didn't say much. I think he'd already had his mind made up. And Sam . . . Well, he persists in feeling cheated out of the love of his life, and who can blame him? He's idealized Grace's memory, and, in a way, I don't think it matters to him whether she did it or not. He decided years ago in his heart that she didn't, so I suppose he might feel vindicated that some-one else has dug a bit deeper and come to the same conclusion. As for me, I'm convinced. I don't need to search anymore." I paused. "This has been thirsty work. How about I open another bottle?"

Heather thought for a moment. "Well, only if we can take it upstairs and you let me show off my new dress for you."

I laughed. "It's a deal."

As I opened the wine, I reflected on how our discussion had made me think perhaps more of my own mystery than that of Grace Fox. Not mystery so much as the twisted, half-hidden guilt I had confronted after my talk with Billy. I had thought about it more that night out on the balcony with my wine, and I had accepted what I'd done, made the first tentative move toward forgiving myself. In an odd way, getting to know Grace had helped me do that.

While I would cheerfully have given the moon, the planets, and the stars not to have had to kill Laura, I knew that it had been the right thing to do. You can't let someone you love suffer an agony that gets worse every day and has no possibility of ever abating or ending, except in an even more drawn-out and painful death.

Would I tell Heather what I had done? I didn't know. Those ques-tions were for later. For now, we would go on as we were, playful and easy. I would finish my piano sonata, and perhaps it would even be a success. At least it would be music people listened to. It would have Grace's name in its title somewhere; I knew that much. Spring would come, the snowdrops, crocuses, daffodils. Then the woods would be full of bluebells; the birds would come back from the south and sing, the swallows would return. A turning point would come for Heather and me eventually, of course—they always do—and decisions would have to be made then. But not yet. Not yet.

Extract from the *Journal of Grace Elizabeth Fox* (ed. Louise King), November 1945, Netley, Hampshire.

SATURDAY, NOVEMBER 3, 1945

THIS MORNING, JUST AFTER OUR DEMOB, MATRON GATHERED US ALL together in one of the big, cold lecture halls. I could hear the rain pattering against the large sash window beside me, occasionally getting louder, carried on a sudden gust that made the window rattle.

Matron told us first that she had a number of things to say to those of us who were now leaving the service for civilian life. First, she wanted to thank us for all we had done, and she went on to extol the virtues of military nursing, and of the QAs in general. Then she said that we were now about to face probably one of the most difficult tasks and duties of our lives. After all the things we had witnessed, done, and suffered through, I must admit that we all looked rather askance to hear this. But Matron was a wise woman. We listened.

She went on to say that the transition from war to civilian life is always a difficult one, but that it would be especially difficult for us because we were women. Not only that, but we had lived close to the battlefields, close to the fighting men themselves, not in hospitals miles away, where the guns could not even be heard. We had heard guns. Some of us had even felt their sting. We had been bombed, sniped at, shelled, shipwrecked, and worse. Many of us had also suffered great physical and mental privations in the camps or under life-threatening conditions in the wild. In order to survive, Matron told us, we had had to exist, and to act, in ways that were not always ladylike, and some of us may have been traumatized by our experiences.

Then Matron admonished us to think of our families, present or future. Their world was not our world, she said, but it was a world we had fought for; there was not one point of contact between those at home and those who had done what we had done, but we had done it for them. There was nothing they could understand about what we had been through and how it had affected us. If she were about to tell us not to talk about our experiences, I thought, then she had no need to bother. I think most of us would rather not. But it was more than that.

Whatever our war experiences, Matron concluded, it was now our God-given duty to be young ladies, housewives, sweethearts, and mothers again, not unrecognizable figures slithering around in the mud and blood of a casualty clearing station, or lying in the filth and squalor of a Japanese POW camp. Our loved ones did not want to hear or know about these things. If they did, they would never look at us in the same way again; we would become pariahs.

We had a role and a duty to perform in society, and in order to do so, we had to put the last five years behind us and mold ourselves into the image of the feminine again: the wife, the mother. That was what our world needed now, and that was our role in it. The men would get all the glory, as usual, Matron said, to knowing smiles all around, and this time we should let them have it. I glanced at Dorothy beside me, and she rolled her eyes. I smiled.

It was all a bit too much, I supposed, but at bottom, Matron was right.

Later, after the farewells and the promises to write, clutching my small suitcase in one hand and my travel pass in the other, I walked through the park in the rain, toward the railway station. Raindrops dripped from the bare branches. What a very English November day it was, I thought, and I felt a great surge of love for my country, for the future. Perhaps Matron was right. We needed to lock the memories away and get on with our lives. We needed to rebuild, to look forward, not behind.

The train stood waiting at the platform, puffing steam into the drizzle. I settled back in my seat to watch the landscape go by and opened my journal. In a few hours I will arrive at Darlington. Ernest will be waiting for me at the station. We will get into the car and drive back to Kilnsgate, to home. There, my future will begin.

BOOKS BY PETER ROBINSON

BEFORE THE POISON
A Novel

ISBN 978-0-06-220468-4 (paperback)
"Robinson outdoes Daphne du Maurier in creating the proper atmosphere for the imaginative fancies of a grief-stricken man." —*New York Times Book Review*

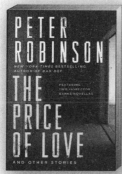

THE PRICE OF LOVE AND OTHER STORIES

ISBN 978-0-06-180949-1 (paperback)
"An excellent introduction to one of the best voices in contemporary crime fiction."
    —*Publishers Weekly* (Starred Review)

GALLOWS VIEW
The First Inspector Banks Novel

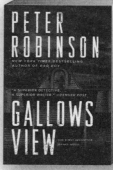

ISBN 978-0-06-200938-8 (paperback)
"Intimate . . . suspenseful . . . and satisfying in its resolutions." —*Los Angeles Times*

PLAYING WITH FIRE
A Novel of Suspense

ISBN 978-0-06-082464-8 (paperback)
"Refreshingly down to earth . . . Robinson, like his hero, understands the deeply mixed emotions that accompany a return to the past."
—*New York Times*

THE FIRST CUT
A Novel of Suspense

ISBN 978-0-06-073535-7 (paperback)
"Taut . . . . Robinson keeps up the suspense."
    —*Kirkus Reviews*